Edited by Caren Irr

Environmental Futures

AN INTERNATIONAL LITERARY ANTHOLOGY

Brandeis University Press
Waltham, Massachusetts

I0806818

© 2024 by Brandeis University Press
All rights reserved
Manufactured in the United States of America
Designed by Mindy Basinger Hill
Typeset in Garamond Premier Pro

For permission to reproduce any of the material in this book,
contact Brandeis University Press, 415 South Street,
Waltham MA 02453, or visit brandeisuniversitypress.com

Library of Congress Cataloging-in-Publication Data

Names: Irr, Caren, editor.

Title: Environmental futures: an international literary anthology / edited by Caren Irr.

Description: Waltham, Massachusetts: Brandeis University Press, 2024. | Summary: "This volume is an anthology of fiction and poems by authors from around the world that highlights the diversity of stories that flow from experiences of the natural world, giving particular emphasis to those that wrestle with the legacy of colonialism and its approach to nature as a resource to be exploited"—Provided by publisher.

Identifiers: LCCN 2024001530 (print) | LCCN 2024001531 (ebook) | ISBN 9781684582129 (paperback) | ISBN 9781684582112 (cloth) | ISBN 9781684582105 (ebook)

Subjects: LCSH: Human ecology—Literary collections. | Nature—Literary collections. | Colonialism—Literary collections. | BISAC: LITERARY COLLECTIONS / General | FICTION / Literary

Classification: LCC PN6071.H78 E58 2024 (print) | LCC PN6071.H78 (ebook) | DDC 808.80353—dc23/eng/20240125

LC record available at https://lccn.loc.gov/2024001530

LC ebook record available at https://lccn.loc.gov/2024001531

5 4 3 2 1

ENVIRONMENTAL FUTURES

In any weather, at any hour of the day or night,
I have been anxious to improve the nick of time, and notch it on my stick too;
to stand on the meeting of two eternities, the past and future,
which is precisely the present moment; to toe that line.

Henry David Thoreau · *Walden*

Contents

Introduction

Decolonizing Environmental Futurisms

CAREN IRR AND ANIK CHARTRAND

In May 2013, scientists at the Mauna Loa Observatory in Hawaii documented average atmospheric carbon dioxide levels exceeding 400 parts per million (ppm). Far above the limit of 350 ppm considered safe for a stable global climate, this new high signaled a future of unpredictable storms, melting ice, extreme heat, and desertification. In the following years, increasingly ominous environmental events linked to climate change have filled the news and slowly colonized the collective human imagination. It now seems impossible to describe the present or near future without making reference to environmental concerns.

At the same time, we must recognize that the perspectives that inform climate science have been shaped by a history of imperial exploitation. A mere thirty-seven miles away from the Mauna Loa Observatory lies Mauna Kea, the highest peak in Hawaii and the site where thousands of protestors gathered in 2019. At issue was the construction of another massive telescope on a site sacred to native Hawaiians. Holding the ceded land of the dormant volcano in trust for future generations, the indigenous land-protection groups set their vision of the future in direct opposition to the gloomy scientific empiricism of the observatory. The slow collection of data that allows the projection of future climate trends found itself face to face with cultural continuity and a future that honors sacred geography.

Without denying or discrediting the importance of scientific inquiry into climate change, this volume attends to the many perspectives that confront the single story of an environment doomed by industrialism. We highlight the diversity of stories that flow from experiences of the natural world, giving particular emphasis to those that contest the monotonous blare of the colonial sensibility and its treatment of earthly abundance as a resource to be exploited. We begin from the premise that while a single line on a graph may trace the rising carbon levels, no single story can represent the environmental future that line represents, just as no single action will prevent further carbon dioxide from continuing to alter the atmosphere.

Many languages, authors, moods, and genres are required if we are to reckon with the environmental changes already underway. Many voices must be enlisted to describe the consequences of climate change that we are already living with. And even more will be needed to find some paths out of the present morass. Collecting and sharing environmental stories from traditions that have to date had too little purchase in the empirically dominated traditions of settler colonial societies is an urgent task.

Fortunately, we have a wealth of writing to consider. Storytellers around the world have been examining human relations with the natural world for as long as stories have been told. Some of the most ancient narratives concern themselves with just this matter. Think of Enkidu's battle with the forest in *The Epic of Gilgamesh* or the symbolic animals that are everywhere evident in ancient rock art. Human engagement with the natural world has arguably provided the primary subject of storytelling over the thousands of years of our existence as a storytelling species.

In the past one hundred to two hundred years, however, human actions have triggered a massive turning point in natural history. As Paul Crutzen and Eugene Stoermer argued in a landmark 2000 essay, the geologic strata of the earth are now indelibly marked by human activity. Everything from synthetic waste and petrochemicals ripped from below the earth's surface to radical shifts in the temperature and weather has left its mark. In recognition of the massive impact of humanity (or *anthropos*), Crutzen and Stoermer proposed that we call this new era the Anthropocene, and the name has stuck.

The Anthropocene has inspired writing filled with new characters, locations, forms, and moods. Many pieces from that inventive and exhilarating array appear in this anthology. From the traditions of the formerly colonized (and a few colonizers) from around the world, our editors have chosen work that experiments in tone and subject matter while appealing to the heart and body as well as the mind. Their selections dive deep to converse with fearsome creatures at the ocean floor and look upward toward the stars that are still visible through the fumes of burning oil. These writings speak to our attachments to charming little dogs and our terror at the prospect of irreparable solitude in a world denuded by extinction.

In voices that range from lyrical to satirical, they convey the abundance of human reactions to a changing world, even as they testify to the consistency of a desire to imagine some mode of survival—that is to say, a future.

Across this range of styles and voices, some recurring themes emerge. Oil and soil form one important strain, and streets and trees another. The former speaks to poisonous desires and the modes of destruction that tear up the very ground on which we walk. The latter concerns cuts, regrowth, and mobility—conjuring visions of movement across landscapes of recovery or adaptation. The first set of motifs might be understood as leaning toward the apocalypse while the second bends toward something like Eden, although these Abrahamic references are certainly not shared by all the authors whose works appear in this volume.

What does unite nearly all the perspectives presented here is the historical experience of colonialism. The imperial projects that spread out of Europe during the eighteenth and nineteenth centuries and shattered during the anticolonial struggles of the twentieth brought with them a whole network of travel and goods; they crossed the earth and in so doing changed it. The worldwide redistribution of plants and animal species followed many of the pathways established by colonialism, and the circuits of energy transmission share much of the same orientation. From the perspective of the imperial center, poisons were exported and exotic species imported. At the same time, a program of terraforming led to efforts to remake colonial terrain in accordance with the norms of the European temperate zone—to plant gardens in deserts and contain the abundance of tropical forests. Accompanying these terraforming projects was a tradition of nature writing that took for granted the seasons and species of the colonizers while registering terror or horror at deviations from those implicit norms.

In full recognition of the dominant role that temperate zone European-language writing has played in establishing an environmental canon, the editors of this volume have made a concerted effort to provincialize that work. Our goal has been to foreground writings that speak to the situations of formerly colonized peoples both within and beyond the sites of imperial power. Writing from these perspectives recognizes with clear and sober eyes the damage inflicted by colonialism, and it often makes a strong case that survival in the future requires some reckoning with the injuries of the past. Whether speaking in the archly imaginative voice of a Neanderthal or the agonized surprise of a human in the process of turning into an ape, the decolonial writings included here insist on the value of becoming disoriented in relation to the technological modernity that emerged from imperialism. They turn critical eyes on the overly familiar stories of the heroic trekker alone in a pathless wilderness and introduce readers to surprising new takes on tradition and wild leaps into a fundamentally altered environment.

The editors have made the inclusion of decolonial and indigenous voices a priority while also recognizing that no collection of this sort could be entirely comprehensive. We have had to make some hard choices along the way. We have elected, for instance, to emphasize the eastern perimeter of Europe in hopes of correcting for a habitual North American focus on the Western powers; this has meant giving short shrift to the influential traditions of environmental writing in Germany and the United Kingdom. Similarly, for reasons related to the challenges of translation, the prolific and varied literature of sub-Saharan Africa is here represented only by Anglophone work. In the same vein, rather than attempting a superficial overview of the most readily translated writing from across all of the many languages and cultures of Asia, the selections included here derive only from South Asia and China. Finally, our group of Latin American writings includes only works written in Spanish, neglecting Portuguese as well as indigenous languages, and too few works from the Caribbean appear. We are aware of other important absences—such as the complete lack of works from the Arab world and the miniscule presence of Oceania in this volume. Despite these absences, we believe the work presented here will invite many new voices into conversations about environmental literature.

In assembling this volume, we have prioritized adventurous writing with a strong environmental concern and an appealing style. We hope that every reader will make at least one new discovery in these pages. We hope that, whether they encounter this work in the living room or the classroom, readers will leave this book with ideas for envisioning other environmental futures. It is only by facing up to the futures that now seem to be in the process of arriving that one can wade in and possibly, just possibly, redirect the flow.

WORK CITED

Crutzen, Paul J., and Eugene F. Stoermer. "The 'Anthropocene.'" *Global Change Newsletter* 41 (May 2000): 17–18.

1

AFRICA

Introduction

CAJETAN IHEKA

African literature has always been environmental. It has an enduring preoccupation with human relationships to the land, contestation over territories, and the extraction of human and other-than-human lives from the land in the form of slavery and colonialism. As early as the sixteenth century, Africans were forcibly brought to the New World to produce wealth. As the practice of slavery waned, it was replaced by colonialism, a process that brought much of the continent directly or indirectly under European administration. To service their industrial expansion, the European powers convened the Berlin Conference of 1884–1885 under King Bismarck's leadership; they balkanized the continent and carted away its resources. Walter Rodney captures the negative effects that colonialism had on the continent in his well-known treatise, *How Europe Underdeveloped Africa*.

After colonialism, new nation-states arose. Some scholars view those nation-states as failures because they continued colonial projects and disparaged indigenous structures of governance in their constitutions. Whether or not one agrees with this assessment, one can state unequivocally that the national elites squandered the opportunities of independence by bringing corruption to public office. What emerged across the continent, in Patrick Chabal's words, were "clientelistic and/or patrimonial regimes that have, more or less reluctantly, adopted the procedures of multiparty elections." Corruption led to public unrest and social conflicts, including civil wars and military coups across the continent. By the end of the oil boom in the 1970s, the economies of many African countries were struggling, and they turned again to the West for assistance. The 1980s saw the imposition of rigid policies required by the World Bank and the International Monetary Fund in order to access aid. These structural adjustment policies further deepened social divides by shrinking the welfare state, enshrining austerity as a matter of state policy, and privatizing public assets and services. As Joseph Stiglitz, former chief economist of the World Bank, explains it, these uniform policies did not consider the contexts of application and were thus doomed to failure at inception. And they indeed failed across Africa, further weakening African nation-states while international organizations and transnational corporations became stronger. To discuss the weakening of nation-states does not mean, however, that they have become obsolete in Africa or in other parts of the world. The surveillance and coercion of the state are operative in Africa where governments collaborate with local business interests and multinational corporations to exploit the people and squash the opposition to said oppression.

While environmental concerns have been central to the exploitation of African communities, they also have served as catalysts for resistance. For instance, on March 26, 2021, women in the Niger Delta occupied a facility owned by the oil company Chevron to protest a leaking pipeline that was endangering the health and livelihoods of people who rely on fishing and farming for survival. These women refused to leave until they received Chevron's promise to address the leak and pay compensation. This mobilization of human bodies against the despoliation of the environment has many precedents in the Niger Delta and across Africa. Ken Saro-Wiwa and Wangari Maathai—to take two of the most well-known African environmentalists—also put their bodies on the line. In the case of Saro-Wiwa—the writer, businessman, and activist—his resistance to the degradation of the environment created by oil exploration in the Niger Delta resulted in his death on November 10, 1995, when the Nigerian state led by General Sani Abacha hanged him. The late Nobel Peace Prize winner Wangari Maathai was spared death by the Kenyan state but faced imprisonment for mobilizing resistance against privatization of the commons including Kenya's Karura Forest. Maathai's Green Belt Movement challenged the allocation of public land and forests to commercial interests and planted trees to thwart deforestation in Kenya.

These examples of resistance from Kenya and Nigeria are temporally and thematically different, but they share a focus on the environment and the project of futurity—that is, environmental futures. There is a concern for survival, whether it is the women occupying Chevron's facility in 2021, in the agitation of the Saro-Wiwa-led Movement for the Survival of the Ogoni People (MOSOP), or in the activities of Maathai's Green Belt

Movement (GBM). Maathai, for instance, was concerned about the threat to both present existence and intergenerational continuity resulting from the destruction of the commonwealth—the forest and land. In choosing to plant trees as a solution to the sociopolitical and environmental crisis in Kenya, she elaborates a theory of environmental futurity for humans and nonhumans: "The trees would provide a supply of wood that would enable women to cook nutritious foods. They would also have wood for fencing and fodder for cattle and goats. The trees would offer shade for humans and animals, protect watersheds and bind the soil, and if they were fruit trees, provide food. They would also heal the land by bringing back birds and small animals and regenerate the vitality of the earth" (126). It is interesting that Maathai foregrounds food, an essential need, in her rationale here. With poverty exacerbated by postcolonial dysfunction and the extractive disposition of the Kenyan state, the people and the environment needed the kind of nourishment that trees provide—food for humans, for plants and animals, and even for soil that needed to regenerate. Trees are also significant because they not only provide immediate sustenance; they also amount to an investment in the future for food and carbon capture during a time of climate change.

The survivalist and futuristic ethos underpinning Maathai's work in Kenya animates the history of resistance in the Niger Delta as well. In response to the alarming dissonance between the oil wealth generated from the Niger Delta and the extreme levels of precarity in the region, Rob Nixon asks, "Who could have dreamed in 1958 that four decades and $600 billion of oil revenues later, some 90 million Nigerians would be surviving on less than a dollar a day?" (106). Nigerians may lack wealth, but toxicity abounds in the Niger Delta. Significantly, Saro-Wiwa framed the injustices against the Ogoni people as ecocide and foregrounded survival in the naming of MOSOP. As in the Kenyan example, *survival* and *ecocide* imply present and future threats. As rhetorical devices, these terms situate Saro-Wiwa's and the larger community's concern about oil's toxicity and its lingering effects in the environment within the context of environmental justice and the right to self-determination.

African writers have always grappled with the social problems of their societies, from slavery and colonialism to the current realities of globalization.

Early literary writings from Africa showed Africa's complex ecosystems by depicting humans in relationship to the land and environment, partly in response to the racist categorization of Africans as ahistorical, brutish, nonhuman, or lesser beings. In Thomas Mofolo's *Chaka*, for instance, the land is crucial to self-actualization, and communal belonging depends on it. Writing in the 1950s, Amos Tutuola and Chinua Achebe portrayed African people in complex relationships with animals, forests, and denizens of the supernatural realm. Elsewhere, I have described this preoccupation with humans and their interactions with the environment as producing an "aesthetics of proximity" in African literature.

This proximity has not abated in African literature, but the often-harmonious relationship between humans and Others has been overshadowed by an exploitative sensibility manifesting in toxicity from resource extraction, pollution, and other environmental problems. In the selections from Tanure Ojaide's and Ogaga Ifowodo's poetry collections on the Niger Delta, the melancholic tone adumbrates the losses occasioned by decades of oil exploration. In the search for the appropriate form to carry the weight of the putrescence and destruction in the Delta, what Jennifer Wenzel describes as the "petro-magical realism" of oil production in the region, Ojaide and Ifowodo plumb the resources of oral tradition and appropriate the techniques of bioregional writing. The resulting cultural products catalog the physical and psychological costs of mineral extraction and the threats they pose to continuity in the region. In representing polluted landscapes and the exploitation of environmental resources in Africa, these writers secure these locales in the imagination. As climate change and sea-level rise threaten the Niger Delta and other parts of the continent remain ravaged by centuries of exploitation, the imaginative work of literature thwarts the erosion of these spaces. In other words, these spaces survive in the act of literary inscription.

As an aesthetic and instrumental artifact, literature is a portal for African environmental futures. As resilient objects, literary works have an unparalleled conservationist ability. They hold and keep spaces alive despite the threats to their territorial integrity. The critiquing function of literature also introduces the possibility of redress. By drawing attention to social problems, literature begins the work of dismantling the status quo. Mindful of Africa's disadvantage in the distribution of the gains of globalization and its marginalization in futuristic engineering and design, African writers and their counterparts in the diaspora have turned to the arts for emplacing the continent and its people at the core of imaginative prototypes for the future. Under the term *Afrofuturism*—and the more recent *Africanfuturism*, proposed by the writer Nnedi Okorafor—writers and other artists have drawn resources from indigenous cosmologies, Western science, and speculation tools to propose worst-case scenarios if current consumption levels remain unchecked. These artist-thinkers have also offered alternative conceptualizations of the Earth based on planetary ethics.

The works collected here tackle directly the question of the future while taking cues from the past and present. They have been selected for their formal complexity and innovativeness but also because they deal with the central themes of contemporary environmental writing in Africa: resource extraction, pollution, toxicity, repair, and either apocalyptic or positive renderings of futures. The works here represent the different regions of sub-Saharan Africa, although they are not exhaustive of the literary traditions of the continent. Works in indigenous languages and in metropolitan languages other than English are unrepresented, and North Africa does not make an appearance. Given Africa's geographical vastness and its complex linguistic ecosystems, we can only begin the work of curating contemporary African environmental writing here.

WORKS CITED

Achebe, Chinua. 1964. *Arrow of God*. London: Heinemann.

Caminero-Santangelo, Byron. 2014. *Different Shades of Green: African Literature, Environmental Justice, and Political Ecology*. Charlottesville: University of Virginia Press.

Iheka, Cajetan. 2018. *Naturalizing Africa: Ecological Violence, Agency, and Postcolonial Resistance in African Literature*. Cambridge: Cambridge University Press.

Maathai, Wangari. 2006. *Unbowed: A Memoir*. New York: Alfred A. Knopf.

Nixon, Rob. 2011. *Slow Violence and the Environmentalism of the Poor*. Cambridge, MA: Harvard University Press.

Okorafor, Nnedi. 2020. "Africanfuturism Defined." In *Africanfuturism: An Anthology*, edited by Wole Talabi, n. p. Brittle Paper.

Tutuola, Amos. 1952. *The Palmwine Drinkard*. London: Faber and Faber.

Wenzel, Jennifer. 2014. "Petro-Magic Realism Revisited: Unimagining and Reimagining the Niger Delta." In *Oil Culture*, edited by Ross Barrett and Daniel Worden, 211–25. Minneapolis: University of Minnesota Press.

Lekki Lekki

MAME BOUGOUMA DIENE

African writers are routinely criticized for fetishizing the challenges of postcoloniality, but they are also at the vanguard of experimenting with alternative visions. Mame Bougouma Diene's "Lekki Lekki" is a significant addition to a corpus invested in the work of repair and environmental transformation. Diene's Africanfuturist text contemplates the possibility of an organic world where humans, plants, animals, and technology interact ethically as well as the challenges of creating such a world. In a memorable passage, we learn that in this future "we'd be a planet with a conscience. A planet that could guide life instead of suffering from it." Diene is a Franco-Senegalese writer of speculative fiction. His collection *Dark Moons Rising on a Starless Night* (Clash Books) was nominated for the 2019 Splatterpunk Award.

The back of her hand glided under her red and yellow head wrap, wiping the beads of sweat receding into her midnight skin in the shade of the giant tree.

Wind rustled through the leaves and whistled through holes in the trunk, to the shrieking of bats bothered in their sleep, buried in its crevices.

Djoulde dipped her painted fingers in a wooden bowl, relishing the fresh feel of water. She sprinkled droplets on the roots digging deep into the cracked and dusty soil, sucking her fingers for a fleeting taste and repeated, singing a light melody under her breath.

Sukaabe e mawbe ngare niehen . . .

She knew the tree could hear her, and know her love. At times it felt as the trunk pulsed like a wayward heart, that somewhere inside the calcified bark the memory of sap bled pungent dreams.

. . . Goto e men fof yo aw lekki . . .

The behemoth rose above and around her, branches long as it was tall, like twenty men or more. Wide enough to dance and spin on, though Cheikh never wanted to.

Children and grownups, come with me . . .

There was so much it had seen. So many secrets through the centuries of patience and sheer will for life, so much she would share with it soon, that the whole village would share.

. . . May every one of us plant a tree . . .

"Still singing that old song?"

Cheikh's gritty voice irked her sometimes.

"Why are you always so bitter?" she asked, dusting her hands on her dress and rising.

He stared into the large oval hole in the trunk, large enough for a tall man to step into its caves.

"It is old," he snapped. "What does it mean now? What is there left to plant? Maybe it made sense to someone two thousand years ago . . . someone stupid . . ."

"It makes sense to me . . ."

"I didn't mean you, I meant . . ."

Cheikh didn't finish his thought, and Djoulde wasn't sure she wanted to hear it.

He picked up her bowl and they walked back towards the village together. She hadn't seen time fly as she cared for the old bokki. Twilight was dying on the edge of the earth, the village lights blinking the stars out one at a time.

The call to prayer rang from the minarets. Djoulde saw other villagers hurrying home before the protective dome rose against the evening storms, green, blue and multicolored dots against the broken night, and sighed. Perhaps Cheikh would understand one day.

The combined blaring of her father yelling for her to get up, and the whooshing of the giant turbines blowing away the dunes delivered with tender fury by the storm, tore Djoulde out of her slumber.

The sun wouldn't shine through the dusty vortex until the turbines had worked their magic, but cattle always knew, the three cows in the yard bleating for water.

She pulled a rough blue dress over her head and tied her braids in a bun before leaving her room. She clapped her hands and the air conditioner went out, the whiplash of desert heat finishing the job of waking her. Her head still cloudy with the flames of her dream.

She yawned as she walked into the kitchen.

"You took your sweet time this morning," her father said, gulping down a cold glass of bohe juice. "Grab yourself some breakfast; we're taking the cows out soon as the dome is lifted."

She sat at the large round table. Her mother handed her a plate of whitish-brown fried bohe bread and a glass of juice. The thick, sweet liquid clashed bitter cold against her teeth. She bit into the bread.

"Today? Isn't it Hamady's turn?" she said, spitting little bits of crumbs, and wiping her mouth.

Hamady laughed, sitting across from her. He stood up, wearing his light blue worker's boubou. "Not today, sis," he said, pointing at his uniform. "Working the Engines in case you can't tell."

"At least you'll be nice and chilled in the forest . . . Yerim, then?"

"He's on maintenance duty at the solar plant today. He's been gone for hours," her mother said, picking up her father's glass. "You can't sing to the trees every damned day. Gidelam," she told her father, "I'm not your maid; you'll find your plates waiting when you come back."

Her father barked a laugh. Something both her brothers had picked up from him.

"Get married, they said. It'll make your life that much better . . . Duly noted my love. Djoulde, you done?"

Djoulde finished her glass.

"If no one else will . . ."

The expanse of long grass stretched ahead and around Djoulde. A green sea full of whimsical currents drawn by the winds. She couldn't tell where the grasslands ended from where she stood now, the three thin, white cows grazing quietly, their long horns leaving furrows in the meadow. She had walked the length of the plain as a child, to the sands lost on the horizon, a desert so vast it swallowed the world whole.

She had seen it burn and turn to glass in her dream. The flames crackling through the grass until they licked away at the millennial trees. The bokki's branches flaying in panic, the defiant roar of bark about to split and burst. She slept in its bosom, reveling in its warmth until her hair caught fire . . .

Her father's cane slapping the cows' buttocks brought reality back, and the softness of the grass on her sandaled toes.

"Do you think there's anybody else out there?"

Her father cleared his throat and spit in the grass.

"You've asked me that five times now. Today, when you were six, nine, eleven and fourteen. Took you almost four years this time."

"But you never gave me a real answer."

He shrugged in his black boubou, looking up to the sun settling at noon.

"The last recorded newcomers go back almost five or six hundred years, not quite sure. You can check the archives if you want but . . . I don't know, somewhere on the other side of the oceans maybe, or the other side of the universe. Maybe they're asking themselves the same thing, maybe they're all dead . . . Happy?"

It was her turn to shrug.

Other herders were scheduled for grazing this morning. All with the same emaciated cows. Goats had gone extinct with good riddance. Goats were a plague on the grass.

She turned towards the forest. The Soul Engines, installed inside the bokki, vibrating and rumbling in the distance.

"It doesn't matter, I guess. We're all going back to the earth anyway."

"I guess so," her father replied.

"Then why bother with the cows every day if that's how you feel? We get our food from the trees, our water from the roots. We hardly eat any meat at all, we barely use the milk for ceremonies. We won't be here much longer. But you get up every morning, you wash them, walk them all the way out here every day. What's the point of dancing by yourself?"

Her father smiled. "You and your mother . . . It's who we are, Djoulde. We herded cattle before the world knew we existed. When other people flew overhead, we herded cattle below. When the world crumbled and the towers fell, we herded cattle. Two thousand years later we herd cattle. It doesn't matter where we're going. It doesn't matter where we came from, it doesn't matter if we're here or on the moon, Djoulde. We herd cattle, it's our tradition . . . And that's why I take you all in turn with me in the morning. To remind you of that . . . Speaking of tradition, how are things going with Cheikh? You getting along?"

"It's alright," she said. She didn't know how she felt about Cheikh. She had expected to feel differently. "He's just always so cynical. He doesn't believe in anything; I don't know . . ."

"Can you blame him?"

She took off her sandals and dug her feet in the ground. It felt so firm, so real, but it wasn't. It was a dream. When the generators crashed it would wither, dry, and fade to the sands. The dome would never rise again and the trees and the village would disappear. Perhaps that was why her father really kept the cows, to forget that none of it was real.

She shook her head.

"Good. Then maybe you should spend some time together this afternoon. If you're gonna be married, you need to know each other."

"But Baaba, I was . . ."

"You heard your mother. Someone else will daydream in the trees for you today." He handed her his stick. "Round up the herd. I could use some lunch."

"How can you say that?"

"Say what, Djoulde? That a halfcocked plan to transfer people into the roots of monstrous trees and live on like that is crazy? You wanna know what I think? I think Chief Tenguela, the Council of Elders, the whole lot of them, want to kill us. Or a lot of us. There's too many of us, we're all freaking related. Even our marriage is based on an algorithm. How long do you think we can last like this? Do you even think at all?"

There it was again, that spite for the sake of jabbing her. Couldn't they just talk? Just once?

He reached across the bed and caught her hand, but she pulled back. Sitting on his bed, his parents' prayers making their way through the door, she wanted to grab Cheikh by the braids and throw him into the desert.

"Do you have faith in anything? Don't you want anything better than this?"

"I don't mean it like that . . ."

"You never do . . . What if it works? What if we could live on? One with the earth?"

"What if we could?"

"We'd be a planet with a conscience. A planet that could guide life instead of suffering from it. When a new people are born to this world they won't be blind like us humans were. Ravenous like we were. They will learn. From us."

"Yeah, because we're such a sensible bunch. Look, what happens if it doesn't work and you die? You wouldn't even know. I was with the crew that removed Oumar Bayal's body from the pod and buried it. Remember the test run?"

"Of course I do. The Elders said it worked."

"Maybe. Maybe his soul is really in the roots. Maybe he's just dead. Worse than dead. I've seen dead people. This guy wasn't dead, he was just an empty sheet of skin, the wind could have blown it away. Look. I get it, you want it to be true. But I haven't heard the old man since, have you? Didn't think so."

"I hate you . . ."

"Then don't marry me. What bloody difference does it make?"

She didn't answer.

Cheikh smiled. "Let me guess, your mom gave you the talk too, huh?" he asked, poking her waist with his elbow.

Djoulde shook her head and laughed. He wasn't always bad.

"Was my dad . . ."

Cheikh laughed in turn and took her hand.

"What are we without tradition, right?"

Djoulde rolled Cheikh's heavy arm from her shoulder as she opened her eyes to the call to prayer, their sheets still humid with sweat. She couldn't sleep, who could have? The only way she'd found to exhaust herself was . . . The one thing they seemed to get along doing.

A nervous shudder rocked her body. Delirious excitement clashed with sheer terror. Cheikh snored. The Soul Engine trials were today. They were still of two minds on that. Three months into their marriage.

Cheikh stretched and yawned.

"We're not scheduled until noon. It's barely fadjar. Go back to sleep."

"I'll make some breakfast," Djoulde answered, rising.

She reached for the towel sitting on the chair by the bed, and wrapped it around her waist.

She wasn't going back to bed, the trees called her, they would be one soon.

They would all be one.

The overlapping waves of light drew sly rictuses on the trees, grinning deep shadows where there were none, while dizzied steps carried her closer to the heart of the forest.

It was the first time she had wandered this deep. The pulsing glow of the engines, while overwhelming now was invisible outside. In the daytime, the sun drowned it out and at night, the storms blinded everything. She wasn't alone, guided with Cheikh and the hundred more scheduled for the day's trials by a tall, dark woman in a white dress stained at the ankles with dust and dirt, but Djoulde felt like she wasn't really there, that none of them were really there. That she was marching amongst ghosts.

Djoulde wondered if the others felt the same, that they had crossed a threshold into the forest that connected all worlds, that in an infinity they were none, that a step into the shadows was a step into oblivion. Maybe they didn't feel anything at all.

Her eyes adjusted to the light just as her body shivered from mechanic rumbling.

"We're here," the tall woman said as they all stopped.

"Where else could we be?" Cheikh mumbled.

The trees before and beyond them glowed with a reflective light, trunks and branches laced with slick metal, connected across the soil by slithering black cables to large gray cubes, vibrating with a collective hum, like the voices of a million bugs calling to be born.

A flurry of scientists in white dresses and boubous busied around them. Maintenance workers in blue tended to individual trees and power sources. Perhaps Hamady was one of them, but there were so many trees so far ahead she wouldn't see him even if he was.

Cheikh spat on the ground beside her.

"Look at all this wasted energy. I'm telling you th—"

"Men, follow Oulay here," the woman said, pointing at a colleague settling next to her. "Women come with me, I'm Ayida Boucoum."

Djoulde exhaled relief at not having to answer Cheikh.

"See you later," she said. "Don't make a fool of yourself."

Cheikh grunted and followed the others.

Ayida led them deeper into the woods. Chrome reflected on chrome, projecting their reflection flowing from trunk to trunk and back. She caught herself facing herself and walking away in two directions all at once.

She stumbled and rested her hand against the nearest trunk.

"It's OK," Ayida said, helping her straighten. "I thought I would lose my mind after weeks in here. You'll be fine, we've arrived."

Two women slid between the trunks to meet them.

"Thanks Ayida. We'll take it from here. Ladies. Welcome to the Soul Engines. We will brief you on the procedure and have you take the trials. We know this is overwhelming, believe me. I'm Sokhna Boiro, some of you know me, some of you don't. And this is Khady Ndione."

"Same story," Khady said.

Djoulde caught a glimpse inside the hollowed trunks, lined with open pods, of the same shiny metal that coated the trees, tall enough to fit a person, with what looked like red cushioning inside.

"Intriguing, isn't it?" Sokhna asked, catching her glance. "I know they say a lot of things in the village, many of them scary, most of them untrue. Let us explain. Khady?"

"Sure. The Engines are very complicated but quite simple. The world is a network, everything is interconnected. We all evolved from the same original organism. Billions of years ago. Down to our DNA. We are one with the earth. One with the wind. And yes, one with the cows we herd in the morning." They laughed as she caught her breath. "The trees and plants around us too. And they communicate. Organically. They know who we are and fear us when we wish them harm, and love us when we give them love and they let the others know, through their roots, through their spores and sap. We have mapped these networks and now, we can connect to them more directly through the Soul Engines. These engines parse out our human consciousness and pulses it into the network, mimicking the bokki's own bio-chemical signals, those signals are transmitted into the roots of the trees and conducted into the earth where they become one with the planet. Growing with new saplings, spreading through open spores. Our way of life is no longer sustainable, if we want to survive we have to adjust to the world, adapt and embrace it. For thousands of years humanity has tried to shape the world in its image. We failed and did so much damage to the world in the process. Now, we pay it back."

Djoulde could barely breathe. They'd worked on the engines when she was a child. When her parents were children. She hadn't thought she would see the day. But it was here. Almost here.

"You'll be scanned and fitted into a transmission pod for testing. Today and on the day of. Don't worry, it's painless. We just need to verify a few things. Many of you are married women, we need to check that you are not with child before we can try the machines. We must also ensure that your own brainwaves are compatible with the bio-chemical matrix. Is everybody with me?"

They all nodded agreement, some slower than others. Djoulde pictured Cheikh snickering in the manner of men.

Khady smiled.

"You are brave, and strong. You will do the earth honor. We all will, I'm sure. Alright, the following come with me, the others with Sokhna. Nani Sow. Djoulde Diallo . . ."

Djoulde came to in midafternoon warmth, the forest a few hundred feet behind her, Cheikh shaking her by the shoulders.

How she got there was as clear as his lips moving soundlessly to droplets of spit.

It was real. All of it.

The pods had slid shut, the red cushion squeezing her warmly into darkness. Not sleep, not quite sleep, fully at rest yet aware of herself, and she heard him. Late Oumar Bayal calling her name, unsure she could hear him. *Djoulde,* he had asked. *Djoulde, are you there?*

She hadn't said a word, but felt his relief at her presence, a smile and mischief.

Watch . . . , he whispered.

She'd sunk deeper into the darkness, her head bursting through the soil into sunlight. A city gleaming in the distance where the desert stood now, a river streaming through it to a sky of deep blue abysses. In a flash she stood fifty feet above, in another a hundred, and as she grew the city shrunk, her arms impossibly long and stiff, until there was nothing but dust swirling woolly death to the horizon.

And all the while a murmur, soft with radiant energy calling her into its roots . . .

"Djoulde! Djoulde dammit, wake up!"

"Cheikh!" she screamed, throwing her arms around him, her head on his chest. "Did you hear? Did you see? Don't you see now? It's real, all of it!"

Cheikh pushed her back and turned around.

"I didn't hear anything," he said. "I'm not going . . ."

Cheikh downed a glass and poured himself another. His fifth today. Takussan, afternoon prayer, was still hours away.

"The pitcher's empty," he snapped, waving it at her.

Fode Dem had walked into the desert this morning. Fatima Kane, Ibrahim Dia, and Pape Mor Sylla yesterday. Twelve-year-old Adama Ba two days ago and Friday had seen a record of thirty that she knew of. They had finished praying and wandered off into the desert.

A week since the trials ended, two more before they left.

Djoulde grabbed the pitcher from his hand. Cheikh was meaner drunk than usual, but at least he was still here.

She filled the pitcher from a bottle of fermented bohe and handed it to him, reaching for his shoulder for comfort. He grabbed her hand and pulled her close to his face.

"Is that what you want for me? Leaving me to die with the others?"

Someone else would walk into the desert and never come back before nightfall. Thousands more would follow.

He was mean. Bitter and mean, but wouldn't she be if she'd been told she couldn't go? If her mother and father were left behind too? In spite of all the spite, deep down, he'd wanted to leave too.

She pulled her arm away, grabbed his face and kissed him. Could she leave her husband behind? Should she?

Yes.

Yes, she would.

Until then they could do the one thing they were good at together, and kissed him deeper.

Djoulde's dress slipped from Cheikh's hand, but stayed caught in the door sliding shut behind her.

There was nothing to it. Between Cheikh crying, screaming and begging, and the excited buzz of the throngs of people she hadn't had thought of what to wear.

What did it matter? They were almost there.

Her parents and brothers waited for her outside, catching her stumble as her dress ripped in the doorframe.

"Took long enough!" Hamady laughed as he helped her stand.

Her mother hugged her.

"How are you?" she asked.

She had no idea.

"And how is Cheikh?"

"Who cares?" Yerim said. "Guy's a goat."

"Be quiet," her father said. "Think of all those who wandered off to die. They weren't all bad people. Leave it all behind son, don't carry that anger where we are going."

They melted into the crowd. She couldn't feel her legs, somehow, she moved forward, the crowd singing a deep and joyful yet almost weeping melody.

Lekki ki do lekki,

Aadi nafore waalii ngourdam
Tree. This tree so useful, has changed our life . . .

It was the perfect rhyme for the time. She should have felt happy, excited, nauseous even, instead she floated numb into immortality.

Would Cheikh live? If he died would they find him in the roots? Soon they would be everywhere, surely they would find everyone. Everyone and everything that had ever died. Strata through strata of long-gone life but persistent memory.

Did she leave him to die? Could she forgive herself? Carrying that weight forever? She only had a few minutes to figure it out, the sky already darkened by branches.

Her heart pounded so fiercely the world around her turned to blinding light, her head spun and she retched on her sandals.

Her brothers laughed.

"You had to leave your mark didn't you?"

She wiped her mouth on her sleeve as her mother handed her a sip of water and smiled.

"It's gonna be alright. We're all gonna be alright."

They reached the engines and hugged each other. They all did. Family and friends, and people who'd hated each other deeply. She expected to hear sobs but didn't.

"We'll see each other soon," her father said, beaming as he hugged her last. "Look out for your mother. She might run off."

"Anything but an eternity with you Gidelam. One life was entirely enough . . ." She kissed his forehead. "I will see you soon . . ."

They walked off as Djoulde and her mother lined up with the other women. Singing the song, scanners flashing a soft blue as they walked towards their pods, reflections of thousands melting into each other on the trunks of the giant bokki.

Her mother turned to her and smiled as she passed through the scanner. Every wrinkle on her face smoothing, a glimpse of who she had been, of who she saw in the mirror, as she still saw herself. She held out her hand as Djoulde followed her, and the scanner flashed red.

Her mother's smile dropped, her face aging in a frown, their fingers brushed each other as two women in white approached them and turned to Djoulde.

"Salaam aleikum. Don't worry. We just need to run a quick test. Please follow us."

"Wait! That's my daughter! That's . . ."

Two more women approached her mother, smiling.

"It's fine. She'll be back in no time. Please. There are other women waiting."

"I'll be fine, Nene," Djoulde said, "Just go, OK? We'll be alright. I'll see you soon." She smiled. "On the other side."

The flood of women didn't abate, the scanner flashing blue, blue, blue, her mother dissolving in the flow.

"I'm Reyhanna," one of them said as they reached the last of the shinning trees. "What's your name?"

"Djoulde. Djoulde Diallo."

They stopped and the two women stepped back, arms folded under their breasts.

"We're sorry, Djoulde. We are very sorry. You are pregnant. You can't go."

Djoulde sat on her bed, the air-conditioning unit roaring behind her. She had never noticed how loud it was, but in the silence of the empty village it was all she could hear.

Cheikh slept in the kitchen, passed out on the table.

She should have been cold, but the hilt of the knife pressed against her stomach slipped in her sweaty palms.

The tip slid through the threads in her dress, grating against her skin. Just a push. Not even that hard, just a small push.

The life she carried had cost her hers. Had cost her her dream. Her only dream. Her family. How could she ever carry it? Birth it? Love it?! It would be so simple, just a small . . .

A droplet of blood pearled around the blade and the knife clanged on the floor to a single sob.

She couldn't do it.

Three children played in the grass as Djoulde and Arsike walked past them towards the forest. They had tied strings to a small wooden post and ran around it until the string tensed, and light as they were, they bounced off their feet, taking off, spinning to delighted giggles.

Something had changed. The children were inconsolable at first. Their friends gone. Their parents gone. Everyone engrossed in their own misery and no one to guide them. Beside the wailing wind the only sound the village knew for months was infant sorrow. But not for the past few weeks.

Arsike tugged at her arm, eager to join them. Her small hand almost slipped through Djoulde's fingers.

She looked just like her grandmother. She had told her that herself.

"I look like Grandma!"

"Who told you that?" Djoulde had asked.

"Grandma!'

She was a bright child, so alive. So happy. She had no fear, an imagination that changed her world with each passing thought. This world was new to her. She didn't know pain. She didn't know loss. Not yet.

"You'll play later. Your father doesn't like to wait."

She nodded hard and pulled closer to her mother.

For two years Djoulde hadn't come near the forest. The thought of leaving the village, of feeling the cool shade on her face froze her very soul. She couldn't walk. Will them though she might, her legs wouldn't move. Her mind would go blank. She would faint. Neighbors would drag her in and she'd wake up in bed, Cheikh looming over her, yelling about embarrassing him.

When Arsike turned three she started asking about the trees. The trees called her she said. She had to see the trees. And so she had. She was exactly like Djoulde'd been as a child.

"Let's sing, Nene!"

She knelt by her daughter and let her start. Hearing her shrill voice she felt the knife against her stomach and shuddered, picking up the melody.

How could she have thought of killing her? She loved her so much.

Arsike giggled, pushing her lips to the trunk as evening prayer rang in the distance. They'd been there for hours.

Hours. Months. Years. It made no difference. She opened herself with all her heart, sang to rip out her throat, every day, and yet, she didn't hear her family or the others. Four years. Four years now.

Cheikh was right.

They had all walked singing to their death.

The door slid open slowly and Djoulde tiptoed inside. Arsike breathing softly on the back of her neck, sleeping as the storm blasted the dome behind them. Cheikh would be out cold, he'd been restless for weeks but too much noise and . . .

"Sneaking in?" he asked, sitting at the kitchen table in the dark. The thin glow breaking in, lighting bloodshot, angry eyes over his dark face. He stood up, knocking a glass to the floor, rounding the table towards her. She circled away, the sourness of fermented drink on his breath wafting vomitous into her nose.

He wouldn't touch Arsike. He never had.

"Think you can keep my daughter from me, do you?" he asked, reaching to grab her and missing. "You try to leave me and now you want to steal my daughter!"

She slipped and almost fell, barely avoiding another lurch.

"Nene?" Arsike asked, yawning against her back. "Nene, where . . ." She saw her father closing in over her mother's shoulder. "Baaba? Baaba, no! Not again!"

Her mother hugged her in a field of crops. Cattle by the thousands drifted on the horizon, invisible but for the cloud of dust surrounding them.

Her father and brothers conversed with a man of light skin, sharp eyes and strange, shiny, smooth, green and gold clothing, throwing their heads back and laughing.

The village was nowhere in sight, the forest neither, but crowds of people congregated throughout the field, some sitting and eating, children playing games and rolling in the grass.

They weren't all her people; most weren't but she distinguished a known face in every group she saw.

"My daughter. My first-born. We didn't want to leave you. I didn't know. But we are here. We will help you."

The bruises on Djoulde's cheeks stung at her mother's words.

She pointed to her bruised face.

"This is what you left me to! This is how you help me? You left. You left me. But I don't need your help. I am not a child anymore. I have one of my own. I won't let this happen again. She will . . ."

Her mother's face hardened.

"What are you whispering to me?"

Djoulde froze; her mother grabbed her by the shoulders, digging nails into her skin.

"Stop whispering to me!"

The field went silent. The thousands of people sitting and talking stood and closed in on her, arms out, clawing at her hair and face.

"Stop whispering to me!!"

Djoulde awoke to Cheikh shaking her furiously, screaming at her face while Arsike cried in her bed.

"I won't walk into the desert! I won't!" He ran naked out of the bed, climbing over her and into the kitchen, his hands on his ears. "Stop whispering to me!"

Djoulde ran to cradle her daughter's head. The warm wetness of her cheeks slipping against her breast.

"Why is daddy like this?" she asked, words setting Djoulde's bruised body aflame. "What have we done wrong?"

"You've done nothing wrong," she said. Arsike's curly hair caught between her fingers. "We've done nothing wrong."

"Why isn't Grandma helping us? She promised."

Djoulde held her at arm's length.

"What?"

"Grandma, Mommy, Grandma. She was telling me she would help us. Just before Daddy started screaming again."

Cheikh's voice boomed from the kitchen.

"Stop talking to me!"

Djoulde put Arsike down.

"You stay here. I'll be right back."

Cheikh sat in the kitchen, holding his head and banging it on the table in turn.

"Leave me alone!" he screamed and saw Djoulde standing across the table from him. "You," he snarled, rising slowly. "You. It's you!"

He charged, but Djoulde didn't move. She bent down, picked up a shard of broken glass and walked towards him.

"You won't touch me again." She slashed the air before her, missing his nose by a breath. "You'll never." She sliced again, blood running across his cheek. "Touch me. Again!"

She lunged forward, Cheikh fell back, crawling towards the kitchen door.

"Leave me alone! All of you leave me alone!"

The door slid open and Cheikh bolted out.

Djoulde stumbled after him. She had never spent much time outside at night. But the dome's faint orange glow, lacerated with gritty static at the onslaught of sand and debris, felt like a reflection of her fractured soul.

"Nene!" Arsike called from a crack in the door. Djoulde picked her up and ran.

Cheikh sped on ahead screaming, lights blinking in windows as he passed.

He didn't slow or stop. Djoulde doubted he could see anything at all.

His head slammed into the dome.

He fell back. Djoulde put her daughter down and reached for him.

He got back up and ran headfirst into the dome again. And again. All the while screaming to be left alone, for the whispers to stop. Again. And again, and . . .

His skull cracked and gurgled. He fell back, wracked with spasms, the imprint of his face in blood sliding down the dome like raindrops on a window.

Djoulde didn't move when the convulsions stopped. The buzz of bystanders fading. He was gone. She felt no shame at the lightness in her shoulders. At the strength she felt in her legs.

"Thank you, Grandma," Arsike said, hugging her thigh.

The wind carried hints of a rain that would never fall. Instead a thin sheen of wet air sprinkled Djoulde and Arsike's faces, as they sat in the shade of the baobab, Arsike sprinkling the roots to soft giggles.

Djoulde hadn't allowed the villagers to bury Cheikh in the forest. His body was left in the desert for the night's storm to shred to dust.

Arsike didn't seem to care. She sprinkled the roots and listened to something before nodding her head.

"How long have you heard your grandma?"

Arsike shrugged and lay her head on her mother's lap.

"Since I was in your belly?"

Djoulde's eyes filled with tears.

"Are you talking to her now?"

Arsike nodded.

"I talk to Grandpa too sometimes."

"Can I ask her something?"

"She says you can ask anything you want. Just ask me and she'll hear you."

Djoulde hesitated.

"She says she's sorry. That she should have stayed. She never wanted to leave you."

Djoulde waved her hand.

"She doesn't need to," she said "There was nothing she could have done. It wasn't her fault."

"Do you love me Mommy?"

"Of course!"

"Do you forgive me too?"

She pulled her daughter closer.

"There is nothing to forgive, Bingelam, nothing... Can the other children hear her too?"

Arsike nodded.

"Why can't I?" Even Cheikh had.

"It's too late for the adults. If you did you would go crazy, like Daddy."

"But in the dream I saw all these people and . . ."

"It was just a dream, Mommy."

Djoulde's breath stuck in her throat, there was something she needed to know but didn't want to.

"And will . . . will I ever see you again?"

Arsike looked up at her mother.

"No."

"No? Not even when I . . ."

"No."

Tears ringed Djoulde's eyelids like pearls.

"Grandma, Grandpa, my uncles, none of them will be there forever either, Mommy. Not as they were. That's not how life works. I'll walk into the engines one day too, and others after me. We were always one with nature," she giggled, "It's our tradition! Grandpa says." She laughed some more.

The tears bubbling in her eyes streamed down her cheeks. Arsike wiped one off with her finger.

"Don't cry, Mommy. Grandma says that's the lesson. The mistake we made all those thousands of years ago. The world cried and we couldn't hear it, but just because you can't hear, doesn't mean you shouldn't listen . . ."

Djoulde cleaned her tears, breathing in the dry scent of the trees and nodded.

Arsike caught her hand.

"Come Mommy. Let's sing now."

Sukaabe e mawbe ngare niehen,
Goto e men fof yo aw lekki . . .

Acknowledgments With thanks to Baaba Maal and Double Servo

Selections from

The Oil Lamp

OGAGA IFOWODO

Ogaga Ifowodo is a Nigerian poet, scholar, lawyer, and human-rights activist. His poetry collections include *Homeland and Other Poems* (1998), *Madiba* (2001), *The Oil Lamp* (2005), and *A Good Mourning* (2016). The selections from *The Oil Lamp* that follow adopt a melancholic tone to describe the losses occasioned by decades of oil exploration in the Niger Delta region of Nigeria.

I saw so many flocks of naked souls, all weeping miserably,
and it seemed that they were ruled by different decrees . . .
Above that plain of sand, distended flakes of fire showered down . . .
The dance of wretched hands was never done; now here,
now there, they tried to beat aside the fresh flames as they fell.

Dante · *Inferno*

Numbers, too, have significance: . . . 1,001, the number of night, of magic,
of alternative realities—a number beloved of poets and detested
by politicians, for whom all alternative versions of the world are threats . . .

Salman Rushdie · *Midnight's Children*

A WATERSCAPE

Hung above water, hands in the air,
whited tongues and breathing fibrous hair:
roots, white mangrove roots.

Blacker than pear, deeper than soot,
massive ink-well, silent and mute:
water, black water.

Floating hats of lily, yellow plume,
plankton and shrimp, egg-and-fish in bloom:
lakes, ancestral lakes.

Rich mud of eels, water-holes of crab,
sink-place for fisher of dig-and-grab:
bog, mudskippers' bog.

And in the mangrove waters, where tides
free the creeks of weeds, fishermen glide
home to the first meal.

PART III *Ogoni*

XXIX

Major Kitemo, boss of the mob,
chief pacifier
of the lower Niger's

still primitive tribes, had at last laid waste
the prickly land. And speaking to the press
about the good job he had done for

country
conscience
posterity,

showed what a half-breed the people were
to claim and fight for what they did not own,
to deny the owners what was theirs

by decrees duly made and in the books;
showed why extreme measures were called for
to teach the needed lesson, stem the tide

of defiance which, for three years,
had shut down Shell's oil wells
and slimmed the nation's purse;

showed how deficient words had proved,
how efficient persuasion by other means.

XXX

I went to their leaders—no, not the Ken Saro-Wiwas
of the foreign-sponsored MOSOP and NYCOP—
I went to the women, fishermen, farmers,

and jobless youths they had brainwashed,
to bring them to reason, and I asked them,
"Do you really believe you own the oil?"

"Yes," they said, as I knew they would.
"And how did you come to own it?"
"By its being on our land," they said.

"The land is Nigeria's," I corrected them.
And then an old man, parched and cracked
far worse than any sun-sucked patch

of spill-soaked land I have seen, asked in return
"And how did Nigeria come to own the oil?"
Oh, I should have paused to give thought,

should never have presumed a hoary-headed man,
but I answered too quickly, "By its being
on her land." It was a minor slip,

a momentary lapse of no consequence
to the crack prosecutor's cast-iron case.

XXXI

The old man, ready with a riposte,
was speaking again. I was losing patience,
but I have an old father, his head a hat of wool,

so I let him speak, just one more time.
And what treason! what outrage! He said:
"Can you tell me, my son, how old Nigeria is?"

I can't tell now why I was so rash,
expert that I am at squelching mischief
before it buds, but I spoke too soon:

"Born in 1914, she's seventy-nine this year," I said.
And he: "That's Lord Lugard's colony, the cartographer's
trade map for British expropriation. But I

will take your word for it. So tell me, my son,
How long do you think we have been on this land,
how long the oil, the trees, the creeks and the rivers?"

Oh, never take an old man for granted
nor the mist and webs of times past;
still it was no case for history,

nor the error more than a minor slip,
but I had seen the strength of their delusion.

XXXII

I had to regain lost ground, be interrogator
again, and steer clear of foggy waters,
so I said: "By decrees and edicts

duly made, the land is not yours
nor all that lies in it. The powers
that rule the country—your colony

that make you citizens
of a nation, known to law
and safe from plunder,

decree the land and its wealth not yours."
It wasn't the old man again, God knows
I would not have let him; it was a woman

and I thought, What can a woman say
to loosen one rivet of the law?
And she said, in plain pidgin,

No vex o, Oga soja, but who
or wetin make up dis Nigeria?
There were many hands now up, no doubt

with more cheek and treason,
the hard rote of lawlessness.

XXXIII

I'd had enough, but now it was a child
barely through high school, in ragged
uniform. I'd noticed his fixed stare

at my crisp khakis and mirror-clean boots.
I raised my hand to say, Listen to me,
there'll be no more impudence, no more false

claims and clever arguments, but he spoke—
too calmly for a child, I must say—
and as I kept my hand up, the old man said,

"Do you fear a child's words too?"
I had to let him speak. "Excuse me, sir," he said,
"but in whose name, and by whose powers,

were the laws you cite made?" It was unreal,
an ancient, a female and a sapling,
had taken words from me! But though to a soldier

that's nothing of shame, I had to have
the last word, show an officer is brains
and brawn, as sharp in mind as his hard-pressed

pleats. I said, "So you own the oil, but what
did you do with it buried in the ground?"

XXXIV

They were rattled; no hands were up now,
so I chased the enemy home
back against a wall of his own.

It was true. What did they know of oil
other than the fruit-red extract of palm trees?
The bounty of the sea, of the creeks and rivers,

the barn-busting yield of arable land
rich in organic silt and loam
had not caused a quest for riches

hidden deep in the heart of the earth.
When they dug wells, it was for water;
They didn't have to dig too deep for the table,

didn't have to drill to the heart
or mine every vein for fossil ooze,
until the colonial find in '58

at Oloibiri—not even in their land!
But they found their tongue once more,
in a former teacher, the plucky child's father:

"But for the theft by law, we would in time
have seismographed and drilled, or hired Shell."

XXXV

There was nothing for it: words had failed.
No child, man or woman could be swayed;
they had the script in their heads,

answers for every question. I
had now to follow my own script,
outlined in my Memo for Peace

to the Commander-in-Chief.
First, cure them of the lies
drilled into their bones by rabble-rousers;

if that failed, set them against themselves,
cause feuds with neighbors,
and if still true to the rote, still starving

the treasury of petro-dollars, launch
the last plan: Wasting Operations,
group infiltration, mass deportations.

"Can you do it, can you secure the target?"
the C-in-C wished to know. "Sir," I said,
"I have the best skills your army can give,

"I have excess of zeal. What is more, I know
two hundred and twenty-one ways to kill a man."

XXXVI

I had used two centuries of killing skills,
yet they clung to their claim.
There were, of course, some gains: only

the cause-crazed, craving martyrdom,
dared come to rallies or picket oil wells.
But I knew I was far from winning

when one said at gunpoint,
mouth and nose frothing blood,
"If I starve to death on a Shell-shocked

bog, or fall off a deep-sea rig and drown,
taking my tears like coal to Newcastle,
I will have died as I lived—to no end.

But if Major Kill-Them-All (yes,
that's what they had begun to call me)
shot or tortured me to death

for linking hands with my brothers
to stop the drilling of another barrel
then my death might dig deeper into the land

the anger that chokes me when I sleep,
make me a landmine to trampling boots."

XXXVII

Far from winning, the C-in-C's trust waning,
I had to go for the last plan, secure the target.
But I lacked a pretext, the aggressive

act of folly gladly embraced. I was charged
to go shooting from the hip, but I'd had
truly bad press: none of you here now helped

my cause an inch. You made a monster of me,
accepting like holy writ every word Ken spoke;
the playwright and poet, he made plain words

cry false wrongs on your desks till you reached out
a hand to console him, picked your pens for the scoop,
and I could never match him word-for-word,

if I couldn't have the last word
with children, women and old men.
I was close to despair, ready

to give you the prize headline, shoot myself
in the foot. Then they sprung the trap! I
had set it with the perfect bait, prepared

with inhuman patience. It was time,
and I flung my arms in the air.

XXXVIII

I preferred the nights when oil lamps twinkled
over the evening tide catch in wet nets,
fish-women smelling of *eau de poisson*

and buyers bent like shrimps over trays and mats,
haggling over prices without a care. We'd
surround the town but keep the roads clear.

At my word, big guns would go off
and at first, the fish-market, always
a hubbub equal to the sea's roar,

would be dead-still, and you could hear
a lamp, its oil drying, splutter its rage,
or the chink of change dropped by shocked hands.

We paused for the awe to revive them,
till we saw them fling away the fish
as if they were marine bombs! We sustained

fire then till all the lamps gasped and surrendered
to night, till only the light of our fire streaked
in the bloated darkness as houses quenched

their lamps to hide their fear, and their occupants
fled to the bush through the paths of flight I'd kept open.

XXXIX

Major Kill-Them-All. At first I was mad
at the brave wretch. Soldier or not, it wounded
my Christian heart. I yelled at him:

"It's Major Kitemo, understand? you
bloody Good-for-Nothing! No one fools
with my name, you hear?" Then I was glad

to know they'd killed four men, calling
them traitors, vultures gorging on kinsmen's
corpses. Yes, I'd set the trap, unspooling

threads of suspicion, spinning webs
around them with words that failed
at town meetings, grown forceful with bribes

and slander. Multiple murders: I had now
the aggressive act of folly, so I said: "Kill-
Them-All, not so? Well, you'd better run! I

will wipe out every damn one of you, if I must."
Guns and grenades yelled my new name for fifteen days.
I drove them all into the bush, sent them rowing

into the creeks with fireflies as their light. Then we dug
in to hold the town, shooting to keep them in the bush.

XL

Shooting and bombing to keep them in the bush
we were running out of ammo by the tenth day,
but Shell shipped in caseloads of what we lacked.

Fifteen nights and days in swamps and creeks
broke them. First, they pushed out two little girls,
who kept running back, scared to death. Then, a boy

and a girl. As the matinée grenades went off,
they fainted. I'd waited for the surrender;
we took them in and kept shelling. I wanted

the smart-ass quartet: the old man, the schoolboy
and his father, the woman. I didn't have to wait long,
They came out among a crowd and fell on their knees:

Please, please, we will do what you say, anything
you want. But stop the shelling. Please! Please!
"What about your oil, you don't want it anymore?"

Three have died of snakebites, four of malaria.
Two women have given birth under trees. Five elders' hearts
expired with the last bomb. Our stomachs are raw with roots.

Let us live. Please! Please! I let them live,
took prisoners, and brightened my epaulettes.

PART IV *The Pipes War*

XLI

They hanged nine
for murders pre-planned
and Colonel Kitemo

had, at last, his last word.
The troubled peace of surrender
churned stomachs, threw up

the bile of raw-root meals
eaten in the bush, renewed the taste
of uncontainable grief

for all too weak to be right,
    too few for a moment's doubt
    in the mind of the well-paid hand,

money-on-the-barrel to the oil cartel
for containment strategies
when the natives get restive.

"After fifteen nights and days in the bush,
they came to me, begging, *Let us live. Please! Please!*
Anything to stop the bombing. Please! Please!"

That was the swashbuckler's boast in barrack pitch,
hear it from the bureaucrat's well-oiled tongue:

XLII

Can anyone think of the Niger Delta
and not feel an ache in his heart?
So inhospitable, it is like all terrains

in the world where oil might be found: under
seas, desert dunes, snow-capped wilds, malarial
swamps. As if He who desolated

those places thought it too cruel to plant
humans in some of them without recompense;
still I think He erred to give in remorse

to so few what must belong to all.
But a good man's conscience
will sting him like bees to see how abject

they are that live amidst such wealth in our
land; to hear them bewail the dissipation
of their share of earth's bounty, the devastation

that pours oil on rivers to float fish
lure the flamingo to a lethal meal
and quill the secretary bird's death on sludge;

that irrigates lowland crops to rot their roots,
and wells resentment like ocean tides above their heads.

XLIII

I would be first to plead their case, and say,
Pamper the goose that lays the golden eggs!
But so difficult is the land, so absurd

their claim for redress, that it should empty
the coffers and deny the nation's engine
its lubricant. Rust would follow; there'd be an end

to motion and a nation to call our own.
But though resentment swirls and eddies
in every house and raft in the Delta,

the demographics of their grief makes it easy
to contain, blunts the sharpest arrow
that may fly from any fray they are forced to start.

The wealth of nations, by fair distribution,
makes no fortunes. And Nature, unjust
sharer of its gifts, favors the stronger arm.

Unable to threaten
the settled peace
of the realm

there's nothing to fear; we can let them weep
rivers of blood till despair drives them to sleep or folly.

XLIV

Such folly
as Major Kitemo's pretext in Ogoni,
as flattened a town for a felony,

as burned one thousand officially dead,
as turned a scrapping for used pipes
—so rusted Shell could dig them up!—

into a war for territory
between Oleh and Olomoro:
with oil wells and pipelines, without piped water,

(but also without tribal feuds
over ancestral lands or lakes);
they had shared peace and poverty

till pipes too old for hot crude
called for heated blood in their hollows.
Oh, do not ask history's questions,

know only that claims clashed over rust,
a youth from Oleh died, and Olomoro's
equaled the spillage, and guns and machetes

leapt into hordes of hands, and there was a pretext
to shoot and burn, and drive more into the bush.

XLV

They scrap for a living where the land's promise was boundless ease.
The fisherman throws his net, rejoices

for a single meal's catch, as trawlers
haul in schools of fish. Tankers,
whose docking and leaving make his canoe

rock to the wild tune of their wakes, sail away
with Bonny Light crude. And far
from the lighted Jetty, he paddles home

by the flame of Iron-Dragon—
the gas-flaring stack whose awful mouth spits fire:
without cease near his village. Born before

the first built by Shell, he too had
cursed the dragon, called it Hell's Gorge,
sure to retch on every head afflictions and deaths

sucked from the depths of the earth;
till the women found its oven heat perfect
for drying tapioca. Till he—in the absence

of eletiriki—renamed the red tongues snarling
at the inky skies, Oil Lamps of the Delta.

PART V *Cesspit of the Niger Area*

XLVI

What tears have not been shed
cannot be shed now,
what grief still unprinted

has no tree to pulp
its words that burn the tongue,
that choke the windpipe.

Broken verses, wept
far from the hidden pit,
where they flung the famous nine,

after the under-
taker's conjuration acid
(which, as we heard,

was to erase their bones,
wipe out every trace
of a deed too foul

to stay under the ground)
have dinned the air, etched
the proof on every soil.

But the many scars that itch and wounds that bleed
far from the eyes of the world beg a few more songs.

XLVII

Such as this I heard a mother sing:
The child was down with a fever
so we boiled herbs and barks for him,
still the heat rose higher and higher

till you could roast yam by his side,
so high I feared he would die.
But there's no doctor in Asaba-Ase,
no clinic in a hundred miles,

and no motorway to where he aches.
So I said to his father,
"Quick! quick! we must go to Port Harcourt,
and he said, "Dear wife, it's midnight!

Tomorrow at crack of dawn
I will go by speedboat. The times
are past, my dear, when we sang:

If you must go to Port Harcourt
and be there before it's dark,
take enough garri *and smoked fish*

say a prayer to Mamiwata
and paddle off in the dead of night.

XLVIII

Wonodi's wife's waters broke too soon
now sighs have replaced our song,
Wonodi's wife's womb is too fertile
now worry stiffens our smiles,

for she has given birth to five
a month and a half before her time
and old Tobrise the midwife
has only pots and pans and hot water.

Quick! quick! we must hurry to Warri!
where they say there's a machine
to save the ones that come too soon,
quick, quick, pull out canoes and paddles.

And you ask: Did life reward the journeys?
Did your man reach Port Harcourt by dusk
Is the ailing child back in your bosom?

Oh you ask: Did they make it to Warri
Did Olokun calm the waters,
and the machine quicken them for her arms?

I will not answer! I will not answer!
Look at my arms! Go to her house!

XLIX

And this from a man with a grudge in Warri:
The whole town in darkness
because Never Expect Power Always
is working hard for its name.

First, there was light every other day,
then every two days, then four, then . . .
Forty-five days! Can't sleep at night—
without the fan to stun mosquitoes.

See where I live—a shack in the swamp!
But light shines on the oil staff estates—
well-drained and paved and mosquito-proof.
Went past one today as I tramped for work,

and seeing those carpet-lawns, the quiet
order of the place, shamed me to the bone;
didn't want to go home then, I felt like a sewer rat!

That's when I said, "Listen, Solomon,
you're nobody's fool. Be wise! Good job,
fine house, sleek car and beautiful woman

are for Solo too. That's your money, man!
And I'm going to live even if I die first.

L

And now with naked malice, I must deny
Major Kitemo (and his ilk) the last word,
give it to his nemesis, the schoolboy,

now a sophomore at law, unaware
what paths to even sharper perception
the gods, offended by bombs, prepare

for his itching feet as he writes under a tree
—and I copy—the words of the shaping
poet, peeling the scabs to regrow the skin:

The Niger flows down to us the pus of the land,
East and West of the putrid heart, two valves
pump dead blood into our open veins. And we

are silted gutters, swamp and swampdwellers.
The Niger flows down to us its floodwaters,
swells our rivers with the dread tributes

of seasonal carnage washed in from the fields.
And we stay afloat by treading tears, reclaiming
footholds with the humus of hate and envy.

And when they rise to spit on our heads the rinse-water
of their early morning mouths, I remember the dew,
the one thousand and one gone, and what will remain true.

Eclipse Our Sins

TLOTLO TSAMAASE

Tlotlo Tsamaase is a Motswana writer. Her novella, *The Silence of the Wilting Skin*, was a finalist for the 2021 Lambda Literary Award and was shortlisted for a 2021 Nommo Award. In her "Eclipse Our Sins," Mother Earth seeks revenge for human-induced climate change. With a fire motif that runs throughout the novelette, Tsamaase's work foregrounds a sick people inhabiting a ravaged earth. As the story puts it, "you only become sick when you've sinned against Mama Earth."

I pray to You, Mother Earth, Mama Earth, Mmê Earth:
Sun, hide your eye, eclipse your birth from our sins.
When Climate Change came,
It tore into Your womb, Mama Earth, sodomized it
—and we watched.
We stood and watched You, Mama, crying.
Still we didn't listen:
We were the wildfires
The sky's mouth was wrapped around smokestacks and tailpipes,
muzzled, Your lip hog-tied around that foul,
folding the poison into Your lung,
burying it into Your oceans, making fire of soft bodies, perfumed in oil.
We slit Your womb to throw out the children who lay in Your bellies
across nations,
across oceans,
across skies,
distances they sacrificed,
as if Mama Earth is not their own,
Claiming the crime as many names like xenoph—I don't want to say it.

Reality evolved to punish us for it was us who solicited climate change
as Your murderer:
We have sin-fever
Your oceans swallowed continents.
What was once a relic, is our savior.
We can't rely on technology when it relies
on electricity wi-fi fossil fuels that are no more.
A relic relies on nothing but itself.
Our souls were the only things we could rely on; from solar energy
to soular power.
We had no other hope but to use them to light the streets and
our homes to give warmth in the long, rainy heat wave-winters.
Soon our actions, our thoughts became our enemies.
Mama Earth, we heed Your warnings, forgive us, forgive us for our sins.

The morning prayers ended, and we dispersed from the heat wave of the mosques the churches and tents in our respirators and cooling suits and the skyscrapers that raised their fingers to God's eyes. Maybe one day Mama Earth will hear our prayers, maybe one day She will forgive us, and maybe She'll set Her hound dogs—reality and the new culture—off from our bloodline.

a-burning-soul

It starts like always, a burning soul, a still sky, a quiet universe. A white rooster croaks, a death has been foretold. A quinquennial affair. The earth moans under our breath.

It is dusk. The sun is menstruating, smearing a rosy tinge across the bleak industrial skyline. It has teeth. Teeth to catch. Teeth of metal and jagged glass. Nothing homelike about this city. The smoggy vapor of every citizen's breath obscures the solar-powered streetlights. I gaze out our cinderblock apartment windows at the masked commuters below in the streetways unable to tell who's human, who's not. Every machine's gait is seamless, the joints oiled with the occult of the upper-city citizen's desire and our rigged poverty. In the misty-sandstorm-laden morning, I watch some of the commuter's smog-voices and smog-words rise into the air, like round shiny balloons, turning the skies rowdy and gray, tearing open the ozone layer. Even the poorest don't have access to at least one basic human right: a respirator.

I lean against the window. Huff my breath until the glass fogs, and with my index finger, I draw the words "freedom is extinct." My breath is smog. The window clears. I replace my mask, listen to the intermittent buzz-buzz sound of the breath purifier, the air purifier in our household, a secondary precaution in case the former fails. Every apartment window is a widow, staring back with lack of want and light, carved too deep into the façade to protect tenants from the penetrating hot eye of the sun, its fingers always hot and abrasive. We know it too well, for it probes our thighs, molests the unknown parts of ourselves.

It is morning, burning with too much sun. But in the other room, a darkness segues into a deeper dark, the air humid with a breath laden with too much evil that our masks rust by the second. Mama is in death throes with an immense force we can't see, but we can see the slashes it leaves on her arms, back, and legs. It wants to silence her. But her voice has been to God and back, nothing can stand in its way. Even the shaman takes his shit and leaves, his shame tucked in between his legs.

"Fuck," I yell, grabbing him. "You can't do this! You can't just leave. We paid you. We paid you."

He lifts his palms. "Sorry, sisi. You paid me for the work, not its success rate."

"What kind of bastard are you?" I shout. "Save her. You can't just leave her like this." My glare turns to Mama, her skin wet with sweat, exhaustion an axe in her mouth.

"I'm not God." The shaman struggles with me by the doorway. "You can't force me to be God." My grip is viselike, so he snarls at me. "Aren't *you* the hypocrite? How can you force a stranger to be her savior when you couldn't live up to the task, yet she got you, birthed you for that reason? So *you* save her. *You* can't just leave her like this."

"Don't talk about my birthright." But my voice is weak, not as poisonous as my anger.

"*Fong-kong* human," he spits, and the words wash over me like acid.

"I swear this is going to come back and haunt you, like all these diseases," I say, my voice wet with pain. He pauses at this; for, an unfair treatment begets the owner a fatal disease. "Isn't that how your wife died? She was racist, wasn't she? She maltreated someone because of their skin-shade. The disease got her. It'll get you, you fucking swindler."

He falls to his knees, misery torn across his face. "I can't be God. I can't save everyone."

My sister's tiny arms wrap around my waist; her lisp weepy. "Tsholofelo, no, please, we're burning up the minutes we have with Mama. Just let him go. Let him go."

My grip slackens. The shaman shuffles and disappears out the front door.

Mama's giving birth to death; thirteen hours so far of labor. Our uncle, he stands in the bedroom threshold, the daylight from the other room sharp against his back, promising to bring a hopeful help. That bastard man. From the nook, where each of our melanin hangs, my uncle yanks his skin-color coat, throws it over his shoulders, ties it to his bone, taut as ours, black as ours. He wears our skin color, but he's not like us.

"I'll be back," he says gruffly.

My sister, Botshelo, nods politely. My head refuses to move, but my palms fold into rage. The coat belonged to my brother who lost the war to this family. My uncle wears it proudly as if he faced the war. Bastard. He has a slew of habits, terrible habits. My uncle, his terrible habits have become the sewage of our city.

Mama screams again. So I have to pin her down from breaking more bones. And I remember how it started. When she returned from work two weeks ago. I'd visit her at work, bringing her lunch I'd cooked. I'd watch her as she sat in her factory chair with knotted fingers, her illness weaving the time-holes, the laptops, the eye-held for the rich, the bones in her back screaming out of her skin. Her skin was too tight to hold anything. I stare out her bedroom window at the shock of sun's glare, refusing to enter. I stare at the miles of the city, sprawled out. The city rests on tribal land in a metallic voice devoid of adobe sultry notes. Architecture is a refugee of this torn world, unable to run, its feet frozen to the ground. The city has teeth, and it devours the land with its politics and materialistic gluttony. It devoured its way through nearby villages, upheaving homes for "better" franchised architecture. It's not urban sprawl, it's rural devouring; sharp glamorized buildings glooming above shacks and poverty. We, the city, stand in the tribal land of Kang.

The country is the city, and it's devouring its way into my mother's body.

Mama's back cranes as she screams. Her teeth gnash, a few topple to the ground. I collect them quickly, shake them like dice for a miracle, and put them in the jar, place it on the shelf next to my great-great-grandmother's. Mama refuses to die. Not yet. "Please, Mama," I cry. "Please."

Her skin sizzles with boils, her scream penetrates everything, like steel boring into my bones. Something beyond us harbors in the air. Botshelo foolishly tries to plead with this thing.

"Please, we'll give you anything," she cries, spinning around, unseeing. She's naive. She doesn't know that to give is to sacrifice soul-blood. I cup my hand around her mouth.

"To live is evil," something in the air says; maybe the air is not an accomplice, maybe it's the victim to the voice-holder that hides itself in its folds, camouflaging itself to taunt and haunt us. But that voice came when we hurt the earth; now Mmê Earth hurts us in turn. In our tribal land, the human soul is tied to the land; what hurts the land hurts the soul. I listen to the burrowing screams, seismic, of Mama's cries as she gives birth to death, fighting it too. Trauma punches a hole into our family's time—time-hole—because he left, my father.

"To save someone, it is better to kill them," the voice in the air says.

But why, why why why?

This urban sprawl continues to eat into Mama's blood, bones, her mind, destroying the culture that once disseminated in her bloodline. The still night is mixed with the sound of rattle-shakers, like cicadas imprisoned in beads, singing into a heated crescendo. The mourning voices of the choirs, a funeral song, as they beat their palms and thrust their illegal unfiltered breaths into the balmy air. The treetops inhale the wind, tossing it back and forth, collecting sin-dust and disposing it into our mask-less faces.

Mama bleeds and screams, breaking bones that recalibrate themselves. "Someone is killing our land. Someone is our enemy. Someone in our midst hides in our color. Catch them! Catch them; if your land dies, you die."

Those were the last words as Mama fought death, a death that tried to silence her, but her voice rose higher than any flesh, a bigger purpose than us. Her voice, her words are immortal, lived longer than the people who thought killing her would stop her entirely. But she lives in those words and many more:

"Only non-sinners cast stones," Mama used to say, "which is why I cast my voice to you."

"But how do I cast my voice when it was stolen from me?" I'd ask her.

My world ended on my mother's tongue. She was the only one whose voice wasn't a murderer. Mama wasn't a believer, but she survived on her beliefs for a while. "Nana, I will only believe what I see," Mama used to whisper as she kneaded bread, "therefore all these superstitions are just make-belief hallucinogenic kak that people like to eat." Kak; crap, shit. We covered her corpse to prepare for her burial, but hours later we found it twisted; the apartment yanked the voice box from her throat, and days on end, the apartment whistled a hazy dark into the folds in between our legs. I hate this apartment. I hate this architecture.

I don't know why she had to test reality like that. Now she's dead. She's left us alone. And I wonder if she became a believer when she saw what was happening to her. Sometimes faith keeps you alive, but sometimes it kills you. So I hardly hold on to things or people. There are those before us who have sinned more than we have sinned, but they enjoyed the mercy of Mmê Earth, unlike us today.

Our sinful habits are the cause of everything that's happening in our city—every action must birth a more powerful insidious reaction. Our sins are here to reap our sorrows into our corpses.

Mama's gone and we are without her protection. We are demons; we can't be exorcised.

Each week, on a Sunday, we rose early, went to church, sang hymns, waited for the priest to slap our heads desperately trying to extract the demons in our bodies. We'd return in our Sunday church-anointed bodies, and in dark rooms and secret-encased closets, we'd remove our skull-covering, clean the sticky residue of toxic thoughts. Sometimes we'd lick them, gluey and chewy, push them down our throat, wondering how something sweet and delectable was a danger to the environment.

Sun, Hide

I pray to You, Mother Earth, Mama Earth, Mmê Earth:
Sun, hide your eye, eclipse your birth from our sins.
Earth's hands taste like smoke and suicide.
We held our unborn,
lay open beneath the cirrus veils of sky,
catching sunlit stars without knowing the death we salt their throat
with—
our babies, their eager lungs slurping, thinking all is oxygen, all is milk.
In the mornings, we pray.
Because of infertility from this global war,
men have taken children from the streets, to have their children.
It's sick; Sun, hide your eye, eclipse your birth.

living-as-an-orphan

My bed is a comforting grave at times. The night is still, sleep is a villain, taunting me to lull in its quietude waters. Death is a silent walker. I am drowning in a room full of oxygen. Oh, dear God, no, has the sickness come to get me? Has Mama Earth's hounds come for me?

I don't want to die like my brother, Itumeleng. Mmê Earth was angry. Her tides were high, her labors strong. She was purging a group of them one by one by their sins. By their lack of consideration for the other. The natives who looted the foreigner's businesses, burning them down, beating them up—they were found walking about like ghosts, in incomprehensible chatter. My brother, Itumeleng, was one of them. We pulled him home. Several days later, he died. His xenophobic predilection killed him. Sin-fever is fatal.

But no, I am not sick. Something else must be the problem. A loud siren flares in the darkness, my bedroom, supported by intermittent flashes of a warning red light. My respirator screeches into the midnight hour, wailing. I sit up, pinwheeling; my lungs burn with pain as I gulp for the excruciating unfiltered air that scrapes its way through my nostrils, frying my alveoli. The respirator continues to cry, clamped to my nose and mouth, a gaudy beast, unlike the sleek expensive models that my friends have. It has a chute leading into my esophagus as thick as a python that swells and assesses the safety of food that enters my body. Tonight, it gags me.

Warning! Replace your respirator immediately. I need to change it. Warning! Pollutants rife in the air, in the city: carbon emission, racism, oil spills, sexism, deforestation, misogynism, xenophobia, murder... I'm not the only one screaming in our neighborhood tonight. Someone is dying because of a simple skull-escaped thought, and as they exhale their smog-breath into the air it contaminates us all. We hurt the earth, and so shall we hurt each other.

I fall onto the floor, banging my fists, trying to reach for mercy, gulping for air, but choking from its excruciating asphyxiation. I yank open my side table drawers desperately looking for another respirator as I would a sanitary pad when I leaked onto the bed. *Dear God, I don't want to die, not today, please, I'm only eighteen years old. Please, God.* I'm hiccupping and sobbing, desperately pleading to God that I hope I didn't forget to at least leave one spare respirator. Several rustic ones sit aside for return-and-exchange purposes.

As I rummage, the glinting eye of a respirator calls my attention as my bedroom's soul-light licks its reflective surface. I yank the current respirator off my face, and it swivels to the ground, the chute covered in mucus as I choke out stomach-sac produce. Sin-dust quickly steals entry into my nostrils, making me sneeze and cough. I slowly dangle the new respirator's chute like a spaghetti string into my mouth, and slowly slide it down my esophagus, and to avoid a gag reflex I attempt to do this with ease as I'm dying; it is a skilled art I learned the hard way.

Eventually, the mouthpiece fits snugly into my mouth and nose. A green glow fills my face, the new respirator hums gladly, filtering the air that enters smoothly and cleanly into my body. Fresh air is as rare as a non-manufactured human being. Respirator installed into the body successfully! I made it in 2 minutes 39 seconds, but the poisonous, unfiltered oxygen slimes the surfaces of my lung sacs, deteriorating them further.

I fold into the floor, tears dampening my face, panic gripping me. The soul-lights in our home flicker. As renewable as they are, the bandwidth of our souls is bone-thin, in need of being replenished. Darkness will fall soon. Life, for the generations before us, used to be easier, air floating around their bodies, easy to inhale, easy to exhale. Mmê Earth, You used to be so healthy for us . . . until we destroyed You. I understand now why You want to purge us from Your womb. But it is unfair. How come we are the ones to suffer for the before-generation's desires that smoked our future? I hate them. I hate them all. And now this is who I have become; I sinned by breathing more pollution into Mother Earth's belly. Nonetheless, I must show gratitude to Mother Earth, God, and the Universe. I prostrate, take a deep breath, glad and desperate for clean air.

My respirators last only a month each. This is my last one. I need to buy a new one, tampons, period-pain medication, anti-depressant medication, food, water—these are all necessary things that I can't do without. Maybe I can do without food for a bit, but with my anemia, I need some iron at least. All my uncle has to worry about is food, Chibuku, and porn. Normally, Mama was the only one who'd remind us to change our respirators the day before they expired, or when we needed to buy more food supplies. These are the holes in our families, the holes we must survive with. Even now, I can't maintain the tasks she managed. How did she even manage our water harvest, for when we open our taps, the droplets grip to the metal mouth, refusing to release; how did she ration and stretch our food storage for months long?

When Mama died, I had to become a mother to people and grown-ass men I didn't even give birth to. I only care for my sister. But my bones are tired, they want a rest I'm too afraid to give.

the-time-hole

Every girl-child is given one of three roles: warriorship, housewifery, birther of death. My sister is neither, so she is considered useless. It's only been years since my mother died, but it feels just like yesterday. The time-hole initiates the memory every month. We can't run away from it. My cousin is rattling through the house, carrying away dust and sin, which coagulates to the upper-roof of the soul-blood, slick and sticky. She came when the time-hole reported my mother's funeral to every family member. Everyone is here. She keeps bustling about every room. I want silence and shadows.

A low frequency forces itself into our ears, a burning signal, Morse code. The disparate breathing of the earth, its belly. By rote, I rise. Unfold my skin-coat; it ages slowly. I pick my thought-dial, it refuses to connect. Our soul's bandwidth isn't strong enough to carry our message, it needs funds, and maybe in many lightyears, someone will hear our story light the sky. Communication and commerce have merged with our bodies, tore its way into our minds with no need of access codes and passwords. It needs our bodies more than we need it. When we were young, Mama used to chide my sister, Botshelo. Botshelo thought of every unforeseeable bad thing. The divorces in our family. Men who weren't supposed to touch girl-child nieces a certain way. Affairs that clung to the dark in the closets. And every time Botshelo woke up, she wondered if the city had shat her out yet, had purged her yet. She'd see me and hope ceased to light her eyes, so she'd lie back hoping one day that she'd actually die.

As I enter my sister's room, her soul-light flickers as my shadow stomps on it. Her sickness is a gauzy yellow veil in the bedroom. Soon I swallow its acrid taste, bitterer than bile. On the other side of the house, I hear her thought-dial ringing, endless, the hour hanging fruitlessly on the limb of the only technology that connects us. She hardly opens her mouth. But her thoughts always crowd me in the kitchen as I knead bread, hoping to deep-fry magwinya for us. And now, whoever is calling us is impinging on our thought-dial's bandwidth—we bought two to share five winters ago; we may as well share the same skull. I feel Mama Earth's force clench around my body, and I do a quick prayer, *I will police my own thoughts before they're skull-born, before You feel their whisper bend Your bones.* It's a hard thing. Our bodies are no longer the refuge of our souls. The flesh soul-holders are grief-stricken.

Botshelo sits in the dim light, her feet dusty with not-belonging as she ropes sectioned parts of her Afro in wool. For days she looks like this, a medusa with maphondo-styled hair. Her time-hole is rusted and old and hangs next to the rain-wet umbrella by the door. That's how I remembered that tornado day. The mud footsteps that led to her bedroom. The miasma of her sickness and sweat that hung humid-thick in the air first notified us she was sick, but she wouldn't tell us why. That's how I remember my sister. Her time-hole, a metal thing that stored everything about us: biometric data, digital life, AI assistant, bank accounts, medical aid info—everything, yet it wouldn't tell us what she did.

I pull aside Botshelo's tattered curtains, and a bird, something rare in our city, sits on the windowsill pecking at our window.

Botshelo sits up from her bed, joy brightening her eyes. "Death's coming," she says, staring at the bird. "It's knocking on our window. My window."

"That's not a good sign," I say, sighing. I knock my fist against the window. The bird throws itself into the air, flapping its wings.

My sister crosses her arms, a sour twist to her lips. "Why won't the doctors just kill me if they won't save me?"

"You know why they can't kill you," I say, crying. "The city still needs your body connected to the grid. How else can they connect to your soul?"

Our souls light up the riches' avenues and streets we can't even call home.

"Now, here, it's time to go for your meds," I say, dragging out her wheelchair from the closet.

She pushes herself into her pillows, sulking. "Please, tomorrow. I hate that place." She raises her pinkie. "I promise I'll be more agreeable tomorrow."

"It's the only way they'll let us live here," I say, folding the wheelchair back.

"But this was our grandmother's home. It's our home," she cries.

I walk toward the bed, wrap my arm around her. "Things will work out, let's just be a bit more patient."

"People used to live longer than this," she whispers. "Sisi, we expire so fast, but why us? Why not those who had the chance to enjoy Mmê Earth? Why are we living in their shit?"

I hold my head in fear of it snapping off my neck. So, like always, my sister counts my fingers hoping that they stay even.

"I shouldn't have sold my eggs," she whispers, "to the manufactures. Look at all those abnormal manufactured humans. Yes, they live longer, they're resilient, but still, we're still humans, we matter as well. I shouldn't have signed up for the experiments to save this family—look at me now, they destroyed my body. When it wasn't satisfactory for them, they fired me, took me off their payroll. They don't even give a fuck about me."

"You were gone for years," I whisper, "what exactly happened?"

She realizes now the acerbic rise of the past, existing in this little room of ours, burning her tongue. Realizes how she never spoke of her experience. Realizes how her discomfort triggers the trauma. I watch her, silently calculating, sifting through her thoughts, editing them then throwing them away because neither one sounds good.

She pulls her knees to her chest, peers at me through her thick eyelashes. "Why am I the one who's ashamed when it should be them who's ashamed?" It surprises me, this response of hers, the light sharpening her pupils to a dark pinpoint in her brown eyes.

"What did they do to you?" I ask.

"There are many of them out there." She rests her chin on her knees. "I don't know how many. I'm going to die without knowing how many . . ." She hiccups. A sob. A tear streams down her cheek.

"How many what?" I ask.

Her grip tightens around her knees, her shoulders clench forward, as if gripping onto her secret. Maybe she realizes that she doesn't have long to live, maybe that's why she's slowly opening up to me every day.

I catch her teardrops and massage her shoulder. "How many what?" I ask softly.

"Children."

"Children?"

"My . . ." She sighs, digs her head into her knees, then in a muffled voice, whispers. "My children. The manufactured ones."

No one in our family likes her mouth except me. They'd gagged her with soap once. She woke up to find him with his arm down her throat, soapy and acrid. She couldn't even scream. His thought-dial, unlike ours, was portable. He was authorized by the family to do that. Their reputation was more important. Perhaps, at a microclimate level that's how it started—accumulated from every family, from every district, from every nation to the whole continent until it overwhelmed Her, Mmê Earth. So when my sister tells me she has children, I think it's just her typical mouth speaking silly stuff.

"The plan behind the experiments was to migrate the upper-class citizens into a more resilient body that can withstand our climate," she whispers. "They've already paid body rentals and purchases of the manufactured bodies."

My respirator makes a hoarse noise, then I realize it's me gasping, choking. I clasp my hand to the respirator, as if it's in the way of my breathing.

It's the shock, filling my bloodstream with adrenaline. Is this what Mama meant? *Someone is killing our land. Someone is our enemy. Someone in our midst hides in our color. Catch them! Catch them; if your land dies, you die.*

Our land is our bodies.

I'm supposed to love my sister, to care for her, but each time I look at her, I feel this grudge, its furnace burning in my body. I stare at her as if she's holding a knife to my back. I could be next. I could be Mama. I grip her shoulders, my sudden movement stunning her. "Why is She doing this to you?" I ask. "What did you do to Her?"

"To who?" she shrieks.

"Mama Earth!" I yell. "What did you do to turn Her against our family. Are you telling the truth?" I ask. "Is this why you're re-sick? You only become sick when you've sinned against Mama Earth."

"I became part of their experiments, part of their sins, and yes, I may have sinned."

"What did you do to Her?"

She clasps her ears with hands.

"Please don't be ashamed," I say. "Just tell me."

"Everyone sins against each other thinking they're going to live forever, thinking they can trick Her. You can't. Sin leads to death."

"You're the only one sick in our family," I say.

"Even Malome is sick," she yells. Malome; uncle. "He thinks I don't hear him at night, creeping through our passage into the toilet, vomiting every night, his diarrhea filling the toilet bowl, him wearing heavy garments in this heat wave. He's trying to hide the rash from the sin-fever." Her eyes turn deadly on me. "Soon you'll fall sick."

There are secrets in our family. Terrible secrets that lie on our skin like rash. The rage in me burns. I stare at the blatant, gaudy sickness clinging like a batshit lover to her skin. The rash. The boils. The scathing lies. *What did you do to become like this? Are you still my sister? Why do you cling to your secret like this disease clings to your bones? What pollution did you impose into the environment that it turned on you? Did you burn down someone's house? Did you talk down to someone because of their religion? Did you kill someone?* Mother Earth no longer stands for such pollutants anymore. I ask these questions only to myself because she won't say. Who are you? I hate that there's a part of her that I don't know. Mama Earth knows all our secrets, Her and God and the Universe, and They will not let us live freely with them.

"Haven't you learned anything from Itumeleng?" I ask her, reminding her of the family fable, the death of our brother.

A family fable:

The only reason someone becomes sick is because they sinned, did something terrible. Last summer when the sun was boiling the air, my brother was one of many behind the xenophobic attacks on foreigners' businesses—looting, burning, killing. The next morning as I made breakfast for the family, he sat in the middle seat as usual. He tried to eat the bread. He tried to drink the coffee. But his mouth was skew, and everything slipped out. The next morning, his mouth was slack, teeth unhinged. He had a knife. Scratched at his skin.

He was allergic to his skin.

He scraped it down to white flesh that was just as quickly flooded with bright-red blood. He became allergic to himself. The only cure was death. Mama Earth was trying to purge him as he tried to purge the outsiders; but not as quickly as he snuffed them. She did it slowly and painstakingly so that perhaps remorse diluted his rage. Only good and God and Allah or whoever holy you believe in will exist. All evil will be extracted out like a bad molar from Mama Earth's mouth. The rest, She will purge unto death. The racism and exclusion too, hit back like a bad wave of locusts, harbingers, a pandemic of encephalitis. The population was low. They tried to manufacture new people who'd be more resilient to this new climate.

Tomorrow is looking for Future

We still continue to sin. I have been out, looking for a second piece-job; it's been a failure. I am brilliant, I am smart, I am talented—I know that, but I lack the privilege and wealth to get into "somewhere, somewhere." Every department's response: "We are looking for someone with mass appeal," they say, every snow-white strand pulled tautly from their scalps.

"Your work, your body is not a fit for our list . . . unless you are interested in signing up for our experiments."

I was desperate, but not that desperate. Look at what they did to my sister's body, and I still have to take her to them for meds. But I didn't want to be blacklisted for my attitude, so I bowed my head, smiled, and thanked them for their consideration. When I stepped outside, I couldn't breathe. I was filled with a burning panic at the truth: there are walls built around me. I can't see them, but I can feel how they suck at the air around me leaving me unable to breathe. All the things they want me to censor about myself will eventually censor my existence in their eyes; from this, as Mother Earth has dictated, they will die. But they don't believe in this "superstition" like Mama didn't. And now she sleeps in a grave.

On the way home, I tried contacting my sister, but she was not responding to my thought-dial, so I had to storm up the dirt-stirred concrete stairs. She's probably with her boyfriend. Lung-borne pollutants proliferate the air, obscuring the hallway's path. I bang on an apartment door—her boyfriend's. I bang it again. He, the boyfriend, yanks it open. Climate change has made a home in the marrow of their bones. His studio apartment contains doctored air hyped with amphetamines, secondary meth-smoke.

The lady downstairs selling gene-hacked vegetables told me that she heard from a neighbor that my sister and her boyfriend stoned a young couple a few days ago.

I refused to believe her. "They're not violent people," I tried to tell her. "No, not my sister."

"They called the couple terrible words, said they're sick, yet your sister and her boyfriend are the sick ones. What fucker does that to another human being? Bashes their head in because of their love?" she'd asked. "They're sick, I tell you. Demented."

Then the old woman hobbled to her workstation to pick up her thought-dial and sent me the image that was circulating through many thought-dials. The couple, two young girls in love, lying huddled in the street. My sister and her boyfriend, their hands bloody, their eyes rabid and fierce.

I staggered backward. "This is not my sister, no, she's—she's not capable of this."

"You're so foolish with your faith in your sister," she'd said.

I want to rid our city of this pollutant that continues to destroy our world. This pollutant that infests my sister's body. If my sister dies from sin-fever—no, I can't watch her die so that the world continues to live. She is my world more than this Earth is. It's not her fault—but this is her, hurting another human being, for what reason?

"My sister, she's only fourteen," I whispered. "She's just a kid. He's twenty-three."

"Dating a kid. Perhaps that's why he's doubly sick." The old woman grabbed her thought-dial back. "The police don't need to lift a finger," she said, "Mama Earth will sort these criminals out. They deserve what's coming to them."

Actions and thoughts lead to real sickness. Stoning someone can give you a disease worse than cancer. And I see it now, what Mama Earth is doing to them, the encephalitis sickness of their consequences, gripping to their sharp cheekbones, as they limp around the small apartment, looking puny and pitiful. A cackle of thunder as if Mama Earth laughs over this. My sister's boyfriend is shaky, at first, bones brittle, cytosine rife with anxiety and depression like every other citizen, and saturated with commercial ads that probably sprayed every tester at them from every façade with cleaning agents to protect society from their sickness, charging them an automatic "small" fee that they couldn't pay.

"Why?" I ask. They both stare at me stupidly.

"I'm sorry, I was puking," Botshelo says. "I didn't have my thought-dial. Just saw your message. I'm ready, we can go."

"Is it true?" I ask. "Did you hurt those women?"

Her lips tighten into themselves. "Don't believe every rumor you hear."

I raise my rusty thought-dial. "I have evidence of you and him"—I point at her boyfriend without staring at him—"hurting them."

"It was a misunderstanding." She picks up her luggage and drags her body to a stand. "We're going to be late."

I stand in her way. "Why did you hurt those women? They're barely holding on to life at the hospital."

"Speaking of the hospital, if we don't leave now, we'll be very late."

I shake my head. "Take your damn self."

As I turn my back on her, her voice reaches out to my neck. "You think you're so innocent. Don't neglect your family or Mama Earth will punish you like She's punishing our uncle. You'll be next soon."

I turn to her. This is my sister. When did she change? Become this way? Is it the sickness now changing all that remains of her? In the days to come what will she turn into before she dies? Does she still love me? No, not if she will stoop so low to threaten me so as to do what she needs.

Chemical weapons fondled Earth too much. I guess the environment became sick and fed into her, then she became sick and fed into the environment—this cycle, no quarantine. I remember we'd drive for miles, the fields barren, the quarry a white-torn wound in the earth. The earth tried to swallow back its ocean, but it came back in tsunamis, washed aside our homes in toxic acid. My eye-feed blurs, another village has gone down. Everyone is living in temporary housing, but the rich stay in the sky, smoking it up, because they can afford it.

I slam the door leaving them alone, wiping tears from my face with my fist. *My family is falling apart, Mama Earth. I'm sorry, please forgive them,* I yell at the sky.

I step outside, the heat boiling the air. Fuck.

We have become foreigners to Earth, and it has turned xenophobic.

hidden-by-night

Darkness falls. The moon clicks into place, like a bullet into the chamber. I must hide. I catch sight of the moon, half-slain, a stranger. Why is Mama Earth punishing my uncle? What has he done?

Nightly. Moonlight sways through the air abnormally, and once in contact with skin, a rash quickly develops. Severe asphyxiation initiates. Soon death befalls the body. The moon is a toxic beauty. We must remain indoors; the tectonics of architecture are built to restrain outside toxins from us, and our toxins from the natural environment. It'll be only an hour before the city shuts the moonlight out.

Night; the world dissolves into black. All I hear is humming rain, panting breaths. Every noise slows down to a heartbeat. Soul-lights flare. Only the broken moon's shadow tells us the time. I can leave my residence now. I will follow him, the honorable uncle, to see what he does under the cloak of night.

Maybe once I witness his ugly actions, then I will understand the sickness that pervades my sister, that is killing my family one by one. As I follow him in the dark—through the backstreets, the gravel road, the barren fields, to a lowly place between two hills, a tavern overlooking a bonfire—my thoughts burn a feverish gloom, evaporating from my skull, almost exposing my hiding place. It's not just us, there's a tavern of them. Oh, dear, God, Mama Earth—it disgusts me what they do. I crouch lower behind a cactus. *Moon, hide your eye, eclipse your birth from our sins.* A tavern of them stand, dancing and drinking around the bonfire. Laughing. Little children. There are little kids here. How can these people laugh at this evil they create?

Who can I cry to in this very second that can stop this cruelty? Even if I ran back to the city to report them, they'll be gone by the time I get back. My thought-dial has no network. Mama Earth, there are people made of devil-skins unburned by God hands. These are the people I see in our newsfeed in our government in our schools who act as our guardians—these are the people that make a noose out of bible pages, wrap it around our ears and eyes, and hang You dry. They wrap it around the night, saying, "This is the lung of Earth." I know these men with starving throats so full of fire to evade the teeth of ethics; they're carving hunger into the belly of our children, saying our food security is compromised, saying there is drought, yet they're taking these children's hunger to dress their dinner tables. They light the torch of hunger in our bellies and parade streets and slums saying, "Here is light, here is star."

I press my fist against my mouth to stop me from screaming at the horror. Behind closed skins, and even in the sockets of eyes, they bury themselves in wombs of little children to carve their names inside them, until their bellies balloon to sky, their hearts nowhere found. Is this what happened to my sister in her experiments? I can't watch this anymore. Sun, moon-stain your bloodied ribs. We're a spatter of sky, there are sinless stars broken from the voice in our throats. These men, there are deserts in their heartlands. They've learned how to open children-thighs, their mouths are spraying evil into the crooks of their knees, breaking the language from them in villages where the tongue is tender, the brain soft.

The village, a mecca for men
who still fondle the night with their wife hung around their necks.
They make a shebeen of children's limbs,
turning their hearts into sorghum and dust,
teeth nicking their magic from children's milk,
children who don't know what it means to be the hourglass of birth
as death lilts at the cages in their chests.
It snows in parts of them that didn't know the sun.

"Child, do you understand my anger now?" The voice in the fold of the air enters my ears, quietly. I jump, turning around. There's no one near me. No one has seen me.

Mama Earth is intimate with my thoughts: *Mama Earth is that you? Has it been you all along?*

"Child, do you understand my anger now?" She asks.

All along it's been Your voice in the air, Mama Earth?

"Child, do you understand my anger now?" the air-voice repeats into my ear.

I understand Your fury, Mama Earth.

"What must I do now?" You ask. "Must I let such people live?"

Stop them, stop them, the kids—the poor kids!

"To live is evil," Mama Earth's air-voice says. "Do you see that now? Now tell me, what must I do?"

Stop them please.

"How must I stop them?" She asks. "Don't you remember this? Remember we have been here before?"

There are so many memories in my head. We became man, the machine that decimated the planet, hastened its way toward its end. The phantom of our thoughts rose from our limbic systems as we slept and night's tentacles fed into our nervous system. Anxiety and depression grew like the urban sprawl of our cities into the marrow of our bones.

"What else do you remember?" Mama Earth asks.

Our home villages were gone, replaced by cold foreign skyscrapers, its mother tongue guillotined. With toxic lungs, our thoughts carried weapons through the night, tore the trees down, sullied the waters. I remember seeing an angry moon that night, leaking death into our time-holes. Time-holes, the only thing close we had to sanity, to humanity. That night, we silenced our thought-dials, watched our time-holes glow in the dark. My sister was bone-tired. "Climate change has crept from the built environment into the marrow of my bones," she'd whispered in that raspy voice of hers. "That's what's wrong with me. Climate change lives in me. The old are lucky to have died and lived in a safer Earth. This one wants to purge me—Earth doesn't want me born."

I remember she'd stared at her time-hole hoping for a better reincarnation, but time was a ceaseless, indifferent creature. Her time-hole sat on the mantelpiece, anachronistic, beeping at the endless updates it starved for. During the night, we listened to the hoarse grumble of taps that were thirsty for water. She checked her time-hole where every part of her life resided. There were no funds. There were no jobs. There were no opportunities, except the hole in between her thighs to hold men who didn't want children.

"You can start afresh," Mama Earth's air-voice says. "But to live again you have to die. It's the only way I can stop or save them. Tell me, how must I stop them?" Her air-voice fills me. And I know what she wants me to say. "Why do you keep choosing to relive your family's past and trauma. Let's stop it now. Do not be afraid, child."

I stand on the edge of a rock, whisper to the wind, "I know what I'm going to do will be considered evil, illegal. I do not care." Summertime languishes on winter's skin. Sky tears are saltier than ever. Forests and grasslands are scraped back like alopecia of the land. We're buried in this tombstone of tar; a desert gives birth to anorexic trees.

How can they not feel that? How can they not taste that? Our evolutions are running through Mother's bloodstreams.

Sun, Earth: your truth needs pain.
I'm sick of it.
I.
Am.
Sick.
I do not care;
so Sun, hide your eye, eclipse your birth.
Tonight, the city goes.
Sea-rise will be our baptism, brushing Her breath of our toxin.

That's when the fissure tore through Your layers, it's Your anger Mama Earth, and rocks from the hill eclipsed some lives. That's why You drowned some continents, Your bile swallowing whole civilizations. Many times this has occurred based on such morbid actions. You're sick of it. So sick it hurts. You, Mother Earth, taste like suicide, smoke, smog.

a-sleeping-earth

I don't know where I am currently. I am a being freed of flesh. I am sight without bone, without structure. Hope is a sun that never rises. A moon that never "woke." All it knows is a night full of stars it pulls from people's hearts.

There's no existence in the constellation. There is only smoke and no God in the horizon. Look at Her, Mother Earth, Her womb protruding into a constellation of space and dark matter—*we* matter. The heat warms Her globe, She is lit, She is lava. Atmosphere is our gas mask, forests are an underbrush of sky, and ocean waves emulate amniotic fluid. Gravitational pulls, the labor pains. The ozone layer unfolds, the gases choke. The sky is screaming. The sun broke, and he's bleeding past our horizon.

I am gone, I am going, but I am here too.

Everything hurts. Everything—it hurts. The Earth, She hurts—we degrade Her skin, discriminating it with war, bombs, shootings, and pollution . . . there are parts of Her body desecrated, forcing people to flee, leaving Her naked. Don't you see? She's human too. We live in *Her—Her* womb. Earth can't commit suicide; we commit it for Her. I am gone, I am going, but I am here too. Everything hurts. Everything—it hurts. Don't you see? But the pain. Tell me you can't smell that? The summer sky smells smoke. I smell smoke. Her soul, a pyre for our desire, burns. The summer sky . . . my starry eyes are smoked. This is what we became; Her ozone layer is torn, the sun leaks through. She is bleeding moon. Everything hurts . . . the oceans, the ecosystem—Her heart, it beats outside Her.

Our heartbeats were cataclysmic, a big bang, giving birth to pandora-things. Every creation gives birth to chaos as well—we know this now and we will be reborn.

And that Woman, soft rivers run in her throat, volcanoes thunder in her voice

She is lady,
She is monster,
She is Sun,
Hide your eye,
Eclipse your birth,
Sea-rise will be our baptism
We will be reborn.

Selections from

The Tale of the Harmattan

TANURE OJAIDE

Tanure Ojaide is a Nigerian poet and scholar of African literature and culture who has published poetry collections and volumes of literary criticism. His poetry collection *Songs of Myself: A Quartet* (2017) won the 2018 Wole Soyinka Prize for Literature in Africa. In *The Tale of the Harmattan* (2007) and across his writings, Ojaide plumbs the resources of oral tradition and appropriates the techniques of bioregional writing. His poetry catalogs the physical and psychological costs of mineral extraction and the threats they pose to continuity in the Niger Delta region. In representing polluted landscapes and the exploitation of environmental resources in Africa, Ojaide secures these locales in the imagination.

The goat song

I

I sing the community's goat song.
Folks wear gold over tumors of hope;

they are rounded into a guarded prison
south-south of the mountain palace

where the king and his consorts carouse;
a bacchanalia that breaks the rock of reason.

The capital so afflicted with flatulence,
only thunder can halt insatiable hands

from clearing the commonwealth's table
of cornucopia into paunches of the lords.

Those sitting on wealth are rickety, groveling
on sand; globules of anguish their only share.

And who cares if foreigners found deep
under their bare feet divine gifts of pools

and started to tap the earth's underbelly
for fuel to blaze brushes of progress?

II

All along wells brought forth rusty coloration;
folks wondered about the sign from beyond—

all along the taste of water from wells exposed
what kind gods held underground for the people;

the gods know best what their devotees know not,
they bless the people with their measures of wealth.

Is health not the greatest wealth? Ask the old
what blessing exceeds the wealth of health.

Must you uncover the wrapped gifts of gods
if you have absolute faith in their benevolence?

I sing the people's goat song—
they wear smiles over deep wounds.

III

They incinerate our dead heroes with flares;
no hardwood for caskets to accord them honor.

Ozidi will not forgive the humiliation.
Ogidigbo will not forgive the insult.

The blackened stream is ancestral blood
tapped away by giant pipes into ships

to rejuvenate foreign cities, invigorate markets;
distant places lit with wonders; here, a blackout.

Agitated, Mowoe flaunts his right forefinger.
In self-defense Saro-Wiwa exhorts foot soldiers.

The wind laments, its fans are burning out;
the trees have been shaved of their coiffures.

The snake is sliding closer to the heart
and its venom intensifies with every strike.

The big family is dying out—irokos fall; game
leave in droves, and humans flee to hunger.

Soon the whole landscape will be a cemetery
south-south of the carousing palace of the king.

The carrion lord cares not for the rot he stirs;
he pranks with consorts in the death-field

Government and the coalition of global lords
have snatched away what ancestors sat upon.

I sing the land's goat song;
the last cry of its warriors.

Priests, converts, and gods

Pentecostal converts burnt down the primeval grove—
there, they believed, witches metamorphosed into owls;

they did not even know what animals they had become,
when they were *born again*, living in self-renunciation.

The developers tore down the forest that covered us
with green foliage, trashed the natural canopies—

they argued we needed roads to go out, as if we knew
nothing of adventure or did not visit other places.

They also argued we needed schools and football fields,
not to continue living in the bush where they found us.

It was futile explaining to them the divine splendor
when the archer sun shoots gold-tinted arrows between leaves;

it was a shame that those who loved colors didn't see
the spectacle of rain, wearing reeds, perform a stilt dance.

After school I looked out for the public park,
the community of plants and animals, they promised

but they only felled more trees for cemeteries, forbade burials
in homes to confine ghosts to fenced lots and make towns safe.

Worshipping a foreign-accented god, they thrust a blazing
firebrand

at the behind of the war-god who fled his guard without
looking back.

Up north the Sahara devouring plants advances ferociously
after gulping the River Niger in a generation-long fit of thirst.

In the south campfires of oil barons litter the landscape;
stoked all year round by helmet-wearing graduates

who consider themselves lucky, paid foreign currency
instead of the naira; an astute ploy to buy their loyalty.

The streams and creeks clogged to keep ocean tankers full,
we no more boast of fresh water or the abundance of fish.

We know the capital gain from the blessed but besieged land
will go down the drain for a caste to maintain its smug smile.

The priests that came from abroad warned of the inferno
that would consume those who did not heed their
commandments—

they were wrong in attributing hell to another life; it is
here victims already suffer daily pangs from profiteers,

condemned to burning winds of gas flares and streams
of boiling oil so combustible they burn all in their wake.

Quatrain suite

1

To have loved Mami Wata in her underwater palace of coral:
to have had trysts with the moon in her days of full glory,
to have tasted one dish and never wished for another,
and to have lived here when it was a different country!

2

My memories chase out the army of poachers.
In their green outfit of old seasons they restore
the tattered map of the country. Now the starving
amongst us trip over carcasses they won't even touch.

3

I look for the reed in the tide, the resilient spirit
bending but never breaking; the slim one
that relishes its God-given supple limbs—
now another casualty drowned in oil slush.

4

Before the fisherman could finish building a boat to evacuate,
the river dried up and horses galloped through to capture him—
in exile he remembered the moats of Benin did not stop swarms
of locusts
from devastating the city and having their fill of blood and
bronze.

5

The map of my homeland has changed.
The cartographers blot out forests and rivers.
Oil wells and flares dot the new landscape—
now nobody recognizes the beauty queen's face.

6

The primeval inhabitants of the land
suffer martyrdom at the hands of poachers
who blast them out of their naive existence.
The Niger loses draughts; memories of majesty.

7

For good luck I carry about memories of floodwater,
primarily the seven-day storm that sank sun and moon
in gurgling streams and creeks, the entire land a seascape
when my bait-free new hooks caught catfish and mudfish.

8

The apiapia cries hysterically, flying over its former haunt:
"It's another planting season and what a cheerless sight,
hardly any farmers!" They fled to be servants in the city.
Who blames bird or migrant, the soil one barren crust?

9

Evergreens bald, every head bowed in disgrace.
No season grows back flared or suffocated leaves
and the cycle of self-succeeding generations dies.
Green is now a scarce commodity in the rainforest."

10

The eye of the earth beholds a vandalized fortune.
The ears of the earth numb from the deep silence,
Its veins clogged by an abundance of oily grease,
its heart beats an irregular drum that fades away.

11

When wood copulates with iron,
the axe is born and groomed
to chop down more trees.
Suicide goes by many names.

12

The iroko knows not how it can survive the iron era
to welcome eagles to its crown. I wish I knew how.
Globalization is a category-5 hurricane; its direction
escapes forecast—it leaves litters in an insane trail.

13

We have plenty of bait but no fish in the water—
decades of genocide, millions of victims.
Once earthworms begin to consume themselves,
the world would've run its cycle; a predator's paradise.

14

The rich among us used to boast of the many barrels
of palm oil they produced in the season of industry.
Then came spills and flares that burnt out palm trees.
Today the government and Shell toast their oil fortune.

15

The birds and beetles lost their refuge, as people
of the creeks lost their sun, moon, and stars to fumes.
Why are survivors of the globalization assault only
the insignia of commanders-in-chief, vultures and cobras?

16

When the migrant birds return, how will they know
their homes from others in the wilted dominion?
If they stray from the native soil, it's because
flaring winds blew them to where nobody lives.

17

In town there are new roads and signposts
as well as waves of rats and migrants—
democracy demolished monuments of dictators
for good, but still we bleed . . .

For my grandchild

My children have had no scholarships;
they can't fish or tap rubber as I once did,

the river transformed into a snake of a tomb
and the forest fraught with flares and fumes.

With crude oil gushing into slave ships
refurbished as free-market super-tankers,

the government assures people of development
with proceeds from export and spot-market deals.

No jobs for the graduates in the oil sector
even as wells litter the family's farmlands.

In the daily dearth of prospects staring at all,
mobile policemen brandish guns in the sun

and, from a safe distance above the ground,
hired retired marines keep the pipelines safe.

Villages of imploring eyes marching, hands up-
raised with green-leafed branches, mowed down.

CNN & BBC embedded with Chevron and Shell
report that local women, stripping before cameras

to save their dying children and men, are primitive.
In their secure wings they know not Ogoni's agonies.

With my grandchild born, the new Stone Age
of a nation very black in the books has begun

with refilled slave ships refurbished as super-tankers
anchored at Escravos and poaching inland as centuries ago.

Tale of the harmattan

It is harmattan, time to prepare every hearth
to combat northeast winds, fierce warriors

that this year have lost their frostbite
but still stir swirls of inescapable dust.

They say in their home country the dunes
have never enjoyed such massive fortune.

On the way hosts slashed and burnt trees
for the desert to advance without hindrance.

Season of brush fires, kites fly overhead
in festive formations in smoke-smothered skies;

still we lose not thatched homes or barns
since we keep a wide buffer state, a clearing.

The season's blaze diminishes the hard labor
demanded in preparation for the next planting.

But this season's like no other in the minstrel's memory;
the rubber tappers are frustrated with anemic trees

suffering hardship and baldness from a neighboring
business that devours whatever stands before it.

The exciting spirit of the harmattan is lost on us,
there is nothing to celebrate with bonfires

because the regular visitor failed to arrive
with the good luck that follows its wake—

the swarm of generous djinns that invade us
barred from the land by free marketers of oil.

In place of heat from the log-stoked hearth,
we burn from gas flares and oil blowouts

on insomniac nights in the big compound.
We no longer swathe ourselves from cold

in one blanket, warm and inhaling body odor;
the sparkling hearth telling our tale of the harmattan.

At the Kaiama Bridge

I see them retreat, flotillas of river spirits
who for centuries brought their spectacle to town
in yearly masquerades—they retreat seaward.
What becomes of us without their presence?

Along in the southward flow, all other water
borne names, once guests on land, return—
they are no longer safe in the drilling wetlands
that from beginning hosted the congress of life.

All with the property of land gone into water
to relieve themselves of the scathing noise above
return to the hard soil posthaste because now
the waters have turned to a poisonous brew.

We have organized a resistance army,
declared sovereignty over our resources;
but have not pushed back the poachers.
Outside forces pillage the inheritance.

I see the oil-blackened current suffocating
Mami Wata and her retinue of water maids;
they leave fast the inhospitable dominion
for the freedom and health of the open sea.

I have not seen a regatta in three decades.
Nor have I seen the island's boat of songs
raise its ritual paddle in salute to high gods
that astronauts now suffocate with satellites.

Oil spillage has fueled water hyacinths
to multiply astronomically across rivers.
Refugee gods are taking the last route
before the entire waterway is clogged.

Neighbors are surrendering their homes
to destruction by the fires from above.
Others have the soil burning underfoot,
their shield of green gone; mere ashes.

The refugees are removed from the fields
in company buses, a humanitarian gesture;
then in diarrhea-infected camps force-fed
genetically modified corn meant for cows.

Do I want to shed blood defending the wealth
that the gods themselves have given up
because they know in their serene silence
the barbaric charge of godless ones after them?

Is revolution dead and must the Egbesu Boys
surrender rights of ownership and humanity
to the brigand lord and his fierce livery
of insatiable appetites raising a flaming flag?

At the wobbling Kaiama Bridge that holds the Delta
together, I see a procession of oil-soaked water spirits
wailing their way out. No boats of fishermen plying
the waterways; no regatta and no swimmers in sight.

The fortune

Where the creeks enter the sea
Olokun filled me a boat to keep.

It was left for me to take home
without crying for more help

through pirates betting their lives
on unescorted cargoes passing—

robbers keep mirrors in closets
to foresee the fortune of others.

I steered upstream as I must;
the boat mine to take home

but it was too large and loaded
for the creeks that took me home—

the fingers of the Niger did not
always reach everywhere nearby.

At the last deep-water station,
destitute hands waited to off-load

the cargo and be head carriers
for the rest of the shallow way.

No road for boats to my home,
only logs floated there in floods—

the sky turned off its sprinklers
and rafters sat at home, waiting.

Among my helpers pilfering ones
that I can't convert into clean souls.

My home is large but not loaded
though Olokun filled me a boat.

Swimming in a waterhole

We grew up to love rivers and lakes, open refuge
that saved children from the hard labor at home—

every parent knew where first to look for a missing child
before ever alerting the town-crier to beat the drum.

Many of us did not concentrate at school in anticipation
of going straight to swim until dusk when eyes turned red.

Rivers and lakes must have cried themselves into silence—
we spent nothing of our millions of earnings to save them.

For decades water hyacinth overran the pristine waterscape
in convoys of weed and started stifling the beautiful host.

With the oil companies only looking after profit margins,
oil slicks easily found their way to bury the waters alive.

Parents still make demands of children as never before;
the ageless sun remains master archer in the dry season

and young ones ever restless seek new bathing spots
to relieve themselves of the sun's scorching gaze.

Burrow pits of road builders, deluged into perennial
waterholes, provide respite from hard labor at home

but there no fish, no water spirits borne by currents;
no Mami Wata and others to share the salt of life.

In these holes abandoned caterpillars and other monsters
drag down the swimmer without recourse to a treat.

We are fortunate we still swim in groups in the open.
After gas flares, oil slicks, and hyacinths converge

to turn rain into acid and all the methane seeps in
to raise new syndromes that destroy the body,

where next to seek refuge from step-mothers
when the sun flares up in its sadistic fit?

Without the trees

Without the trees
the wind no longer gestures playfully to me

without the evergreens
nobody speaks the lingua franca to me

without the creeks
the rains no longer sate my voracious appetite

without the currents
the flying fish no longer makes sorties into my soup pot

without the sun (now fumigated)
the sunbird no longer plays patiently with me

without the shrubs (already devoured by fire)
the dew no longer delivers to me the message of dawn

without the forest (now poached to death)
the choral ensemble of hyrax, woodpecker & co. no longer
performs for me

without the farms
the butterflies no longer indulge me with a colorful pageant

without the stars (all smothered)
I nightly lose my way to the congress with ancestors.

Transplants

I see transplants of my youth's landscape
first at Hawthornden and now at Steepletop:

the pristine streams, the multiethnic population
of plants, costumed birds, and graceful game.

Surely no bears, coyotes, or foxes there
but deer, antelope, and porcupine dazzle.

Birch, eucalyptus, maple, and pine are
older than me—their barks recount centuries of seasons.

Iroko and mahogany are hardly seen; the forest fell
foul to fires of oil blowouts and poaching raids.

These streams still flow as they did centuries ago;
the creeks I fished in without care now clogged.

This orange dusk on a forest trail with colleagues
brought home Godwin, Boyi, and Obatavwe—

we no longer have a place to meet, chased from
home into Warri and Port Harcourt to seek jobs.

At early dawn I will break dew on a trail; mere exercise—
not with Grandma Amreghe to the farm, long planted.

In a half-century one world disappeared; another persists.
Only outside do I now see the landscape of my childhood.

(August 13, 2004)

For the Egbesu Boys

With your white headband the god you serve
recognizes your steadfast faith in his power—

Egbesu retreats not from a war thrust upon him!
Supreme warrior, Egbesu runs not from a fight.

Let the overlords call you obscene names.
Let the benefactors of robbers vilify you.

Let favorites of tyrants harass you without rest,
let criminals and outlaws call you callous names;

let their cohorts aim guns and grenades at you,
let them burn your villages and green refuge—

the state lord and his mercenary army
stand guilty of crimes against humanity.

As for their individual or corporate end,
let the minstrel not speculate their hell.

Who breaks into your home to kill you
draws from you all means of self-defense;

who trespasses into your inherited land
draws the wrath of your ancestors and gods.

What are offspring that cannot keep their heritage;
what are devotees that cannot protect their faith?

Who comes to your home to rape your bride
tests your courage before the vile act—

what man cannot cover his love with his body
deserves a shameful appellation, nothing better.

I call on you, Egbesu, marshal of the mangroves,
acclaimed war-god of born fishers and farmers,

to stand steadfast behind your great boys—
true devotees ready to be martyred for you.

For the same reason I sang praises of Ogoni youths,
I praise you Egbesu Boys in song—you cannot be

shackled from enjoying your own land's blessings;
you do the honorable duty of brave sons—fight on.

I, devotee of Ivwri, colleague of your Ifri, sing this.
Egbesu, I invoke your warrior spirit for the boys

to triumph over multiple cavalries of capital forces,
triumph over those come to throw them out of home.

Egbesu Boys, dismiss with your blood the charge
of robbery by the coalition of global powers.

You cannot live on your rivers, primeval providers;
they kill the fish population with a sludge of poisons.

You cannot even drink water from anywhere—
they pissed down barrels of arsenic into it.

They flare gas to raise demands for the commodity
and in so doing mangle every farmer's harvest;

they spray the airspace with methanol and insidious
chemicals—you cannot breathe clean air any more

with the particulate matter of fumes breeding
an asthmatic and cancer-prone generation.

They set hunger on the loose after you;
they unleashed diseases to devour you.

And do they expect you to sit and be enslaved?
Do they expect you to die without fighting back?

Those who bring a running fight to the iguana
will lose their breath and withdraw before long—

the poaching army will stop by the waterside;
the Navy cannot penetrate the fingers of the Niger

and those who know their land from birth
cannot be pushed out by armed invaders

because they have the ultimate weapons
that frustrate the occupying armada—

history is replete with withdrawing troops
of occupiers; shame and death await them.

And so the amphibian forces of young and old,
men and women, hold their own defying threats.

True sons you are, Egbesu Boys, to come
in front to cover your people from death;

true devotees, you have shown deep faith
and Egbesu arms you with an arsenal of justice

that will always triumph in the prolonged battle.
Justice is invincible and robbers will be routed

despite massive superpower arms they import
and multiple billions they commit against justice.

One should not fear death and become a slave
because slavery deprives one of life itself;

one cannot live giving up to another what
makes one's life. That is no life, without life.

When they bring a fight to you in your home,
let them come over your body to take yours!

Dialogue

Delta: A dozen nations and a hundred tongues
serenade you dusk to dawn and daylong.

Niger: Farmers and fishers chant you praises
to bring down the sky's tears every season.

Delta: No longer the seniority of the mountain source,
since from the same earth we rise and fall.

Niger: Nor of the sea in the life of the river;
both are waters, coevals of the earth.

Delta: Your course of majesty blazes the soil.

Niger: Your boundless wetlands sustain lives.

Delta: The feet that stand the head upright
have rightful claim to its revered height.

Niger: I cannot bring back my youth from the Futa Djalon;
hunched at Djenné, I must stretch my feet seaward.

Delta: I am deep to the neck in mud, trampled
by the green foliage that is my robe.

Niger: Is there a flag without flaring colors?
My name is your shield!

Delta: My shield more than sustains you!
My name is only complete after yours.

Niger: This reciprocity springs from both.
We come to each other halfway.

Delta: My bosom gives you the energy to live
despite your complicity with inland lords.

Niger: What child is older than its parent?
You cannot live without me.
Row the boat to the sea.
Fast and fast, row the boat.

Delta: The boat always passes here to the sea.
What course stronger than this current
in hundreds of draughts can drown
the vast calabash that is my dear life?

Poison

HENRIETTA ROSE-INNES

Henrietta Rose-Innes is a South African writer. She is the author of the 2010 short story collection *Homing* and novels including *Nineveh* (2011). The consequences of human pollution of the earth undergird both the form and content of her short story "Poison." In this story, which won the Caine Prize for African Writing in 2008, an African city—Cape Town to be precise—is the site of an apocalyptic chemical explosion that displaces its inhabitants. We find Lynn, in the aftermath of the disaster, at an abandoned highway gas station, unable and unwilling to move on.

Lynn had almost made it to the petrol station when her old Toyota ran dry on the highway. Lucky me, she thought as she pulled on to the verge, seeing the red and yellow flags ahead, the logo on the tall facade. But it was hopeless, she realized as soon as she saw the pile-up of cars on the forecourt. A man in blue overalls caught her eye and made a throat-slitting gesture with the side of his hand as she came walking up: no petrol here either.

There were twenty-odd stranded people, sitting in their cars or leaning against them. They glanced at her without expression before turning their eyes again towards the distant city. In a minibus taxi off to one side, a few travelers sat stiffly, bags on laps. Everyone was quiet, staring down the highway, back at what they'd all been driving away from.

An oily cloud hung over Cape Town, concealing Devil's Peak. It might have been a summer fire, except it was so black, so large. Even as they watched, it boiled up taller and taller into the sky, a plume twice as high as the mountain, leaning towards them like an evil genie. As afternoon approached, the traffic thinned. Each time a car drew up, the little ceremony was the same: the crowd's eyes switching to the new arrival, the overalled man slicing his throat, the moment of blankness and then comprehension, eyes turning away. Some of the drivers just stood there, looking accusingly at the petrol pumps; others got back into their cars and sat for a while with their hands on the steering wheels, waiting for something to come to them. One man started up his car again immediately and headed off, only to coast to a halt a few hundred meters down the drag. He didn't even bother to pull off on to the shoulder. Another car came in, pushed by three sweaty black men. They left the vehicle standing in the road and came closer, exchanging brief words with the petrol attendants. Their forearms were pumped from exertion and they stood for a while with their hands hanging at their sides. There was no traffic at all going into the city.

Over the previous two days, TV news had shown pictures of the N1 and N2 jam-packed for fifty kilometers out of town. It had taken a day for most people to realize the seriousness of the explosion; then everybody who could get out had done so. Now, Lynn supposed, lack of petrol was trapping people in town. She herself had left it terribly late, despite all the warnings. It was typical; she struggled to get things together. The first night she'd got drunk with friends. They'd sat up late, rapt in front of the TV, watching the unfolding news. The second night, she'd done the same, by herself. On the morning of this the third day, she'd woken up with a burning in the back of her throat so horrible that she understood it was no hangover, and that she had to move. By then, everybody she knew had already left.

People were growing fractious, splitting into tribes. The petrol attendants and the car-pushers stood around the taxi. The attendants' body language was ostentatiously off-duty: ignoring the crowd, attending to their own emergency. One, a woman, bent her head into the cab of the taxi, addressing the driver in a low voice. The driver and the gaardjie were the only people who seemed relaxed; both were slouched low on the front seats, the driver with a baseball cap tilted down over his eyes. On the other side of the forecourt was a large Afrikaans family group that seemed to have been traveling in convoy: mother, father, a couple of substantial aunts and uncles, half a dozen blonde kids of different sizes. They had set up camp, cooler bags and folding chairs gathered around them. On their skins, Lynn could see speckles of black grime; everybody coming out of the city had picked up a coating of foul stuff, but on the white people it showed up worse. A group of what looked like students—tattoos, dreadlocks—sat in a silent line along the concrete pad that supported the petrol pumps. One, a dark, barefoot girl with messy black hair down her back, kept springing to her feet and walking out into the road, swiveling this way and that with her hands clamped under her armpits, then striding back. She reminded Lynn a little of herself, ten years before. Skinny, impatient. A fit-looking man in a tracksuit hopped out of a huge shiny bakkie with Adil's IT Bonanza on its door and started pacing alertly back and forth. Eventually the man—Adil himself?—went over to the family group, squatted on his haunches and conferred.

Lynn stood alone, leaning against the glass wall of the petrol-station shop. The sun stewed in a sulfurous haze. She checked her cellphone, but the service had been down since the day before. Overloaded. There wasn't really anyone she wanted to call. The man in the blue overalls kept staring at her. He had skin the color and texture of damp clay, a thin, villain's moustache. She looked away. The black-haired girl jumped up yet again and dashed into the road. A small red car with only one occupant was speeding towards them out of the smoky distance. The others went running out to join their friend, stringing themselves out across the highway to block the car's path. By the time Lynn thought about joining them, it was already too late—the young people had piled in and the car was driving on, wallowing, every window crammed with hands and faces. The girl gave the crowd a thumbs-up as they passed.

A group was clustering around one of the cars. Peering over a woman's shoulder, Lynn could see one of the burly uncles hunkered down in his shorts, expertly wielding a length of hose coming out of the fuel tank. His cheeks hollowed, then he whipped the hose away from his mouth with a practiced jerk, stopped the spurt of petrol with his thumb, and plunged the other end of the hose into a jerry-can. He looked up with tense, pale eyes.

"Any more?" he asked in an over-loud voice.

Lynn shook her head. The group moved on to the next car.

She went to sit inside, in the fried-egg smell of the cafeteria. The seats were red plastic, the tabletops marbled yellow, just as she remembered them from childhood road trips. Tomato sauce and mustard in squeezy plastic bottles crusted around the nozzle. She was alone in the gloom of the place. There were racks of chips over the counter, shelves of sweets, display fridges. She pulled down two packets of chips, helped herself to a Coke and made her way to a window booth. She wished strongly for a beer. The sun came through the tinted glass in an end-of-the-world shade of pewter, but that was nothing new; that had always been the color of the light in places like this.

Through the glass wall, she watched absently as the petrol scavengers filled up the tank of Adil's IT Bonanza. They'd taken the canopy off the gleaming bakkie to let more people climb on. The uncles and aunts sat around the edge, turning their broad backs on those left behind, with small children and bags piled in the middle and a couple of older children standing up, clinging to the cab. What she'd thought was a group had been split: part of the white family was left behind on the tar, revealing itself as a young couple with a single toddler, and one of the sweaty car-pushers was on board. The blue-overalled guy was up front, next to Adil. How wrong she'd been, then, in her reading of alliances. Perhaps she might have scored a berth, if she'd pushed. She sipped her Coke thoughtfully as the bakkie pulled away.

Warm Coke: it seemed the electricity had gone too, now.

Lynn started distractedly picking at the strip of aluminum that bound the edge of the table. It could be used for something. In an emergency. She opened a packet of cheese and onion chips, surprised by her hunger. Lynn realized she was feeling happy, in a secret, volatile way. It was like bunking school: sitting here where nobody knew who she was, where no one could find her, on a day cut out of the normal passage of days. Nothing was required of her except to wait. All she wanted to do was sit for another hour, and then another hour after that, at which point she might lie down on the sticky vinyl seat in the tainted sunlight and sleep. She hadn't eaten a packet of chips for years. They were excellent. Crunching them up, she felt the salt and fat repairing her headache. Lynn pushed off her heeled shoes, which were hurting, and untucked her fitted shirt. She hadn't dressed practically for mass evacuation.

The female petrol attendant pushed open the glass door with a clang, then smacked through the wooden counter-flap to go behind the till. She was a plump, pretty young woman with complexly braided hair. Her skin, Lynn noticed, was clear brown, free from the soot that flecked the motorists. She took a small key on a chain from her bosom and opened the till, whacking the side of her fist against the drawer to jump it out. Flicking a glance across at Lynn, she pulled a handful of fifty-rand notes from the till, then hundreds.

"Taxi's going," she said.

"Really? With what petrol?"

"He's got petrol. He was just waiting to fill the seats. We arranged a price—for you, too, if you want."

"You're kidding. He was just waiting for people to pay? He could have taken us any time?"

The woman shrugged, as if to say, taxi-drivers. She stroked a thumb across the edge of the wad of notes. "Are you coming?"

Lynn shrugged back at her.

"You don't want to come in a taxi?"

"No, it's not that—it's just, where would we go? I'm sure someone will come soon. The police will come. Rescue services."

The woman gave a snort and exited the shop, bumping the door open with her hip. The door sucked slowly shut, and then it was quiet again.

Lynn watched through the tinted window as the money was handed over, which seemed to activate the inert gaardjie. He straightened up and started striding back and forth, clapping his hands, shouting and hustling like it was Main Road rush hour. The people inside the taxi edged up in the seats and everyone else started pushing in. The driver spotted Lynn through the window and raised his eyebrows, pointing with both forefingers first at her and then at the kombi and then back at her again: coming? When she just smiled, he snapped his fingers and turned his attention elsewhere. People were being made to leave their bags and bundles on the tar. Lynn realized she was gripping the edge of the table tightly. Her stomach hurt. Getting up this morning, packing her few things, driving all this way . . . it seemed impossible for her to start it all again. Decision, action, motion. She wanted to curl up on the seat, put her head down. But the taxi was filling up.

Her body delivered her from decision. All at once her digestion seemed to have speeded up dramatically. Guts whining, she trotted to the bathroom.

Earlier, there'd been a queue for the toilets, but now the stalls were empty. In the basin mirror, Lynn's face was startlingly grimed. Her choppy dark hair was greasy, her eyes as pink as if she'd been weeping. Contamination. Sitting on the black plastic toilet seat, she felt the poisons gush out of her. She wiped her face with paper and looked closely at the black specks smeared on to the tissue. Her skin was oozing it. She held the wadded paper to her nose. A faint coppery smell. What was this shit? The explosion had been at a chemical plant, but which chemical? She couldn't remember what they'd said on the news.

She noticed the silence. It was the slightly reverberating stillness of a place from which people have recently departed.

There was nobody left on the forecourt. The battered white taxi was pulling out, everyone crammed inside. The sliding door was open, three men hanging out the side with their fingers hooked into the roof rim. Lynn ran after it on to the highway, but the only person who saw her was the blond toddler crushed against the back windscreen, one hand spread against the glass. He held her gaze as the taxi picked up speed.

The cloud was creeping higher behind her back, casting a dull murk, not solid enough to be shadow. She could see veils of dirty rain bleeding from its near edge. Earlier, in the city, she had heard sirens, helicopters in the sky; but there were none out here. It was silent. Standing alone on the highway was unnerving. This was for cars. The road surface was not meant to be touched with hands or feet, to be examined too closely or in stillness. The four lanes were so wide. Even the white lines and the gaps between them were much longer than they appeared from the car: the length of her whole body, were she to lie down in the road. She had to stop herself looking over her shoulder, flinching from invisible cars coming up from behind.

She thought of the people she'd seen so many times on the side of the highway, walking, walking along verges not designed for human passage, covering incomprehensible distances, toiling from one obscure spot to another. Their bent heads dusty, cowed by the iron ring of the horizon. In all her years of driving at speed along highways, Cape Town, Jo'burg, Durban, she'd never once stopped at a random spot, walked into the veld. Why would she? The highways were tracks through an indecipherable terrain of dun and gray, a blur in which one only fleetingly glimpsed the sleepy eyes of people standing on its edge. To leave the car would be to disintegrate, to merge with that shifting world. How far could she walk, anyway, before weakness made her stumble? Before the air thickened into some alien gel, impossible to wade through, to breathe?

It was mid-afternoon but it felt much later. Towards the city, the sky was thick with bloody light. It was possible to stare straight at the sun—a pink bleached disk, like the moon of a different planet. The cloud was growing. As she watched, a deep rose-colored occlusion extended towards her, pulling a wash of darkness across the sky. A strange horizontal rain came with it, and reflexively she ducked and put her hands to her hair. But the droplets were too big and distinct, and she realized that they were in fact birds, thousands of birds, sprinting away from the mountain. They flew above her and around her ears: swift starlings, laboring geese. Some small rapid birds were tossed up against the sky, smuts from a burning book.

As they passed overhead, for the first time Lynn was filled with fear.

Approximately fifty packets of potato chips, assorted flavors. Eighty or so chocolate bars, different kinds. Licorice, wine-gums, Smarties. Maybe thirty bottles of Coke and Fanta in the fridges, different sizes. Water, fizzy and plain: fifteen big bottles, ten small. No alcohol of any kind. How much fluid did you need to drink per day? The women's magazines said two liters. To flush out the toxins. Would drinking Coke be enough? Surely. So: two weeks, maybe three. The survival arithmetic was easy. Two weeks was more than enough time; rescue would come long before then. She felt confident, prepared.

Boldly, she pushed through the wooden flap and went behind the counter. The till stood open. Beyond were two swing doors with head-high windows, and through them a sterile steel-fitted kitchen, gloomy without overhead lighting. Two hamburger patties, part-cooked, lay abandoned on the flat steel plate of the griller, and a basket of chips sat in a vat of opaque oil. To the right was a back door with a broad metal push bar. She shoved it.

The door swung open on to a sudden patch of domesticity: three or four black bins, a metal skip, sunlight, some scruffy bluegums and an old two-wire fence with wooden posts holding back the veld. A shed with a tilted corrugated-iron roof leaned up against the back wall. The change in scale and atmosphere was startling. Lynn had not imagined that these big franchised petrol stations hid modest homesteads. She'd had the vague sense that they were modular, shipped out in sections, everything in company colors. Extraneous elements—employees—were presumably spirited away somewhere convenient and invisible at the end of their shifts. But this was clearly somebody's backyard. It smelt of smoke and sweat and dishwater, overlaying the burnt grease of the kitchen. Through the doorway of the shed she could see the end of an iron bed and mattress. On the ground was a red plastic tub of the kind used to wash dishes or babies. Two plastic garden chairs, one missing a leg. A rusted car on bricks.

Lynn laughed out loud. Her car! Her own car, twenty years on: the same model blue Toyota, but reduced to a shell. The remaining patches of crackled paint had faded to the color of a long-ago summer sky. The roof had rusted clean through in places, and the bottom edges of the doors were rotten with corrosion. Old carpeting was piled on the back seat and all the doors were open. Seeing the smooth finish gone scabrous and raw gave Lynn a twinge at the back of her teeth.

She walked past the car. There was a stringy cow on the other side of the fence, its pelt like mud daubed over the muscles. A goat came avidly up to the wire, watching her with its slotted eyes, and she put her arm through and scratched between its horns. The cow also mooched over in an interested way. Smelling its grassy breath, Lynn felt a tremor of adventure. She could be here for days. She felt no fear at the prospect: nobody else was here, nobody for miles around (although briefly she saw again: the hand sliding across the throat . . .).

Out back here, the sky looked completely clear, as if the petrol station marked the limit of the zone of contamination. She shot her fingers at the goat and snapped them like the taxi-man, and spun round in a circle, humming. She breathed in sharply, stepping back hard against the wire. "Jesus Christ." Someone was in the car. The pile of rugs had reconstituted itself into an old lady, sitting on the backseat as if waiting to be chauffeured away.

Lynn coughed out a laugh, slapping her chest. "Oh god, sorry," she said. "You surprised me." The old lady worked her gums, staring straight ahead. She wore a faded green button-up dress, a hand-knitted cardigan, elasticized knee stockings and slippers. Gray hair caught in a meager bun.

Lynn came closer. "Um," she began. "Hello?" Afrikaans? Lynn's Afrikaans was embarrassingly weak. "Hallo?" she said again, giving the word a different inflection. Ridiculous.

No response. Poor thing, she thought, someone just left her here. Would the old lady even know about the explosion? "Sorry . . . tannie?" she tried again. She'd never seriously called anyone "tannie" before. But it seemed to have some effect: the old lady looked at her with mild curiosity. Small, filmed black eyes, almost no whites visible. A creased face shrunken on to fine bones. An ancient mouse.

"Hi. I'm Lynn. Sorry to disturb you. Ah, I don't know if anyone's told you—about the accident? In Cape Town."

The woman's mouth moved in a fumbling way. Lynn bent closer to hear.

"My grandson," the old lady enunciated, slowly but clearly. Then she smiled faintly and looked away, having concluded a piece of necessary small talk.

"He told you about it?"

No answer.

So. Now there was another person to consider, an old frail person, someone in need of her help. Lynn felt her heaviness return. "Tannie," she said—having begun with it she might as well continue—"There's been an accident, an explosion. There's chemicals in the air. Poison, gif. It might be coming this way. I think we should go out front. There might be people coming past who can help us. Cars. Ambulances."

The old lady seemed not averse to the idea, and allowed Lynn to take her arm and raise her from her seat. Although very light, she leaned hard; Lynn felt she was lugging the woman's entire weight with one arm, like a suitcase. Rather than negotiate the complex series of doors back through the station, they took the longer route, clockwise around the building on a narrow track that squeezed between the back corner of the garage and the wire fence. Past the ladies, the gents, the café. As they walked, it started to rain, sudden and heavy. The rain shut down the horizon; its sound on the forecourt canopy was loud static. Lynn wondered how tainted the falling water was. She sat the old lady down on a sheltered bench outside the shop, and fetched some bottles of water and packets of chips from inside. Then she urgently had to use the bathroom again.

The toilet was no longer flushing. Her empty guts felt liquid, but strained to force anything out. The headache was back. When she got back outside, the rain had stopped again, as abruptly as it started, leaving a rusty tang in the air. The old lady had vanished. Then Lynn spotted movement out on the road: her car door was open. Coming closer, she saw that the woman was calmly eating tomato chips in the back seat. Having transferred herself from the wreck in the backyard to the superior vehicle out front, she was now waiting for the journey to commence. A neat old lady, Lynn noted: there were no crumbs down her front. She seemed restored by the chips. Her eyes gleamed as she whipped a small plastic tortoiseshell comb out of a pocket and started snatching back wisps of hair, repinning the bun into place with black U-bend pins that Lynn hadn't seen since her own grandmother died. In contrast, she felt increasingly disheveled, and embarrassed about her tip of a car: the empty Heineken bottles on the floor, the tissues in the cubbyhole. She should have kept things cleaner, looked after things better.

"My grandson," the woman said to Lynn, with a nod of reassurance.

"Of course," said Lynn.

Evening was coming. The clouds had retreated somewhat and were boiling grumpily over the mountain. The brief rain had activated an awful odor: like burnt plastic but with a metallic bite, and a whiff of sourness like rotten meat in it too. Lynn sat in the front seat, put the keys into the ignition and gripped the steering wheel. She had no plan. The sky ahead was darkening to a luminous blue. The silent little woman was an expectant presence in her rearview mirror. Feeling oppressed, Lynn got out of the car again and stood with her hands on her hips, staring east, west, willing sirens, flashing lights. She ducked back into the car. "I'll be back in a sec. Okay? You're all right there?"

The old woman looked at her with polite incomprehension.

She just needed to walk around a bit. She headed off towards the sun, which was melting messily into smears of red and purple. The mountain was no longer visible. The road was discolored, splattered with lumps of some tarry black precipitate. She counted five small bodies of birds, feathers damp and stuck together. Blades of grass at the side of the road were streaked with black, and the ground seemed to be smoking, a layer of foul steam around her ankles. It got worse the further she walked, and so she turned around.

There was someone standing next to her car. At once she recognized the moustache, the blue overalls.

Her first impulse was to hide. She stood completely still, watching. He hadn't seen her.

The clay-faced man was holding something . . . a box. No, a can. He had a white jerry-can in his hands and he was filling her car with petrol. Suddenly her stomach roiled and she crouched down at the side of the road, vomiting a small quantity of cheese-and-onion mulch into the stinking grass. When she raised her chin, the man was standing looking back at the petrol station.

Deciding, she made herself stand, raising her hand to wave—but in that moment he opened the door and got in; the motor turned immediately and the car was rolling forward. She could see the back of the old woman's head, briefly silver as the car turned out into the lane, before the reflection of the sunset blanked out the rear windscreen. The Toyota headed out into the clear evening.

Lynn sat in the back of the rusted car and watched the sky turn navy and the stars come out. She loved the way the spaces between the stars had no texture, softer than water; they were pure depth. She sat in the hollow the old lady had worn in the seat, ankles crossed in the space where the handbrake used to be. She sipped Coke; it helped with the nausea.

She'd been here three days and her head felt clear. While there'd been a few bursts of strange rain, the chemical storm had not progressed further down the highway. It seemed the pollution had created its own weather system over the mountain, a knot of ugly cloud. She felt washed up on the edge of it, resting her oil-clogged wings on a quiet shore.

Sooner or later, rescue would come. The ambulances with flashing lights, the men in luminous vests with equipment and supplies. Or maybe just a stream of people driving back home. But if rescue took too long, then there was always the black bicycle that she'd found leaned up against the petrol pump. The woman's grandson must have ridden here, with the petrol can, from some place not too far down the road. It was an old postman's bike, heavy but hardy, and she felt sure that if he had cycled the distance, so could she. Maybe tomorrow, or the day after. And when this was all over, she was definitely going to go on a proper detox. Give up all junk food, alcohol. Some time soon.

Lynn snapped open a packet of salt-'n'-vinegar chips. Behind her, the last of the sunset lingered, poison violet and puce, but she didn't turn to look. She wanted to face clear skies, sweet-smelling veld. If she closed her eyes, she might hear a frog, just one, starting its evening song beyond the fence.

2

ASIA

China

Introduction

SHAOBO XIE

Ecological literature as a burgeoning development in contemporary China has its beginnings in Chinese antiquity. All forms of literary and philosophical writing in ancient China were one way or the other informed by the ideas of *dao fa ziran* (Dao following the way of nature), *tian ren he yi* (harmony between human and nature) and *tiandi da mei* (the great beauty of heaven and earth). What is called landscape poetry (including idyllic poems) has been a popular genre among traditional Chinese literati over the past two thousand years or so because it provides a productive space for articulating affective states triggered by a sight or scene of nature, recording an emotional response to a certain undesirable sociopolitical reality, or creating an imagined existential elsewhere transcending or negating the actually existing order of social life. Indeed, one major function of landscape poetry in ancient China was to offer a vehicle for externalizing the poet's emotion by way of concrete imagery of natural scenery, thus cultivating a spiritual mode of being. To borrow terms from Michel Foucault, writing landscape poetry was a significant part of the traditional Chinese literati's technology of the self. Among the champions of classical landscape poetry are Xie Lingyun, Xie Tiao, Tao Yuanming, Meng Haoran, Li Bai, Wang Wei, and Liu Zongyuan. What landscape poetry signals is an aesthetic taste, a worldview, and a relationship with society and nature or with the natural environment as a whole.

As a self-conscious style of writing dedicated to safeguarding and promoting a healthy environment for humankind and other forms of being, however, ecological literature in contemporary China owes its emergence to a ubiquitous eco-environmental deterioration characterized by anthropogenic climate change, natural resource depletion, loss of biodiversity, water and air pollution, deforestation, soil erosion, desertification, grassland degeneration, water shortage, toxic landscapes, and rising numbers of endangered species. Since the 1980s, the Chinese have been euphorically seized by an anguished desire for modernity, zealously advocating a merger with the global system and reproducing everything that already exists in the West. With modernization as China's new Master Signifier, all forms of enterprise, all projects of urban development, and all pursuit of material and economic profit became legitimized. They "exploited all the country's natural resources" with a vengeance "before realizing that they are doing great harm to nature" (Wang Ning, 740). At the same time, there began to emerge a tremendous wave of ecological literature in different genres. This work addresses the disturbed or lost environmental balance and ecological disasters. Among these works of reportage are Sha Qing's *Beijing Is Out of Balance* (1987), Xu Gang's *Logger, Wake Up* (1988) and *Save the Earth* (2000), Liu Guixian's *Water Pollution in China* (1989), Ma Jun's *China's Water Crisis* (1999), and Zheng Yi's *The Destruction of China* (2002). For ecological poetry, there are Hai Zi's *Facing the Sea: Flowers Blooming in War Spring* (1989), Yu Jian's *An Event: The Death of the Palm Tree* (1995), Li Songtao's *Rejecting the Last Day* (1992), and Hua Hai's *Ecological Poems* (2006).

One other key factor in the rise of ecological literature in China is Western nature and environmental writing that has been translated into Chinese over the past few decades. Henry David Thoreau's *Walden*, for instance, was first introduced to Chinese readers in 1949 by the famous poet, essayist, reporter, and critic Xu Chi and since the late 1980s has been retranslated and republished over and over again. Searching for simplicity, fullness, and depth of life, Thoreau finds the consummation of existence not in human society but in the company of nature. For Thoreau, all forms of natural being are sacred, and what we as humans draw from them is purely positive energy, spiritual nutrition, inspiration, joy, and love. For Thoreau to be at one with nature is to merge into the vastness of empowering, invigorating, divine Cosmic Being, to reach the blissful level of being characterized by content, self-sufficiency, health, and moral strength. *Walden* was passionately acclaimed by Xu Chi, its first Chinese translator, as an amazing work in which every utterance comes "as a delightful surprise, every word shining bright, soothing and refreshing my heart, profoundly touching the innermost depths of my being" (qtd. in Zhang and He, 45). After reading *Walden* in 1986, Hai Zi (1964–1989), a nationally renowned poetic prodigy, admired the author so much that he wrote a poem titled "Thoreau Is a

Real Thinker." When the poet was found dead by suicide, *Walden* was one of the few books he had with him. Wei An, one of the leading ecological essayists in contemporary China, learned about Thoreau through Hai Zi and spoke of him as his spiritual mentor. "Of all the writers and poets who have had a great influence on me, established my beliefs, and shaped my writing," Wei An intimated, "Thoreau occupies the first place" (qtd. in Yu, 159). Another great Western influence on Chinese ecological literature is Rachel Carson's *Silent Spring*, which was regarded by Lu Shuyuan as a major contributor to the rise of Chinese ecological literature in the 1980s and 1990s. Among other Western works translated and introduced to China are Ralph Waldo Emerson's *Nature and Other Essays*, Albert Schweitzer's *Reverence for Life*, Holmes Rolston's *Environmental Ethics* and *Philosophy Gone Wild*, Bill McKibben's *The End of Nature*, Peter Singer's *Animal Liberation*, Serge Moscovici's *Réenchanter la nature* (Re-enchanting Nature), and John Muir's *Our National Parks*. Such tremendous influences from the West inspired Chinese ecological literature and environmental criticism, opening up a wide spectrum of themes and forms of writing and a large variety of rigorous critical frameworks. Embracing all forms of life as kin and equals and prioritizing harmonious relations between nature and humanity, contemporary Chinese environmental writing champions efforts to question developmentalism, the cult of progress and economic growth, profit-motivated economic production, and instrumental reason.

Contemporary Chinese ecological literature, according to the famous eco-critic and scholar Wang Shudong, can be periodized into three phases of development. The first phase covering the 1980s can be conceptualized as the stage of beginning, which, as Wang has pointed out, saw three types of ecological writing with different ideological agendas: namely ecological fiction by educated youth that critically reflects on destructive behavior toward the ecological environment; reportage literature that rigorously exposed how the ongoing modernization wave was jeopardizing the eco-environment everywhere; and nature writing that aimed to promote ecological awareness. Among exemplary works of the period are A Cheng's "Tree King," Lao Gui's "Bloody Dusk," Sha Qing's *Beijing Is Out of Balance*, Xu Gang's *Logger, Wake Up*, and Li Hangyu's *The Last Fisher*. The 1990s saw the emergence of the second phase of the development of ecological literature in China. During this period ecology was increasingly becoming a major concern among writers writing in different genres, exerting an immense social impact on readers. Among the representative works of ecological literature of the period are Zhang Kangkang's *Sandstorm*, Guo Xuebo's *Sand Burial*, Fang Min's *The Great Destruction*, and Zhang Wei's *The Fable of September*. Ecological essays mainly include those by Wei'an, Zhou Xiaofeng, Liu Liangcheng, and others. Since the turn of the twenty-first century, the ecological crisis has been looming as a crisis of modernity or developmentalist ideology among Chinese people confronted with a rapidly deteriorating environment as a consequence of China's role as one of the major manufacturing centers in the global empire of transnational capitalism. Ecological or environmental concerns have been a driving force among writers and scholars, hence a new upsurge of ecological writing, with many nationally or internationally renowned writers contributing to it. This is the third phase of Chinese ecological literature, an apex moment when environmental and nature writing is coming into its own in all genres in China. Among the masterpieces of the period are Jiang Rong's *Wolf Totem*, Chen Yingsong's *The Leopard's Last Dance*, Zhang Wei's *Hedgehog Song*, A Lai's *Empty Mountain*, Han Shaogong's *Between Mountain and River*, Baoerji Yuanye's *The Appearance of Sheep*, Jiang Zidan's *Animal Archives*, Li Qingsong's *Ethics of the Earth*, Xu Gang's *National Disaster* and *Great Forest*, and Fu Fei's *Late in the Midst of Mountains*.

The five pieces of ecological prose writing included in this section were all published after the turn of the millennium. They represent the third phase of Chinese ecological literature and offer a window into its newest directions and achievements.

WORKS CITED

Feng, Xiaojun, and Wang Shudong. 2021. "Historical Review and Prospects of Contemporary Ecological Literature—An Interview with Professor Wang Shudong." http://www.chinawriter.com.cn/n1/2021/0111/c405057-31995847.html.

Wang, Ning. 2014. "Global in the Local: Ecocriticism in China." *Interdisciplinary Studies in Literature and Environment* 21 (4): 739–48.

Yu, Wenfu. 2013. "From Reference to Reconstruction: Western Factors and Local Integration in Chinese Ecological Literature." *Social Science Front* 12: 156–60.

Zhang, Xiaoqin, and He Hong. 2016. "Spiritual Resources of Contemporary Chinese Ecological Literature." *Journal of Gansu Radio and TV University* 26 (2): 41–47.

Chocho

JIANG ZIDAN
Translated by Leilei Chen

Jiang Zidan, adjunct professor of literature at Hainan University and past president of the Hainan Provincial Writers Association, was born in Beijing in 1954. A famous fiction and nonfiction writer in contemporary China, she has won the Shanghai Literary Prize and the Zhuang Zhongwen Literary Prize. Some of her works have been translated into English, French, and Japanese. Among her published volumes are *For Whom Is the Smoke of Fortune Incense Rising?*, *The Color Black*, *An Appointment with Life*, and *When Summer Comes Around Again*. "Chocho," a compelling masterpiece of narrative nonfiction, is about the intimate and inextricable bond of affection between a pet dog and its owners. The story provides enlightening insights into the extent of mutual love and emotional attachment between animals and humans. Throughout, the dog Chocho is described like a cute and adorable kid yearning to love and be loved by those around him.

Chocho was a white, smart Pekingese dog, the apple of Lao Chen's eye. Sadly, Chocho became paraplegic at the age of three and needed help to do his business. The vet told Lao Chen that Chocho suffered from intervertebral disc herniation, commonly seen with Pekingese dogs. He might get better if treated consistently along with daily leg massage, but it would be both costly and exhausting.

Lao Chen owned an auto repair shop. He had some savings, but it wasn't easy money. Auto repair business was very competitive these years. Customer retention depended on speedy service, so for him time was the most precious. He had had Chocho for over three years and loved him dearly, but he knew the disease wouldn't go away shortly. He couldn't tell how costly the treatment would be and how much time he needed to spend. Lao Chen decided to give up after a week's treatment. He told the vet: I'll leave the dog with you. You may give him to whoever would take him. If no one is willing, you may put him down. He paid for the euthanasia; bought Chocho a new basket, a can of dog food, and a big bottle of water; and called it a good end.

When Zhang Lyuping walked into the vet, she saw Chocho surrounded by a crowd. They were blaming his cold-hearted owner. She could tell quickly that Chocho had lived a sheltered family life and hadn't seen so many strangers before: he was lying in the basket and looking fearfully at people around him—quite obviously an orphan. After hearing Chocho's story, Lyuping picked him up with no hesitation. She decided to take him to the animal shelter where she worked and to have his disease treated. She noticed that Chocho kept looking at her with tearful eyes and realized that a dog was actually capable of emotions beyond what humans could imagine. She was deeply touched.

Lyuping's animal shelter was located at Men Tou Gou. She drove a long way to town every day for Chocho's treatments. A few days later, as if returning Lyuping's favor, Chocho stood up. Soon after, he would limp to her when seeing her coming back, shaking hands and bowing, oblivious to the fact that he might injure himself again.

Chocho's owner, Lao Chen, couldn't help worrying after leaving him at the vet. His wife and son insisted that he take Chocho back. Lao Chen heard Chocho was adopted and went back to the vet, hoping to find out where he was but to no avail. They wouldn't tell him. He waited there every day until he finally saw Chocho when Lyuping brought him in for his treatments.

Lao Chen bowed to Lyuping and said: Thank you for rescuing my dog, Ma'am. I wonder if you would allow me to take him back. I will pay what you've paid for him. He reached toward Chocho as he spoke.

Lyuping didn't let him touch Chocho and put him in the car instead. She turned Lao Chen down right away: Don't even think about it. Didn't you want to put him down? He is dead. It's pointless to wait here.

Lyuping had been rescuing animals over the years. She detested those who abandoned their pets and spared no kindness for these people. When she started the car and was ready to leave, she was surprised to see Lao Chen crying. He gripped her door handle and asked for her phone number. He wanted to come to the shelter to visit Chocho. Lyuping had the urge to refuse, but when she saw Chocho dashing to the car window, crying and begging for Lao Chen to take him, she felt touched and gave her number to Lao Chen.

The next day Lao Chen drove the whole family in his minibus to see Chocho, carrying sausages, Kentucky chicken, canned food, etc. Chocho knew as soon as they entered the shelter's yard, sticking his head out of the window and shaking with excitement. A caretaker was startled, noticing Chocho suddenly become restless. Concerned that his illness was worsening, he called for Lyuping urgently. Lyuping, having scheduled Lao Chen's visit, knew that the family must have arrived. She was both moved and sad to see that Chocho was so forgiving.

No doubt, the Chen family loved Chocho. Little Chubby, the son, dashed toward Chocho and held him. The whole family came over and cried at the sight of Chocho.

Lyuping said: You all loved him so much, but why abandon him when he was sick and needed you the most?

Lao Chen's wife replied, crying her eyes out: It's our fault. We regret it and want to take him home. Everyone loves Chocho and keeps asking where he is. We're too ashamed to tell them that we abandoned him and lied that he was sick and that a friend was taking good care of him. You saved Chocho's life. Our whole family can't thank you enough. We'll pay whatever you ask for.

Lao Chen was also begging.

Lyuping realized that, from Little Chubby's arms, Chocho was looking at them talking with apprehensive, tearful eyes. She knew Chocho wanted to go home.

Years later when Lyuping thought of Chocho's love for his family, she couldn't help regretting what she had done to him. She was unforgiving back then, thinking Lao Chen's family was not responsible: you didn't take care of Chocho when he was sick, yet want him back when he recovers. What if he gets sick again? Shamelessly send him back? Who knows what you are going to do?

Lao Chen had been speechless, knowing he was wrong. He sought a compromise, asking to visit Chocho once a week. Lyuping agreed. She didn't know how hurtful it would be for such a loving dog like Chocho.

She still vividly remembered the scene when Chocho was separated from his family. She took him from the son and stood there to see them off. Chocho gave a long, sad howl, looking at her and then at his family, his eyes full of tears. The unbearably wretched scene of a family torn apart.

Since then Chocho had suffered from depression. He didn't eat anything for a whole week. Lyuping phoned the family and told them not to visit until Chocho got better. They came regardless. After a couple of visits, Chocho couldn't even take any fluids; they caused diarrhea. He was languishing and had tears in his eyes all the time.

Lyuping realized he was really sick and took him to the emergency room. The vet diagnosed him with depression-inflicted intussusception and suggested surgery. They cut Chocho open only to find that his intestines were all black and that they could do nothing but remove them all together. Lyuping was immensely regretful. Had she known that Chocho loved his family so much that the separation would be fatal, she would have allowed them to take him back.

The surgery failed to save Chocho's life. He died that night despite how much Lyuping tried to save him.

The next day Lao Chen's family came for the burial, taking with them a few toys Chocho used to play with. They wanted to see him for one last time. Lyuping wrapped Chocho in a brand-new towel and buried him under the tree, sobbing too hard to lift her head. Lao Chen came over to comfort her despite his own grief: Ma'am, it's all my fault. You've tried your best. I'm so sorry for our loss.

That moment changed Lyuping's perspective. Lao Chen was no longer as ruthless as she thought. He was sympathetic. Chocho's death must have made Lao Chen aware of his feelings which he never realized as he was busy with work. It dawned on Lyuping that she was naive and didn't understand the complexities of people. Neither did she understand that dogs can be just as complex with their own ideas and ways of being. It was just that people rarely saw things from a dog's perspective and often imposed their good will only to cause harm. Lyuping realized that her way of doing justice to Chocho was simply a selfish intent. She couldn't tell who was more heartless, Lao Chen's family or herself, but she was sure that poor Chocho died because of them both.

The animal shelter moved away from Men Tou Gou shortly after Chocho's death. Lyuping had not gone back since. Not until she accompanied

China Central Television's camera crew on a filming tour. As soon as she entered the weed-ridden yard, she thought of Chocho, the adorable dog.

Chocho's tomb had long disappeared and the tree grew big and tall beside it. Lyuping felt her heavy heart when she stood under the tree, thinking about Chocho killed by their stubborn love. The tree's leaves rustled with a draft of wind. Their reflections of sunlight shone warmth, reminding her of Chocho's loving eyes.

Plants in My Garden

HAN SHAOGONG

Translated by Shaobo Xie

World-renowned novelist, story writer, and essayist Han Shaogong was born in Changsha, Hunan, in 1953. Beginning his literary career in the mid-1970s, he became one of the leading champions of the Search-for-Roots literary movement in the mid-1980s. Drawing upon traditional Chinese philosophy such as Daoism and Buddhism and folklore, Han's writing also reflects influences from Franz Kafka's novelistic art and Gabriel García Márquez's magical realism. Han has won multiple awards including the Lu Xun Literary Prize, the French Knight of the Order of Arts and Letters, and the Newman Prize for Chinese Literature. His works have been translated and published overseas in many languages. Among his best-known works are *Moon Orchid*, *Bababa*, *Womanwomanwoman*, *Intimations*, *A Dictionary of Maqiao*, and *South of Mountains and North of Water*. "Plants in My Garden," selected from *Between Mountain and River*, offers an intimate account of a devoted gardener's love and care for plants. By way of personification, the piece describes plants and their characteristics in such an affectionate way that it is as if they were all endowed with human thoughts and emotions.

Plants are actually different in nature: morning glory, the most sensitive to light, blooms and fades away quickly every morning, bursting forth with sapphire-like blue fireworks only at the moment when early morning sunshine is fleeting across the wall, which is equivalent to the chirping of plants, or the morning exercise of colors. Osmanthus flowers are the most disciplined team. They have golden or silver-white flower grains, which are either everywhere on the tree or are collectively absent. The change is instantaneous. There seems to be a precise schedule for joint action and a local communication network to ensure timely contact. No one is allowed to advance or retreat on their own.

In comparison, the moonlight flowers are the most doted on. They enjoy the most fertile soil, the brightest sunlight, and the most frequent spraying of insecticides. But still, they do not care to grow, their faces full of fatigue, cynicism, and laziness. When they have to, they will suddenly give forth a long twig with one or two lonely flowers hanging on it, just to dismiss you.

Japanese climbing ferns are naturally the most unscrupulous. Their aggressive encroachment often causes the sudden withering of a tree or a shrub. They look honest, their leaves somewhat resembling potato leaves. This is their hypocrisy. They cling to other plants first, then live off them, and then strangle them, with a full set of snobbish, pretty-minded devious stratagems. The wandering vines they release are silent cyan flying snakes, looking around sneakily, waiting for opportunities, and filled with high ambition to rule and dominate the vast fields. Fortunately, they prove to be no real talents in the end; otherwise it is likely that they would pounce upon pedestrians and treat them as large delicious prey.

My wood knife has to fight against such long snakes several times a year to protect my phone line from being hijacked and crushed by them.

When a tree is blooming, who can say that it is not smiling, like a mature woman smiling sexily and erotically in the trembling sunlight? When a red leaf falls to the ground, who can say that it is not a plaintive coughing up of blood? When melon leaves turn yellow or even black, do you not hear them coughing or moaning? Inside the courtyard walls are some tiny yellow or purple wildflowers suddenly opening up everywhere, just like some noisy visitors, talking in a defiantly boisterous manner. Then they will mysteriously disappear all of a sudden for one or two years, leaving the garden buried in silence. I can only see this as an angry gesture of departure and a determined decision to break up with me—but I have no idea how I have upset them.

Let's take a look at the orange trees that I planted at the same time. Without treating them differently, I have dug holes for them, pruning and topdressing them, all in the same way, but the result surprises me. The three trees by the roadside are growing quickly and are about to bloom and bear fruit. There is another one which, small in size and not yet full-fledged, is already starting to bloom and bear fruit. But then, all the other ones appear listless, tiny, and stupid-looking, their leaves already curling up piece by piece. A peasant woman once said to me: You should talk to them as much as you can, and treat all of them with the same level of care; otherwise, they will look despondent and lifeless.

The peasant woman also warned against pointing a finger at the buds of fruit and vegetable plants, lest they get rotten at the core (my wife has since often yelled at me to prevent me from breaking the ban when inspecting my home or being too rude to them). If you find the plants pregnant, you cannot even say it. Instead you can only whisper from a distance; otherwise they will be mad (that is why my wife has told me to carefully protect the privacy of the plants and, to talk about plants, especially regarding matters such as "pollination" and "fruit hanging," only by using code words, even at the dinner table or in the study).

I am skeptical about these suggestions: how can plants and trees have such thoughts and such alert eyes and ears?

Later on, I learned that plants in the mountains seemed to have super detection capabilities. It is said that when oilseed rape is bearing seeds the owner must not mindlessly praise lard and camellia oil; otherwise rape will be so angry that the empty shell rate will increase dramatically. When Nanzhu bamboo is sending forth shoots, the owner must not carelessly mention bamboo-mat-weaving skills, lest the bamboo shoots die panic-stricken; even if they are already jumping up out of the soil, they will be rotten at the core and at the roots.

One must control one's troublesome tongue at the crucial moment.

Tree Shouts

CHEN YINGSONG

Translated by Leilei Chen

Chen Yingsong, past president of the Hubei Provincial Writers Association and former dean of the Provincial Academy of Arts, was born in Gongan County, Hubei, in 1956. He has established himself as a major voice of environmental writing in China and has won multiple awards including the Lu Xun Literary Prize, the Chinese Novel Society Prize, and the National Environmental Literature Prize. His works have been translated into English, French, Russian, Polish, Romanian, Japanese, and Korean, among others. Among his best-known works are his novels *The Forest in Silence* and *Speechless Village* as well as his novella *The Leopard's Last Dance*. The story included in this anthology provides a fascinating and vivid account of life and customs in a mountainous country area in China. Through the lens of a narrative about a peasant cutting down an ancient tree, the author describes the devastating impacts of abusive human behavior on the natural environment.

Wang Shitang had three sons, one died young many years ago. The other two grew up neglected, bullied, and starved. They were both ugly, neither of them was as good-looking as their late elder brother. The second son is called Wang Erzhao. He married into a widow's home in the mountains and disappeared for good, no one knew whether he was still alive or not. The third son, Wang Sanzhao, was not as smart, but he graduated from a vocational school and ended up finding a job in the city. But he had no luck with women, and he was almost forty. Then, unexpectedly, Wang Shitang got a letter from him saying that he was getting married soon and needed his dad to make him a set of furniture.

What a happy and grand occasion! Wang Shitang was delirious with joy. On second thought, though, where can I get all the wood? You give me such short notice without a single dime, how will I afford to buy all the supplies? Carpentry needs big pieces of wood. Where can I find trees that are big enough? Putting down his chopsticks, Wang Shitang glanced up at the mountain, the leftover trees were only big enough to make chopsticks.

Carrying his axe, Wang Shitang headed into the mountain and began his search. When he returned five days later, he had almost frozen to death. His face pale, limbs convulsing, so much so he didn't even bother getting the leeches off of his legs. Fortunately, he ended up bringing back a batch of wood, it was red birch. He found it in a ravine, perhaps chopped down many years ago and forgotten, or deserted there because the ravine was too deep for people to carry it out. There were several batches, some went rotten. He chose one, taking two days to drag it to the road and fainting three times along the way. It used up his energy and almost took his life.

As if that was not enough, a big chunk of bird droppings fell right in front of him as soon as he stepped into his yard in Stinky Woman Pass. Oh, the smell! He looked up. The white-breasted waterhens were staring at him, their eyes looking like bronze bells. These birds appeared ghostly. If they hadn't brought him small fish now and then, he would have smashed their nests. Their cries sounded weird and sinister, as if loaded with deep meaning. Especially when it was about to rain, they squawked sadly and worriedly as if they had lost their parents, and they dashed in the tree laughing and crying all at once. They made at least ten to twenty nests in the tree, and often brought fish from nowhere, the lengthy, clean, and transparent kind. It was said that the fish came from a cave. It was scaleless and tiny-eyed, with a hardened worm in its cheek. The knowledgeable called it fish lice, later people said it could cure choked-to-death disease, or throat cancer. That was why Wang Shitang kept them and sent them to his neighbors who caught this disease.

People living in the mountains liked smoking and drinking and ate preserved food all year round. They also stayed close to fire and smoke every day, so throat cancer was common. Many came for fish lice ever since Wang Shitang found them, as they had cured many cases in this area, even those at advanced stages. One day Wang Shitang noticed that in the puddle under the tree there were fish swimming. He caught a lot, yet lots remained. He had seen bits of fish in the yard. Later he noticed that the birds couldn't eat it all up, they hid the leftovers in the puddle. That was why these fierce birds stayed. They must have owed Wang Shitang a debt in a previous life.

The locals called the fish Sheep Fish Strips and used it to make hot pot with pickled cabbage. So delicious. The best food in the world!

But this bird dropping was too stinky. He looked up. The white-breasted waterhens were staring at him, squawking hideously. Wang Shitang was furious. He kicked the wood on the ground. What can I make with it? A table, but not enough for the matching stools. This bird dropping is bad luck!

He threw a stone, the birds fluttered, some flew away and returned, squawking even more fiercely as if they were crying. A few leaves fell off the Stinky Woman Tree, peach-shaped, shinily green. He felt dizzy as he gazed upward, cold and hungry. He wobbled, reached for the tree that was too big, and fell into the puddle.

Wang Shitang had never thrown rocks at the birds, and now that he had, there was trouble. Their squawks were so loud like wet ropes binding him with the night. The moonlight shone through the tree. The birds, flying vigorously, tore the moonlight into pieces like the falling feathers. Then, two red frogs in the puddle started croaking, two red snakes crawled out of the tree hole and swam in the puddle swiftly. He couldn't fall asleep, picked up a brick and threw it at the birds. He hit one this time, or a couple, and heard a few painful cries and more commotion. It came to a stop finally, and things went quiet again, only a cry or two lurking in the cold night.

Fuck. You shouldn't have messed with me! he said. The world quieted down, the little red frog croaking gently, the two little snakes getting quiet, too, swimming slowly, leaving circles of ripples. The two red snakes never grew. They never ate the red frogs. The red frogs always remained a pair. Even in spring, the breeding season, there were no tadpoles. It had been like this for at least twenty years, frozen in time, within a dream. Wang Shitang also felt forever young, with inexhaustible energy, half a bottle of liquor was never a problem. His wife died, and he had passed sixty, but neither sadness nor aging had defeated him. What a miracle. The frogs, snakes, birds, fish and other weird animals cohabit with the Stinky Woman Tree; lots of fluffy fledglings hatch in the tree when spring comes, as if they were the tree's light yellow bird blossoms (which turn black when the feathers grow well).

Even more miraculous was that the leaves were edible. His wife noticed it. She took the leaves off the tree, blanched them, added a gourd of wood stove ash, put them in gauze, and kneaded. Green juice came out, solidified after a while, and became semi-transparent like jade. She cut it into strips and seasoned them with soy sauce, vinegar, ground hot pepper, garlic, and ginger. Then, a special jelly was ready.

The snakes swam and danced in the puddle, giving one an uncomfortable itch. The ripples extended toward the tree. Its root protruded a foot above the ground, bearing tumors, looking like a huge winding snake. People called it "dragon root." So, some neighbors put incense and candles under the tree, and tied red knots around its branches.

The morning sunlight cascaded upon the tree crown, illuminating the whole yard. The white-breasted waterhens flew back and forth, dropping fish in the puddle. It rained heavily the other day; many fish must have gathered in the springs. But no one knew, as they hid deep within the valleys and ravines. A neighbor needed fish lice for a cure. He had all the fish taken away, but he didn't say this was the last catch. The tree was really big. Wang Shitang wouldn't notice it every day. It was so big that its branches towered over his roof, enshrouding the house in dense layers of leaves where thick moss and grass grew. He could surely make a whole set of furniture out of it: a wardrobe, a queen bed, a dresser, a TV stand, a dinner table, a cabinet, a square table with four benches, and a cradle. The branches were enough for two chests.

He stared at the tree greedily, already knowing how to put to use every part of it. But he must hide his thoughts from the tree. It was old enough to harbor a spirit that allowed it to read human minds.

Wang Shitang started grinding his axe, threatening the tree.

After deciding to cut the tree, he pan-fried a plate of Sheep Fish Strips, stir-fried bracken fern cake, and saved five hundred to six hundred grams of liquor, ready to duel the tree. Liquor made one bold. He might need to shout at the tree for three days and nights to kill its spirit, or he couldn't touch his axe. This was the rule for the mountain people. Especially when they cut big trees.

Stinky Woman Tree, forgive my rudeness. My son's livelihood depends on yours. No one hates you, we've been on good terms for hundreds of years, you've offered protection over our homes, and in return, generations of people have treated you well. My son needs you, please offer yourself then. No one has said this to you before, but now I'm old, I'll tell you. If

I were still young and impatient, I'd only give a few shouts. Or, even not shout at all. What can you do about it?

Wang Shitang aimed the axe at the root, the sharpened blade reflecting the sunlight. Dazzlingly bright. The grinding sound was thunderous, echoing in every corner of the hollow, as if on the hunt for a hundred wild beasts to slaughter. Tss—tss—tss. The axe was made out of shell casings, fashioned by expert craftsmanship, the blade wouldn't recoil from hitting stones. Why do I grind? To scare you. Kill your pride first. He kept quiet, heavy breath escaped his mouth like stones rolling into the puddle. He kept grinding. His body moved back and forth. Solid movements. This was to gather energies, all the energy stored at the core. The energy to kill.

The axe ground on the whetstone gave off a hardened, depressing sound. Curt, cold, clacking. Full of murderous intent, cutting clean through iron as if it were mud. He suddenly felt empty and wondered why. How come the more I grind, the emptier I feel?

The walnut-like face of Wang Shitang's wife popped out from behind the door. She yelled, "The tree has a couple of godson worshippers. Do you expect them to pray to you? Are you a tree?"

It was a custom for a sick son to pray to a godfather for protection. However, the godfather was not a man but a boulder or a big tree. Every year the son must bring dim sum and wild game, and pay them as tribute: muntjacs, roebucks, bamboo rats.

"Screw off, you stinky woman! Get lost!"

He cursed out aloud. Even his late wife would stop him? He wanted to explode and fight his way through. He was ready to shout at the tree, ready to roar!

He flourished the axe and jumped while shouting. It was the highest note from his chest, the sound meant to conquer all, a hysteric roar from the top of his lungs as if out of struggle or desperation.

"Aww, aww, aww—aww, aww, aww—"

The shout, like thunder cracking in the midst of a fine day, silenced the white-breasted waterhens hopping and squawking in the dense leaves while he was grinding the axe. It was a temporary silence.

The shout caused severe pain in his throat. The sound shot out so suddenly as if a dry loofah was pulled up and stuck in his throat, causing a burning feeling. His belly button swelled from the roar, his teeth exposed, the rotten booze breath erupting all the way to the treetop.

But the shout was so short and the throat so thin that even breaking it was useless. Beside him lay the deep valley, around him were the cliffs. The Stinky Woman Hollow sat at the depth of the valley among huge boulders. Though called a village, it was actually a bird dropping, a patch of moss, totally negligible. From the mountaintops this tree was simply grass, and humans simply insects.

His shout also called forth wind. With the wind blowing from the mountain, the birds resumed their cries. Some flew away like the wind, dropping their wastes. Others kept jumping around, squawking as usual. They were a big flock. Their cries lasted longer than Wang Shitang's. He had to shout again and again until he killed the tree's spirit. There was no turning back an arrow once it has been shot.

"Aww, aww, aww—aww, aww, aww—"

The sun receded behind the mountain. Wang Shitang was almost out of breath. One hand on the tree, the other clutching the axe, he still did not dare to cut. He was also out of energy. The tree leaves remained shinily green, its branches unyielding with an exaggerated posture, standing there calmly, majestic and tall in the shower of twilight. The white-breasted waterhens circled around the tree, squawking noisily. Before flying back to their nests, they circled the tree three times as if performing a mysterious ritual, or perhaps they were simply fearful and in awe of the night. Then, the stars popped out. The tree crown turned into an enormous dark wing, covering the whole yard, the entire hollow. It was also like a colossal god of protection, allowing everything—the village and the villagers that were exposed under the night sky in these mountains, vulnerable to wild beasts and threats of the elements—to fall peacefully asleep under its wings.

He staggered into the room, barely having any energy to cook. He didn't light the candle. He poured a shot of liquor. How come it won't go down? His throat hurt. The air exhaled felt like a knife cutting his throat.

The tree fell asleep, laughing at him. It was so big. At midnight the moon snuck into his bed, watching the puddle in the yard. The frogs were out, so were the snakes, leaping, swimming, croaking as usual as if nothing had happened. His shouts died out. Everything stayed the same. The night was dark, the silhouette of the mountain heavy, the wind roaring.

Sobering up, he realized that this would be no easy job. He used to cut down pine trees. After he shouted a couple of times, the dry bark, flapping like phoenix's wings, closed up like a mangy dog tucking its tail. Then he chopped. The Stinky Woman Tree? Who can threaten it? That's fine, though. I'll simply be mean. Fill the mouth with shits and shout. It must be intimidated. You mountain loafer, tree ghost, you must bow to humans!

He shouted and roared, again and again.

With a night's rest, his throat felt better. He drank some spring water taken from the back yard, brought out a stool, stood on top of it, with a leather belt around his waist and the axe in his hand, and began to shout.

The shout lasted all day long without any stop. He peed on the tree, wiped off the bird droppings that fell on his head and rubbed them in the trunk, spat on it, blew his nose on it. He was standing, sitting, with arms akimbo, punching his fists, and stomping his feet. He shouted his eyes out, bowels broken, heartbeat pausing at random. The tree remained still as sturdy as a boulder, its branches dark and leaves green. Its bark, twigs, crown, leaves, root, even the birds in there all stayed the same, their droppings stank as ever. They perched as usual on top of the branches high above, nestled in their nests, or loafed around carelessly. They squawked, ate fish, dropped some crumbs, put the leftovers in the puddle, and cooed dreamily.

That was humiliating. I must kill you! These birds. They were the most lowdown kind. Squawk, squawk. The cries of pitiful wives in the past who lost their husbands. They were all descendants of child brides. They cried and cried and then turned into squawking birds. If it wasn't for the fish and fish lice you brought me, I would have never let you build your nests and raise your chicks here. The yard stinks, like my family is rotting inside. And the result? The more he thought, the more he believed that they were fucking evil birds of bad luck. His elder son died, his wife died, the second son went missing, the third son didn't have a wife until forty. These fucking birds, wicked birds! I'll kill you! I'll kill you!

He threw a stick at the tree. What's up? The birds were startled as they sang and ate happily. They didn't expect the sudden attack. They cried and screamed, their feathers broken and flying all over the place. He grabbed a broken chamber pot under the roof nearby and threw it into the puddle. Plop. Hide your fish if you don't want it soaking in piss!

Wang Shitang felt blood in his throat.

He wanted to make Stinky Woman Jelly that night. He knew this would be his last time making it. He pinched the leaves fallen on the ground from the bird fight. They were fresh and juicy. The tree was still alive. Let me make some Stinky Woman Jelly to sooth my throat. After three days of shouting, he had lost his voice and torn his throat. As he rubbed the leaves, he started coughing, a mouthful of water with lines of blood gushing out. There must have been bloody soup broiling in his throat.

No one helped. His wife was in the photo frame on the table. She was dead and no longer quarreled with him. Who is next? All will die . . . What emptiness . . .

A cuckoo flitted through the night sky, its call getting distant as it flew away as if saying: "brother lights a fire, brother lights a fire."

Cuckoo cried blood. Its call was sad, it also tore its throat, the way his tree shouts tore his.

The fourth day as he walked out of the door, a flock of waterhens suddenly darted down toward him and pecked his head, face, and eyes with their pointed beaks. They certainly wanted to peck him blind! Wang Shitang didn't expect this. His eyes felt a sharp pain, a piece of flesh was torn from the inside of his nose, his eardrum almost broken. He cried, dodged, and fought back. Dear god, how dare they attack humans? Wang Shitang waved his arms frantically: his hands shielded his eyes but left his head uncovered and his hair plucked off. He grabbed a stick and a broom to fight back desperately, chasing the birds all over the yard. They soared higher, their squawks louder, wings flapping madly, and cursed him with their scarlet tongues sticking out and shot poop bullets at him.

Yiu Huozui lived close to the cliff, the thatched shed he had built remained nicely sheltered and stayed warm in winter and cool in summer. He was an old widower. When Wang Shitang brought him the spicy jelly, he looked at it surprisingly. Such delicious jelly. Why is he bringing it to me?

"My shouts couldn't kill the tree . . ." Wang Shitang pointed inside the bowl.

Yiu Huozui could not hear him. Not knowing what Wang Shitang said, he also pointed at the bowl. Tree? Jelly? Shouts to kill? What the hell was Wang Shitang talking about? No sound came out of his mouth. Farts would have been louder. Seeing Wang Shitang pointing at his own throat, Yiu Huozui didn't know what was wrong there.

"Shitang, let me take a look . . ."

Wang Shitang coughed out blood and spoke again slowly. Yiu Huozui finally understood him. Chewing the Stinky Woman Jelly, he said, "That tree isn't a real deity! You wouldn't dare cut it down if it was. You've worked hard enough. Follow me, I'll show you the way! No wonder the dogs in the neighborhood have been barking like mad."

Yiu Huozui grabbed his axe from when he worked in the logging team and headed toward Wang Shitang's yard.

Yiu Huozui heroically circled around the tree a couple of times without saying a word. He was looking for something. Then he pressed a spot and said, "Here it is—"

In the blink of an eye Yiu Huozui raised the axe and hit right at the bottom of a burl. It cut three inches deep inside. As he pulled out the axe, red juice gushed out.

"Look, how precise! You need to drain its blood and spirit first." Yiu Huozui said, waving his axe.

He then suddenly shouted a strange shout at the tree. "Au-ah—" That was a rare sound, like a Daoist's shout in a ritual expelling ghosts. It startled Wang Shitang, almost scaring the life out of him.

That day Wang Shitang stayed beside the red juice from the axe cut. He watched the flow. It trickled. Consistently. The red juice kept trickling for a whole night, dying the puddle red completely. That was the tree's blood.

That night the waterhens squawked fiercely, their cries permeating the entire tree.

In a single night, all the leaves withered as if frostbitten. The birds no longer cried. Only a few did feebly.

A whole set of furniture was ready. Solid and brand new. Painted, it shone and brightened the whole yard.

Wang Shitang delivered the furniture to town. His son and daughter-in-law were so happy. What a timely delivery! The first day when the daughter-in-law slept in the new bed, she gave birth right there to a big baby son.

One night in town Wang Shitang felt his throat burning. He got up and went to his son's kitchen to find cold water. Seeing a big urn for storing water (because water outage was common), he scooped some. As he was drinking, he looked down and caught sight of a big tree reflected in the water: it was swinging in the wind, its branches dark, leaves green and peach-shaped. Wang Shitang was frightened to cold sweats. Isn't this the Stinky Woman Tree? It was made into furniture, but could its spirit have haunted the wood and followed it to town?

Wang Shitang thought it was his fantasy. He exerted his eyes to look again: clearly, the shadow of the tree was mirrored on the surface of the water. Wang Shitang stayed quiet. He mustn't tell anyone about it. Excusing himself for other business, he said goodbye to his son, daughter-in-law, and big grandson, and quietly went back home. As soon as he arrived, he lit incense at the big pit where the tree had been cut and started kowtowing. The little puddle had turned into a big waterhole, but the pretty red frogs and red snakes had disappeared, along with the fish. A dead waterhole.

A few months later Wang Shitang couldn't swallow food, not even water, his throat felt stuck with a burning charcoal. Ever since he had shouted at the tree and torn his throat, he had been like this, often having trouble swallowing, his voice hoarse, and he coughed blood. He picked up some herbs such as ba jiao lian, qi jin gu, and kai kou jian to make tea. It helped, but his throat worsened again in a few days. As his case exacerbated, his son, Sanzhao, came and brought him to the hospital in town. He was diagnosed with throat cancer.

Throat cancer was what the locals called choked-to-death disease. Wang Shitang didn't wish to trouble his son, so he went back to Stinky Woman Hollow, trying to figure things out himself.

The advanced technology in the city can't cure choked-to-death disease, but the fish lice in Sheep Fish Strips' cheeks can. Where can I find the fish lice now?

The fish are gone because the birds are gone; the birds are gone because the tree is gone. Where have you gone, you fucking birds? You were such a big flock but all disappeared, not a single soul stayed. Where did you fetch your kind of fish? I've asked so many neighbors, none of them could tell where. Those with family members suffering from choked-to-death disease still came to him for the fish lice. He waved them away; he no longer had it, he himself needed it as well.

Wang Shitang had to go deep into the mountain to look for the fish and the fish lice despite his enfeebled health. No one knew where he had gone. No one knew if he had found any fish lice. No one knew where he was.

Salt on the Stars

BAOERJI YUANYE

Translated by Leilei Chen

Baoerji Yuanye, born in Hohhot, Inner Mongolia, in 1958, is the vice president of the Liaoning Provincial Writers Association and the deputy director of the Prose Committee of the Chinese Writers Association. Starting to publish literary works in 1981, he has won many awards. Singer Tengel, painter Zhao Ge, and Baoerji are known as the "Three Talents of the Grassland" in the Chinese literary and artistic world. His famous works include the following collections of lyrical essays: *As Ephemeral as Dewdrops*, *The Appearance of the Sheep*, *Stories of Music*, and *Beauties of the Steppe*. The piece anthologized here is composed of a cluster of mini lyrical essays. The author's affectionate, imaginative depictions of horses galloping in the white snow, quiet, beautiful, distant stars high up in the sky, lovely birds as adorable and intimate company, visible yet intangible clouds as a lived paradox of absent presence, and sea waves playing in the golden evening sun give an impassioned display of love for all scenes of nature and all forms of being.

HORSES WADING THE SNOW

I wonder what horses like watching. I know I like watching horses racing in the snowfield, the snow splashing like a row of waves.

The quiet snow shrouds the ground seamlessly, as if making a huge canvas, accentuating the majesty and vitality of the fleeting horses. The herd stops to have a break, panting, their nostrils puffing white air, the sweat turning to frost around their necks and on their backs.

Set against the snow, the horses' pupils are brighter than dark gems. The maroon horse wears a light yellow mane that runs from its head to neck, a small tassel hanging on its forehead. The piebald horse is the spotted dog of the herd. The white horse is no longer white compared to the snow.

However, the most eye-catching in the snowfield is the black horse, the Mongolians call it *gang gen ha rer*. Its coat shines like black silk, its back covered with frost, its mane slanting along its neck. He is a dream.

When the horses are running, It's hard to tell which one is more handsome. The snowflakes they stir up make them barely visible. Through the waves of snow, I see the horses' forelegs extending straight ahead, their tail paralleling the ground. The herd gallops faster and faster into the white river, clouds of snow rising higher and higher, leaving behind nothing but a black riverbed.

SALT ON THE STARS

Winds make the trees quiver, as if hundreds of snakes wriggle under their leaves. They shake the river, making huge waves along its banks. Yet they can't blow away stars. They are still up there, far away in the night sky.

The biggest winds can't blow away the tiniest stars, the same way they can't uproot the smallest trees on the ground. The stars in the sky are strong.

Twinkling stars remind me of salt. These white rocks called stars do not float or melt. They are like buttons made of salt and sewed to the tent of night. Moonlight falls like cheese on my palm, like Dali's painting.

Stargazing on the mountaintops makes me feel as if I was in a dark cage. Stars line up at the front and the back, their silver bells hanging everywhere in the cage. In such a moment I would think to myself: do stars smell? On this night I smell grass, river, wild animals' feces mixed in the air, the rest being the scent of the stars. It is airy, remote, perhaps a bit salty. I hadn't thought of salt on the stars then.

The stars stay far out of reach from the island sitting low. Ocean waves, like herds of sheep, rush to the shore and disappear. The shore is an abyss for the waves.

The waves have gone to another place, their white laces solidifying into rocks. Aren't they sea salt made by the scorching sun?

Stargazing mocks poor eyesight, as they appear blurrier than the smallest E on the eye chart. On a clear night these stars have rough edges, some stars half-created. Winter stars are coarse salt, piling up at the far side of the sky, waiting to load the carriages that are coming a long way.

Xilingol Grassland has a lake called Ejinur, a salt lake Mongolians call Mother Lake. They drive their ox carts from elsewhere for its salt. The white crystals end up melting in their blood. They kneel down and bow to the salt lake after loading their carts full and before their departure, feeling grateful that the world offers them salt.

The salt in the lake doesn't decrease even though the Mongolians have taken away countless loads of it. Sailing on the ship of waves in the gray lake, the salt moves toward the shore. The salty waves are heavy and slow.

Ejinur is not a scenic spot. Salt lakes usually do not have lush plants around them. Yet the starry sky is beautiful here, clearer than that over other places. The blue dark night is thin and bright, covered with rootless white light (from nowhere).

The ocean is the salts' home. As the sun boils the sea, salts rise, becoming stars. They melt over Ejinur, leaving a hole in the sky.

HOLDING A BIRD IN MY HANDS

When I was a kid, I hoped to have a bird of my own, to be able to hold it in my hand and see its head turn from side to side, feel its warmth, and perhaps its heartbeat.

That was just a fantasy. I never owned a bird. It was fleeting, flying across the sky, and disappearing in a second.

Some birds dart out of a tree and end up nowhere. Some dart into it, also ending up nowhere. They chirp and chat endlessly, but none of their words are comprehensible. Gilbert White, a naturalist, said, "The language of birds is very ancient, and, like other ancient modes of speech, very elliptical; little is said, but much is meant and understood." Li Shangyin's poems are also rich with euphemism and meaning.

If I had a bird, I would inspect every single feather on its body. I would carefully lift its wings to see if both sides look the same. I would touch its sharp claws. When a bird winks at you, its lower eyelids move upward to touch the upper ones. When a human winks, their upper eyelids fall; the lower eyelids can't rise. I tried to wink like a bird, but to no avail.

If I could walk with my bird down the street, I would keep it in my left pocket and hold it with my left hand. If I moved it to my right pocket, I would hold it with my right hand. It's too small and delicate to be hugged or cuddled. The most intimate way is to cup it carefully in my hands, feeding it water and rice, letting it rest on a horizontal stick.

I'm eager to know how birds sleep on a twig at night. They curl up, their lower eyelids moving up to close their eyes. They clutch the twig while sleeping soundly. How can they sleep like that? I wouldn't be able to fall asleep at all when clutching a tree branch. Even if I did fall asleep, my hands would let go.

The bird is impatient, all its actions must be completed urgently, including grooming its chest. Does it need to hurry like that? It seems to have a long to-do list on hand, longer than a human's, an endless list.

I've heard that a wild bird doesn't like being a pet. Some people caged sparrows. They dashed inside and starved themselves to death. I'd love to have a bird, but I won't put them in a cage. The best way of petting a bird is to open your hand and let it fly to the sky. I've never owned a bird. My bird flies in the sky.

I've always loved birds. I wish that birds would see me as a tree. I wouldn't bother them but would have a chance to watch them close by. My wish has more or less become true: a sparrow often comes hopping and pecking around me. It seems that each of its steps is on a spring, it just jumps automatically for a long way, unable to stop. It leaves its tail on the ground while hopping. A way of using their tails. That's why some sparrows have long tails and others have short ones.

The sparrow beside me pecked diligently and then looked at me. I didn't respond. It kept pecking violently and looked at me again. I said, I can't do that. If I pecked like you do, I would have a crooked nose.

The bird flew away. It likes flying. I like sitting under the tree and watching it flying in the sky.

THE CLOUDS WET MY CLOTHES

The Lower Stone Ditch Village perched on the edge of a bottomless cliff of Taihang Mountain. This was what we saw from our car winding its way around the mountains. The village got its name in Tang Dynasty, and it was still in use.

We stayed in a stone house with a local family. All the houses here were made of stone. Bricks couldn't be transported here. No earthen homes, either. When we opened the door the next morning, cotton-like clouds deluged the room. Thank goodness the door remained locked, or the clouds could have flooded during nighttime. Chen Dongjie and I shared a room. As if blind, we fumbled our way out of the room into the clouds, grinning. How dense were the clouds? They were everywhere below our waists. We couldn't see the path under our feet.

We lifted our feet purposefully to hear our confident steps on the slates as we headed forward, but fearing the cliffs ahead, we stopped shortly after. Dongjie said, Let's have a rest.

In less than a minute the clouds disappeared. The village emerged in Tang Dynasty style—houses with stone walls and roofs, braids of red pepper and yellow corn hanging on the door sides. Bright yellow pumpkin flowers climbed over the stone walls. The old and the young were walking in the street. They, too, had just come out of the clouds. Dongjie and I smiled at each other. The clouds came again and blocked our views.

Again we stepped into the cotton candy, wondering if these were the same clouds we met before. I breathed deeply and didn't smell anything chokingly pungent.

I must have breathed in a good amount, as the clouds dispelled quickly, giving way to another scene. A locust tree stood in front of us (incredible on the top of Taihang Mountain—a tree trunk so thick that one can't get arms around it)! Under the tree some old people were chatting. They had also just emerged from the clouds.

We walked toward the old locust tree and hoped to touch it, saying to ourselves: the tree is getting old, and we certainly are as well. A two-meter high cloud sailed over before we got to the tree. We stood still. It was like the game we played when we were kids: when a command was given, the runner stopped right away and couldn't resume running unless being told. I knew the old locust tree was right there but couldn't see it. When the clouds were gone, we saw the seniors sitting under the tree, radiating good health and kindness. They looked at us, smiling, as if it had been them who sent the cloud to enclose us. We smiled back. I smiled because I understood why they enjoyed a long life: clouds were their daily company.

We kept walking and valued everything that came to our sight, including a yellow dog nosing the stones on the road while running toward us. Clouds came from behind the hutong's corner and surrounded us.

This time they dispelled slowly. We stood still in the clouds for two or three minutes. I had a sudden whim of undressing myself. Wouldn't it be cool to have a cloud bath? But it would frighten others if the cloud disappeared before I had time to put my clothes back on.

It was a small village. We walked and paused in clouds, greeting everything we saw with smiles.

I had seen clouds coming out of a steamer when buns are ready, or puffs of steam from the trains at the station. I had never seen clouds floating over the ground. When seeing clouds in the sky, I have wondered what was inside. Then I knew clouds are nothing special. You can't touch them with your hands. They are visible but intangible. Standing in clouds offers a perfect occasion to recite, "Reality is illusionary, and illusions are real." A cloud has nothing in it.

The clouds dispelled, we kept walking forward. The stone-paved roads, stone walls, and houses reappeared. The seniors looked alike and spoke Shanxi dialect. After this stroll in the clouds we returned to our room. Dongjie said, It was such an adventure. I said, What an adventure. We had a good laugh. I touched my clothes. They felt wet. With the moisture, they felt like clouds in my hands.

THE OCEAN WAVES WASHING THE DUSK

Cave Head Island's unique scenery revealed itself as dusk settled on the beach.

The dusk coincided with the tide ebbing. Like thousands of hands, each wave reached toward the shore then retreated deep within the sea, as if searching for lost treasures. The blue sea shimmered golden yellow and, fleetingly, vermillion. The seawater shook, instantly shattering shades of gold and red into pieces. Seagulls circled back and forth frantically, squawking unpleasantly. That was why Yingkou people called them sea cats.

Sea cats didn't like the blue sea to be dyed gold and red. They blocked the sunlight, their snow-white, lengthy wings also dyed gold.

A white sailboat was approaching. A small boat, its sail bearing a line of numbers, but no longer white. The sunset coated it golden red nonetheless.

The earth is turning dark. The tree branches in the woods merged together like a black wall. Clouds gathered on the horizon, as if a fleet was returning to shore from afar.

On this side of the ocean, the sky was immensely wide. The clouds dispelled quickly, revealing the bright, blue curtain of sky. The golden stars were ready to come on stage.

The light of the dusk had receded, and the waves, too. The white lace of waves became blurry. They fulfilled their mission. They harvested and buried the sunset in the sands, turning them gold.

The Pond in the Field

FU FEI

Translated by Leilei Chen

Fu Fei, poet and essayist, was born in Shangrao, Jiangxi Province, in 1971. He is a newly emergent leading figure in the field of nature writing in China. Starting his career as an environmental writer in 2002, he has published several volumes of poems and essays. His writing is well-known and admired for exploring three levels of being, respectively identified as the soul, the spirit, and coexistence of all beings. What defines his poetic and prose writing are his love, care, and compassion for all forms of life. Among his publications are the following collections of essays: *The River above the Cottage Roof*, *Portraits of the Skies*, *The Absence of Wilderness*, and *My Beloved World*. "The Pond in the Field" can be taken as a series of snapshots of wildlife located in and surrounding a pond in the wilderness. The universe inhabited by plants, birds, and fish is a world of fullness, innocence, and simplicity, one that follows its own laws and its own seasons of change and joy, portraying harmonious relations between all beings. Abusive human behavior towards nature threatens to destroy such ecological harmony.

A pond in the field is the Earth's blue eye, beholding only the sky. As the night thickens, the stars decorate like snow wreaths twinkling. Countless flowers wither during the day and bloom at night. The blue eye is like a solitary soul, gazing at a gigantic constellation of wanderers who have lost their way and are waiting in strange lines for a holy meal on the ocean surface.

I have seen such a pond in the field. It sat in the triangle where two riverbanks met. Sand diggers rented two field patches. They removed the earth layer to mine the sand underneath—the white, fine, clean type that can mix with concrete directly for house building. The area had been a beach sixty years ago and became a hundred-acre field only after the riverbanks were constructed. The sand layer was so deep and offered over ten truckloads every day. The villagers stopped the mining when over half of the two fields was gone. They said without the sand the ground becomes loose and the riverbanks will collapse, doors can't lock floods out, no one can stop the flood.

The field was dug and abandoned. No reclamation. The big sand hole is a trapezoid, its long side about twenty meters, the legs about fifteen, and the short side ten. A stone wall was built along the long side where the fields meet to prevent them from falling. The short side is the earth pile from the fields which has become compacted from the constant rolling of the trucks loaded with sand. The legs are the two riverbanks built with limestones. The sand hole is over four meters deep like an underground basketball field.

During the rainy seasons, Raobei River roars with humongous muddy waves, slaughters trees along the way, and ravages the fields in mighty force. The longest rainy season is called Duanwu Rain and begins more or less on the fifth of May of the lunar calendar. Raindrops fall like nails, darting into the ground pitter-pattering. They drop on tree and grass leaves, bouncing like beans fried in a hot wok. The leaves dance in harmony. The bamboo forest rustles in the rain. Endless rain. The fields are a patch of white, where the water and the sky coalesce. Grayish white.

Raobei River floods half of the Chinese ash forest, leaving only the tree crowns shivering violently. The sluice gate is lifted. Big fish fall, their bodies cut in halves or heads exploding. Small fish also fall, are tossed to the tips of waves, then drown or flee. The flood season never misses its visiting schedule. Like a horse descending from the sky, the flood runs clip-clopping across mountaintops and waves of hills, bringing the words of rain to every grass, seed, root, and lowland. The flood season urges dead things to decay and birds to breed.

The sand crater, with water filled to its rim, becomes a pond. Reeds, Chinese silver grass, cogon grass, and desert willow occupy its edge the next spring. The reeds branch out, their stems grow as big as a bamboo basket. They are the tall kind, one leaf is taller than a person. The Chinese silver grass and cogon grass disappear. The willow, taller than reeds, grows alone, its branches drooping, with creeping fig climbing all over.

When the sand crater was abandoned, a few lotus roots and stems of wild rice were left here (or perhaps the flood brought them here). A small patch of wild rice and lotus thrive in the pond's eastern corner. The rice shoots have many broad, tall, straight leaves. In April the lotus sprout sticks its head out of the water's surface like the tip of a writing brush; its tender yellow, white, and green petals curling into a bud. The buoy of spring. The bud unfolds day after day in a clockwise spiral until it's in full bloom, floating on the water.

The water is mesmerizingly blue. For a few times gazing at its surface drew me to hallucination. The water, purified by sand, hallucinates with me. It sees itself as blue sky, willow's reflections, its own dream. The high sky mirrors the deep pond; the peace of the reflections echoes that of the pond; the pond changes like changing dreams. I fantasize a group of women in water green dresses dancing on lotus leaves in the moonlight, their white skirts flying.

The head of the pond is also where I would stop every time I have a walk by the river. Two acres of reeds cover this area. On the one side lies a belt of pristine woods with more than twenty huge camphor trees and ten Chinese wingnut trees. In between the pond head and the woods sits a small vegetable garden. Flocks of birds with long curly tails, jays, turtle-doves, and cawing crows are there, perching on the tall twigs, hopping and playing, or hiding crouched under the tree leaves. From time to time they come to the vegetable garden and the riverbank for food, flying over the field in flocks to make a show, or simply nestling in the reeds for a long while. I can always hear the reeds rustling. In there, too, I see tons of reed warblers and tiny tits. Occasionally, red birds with shiny eyes also visit. A dark cloud of birds.

In hot and humid summertime, the pond has all sorts of fish swimming. Grass carp, crucian carp, common carp. Schools of crucian carp stay close to the pond edge, either at the surface or below, the dark blue backs blending harmoniously with the water colors. I magnify the pond and the fish in my mind's eye millions of times, seeing a floating line of crucian carp mountains with dark peaks on the top. The mountaintops immersed in ocean are free. Grass carp hide under lotus leaves or in reed shoots.

My cousin said to me a couple of times, If we cast a net to catch some, we could make delicious, milky fish soup. Anyone who has seen the fish in the pond would think so. But no one casts a net here. The reeds are too dense and the pond too deep. No one will cut the reeds to get fish meat. Besides, snakes are rampant and the pond edge offers no place to stand.

The reeds, wild rice, and lotuses are always sparse. Perhaps there isn't enough mud to sustain their life. These plants are lean but graceful. My heart swells with loving sympathy. They must be lonely here. The pond feels more like a temple that worships these plants. A temple where no bell tolls in the morning nor drum booms at night. Only clouds of water surrounding their slim figures all the time. The shoals of fish cloaked in dark blue ragged robes are the little monks wandering in the floating mountains—their only companions.

The pond in early summer sees lotuses blooming, but I like it more in late fall. The reeds fall down to the water with their yellow leaves turning white, shining unpainted beauty of the final stage of life. The lotus leaves are nice and round still, offering frogs—instead of doves—a Noah's Ark that sails in cold moonlight.

Many people don't like the pond in late fall, thinking it's too desolate and colorless. But this is nature's true look. No place is eternally prosperous. The cycle of waxing and waning is the principle of life. A form of life. The process of growth is extremely hard: leaves turning green little by little, one centimeter extension of a stem is like miles of trekking across mountains and rivers. The cycle of reeds rising from their shoots, or a lotus plant changing from dying yellow to exuberant green takes months to complete, while the decline happens after a night's frost, an important step of life's cycle in the natural world. What spring offers to nature is taken back in fall. The giving and the taking remain eternally equal.

In the winter of 2015, a dabchick couple came to the pond and made the reeds their home. At daybreak they started diving, swimming, and pecking. The next summer five more little ones were added to the family. The baby dabchicks, coated with gray and black down, sailed proudly on the private yacht of their parents' back, twittering cheerfully as if saying, the world is so big, let's grow up quick and travel wide. When the early summer passed, they were no longer seen on the pond. When winter returned, another dabchick couple came. I wasn't sure if they were the old couple from last year. Standing on the riverbank, I plopped a small stone into the water, surprising it into ripples. The dabchicks flew along the surface, extending their feet and fluttering their wings. They either hid in the reeds or submerged under the water. I saw them diving down but never popping their heads up again. After a long while—about a quarter of an hour, they swam out from the reed shoots, leisurely and cheerfully, asking nothing better.

According to the twenty-four solar terms, dabchicks come back at the Beginning of Winter every year—around November 7—and fly away on the day of Pure Brightness, around April 5. A big family at the time of migration. I have never seen how they move in or out. They're simply committed to spending winter in the pond.

I sometimes think about the pond's previous life—an agricultural field only for planting rapeseed, rice, and cotton to sustain human lives. Now the pond is deserted and no longer offers crops or produce, but it has become home to dabchicks, spacious enough for them to raise a big, happy family. Hence its irreplaceable ecological value. The pond is lucky. So are the dabchicks. Humans have taken all possible lands for food and resources. How hard it is for the dabchicks to find a home!

Flood comes every year, carrying fish from the river to the pond. Some are flushed away, while others—after the flood has gone—are detained in the pond permanently. I ponder whether a fish has memories and remembers itself being a warrior, jumping across boulders and off a dam cliff, marching toward the river's origin in the fast and slow of the torrents. In the pond there's neither waves nor currents. It contains abundant water and never goes dry as the river keeps refilling it through saturating the underground sand layer. Dead reeds and lotuses degenerate, providing fish with humus and plankton. A fish becomes Wang Wei, the Tang Dynasty hermit poet, residing in the cherry blossom paradise of the pond.

Once I had a sudden whim of doing something meaningful. I bought ten baby salamanders from a farm in Zhejiang, carried them back in a Sprite bottle, and dropped them in the pond. I kept asking the expert if they could survive in a natural environment. He said thoughtfully, "Salamanders breed every five years. You need patience." I was full of hope that my salamanders would live on safely and produce lots of babies.

I started to feel guilty two years later. Salamanders are amphibians and crawl a lot. Besides, they were surrounded by too many predators in the pond such as snakes and dabchicks. They might survive snakes' attack but would find it hard to escape from dabchicks' mouths.

A variety of species used to live in the river, but they are now all gone, or are dying out. Otters, eels, perch, and the Mandarin fish I used to see have been gone for over twenty years. These species have high standards for water quality. The river, polluted by wastewater and pesticide, is no longer livable. The water in the pond, filtered through sand, offers eels and groupers a safe home.

Coming back to Shangrao, I found a fisherman living by the Xinjiang River. I asked him to call me when he had eels for sale. He said eels are rare, for a whole year he barely catches one or two.

After I had waited for over a year, the fisherman finally called: he had two eels, weighing over one and a half kilos, sold at two hundred and eighty yuan for half a kilo; come and wait at the market at seven-thirty tomorrow morning. I took a day off work, bought the eels, and hurried to my hometown. I hadn't seen such big eels for over thirty years. I prayed for them not to die. Eels are fish but look like water snakes with white and black dots all over, lengthy and graceful. They feed on small fish and shrimp, plankton eggs, and like hiding in mud.

I left the eels in the pond for a year, not knowing if they were still alive. I could only let them be. Another year passed. My neighbor told me during a walk along the river that his son caught an eel with a creel (which is a basket for catching fish). They steamed it, the meat mouth-filling and delicious. I asked him about the eel's size. He told me: over a hundred and fifty grams. Thank goodness. The eel must have been the offspring of the one I put in the pond. I didn't tell anyone that I brought back salamanders to the pond. I would never tell I brought eels, either. I want to breed harmless species in the pond and help them prosper again in Raobei River. I had even thought of raising hairy crabs and baishui shrimps. Then realizing that their predator dabchicks return every winter, I dismissed the idea. I wouldn't kick out dabchicks for farming shrimps and crabs.

The pond remained full of water for seven or eight years—the level decreased only when water flowed over the dam. No one knew how many fish the pond had and how big the biggest fish was. Fish electrocutors wouldn't come because the pond was too deep. It was surrounded by reeds, half of the willow's crown slanted over the surface.

Zhengfang Basin suffered from drought when the season transitioned from summer to fall in 2019. It only saw a little rain on July 7 and wasn't graced by its generosity until November 20. The Raobei River almost dried out. The pond lost water and showed its mud in late October. White under the sun. There were lots of fish still alive—grass carp, common carp, crucian carp. The biggest grass carp was half a meter long. The place which used to be a paradise for fishes became hell. They had no way out, confined within sand and stone walls all around. They could hardly even move, not expecting the pond to be completely depleted. They rolled in mud, mouths opening and closing, until finally being eaten by birds. The rain comes too late. Useless for the dead fishes.

The rain brings winter and finally fills the pond. Another year of flood follows. The reeds and the lotuses grow bigger than before.

It's a pity that I haven't been to the pond on a moonlit night. It must be a different scene: the stars flying, the moonlight a dream world. The pond then becomes the nature-gazer's heart.

India

Introduction

UPAMANYU PABLO MUKHERJEE

From Afghanistan to Sri Lanka, the region designated "South Asia" by the big beasts of contemporary global geopolitics is comprised of relatively young states carved out during the final days of former imperial powers, notably Britain. It covers 4.8 percent of the world's landmass, but 20 percent of its population, with around 60 percent of the population engaged in agricultural labor (Srivastava, 335). It also has high rates of urban demographic growth and megacities hosting populations of 20 million or more, who are often crammed into unregulated and unplanned residences with fragile and inadequate infrastructure (Fisher, 249–50).

Understandably enough, the most serious environmental afflictions plaguing the inhabitants in South Asia (humans and non-humans alike) include land and water degradation, extreme climatic events, food shortage, and coastal erosion and submersion. Between 1990 and 2008, the total arable land in the region decreased from 203.6 to 198 million hectares; the annual volume of waste discharged into rivers has ranged from a grim 4.5 percent to an astonishing 19 percent of their annual available water flow; the number of severe storms and floods have increased by 10 percent every decade for the past five decades; the air temperatures in the megacities can get up to 12 degrees hotter than that of the adjacent non-urban areas; and India, the country with the second-largest population in the world at 1.4 billion people, is projected to enter a period of severe water-stress by 2025, with per capita availability of water falling below 100 cubic meters annually (Srivastava, 335–53).

To a certain extent, the environmental crises of South Asia reflect that of the continent in general. The most recent (fifth) assessment report of the IPCC on the effects of climate change on Asia documents lower yields of staple crops such as rice, warming and acidification of oceans, massive coastal erosion and submersion, monsoonal deficit combined with extreme rainfall events, and increased mortality and morbidity in urban areas due to more frequent heat waves (Hijioka et al. 1330–47). Yet, to frame our understanding of these continental and regional catastrophes with foreshortened views of periods and processes such as "the contemporary," "globalization," or even "modernity" is not likely to take us very far. Indeed, as my opening remarks suggested, it is only by tracing the *longue durée* of imperial and colonial lineages on the present moment that we can hope to understand the trajectory and velocity of the storm that engulfs us now.

From land degradation to deforestation, food scarcity to water stress, state-led "scientific development" to popular movements against such interventions, most of the problems associated with South Asia today were conceived by and matured with British colonialism and imperialism that displaced the Mughal dispensation there. The opening notes of the new regime were provided by the East India Company's conquest of Bengal in 1757 and the ruthless drive for land revenue there that caused the deaths of 10 million people—approximately a third of the province's population—from famine. The imperial sunset nearly two hundred years later offered a tragic symmetry—the deaths of 5 million people in Bengal once again from food scarcities triggered by British administrative decisions relating to the "eastern theatre" of the Second World War. Bracketed by these disasters was the British Raj's modernization of the territory between the Afghan frontiers and Burma, which more or less involved turning it into a vast zone of resource- and labor-extraction that relegated the region to the (semi-) peripheries of the modern world-system.

Such an extractive drive, sustained by the novel fusion of fossil fuel and expanding circuits of profit accumulation, fundamentally altered every aspect of the South Asian life-world. For example, the Raj succeeded in naturalizing the agrarian—the world of settled peasant agriculture—as the "universal rural" (Bhattacharya, 1). By deploying a battery of administrative, military, political, scientific, and aesthetic devices, it rendered South Asia's rich and complex non-agrarian rural spaces—the dry zones, the scrublands, the forests, the pastures, and the beings whose habitats these are—more or less invisible (Bhattacharya, 8). Thus, what we forget when we celebrate the simplicity and charm of the "traditional" South Asian village today is that they are products of a massive geo-engineering project that was racist and violent in equal measures.

Once we have properly grasped the *longue durée* of South Asian environmental crises, we can begin to address their registration in the literary writing of the region. One of the crucial insights offered by eco-critical theory in recent years has been that the *political unconscious* of the literature of modernity (which is not the same thing as "modernist" literature) is also always already an *environmental unconscious*. The heterogeneous, complex, elongated, and uneven nature of South Asian environmental crises has concomitantly demanded a literature that is unusually open to generic repurposing and formal and thematic experimentations.

I have chosen Mahasweta Devi's *Pterodactyl, Puran Sahay, and Pirtha* (1965) as a paradigmatic example of such a literature. Devi's story takes us into the famine-haunted world of South Asia's *adivasi*—indigenous peoples—who are rendered invisible and disposable by both the colonial and the postcolonial state's developmental imperatives. The *adivasi*'s anguished, resilient, and imaginative response to this violence appears at first to be unreal or incomprehensible to the sympathetic journalist Puran Sahay. But Puran learns, as do Devi's readers, to accept the *adivasi* imagination as a concrete, life-giving praxis in our shared world. Devi's narrative absorbs various codes of the oral and performative indigenous cultures and thereby extends the formal possibilities of the written short-story form. At the same time, Devi scrupulously avoids any romantic primitivism regarding the *adivasi*, presenting them instead as uncannily prescient modern subjects whose conclusions about the relationship between modernization, development, and environmental catastrophes offer life-lessons for the rest of us.

Devi's writing is part of a long, rich, and diverse body of South-Asian environmental literature. That we were unable to present extracts from other writers due to the expenses of obtaining copyright permissions from their publishers tells us much about the cartelization of the publishing industry today. But we hope that readers will be inspired by Mahasweta Devi's vision to seek out this writing for themselves. It might be just the kind of companion they need as they go about the difficult business of learning to live and die in the Anthropocene.

WORKS CITED

Bhattacharya, Neeladri. 2019. *The Great Agrarian Conquest*. Albany: State University of New York Press.

Fisher, Michael. 2018. "National, Subcontinental, and Global Issues in South Asia." In *An Environmental History of India: From Earliest Times to the Twenty-First Century*, edited by Michael H. Fisher, 248–56. Cambridge: Cambridge University Press.

Hijioka, Y., et al. 2014. "Asia." In *Climate Change 2014: Impacts, Adaptation, and Vulnerability. Part B: Regional Aspects. Contribution of Working Group II to the Fifth Assessment Report of the Intergovernmental Panel on Climate Change*, edited by V. R. Barros et al., 1327–70. Cambridge: Cambridge University Press.

Srivastava, Leena. 2013. "The Environmental Challenges in South Asia." In *Democracy, Sustainable Development, and Peace: New Perspectives on South Asia*, edited by Akmal Hussein and Muchkund Dubey, 335–82. Oxford: Oxford University Press.

From

Pterodactyl, Puran Sahay, and Pirtha

MAHASWETA DEVI

Translated by Gayatri Chakravorty Spivak

Mahasweta Devi's 1989 novella, *Pterodactyl, Puran Sahay, and Pirtha*, brings together many of the key interests that animated this remarkable Bengali writer, activist, and educationalist. It is a story of how the "developmentality" of the modern state—whether colonial or post-colonial—destroys entire life-worlds; it is a story of how people designated as "indigenous"—a code-name for the "backward," the dispensable, the un-grievable—bear witness to this destruction; finally, it is also a story about storytelling itself—and how it can save something of what remains and use such leftovers to give birth to a different world.

II

The characteristics of the Indian *Austric* are medium height, black (sometimes very black) skin, longish heads, slightly flat noses, but otherwise sharp features. Perhaps the skin color and the flat nose are a result of intermingling with older Negroid peoples. Were the *Austrics* of a yet earlier time sharp-nosed and light skinned? The *Austric* aborigines spread all over India, and went East to Burma, Malaysia and the islands of southeast Asia (were they then going farther and farther east in search of the sun?), kept moving, moving, moving on, establishing settlements. The *Gazetteer of India* says, "The *Austrics* form the bedrock of the people." To strike a stretched-skin instrument five times means to inform of an emergency. The news is coming and spreading. The Sarpanch shakes and shakes his head. "What to say, revered Sir?" If a terrible, inevitable something repeatedly casts a shadow . . . in the Mushal chapter of the Mahabharata the great constellation of Time himself shadowed the earth again and again . . . Krishna was dark, so was Rama. If you are very dark then you are black, if slightly dark, dusky. The *Austriaco* laid the foundations of Indian civilization. They cultivated rice, raised vegetables, and made sugar from sugarcane. One of the branches of their language is Mon-Khmer, and is alive in Khasi and Nicobari tribal tongues. Again the Munda branch has many divisions, and into these language groups fall sixteen aboriginal tribes. These Nagesia tribals are also among them. When did they cultivate rice, grow vegetables, make sugar from sugarcane? Why are the descendants of the "bedrock of the people," whose forebears laid the foundations of the civilization of India, why are they sounding their signal in such desperation? Puran has seen in his own state of Bihar, in Palamu district, that the Parhaiyas were designated as a "criminal tribe" by the British. And they are all bond slaves. The Nagesias live on hillsides, some collective memory haunts them, they'll see the enemy approach, and fly. But now all around are modern India and medieval Palamu, the enemy doesn't come with war drums, they have nowhere to run.

There are some caste-Hindus in Gabahi. Bhan Singh Shah the Sarpanch [head of the village council or Panchayat] has a turban on his head and a singlet on his back. He introduced himself as the descendant of the Gond king Shankar Singh Shah, whom the British had blown from the mouth of a cannon at the time of the Mutiny. If Puran doesn't believe this he can visit his home and see the well-printed family tree. It is a great injustice that the government of independent India has not given him any recognition as the descendant of a tribal hero of the first Battle of Indian Independence.

—This injustice is because I am a tribal.

Harisharan and Puran look at each other.

Relatively speaking, the Sarpanch is well off. In his fortlike house with high earth walls you can see a separate enclosure for water-buffalo, a granary for corn. Cots in the courtyard. One of his sons is a messenger in the Electricity Office and another has passed an exam to become a clerk in the Post and Telegraph Department.

Harisharan said, "I read the proofs when you had your family tree printed."

—Sure. But his name is in history books. This is what Bhalerao from Gwalior told me.

Puran cleared his throat.

—This is very true. I will discuss it with you later. We'll have a long talk.

—Will you stay in Gabahi?

—In Pirtha.

The Sarpanch looks at Shankar. Shankar keeps his head turned away. An inscrutable, passionless black face against the backdrop of the sky. That face will never give a reply. He's listening with care, in deep, deep thought.

—Dhomra-drum.

Five times . . . five times . . .

—That's how tribals . . . we . . . spread the news.

Although the Sarpanch changed class long ago (when the tribal gets a little education, gains a little safety and moves from his class, does he go up or down? Does the lower middle class or the middle class accept him as a member? If even one percent of the tribals gets a house, a motorcycle, a job, some land, do they enter the well-to-do middle class or the rural kulak class? No, the main point is that he is not of the destitute tribal community, and not of the class which is his in the adjacent community. Is that why he has to empathize with his poor tribal community in troubled times? Why did the Sarpanch first say "tribals" and then "we"? A many-leveled problem. It is improper to pass quick judgment from a safe distance).

—Don't come to a slambang decision, Puran, you know what I mean.

—Mr. Sarpanch! What message are they sending?"

The eyes of the Sarpanch are now vague and distant.

—Well, you have come with the BDO and you will stay here.

The Sarpanch licks his dry lips. Then he straightens his slightly bent body (Puran learned later that before his fortunes changed he used to gather the fruit of the Ritha tree in the extinct forest and a falling tree branch had hurt his spine; at the time peacocks danced on the banks of the Pirtha ditch) and spoke as if in deposition, in a still small voice.

—Now in the whole area we are unclean, in mourning for the dead.

—Why in mourning for the dead?

—What is it that we have seen? Tell us, Mr. BDO! You are an educated man, you are the first government officer ever to come to a tribal area. We had thought that the independent government of India was a fairy tale for our lot. We have seen you, now tell us, what have we seen?

—I don't know.

—You accept that we have seen?

—Yes, everyone can't be mistaken. But what it is, what kind of bird, that I don't know.

—Have you ever seen the picture drawn by Shankar's nephew Bikhia?

—You won't know what he saw.

—You say, our visitor wants to know.

—How shall I explain?

Harisharan says softly, "Mr. Sarpanch! My friend has been to many tribal areas. He is from Bihar. There are many tribals like you there as well, Baiga, Bithath, Gond, Khariya, Khond, Kol, Munda, Nagesia, Oraon, Asur—they are there too."

—How can that be?

—There are, there are.

—We are there as well?

—You are, you are.

—He has seen?

—He has seen them and lived there.

—Is he a moneylender?

—No, a journalist. He comes running when he hears of bad times for the tribals, he writes in the papers.

—Then why has he come now?

—Shouldn't he write about the famine?

—What famine? You tell them, the SDO tells them, and you are the government, still the government doesn't listen. This happens every year, no one knows, no one takes notice. The government doesn't even know that there are human beings in Pirtha.

Harisharan makes his voice even more respectful.

—I know. That is why I keep on trying, so that everyone knows about Pirtha, it comes up in the State Assembly, and the state helps you in some way.

Puran says softly, "So much money is earmarked for tribals, don't you get any aid?"

—How shall I explain to you?

At this point Shankar turns around, clenches his fists, and says in piercing anguish, "We are late by many many moons. Now no one can show us any help."

Moons? Many moons? When the sun is merciless in the sky? When the swordlike heavy leaves of the Khajra trees are still, and when one leaf on the bare pipal tree shakes out of control? How late are Harisharan and Puran?

Shankar goes on talking with his eyes closed. Alas! He speaks Hindi; Puran and Harisharan also speak Hindi, but how can one touch the other? Shankar says his say in Hindi, but the experience is a million moons old, when they did not speak Hindi. Puran thinks he doesn't know what language Shankar's people spoke, what they speak. There are no words in their language to explain the daily experience of the tribal in today's India. Pashupati Jonko, of the Ho tribe of Singhbhum, a native Ho speaker, had said with humble amazement at the time of translating Birsa Munda's life into the Ho language, There are no words for "exploitation" or "deprivation" in the Ho language. There was an explosion in Puran's head that day.

That was during the Sagwana (teak) movement: "Away with teak, save the Sal." Forest Singhbhum was washed over with turbulence. There was firing at Gua. The Ho language has no synonym for "exploitation." There were many bullet charges after that. The Sal is sajom in the languages of Ho, Mundari, Saontali, but in the site of the unfinished Sagwana struggle the word "exploitation" cannot be explained. Then in Ilyagarh, in the resistance against the damming of the Kharkai, the fearless Kol tribal Gangaram Kalundia died. In Gua, Bidar Nag is ruthlessly beaten to death, and Pashupati Jonko says, Brother! The word "exploitation" is not in the Ho language. Puran thinks, Do the tribals, whose life is nothing but exploitation, nothing but deprivation, have a synonym for "exploitation" in any of their languages? But the theorist Kamal, who sticks to the tribal area, even he can't jump over the glass wall of book-learnt theory in his head and says, when he descends to the plains from time to time, "My friend! There is class difference among them and, although small, a class is growing up among them that is exploiting and deceiving their own kind." Saraswati got very angry.

—Oh yes, in our society one person can swindle others and make millions in black money, keep it abroad, that you can accept. And we have taken away everything that is their own, we are imposing our rotten value-system upon them, and then if one of them makes a bit of money, or becomes like us, we abuse them from a safe distance. We say, Look, look! How that man's nature has changed, he is no longer a tribal.

The whole thing is very complicated. To say something too quickly is wrong. What is Shankar Nagesia saying? A warning bell goes off in Puran's mind. He must understand Shankar's words, otherwise no justice can be done to himself or Saraswati in the Saraswati affair. Saraswati had amazed him that day. Shankar speaks.

As if he is singing a saga. They have captured their history by observing the rules of birth-marriage-death-social justice. There is no alphabet, they have caught the past in their songs.

—Once there was forest, hill, river, and us. We had villages, homes, land, ourselves. In our fields we grew rice, kodo, kutki, soma, we lived. Then there was game to hunt. It rained, peacocks danced, we lived. People grew, the community grew, some of us moved to a distance. We asked the earth's permission, we are setting down stakes to build a roof, settling land to grow crops. The Chief of our society told us where we should settle land fit for living. There we built homes, made villages, settled land each for himself. We worshipped the tree that was the spirit of our village. Then we lived, only us.

Shankar ran in a circle and pointed in all directions.

—We buried our dead. We lowered the body at the crossroads. We scattered the seed of the kodo and rice. Then at the time of burial we gave oil, cloth, rice, fruit. We laid the body down with the ancestors. After the funeral we laid a rock on the grave. There are many, many burial grounds like this. The souls of the ancestors were at peace. Blessed us. We lived. And now?

—Ah misfortune! As ants come before a flood, as white ants fly in teeming swarms before the rains, so did our news reach strangers. Did we make a mistake in our worshipping? Did someone tear a leaf from a tree before it was consecrated, before the new fruit, new leaf, new flower came in the springtime, in the month of Phalgun? Did one of us kill a pregnant doe in the hunt? Did someone insult the elders? The community's rule is to protect orphans, was that rule broken somewhere? I don't know where we became guilty.

—Why did the foreigners come? We were kings. Became subjects. Were subjects, became slaves. Owed nothing, they made us debtors. Alas, they enslaved and bound us. They named us, as bond slaves, Haroahi, Mahidar, they named us Hali, named us Kamiya, in many tongues. Our land vanished like dust before a storm, our fields, our homes, all disappeared. The ones who came were not human beings. Oh, we climb hills and build homes, the road comes chasing us. The forest disappears, they make the four corners unclean. Oh, we had our ancestors' graves! They were ground underfoot to build roads, houses, schools, hospitals. We wanted none of this, and anyway they didn't do it for us.

—Alas! In pain we are stone, mute. We failed to give peace to the ancestors. We are coming to an end, rubbed off the soil. And so the unquiet soul casts its shadow and hovers. We didn't know how it would look. This is surely the ancestors' spirit! This is surely the curse of the ravaged land, village, field, home, forest! Now no one can save us. Now we are all unclean, in mourning. Oh Sir! BDO Sir!

—Here, I am here.

—I can't see you. But I say to you in great humility, you can't do anything for us. We became unclean as soon as you entered our lives. No more roads, no more relief—what will you give to a people in exchange for the vanished land, home, field, burial-ground?

Shankar comes up close and says, "Can you move far away? Very far? Very, very far?"

Shankar sways, he faints.

Some carry him under a tree.

—What happened?

—He fainted?

—Now what?

—They will splash water on his face, and he will come out of it.

Harisharan says, "Let's sit down."

They sit on a string cot. Harisharan says, "I have heard these words three times from three people. In three places, Pirtha, Gabahi, Dholki. I heard the same thing from the three. Some mysterious thing is taking place. Each time the man talks and talks, as if in a trance. When he talks, no one touches him, no one speaks. Then the speaker faints."

—What will you do now?

—Listen, man, I can't turn the clock back by five hundred years. Even if some magician can restore them to that archaic freedom, they will again lose it in the hands of newcomers. For they know or knew communism, harmony, co-existence. Is it possible to fight aggression, plunder, exploitation, using of the tribals-with their uncontaminated value-system? This is reality, this is history.

3

EUROPE

Introduction

IRINA SADOVINA

Modern environmental consciousness in Europe emerges from a history of irreversible technological changes resulting from the industrial revolution and correspondingly radical social transformations. These changes have altered nature in both insidious and spectacular ways. In response to these developments, European writers explore modes that have generally been taken up by writers around the world: nostalgic, tech-optimistic, dystopian. What gives European eco-consciousness a specific flavor is its political history. Even as modernization united the continent in a common, if not entirely simultaneous, experience, emergent environmental imaginaries played into Europe's internal divisions.

Visions of the environment and its degradation were enlisted in the building of national identities and images of the Other. In the nineteenth century, colonial projections led Europeans to portray places like Siberia or India as untamed nature, at its best and worst. This lens also operated within the continent, as urban intellectuals went in search of the spirit of the folk, hoping to fuel the construction of the image of a mysterious rural Motherland. These modes—colonizing fascination and national self-discovery—extended into the twentieth century, when nostalgic visions of nature justified nationalist violence, and different modes of conquest, whether industrial or agricultural, ushered in environmental crises. Even as countries on both sides of the Cold War justified damaging experiments and policies, they eagerly projected ecological villainy onto their rivals (McNeill and Unger, 12). As the impact of these political rivalries became more obvious in catastrophic events like Chernobyl, antinuclear and environmental activism grew across Europe (McNeill and Unger, 11). But unlike ideals of "unspoiled nature," environmental degradation exceeds national interests. Environmental futures, both distant and immediate, are sweeping. They are futures on the move.

The texts selected for this section explore how these emergent and pervasive futures unfold in every singular here and now. These specific locations are far greater in number than the states that pursue their political interests. Like any continent, Europe is a space that holds a multitude of languages, positions, and trajectories of speech. This anthology cannot include them all, but it can hint at their multitude.

Maarja Pärtna's poem "solastalgia," which opens this section, begins with a location: "I stand in the middle of a lean harvest / alien like an outdated map in a place / that's changed." These lines describe the condition that gives that poem its name. Coined by Glenn Albrecht, the term *solastalgia* defines a sense of no longer feeling at home in one's home environment as it is being transformed by climate change. Solastalgia is what spatial and temporal disruption feels like; it is "the 'lived experience' of the loss of the present as manifest in a feeling of dislocation" (Albrecht, 48). The term has gained popularity because it provides a reference point for what is often hard to describe. At a time when objective conditions are urgent and overwhelming, the term is valuable in another way: as a gesture of paying attention to feeling. "solastalgia" is a fitting beginning for a series of texts that verbalize the experience of finding oneself in the middle of something that is irreversibly changing.

Each of the seven texts included in this section begins in a place. These are not the places of national origin, though the languages of their authors locate them all over Europe, from Sámiland to Turkey, from Spain to Russia. Rather, in these texts, places are a category of change. Places/changes are there to be mapped, imagined through metaphor, or processed through thick description. In Pärtna's poems, the location is often familiar and unrecognizable. The speaker knows the place so well that she herself becomes its map, even as that knowledge is already expired and the map is already wrong. Evgenia Nekrasova's "The Moscow Museum of Trash" also has a cartographic sensibility, but in place of Pärtna's uncertain maps it provides an all too reliable account of the movement of garbage that connects Moscow with other locations in Russia. Upon closer inspection, this map of cities turns out to be a map of human experiences as they transform into garbage. Plastic containers, beer bottles and used menstrual pads contaminate the countryside with grief, boredom, pain. The impersonal movement of garbage is thus radically personified.

Other texts also explore the tension between impersonal and personal spaces: in Aroa Moreno Durán's "Gravity," the beach is a danger zone between the shriveling domestic life and the expanding sea; in Doğu Yücel's "Under the Seas," the beach is a liminal space where an encounter with non-human agency is possible. Julien Gracq's *Lettrines II* records a traveler's subjective impressions of a French rural landscape transformed by development. In Gracq's short texts, written in the 1970s, the future appears as a fait accompli. Past interventions into the landscape result in the inevitable and already observable consequences; even the distant mountains appear as *not yet* touched by human activity: "a marginal and fragile caprice of a nature still, for the time being, free from the bulldozer."

In these excerpts from *Lettrines II*, as in most texts in this selection, the future appears irreversible. It is not an invigorating alterity, but rather the gradual unfolding of the present. The two selections that tend most toward the mode of apocalyptic warning—Anna Carlier's play *HIDE* and Durán's short story "Gravity"—still foreground the immediacy and the irreversibility of what is unfolding. Set against the backdrop of deadly heat and the rising sea level, "Gravity" is propelled by the speaker's reckoning with a disintegrating personal relationship. This is apocalypse domesticated, and its timing is uncertain: Is it the near future? Is it something that happened this summer? Carlier's play is grounded in the present. At its center is the bed, in which the pregnant narrator is lying, anxious and unable to sleep, and from which several imagined futures spring into immediate sensory being. They are diverging variants of the future of the narrator's grown-up daughter, all of which amount to survival and death during the climate disaster that has already begun.

It is within this inevitability that the texts position their subjects who try to observe, speak, and act. There is something nightmarish about these visions, not because they are dark or frightening (though some are), but because, like in some nightmares, the possibility and nature of agency is unclear: something is happening—is it being done? by whom? and who, if anyone, can do something about it?

The contrast between the subject of knowledge and the subject of action is set up in Pärtna's "weathervane" through a series of statements, in which the poem's speaking subject progresses from being an agent within the landscape ("I ascend through the smoke"), a recipient of someone else's action ("you tie a silk cord around my beak / and hang me from the ceiling"), and a channel that can only embody what is happening but does not explain it: "I spin on my axis carelessly like a top— / I don't plan to tell you / anything at all." If making sense of things is impossible, so is impacting them. Making and speaking sense marks the absence of agency. In Yücel's more optimistic vision, where sea creatures entrust a journalist with the task of making their anger known to humanity, agency may still be possible through translation. One may not be able to explain or even describe the catastrophe, but one can channel another's wrath—and maybe that's not nothing.

The mode of reckoning is also central to Niillas Holmberg's *Underfoot*, which develops an extended metaphor of walking in the world barefoot—or with booted feet. The figure of the shoemaker has hijacked authority and proposes a devil's bargain: "You see he studied the paths of life / and per his studies, the heel doesn't know / and hasn't known for centuries / its own good." Just as Yücel's protagonist must use his skills of translation to impact the world, the speaker in Holmberg's poem unpacks the shoemaker's discourse with probing questions ("Why offer a wooden leg to a woodpecker?") and statements ("The shoe rubs, the foot festers"). But while Yücel's vision allows for the possibility of just punishment or at least of communication from another, Holmberg's shoemaker is not a decision maker to be convinced but a force to recognize and resist through action.

These texts place the reader in the middle of ongoing, often catastrophic, entanglements between humans and garbage, humans and non-humans, humans and places. Unfolding in all directions from the inexpressible condition of something being very wrong at home, the authors trace shifts in temperature, movements of things and people, and inner transformations to get, at least obliquely and partially, at what it is like to be around in the time of climate change.

WORKS CITED

Albrecht, Glenn. 2005. "'Solastalgia': A New Concept in Health and Identity." *PAN: Philosophy, Activism, Nature* (3): 44–59.

McNeill, J. R., and Corinna R. Unger. 2010. "Introduction: The Big Picture." In *Environmental Histories of the Cold War*, edited by J. R. McNeill and Corinna R. Unger, 1–20. New York: Cambridge University Press.

Four Poems

MAARJA PÄRTNA

Translated by Jayde Will and Maarja Pärtna

Maarja Pärtna (b. 1986) is an Estonian poet and translator. She is the author of four books of poetry, the most recent of which, *Vivaarium* (2019), was translated into English by Jayde Will and published by The Emma Press in 2020. Three poems from this collection ("solastalgia," "weathervane," and "vivarium") are included in this selection. The poem "winter" was translated by the author and is published here for the first time.

solastalgia

under the roof of august
hangs a tapestry of rye fields—it's there
I stand in the middle of a lean harvest

alien like an outdated map in a place
that's changed. in this new landscape
north's as near as west

black car tires trundle along unconcerned
spinning round and round

a moment before crashing—
objects in the rearview mirror
are closer than they appear.

next summer it's not a flood
but a drought. the news says in brief
this could be the change. I'm reading a book

where it says it's time to take action—
the future does not wait.

on one side of the world someone says
with a look of importance *change*
opens up new possibilities.

on the other side someone cries out—
a voice that's never been heard before.

weathervane

becoming ever lighter
I ascend through the smoke
hole, exhale and turn on my back

my wings spread through the atmosphere
like azure fans. down on the ground

a heavenly still summer day—
in a farmer's open palm a small cross-shaped corpse
above a sandstone breast two panes of black eyes

behind the panes
the starry landscapes of deep fields.

inside you tie a silk cord around my beak
and hang me from the ceiling so I display
the changes in the weather

but I spin on my axis carelessly like a top—
I don't plan to tell you
anything at all

despite my bird's eye view
of swirling dervish hurricanes and wildfires
wiping old growth forests from land
now dry and burnt. signs

like falling stars
break up into pieces on the threshold

one after the other—
titles, news, articles
books, shows, conferences.

this debate is older than me
but it's up to me to resolve it.

vivarium

in this landscape I have neither reflection nor shadow. I don't know
where I come from—this house of glass is not my home
more an artificial place or threshold.

an endless sameness in all directions, mute groves of ferns
white branches like torn-off arms—words
no language connects.

in a vivarium a root of thought
feels the shape of the future, discovers
its own strange side. behind a transparent wall

a primate forges a world within an unforged world
to bring life to a distant lifeless place

but I don't want to leave, I don't need
a new home in cold, dark space.

winter

winter is an extreme event that occurs periodically. —kaia lehari

here's a town in a snow globe, except this year there's no snow. i shake it, but no blizzard rises up above the rooftops, swirling round the houses in spirals of pixie dust. it's just a glass orb full of cold water now, cheerless as a child whose world has lost all magic, who has watched it melt like a snowflake in her warm little palm. i'm making my way back home in the drizzling dark, street lights glaring in the puddles, yellow like the eyes of snowy owls. tomorrow it's the winter solstice. the ski races are all canceled; the sledding hills across town are empty and quiet as if they've been flattened out by the warmth. the carols that loop in the shopping centers—the wistful ones, the ones about a white christmas—suddenly feel jarring, out of time like the fossils of extinct mammals someone might find buried here millions of years after we're gone.

Selections from

Underfoot

NIILLAS HOLMBERG

Translated by Jennifer Kwon Dobbs and Johanna Domokos

Niillas Holmberg (b. 1990) is a Sámi poet, multimedia artist, activist, and translator. He has published three collections of poetry in Northern Sami, his native language. This section includes selections from his newest book, *Juolgevuođđu* (2018), published in English as *Underfoot* (White Pine Press, 2022) in a translation by Jennifer Kwon Dobbs and Johanna Domokos.

The sky thickens
trees bear the flurry, the three-winged haste.
Birches like the parents of young children
hide traces, incubate a misleading question
back into its shell.

Time to return to the feet!
But where are the terns?

You who taught me the directions
where are you, Terns?

A wooden leg
one can tell by the tracks.

But memory, the body's memory
of reaching steps, of a linguistic
nervous system and rivers rich in fish.

Why offer a wooden leg to a woodpecker?

Is it too late to raise a child
or merely too late to ask?

This must be one of those gravities
the young must know the grown to grow
or when to scratch their heads.

Looking through the shoemaker's window
is to mourn stones that can't fly.

Barren birches
fallen rights conceal the land

a rake's tooth cracks under a boot.

But yet they rise, children
with ears like leaves, children
with grammar hidden in their bodies.

A tactic of bluebells
proves every word is an adjective.

Look at the meadow, the strategy.

Sense the touching, trace where the body meets earth, see
the foot, ask it to speak, the heel becomes a matriarch

summoning the commission of melt and flood, and as the tern
rips the sole off the boot, a drum is born
and Oneness Verbs.

If the shoemaker protests (stones don't fly!)
challenge him to prove it barefoot
and even if he fixes the boot, it is known
you took responsibility.

Prepare to be called to negotiate, prepare to refuse
prepare, don't wait for spring

spring awaits.

If you seek a verb
the shoemaker is your foe.

But can we judge the followers
who were forced to feel ashamed
of their toes, were forced to produce
booted feet and for blisters
blame the rugged land?

Can you call a wolf your kin?

The shoe rubs, the foot festers
and oh the power we possess
to receive news about the latest boots.

Is industry trampling on bluebells?
According to the shoemaker, enclosing the toes
protects both the feet and the meadows.

You see he studied the paths of life
and per his studies, the heel doesn't know
and hasn't known for centuries
its own good.

He sews the shoe with veins
nails, hair.

Yet it keeps rubbing, the foot still festers
and in the shadow of the three-winged haste
the negotiator is overtaken by night.

Before consenting to trade a wet boot
for a dry one, it is known
a shoe can only be removed
by ripping within.

And he fastened his eyes onto ours.

To unlock the machine, to search the needles for facts.
Which threads, stitches, seams, where, when, on what grounds?

Many set off hunting wolves
many returned howling.

Can you call a wolf your kin?

When the herd's dog
wanders off to the village or forest
the trick is to smile
when it comes back.

He sews veins
nails, hair.

Which verb
contains my fire? I rip as I create
wondering will they follow me
if I pierce the shoe.

A romantic paradox, my identity.

No toes, no grounds
a dog, nor a verb.

The shoemaker's children don't go barefoot—
but not even proverbs fill their shoes.

I've never been caught unaware in the dark.
As a boy I smelled the birches' branched lightning
and while we played hide-and-seek, some of us were seen
with memories of light.

A matriarch
gently sways in a rocking chair
creaking like an oarlock.

She knows what she's doing—with each stroke
the boat floats closer, closer . . .

I ask for a story, but she's weary
and retires like the night mist
rising off the river.

I tend to the fire and sit in the chair
the boat warms me, god
is a verb.

Selection from

"The Moscow Museum of Trash"

EVGENIA NEKRASOVA

Translated by Jane Costlow and José Vergara

Evgenia Nekrasova (b. 1985) is a writer of poetry, fiction, and screenplays. Her novel *Kalechina Malechina* was published in 2018 to wide acclaim. Her long poem "The Moscow Museum of Trash" (2019) appeared in the journal *Neznanie* (issue 1, 2019 and issue 2, 2020). The excerpt in this chapter was translated specifically for this volume.

CHAPTER ONE. The Time of Trash.

Marina Iurevna is wailing from the tower
I hear her
They've hanged her son, the three-year-old baby brigand
Crows fly above Volovichi
Marina Iurevna sees the trash heading out from Moscow,
I see it while it's still in Moscow
I produce it, still in Moscow
And then I head to Kolomna.

Twice they married off Marina Iurevna:
to False Dmitrii number one
in Krakow, in his absence
marriage *per procura*,
Then they married her to False Dmitrii number two
in his presence
The Brigand of Tushino, a wart on his ugly mug, he disgusted her

His smell made her nauseous,
The way you feel nauseous near the dumpster by your house,
And she had to sleep with him
And give birth to a baby brigand
And then go to Kolomna.

They've married off Kolomna to Moscow
Even in the absence of the latter,
There you have it: same-sex marriage and nobody gives a damn,
marriage *per procura*,
marriage by trash,
waste products, leftovers of someone else's life.
Thus they married off Moscow to Tarusa,
Chekhov, Klin, Tuchkovo, Naro-Fominsk,
Syktyvkar, Arkhangelsk
and other cities, sickened
by the smell of Moscow's garbage,
where children are borne
to the smell of Moscow's garbage.

Thus Moscow was married off to Tarusa,
Chekhov, Klin, Tuchkovo, Naro-Fominsk,
Syktyvkar, Arkhangelsk
and other cities,
to whom the time of trash has come.

CHAPTER TWO. The Fork

Marina Iurevna brought the first fork to the country,
Silver, two-tined, impertinent,
Ready to penetrate the Russian land.
The first False Dmitrii used one,
The boyars and the churchmen objected,
Up till then Rus' had only eaten with a spoon,
oval like the Kremlin's earth.
So the fork became a symbol of the troubles,
Of everything false, brought in from outside.

Today's Marina, Angelina, Sonya,
Or Zhenya, like me, order up something tasty
To eat in Moscow, something foreign,
Vietnamese or Italian
Brought to our tower—office or apartment.

A tired young man without Russian citizenship
Brings Marina, Lena, Sonya, or, like me, Zhenya,
a big white cellophane bag, still warm.
Marina, Lena, Sonya, or Zhenya, like me,
Pull out little boxes, plastic, or paper,
With noodles, or a burger, or nem, or sushi,
or spaghetti, or pizza, or Hainan-style chicken.
Plus napkins, sometimes wooden chopsticks,
Often spoons and—definitely—plastic forks,
plasticized, three-tined, sharp,
already scraping, here in Moscow, the gums
of Marina, Lena, Sonya, or me,
ready to penetrate the Land of Kolomna
ready to build a new saw-toothed
plastic Kremlin,
a new, white tower: Marina's, Lena's
Sonya's, Zhenya's Tower.

CHAPTER THREE. A Fairy Tale of Artisan-Processors of Waste Product Experiences

1. PEROVO—KOLOMNA

His heart broke in Perovo.
They held the wake at home.
Two kids, a wife,
She didn't cook.
52 years old, individual entrepreneur,
On the outside the same as everyone else,
In life better than everyone else.
Didn't raise a fist,
Didn't raise a glass,
Fixed the broken faucet.
The kids, whom he never laid a hand on,
Sat quietly on the benches,
Bruised by his death.
In his wife a *kutia*[1] of pills,
Before the eyes of the guests—9 wet napkins.
21 people: friends, relatives,
a few colleagues,
classmates,
and no plastic.
His mother is holding down the fort as the cook,
She's keeping things together well,
She's holding down the fort as the organizer.
She cooked all the dishes,
Borrowed porcelain dishes from the neighbors.
At the table, little is said, and little is eaten,
Hands, feet, heads, wine glasses, mouths
Air, room, wallpaper
Smeared with grief,
Soaked with grief,
In total, there remained from the wake:

700 grams of potato peelings
3 vodka bottles and 3 of their caps
8 wine bottles, 5 caps and 3 corks
150 grams of onion peelings
300 grams of walnut shells
400 grams of chicken bones and skin
10 plastic one-and-a-half-liter water bottles
5 two-liter tetra packs of juice
111 used napkins
17 polyethylene bags and plastic trays of chicken, potato, onion,
beef, dried apricot, cheeses, nuts
7 paper instant rice boxes
4 olive tins
2 glass cucumber jars and 2 tin lids
3 of marinated mushrooms and 2 tin lids

And half of the uneaten dishes.
More than half of the uneaten dishes.

All this reeked of grief,
Was saturated with grief,
And went to Kolomna,
To lie in a landfill and radiate.

Her heart broke in Perovo,
And the scrap metal of grief, the wastepaper of loss
Was sent to Kolomna,
To lie in a landfill and radiate.

A boy on Shchurovsky Beach
Builds his own sandy Kremlin,
And gulps down someone else's grief,
Not from the Oka, but from the air.

Strange goings-on.
He walks around sick for a month,
Languishes, snaps at everyone,
Spits obscenities.
Sticking to tradition, the mother is blamed,
Nothing strange there:
She neglected the boy.
As in the womb, he bumps about,
Languishes, snaps.
Pushes away his mother and grandmother with their interrogations,
How can you give an answer
To something that doesn't have one?

A dumpster of someone else's grief,
The third son of someone else's dead father.
(The boy never knew his own.)

After 34 days the Perovsky waste effect wears off.
It's been reworked into:
3 strikes of a racket on another child,
21 obscenities,
7 crude phrases,
and two attempts to cry.

Kolomna waste-emotions
Don't work on the locals,
They're immune from birth
To their own experiences, to the trash in their own soil and air.

The boy gets better,
He's living like before,
But he refuses to go to the beach.

2. SVIBLOVO—KOLOMNA

It's simply that Serezha got bored in Sviblovo,
Unbearably bored in Sviblovo.
He went downtown,
Thought about running off to war,
But he's still unbearably bored.

He called and said to me,
Zhenya, let's go for a walk,
Or take a spin around the MCC,[2]
I'm unbearably bored,
Deadly bored,
Or come up with something for me,
You're a writer, after all,
Why do you live in my city?
I answer, Serezha, what boredom,
Don't you have a wife and child?
He shouts: you've moved in on us, you Moscow scribbler,
But you can't help a person with a Moscow residence permit.

I'm hanging up, we've worked on projects before,
In Moscow doing joint projects signifies friendship.
I don't have kids, but I have my work,
And it's never boring,
But he's still bored.

Serezha plays *Warcraft* in Sviblovo and watches video clips,
Kisses the necks of beer bottles,
First, second, third, fourth.
His wife kisses his daughter goodnight,
And does yoga on Zoom.
They live in the same room.
Serezha breathes boredom into beer bottles
Instead of pale ale.
First, second, third, fourth.
But he's still bored.

The bottles are sent to Kolomna,
To lie and radiate in a landfill,
To breathe boredom into the local light air.
It flies and pollinates the apple tree,
And in Vlada Andreevna's garden boring apples grow,
Large, green, with a red blush.

Vlada Andreevna is a tough Komsomol boyarina,
She lives in the Kremlin, in a little wooden house,
Not far from Novo-Golutvinskii Monastery,
And secretly believes that her apples are better than the nuns.'

Kolomna is a little bit like a fairy tale from a Soviet cartoon
With kings who have been defeated forever:
The only city in Russia,
Where ordinary people
Settled inside the Kremlin walls.

For women in a country with kremlins
It was rarely boring—
Wars, repressions, revolutions, cold and hunger,
In parallel: children, husbands,
Washing, cleaning, cooking, and plowing,
What's in the Kremlin, what's near, what's far from it.
But Vlada Andreevna,
Komsomol boyarina,
Doer of seven deeds, she particularly did not know boredom,
Even working the press at the Kolomna Factory,
Even in a deficit queue.
After sampling a mealy apple,
From the now boring tree,
Vlada Andreevna for the first time felt boredom.
She chewed it, worked it with her artificial jaw,
Couldn't figure it out, decided that the variety was no good.

She set off for DIXY,[3]
Felt that old why-am-I-here-I-can't-make-up-my-mind,
She worked for a bit in the garden,
Felt that old this-is-too-much-it's not-worth-working
She watched TV,
Felt that old why-am-I-watching-this-junk-it's-time-to-stop.
She called her daughter,
Felt that old why-am-I-talking-to-her-I-should-stop.

So Vlada Andreevna grew bored in Kolomna.
So Vlada Andreevna grew bored in life.
And she, not realizing that this was boredom right in front of her, decided that death had come for her.
She got sick and informed her relatives.
Relatives quickly gathered around the Komsomol boyarina in the Kremlin:
Son, daughter, grandson from Kolomna, granddaughter from Moscow.
They arranged for a medical consultation
That proclaimed the boyarina healthy.
But a neighbor brought a young healer,
Who said that Vlada Andreevna had been cursed
By a thirty-year-old Moscow video engineer,
And advised cutting down the apple tree, pointing to the tree beneath the kitchen windows.

The relatives didn't know what to do in the Kremlin with apple trees,
And Vlada Andreevna grew more and more bored.
It was a powerful waste product for
People who have never experienced boredom.
Like the fallen Sviblovskaya Tower,
The boyarina, large and round,
Lay in a red Soviet calico dress
that hugged her heels
And prepared for death.

The granddaughter brought a Trojan horse
To the Kremlin: a psychotherapist passed off as a gastroenterologist.
He spoke with Vlada Andreevna
And prescribed her treatment, taking her boredom for progressive depression.
The boyarina secretly spit out her pills,
She immediately took a dislike to the doctor,
He's too friendly, so he must be inexperienced.

After two weeks the waste from Sviblovo dried up,
It was recycled:
Into the anticipation of death,
A neglected garden
And four quarrels with relatives.

Kolomna waste-emotions
Don't work on the locals,
They're immune from birth
To their own experiences, to the trash in their own soil and air.

The boyarina's condition improved.
She began living like before: in the Kremlin,
At work in the garden and around the house.
She watched TV, went to DIXY,
Sberbank, and the market, called her descendants.
And, having thought about it, cut down the apple tree
Under the kitchen windows.

3. DMITRY DONSKOI BOULEVARD—KOLOMNA

Lena is a person from a multi-story life
on Dmitry Donskoi Boulevard,
From her parents' fling,
To the queen of her own body,
And as she commands, so it will be.

Lena, the tsaritsa of her own body,
Had been bleeding and suffering for five days.
Her ordinary, priceless way of life
Was reproduced in everything else.

There remained from these days:
7 large used pads,
5 medium used pads.

They went to Kolomna,
They lay in the dump and fed the earth with pain.
From Lena's natal red
The pain become colorless, anonymous,
Made its way with the ground water into a bottle
Clutched by manly palms
As they milked the spring on Dairy Square.

The three sons of the king sat, talking trash,
Under the window of my studio in Kolomna, ate something,
   drank something,
Listened to the song with the words, "Mama, she's in love with
   a hooligan,"
A bit about the story of what happened to Lena.
One talked about how he saw some guys holding hands,
Right here, on the square, and he couldn't believe it,
He was saying, "They've already made it here, to Kolomna!
And they don't even hide, the scum!"

It was hot and sticky, they decided to wash it down with spring water,
All three took a sip from one bottle and froze in silence,
Even the singer from the tape player fell silent,
As if the princes had given him a drink, too.

For twenty seconds a new-terrible-unknown pain
Pierced the princes, their bodies, minds, and souls,
Before it occurred, they had always been the tsars of everything
That was happening to them and even to others.

It was a woman's pain, the pain of choice,
The pain of an eternal readiness for loss.

Kolomna waste-emotions
Don't work on the locals,
They're immune from birth
To their own experiences, to the trash in their own soil and air.

When the Muscovite pain passed,
The princes of Kolomna sat for a bit longer and set off for home.
Thus their experience on Dmitry Donskoi Boulevard
Was processed into:
A twenty-second insight for three young men
And two of my peaceful working hours
in an art residency.
Thus Moscow survived death and moved on.
Thus Moscow survived joy and moved on.
Thus Moscow survived boredom and moved on.
Thus Moscow survived pain and moved on.
Sent out experience-waste products
And kept on going.

NOTES

1. A ceremonial grain-based dish with sweet gravy traditionally served in Eastern Orthodoxy during the Christmas–Feast of Jordan holiday season or at a funeral feast.

2. The Central Circle line of the Moscow Metro.

3. One of Russia's largest food retail companies.

Selection from

Hide

ANNA CARLIER

Translated by David McKay

Anna Carlier is a Flemish playwright, actor, and director. She is a permanent member of the theater ensemble Compagnie De Kolifokkers. She received a master's degree in drama from the Royal Academy of Fine Arts (KASK) in Ghent in 2017. Her play *Kruin* (*Crown*) won the Dutch-German Kaas and Kappes prize for children's theater and the writing competition organized by children's theater ensemble hetpaleis. In 2018, *Kruin* was translated into German by Christine Bais for Verlag der Autoren and longlisted for the Deutscher Kindertheaterpreis (German children's theater prize). In 2020, Carlier's play *Hertenleer* (*Hide*) was published by De Nieuwe Toneelbibliotheek with illustrations by Sofie De Cleene. It was nominated for the Toneelschrijfprijs, the annual prize for the best Dutch-language play. An excerpt from this English translation by David McKay was published in *Asymptote*.

/H/ /I/ /D/ /E/

She sees it in one great glimpse of flashing gold: trees and humans, at war over the land and water and atmosphere. And she can hear, louder than the quaking leaves, which side will lose by winning.

For you. You'll soon. —Eimear McBride, *A Girl Is a Half-formed Thing*

you, soon
me, now

// me

i don't know which way to turn
on my right side
i breathe in the air
drifting out of your father's dry mouth
on my left side
the clock stares me down
but i can't lie on my belly
without crushing you
and whenever i lie on my back
i have time to think
about the trees burning
about the waters rising
about the air
choked up with dust and dirt
about the machines we come up with
to clean the air
as we go on cutting down trees
about the latest disease
and all the new people
who just keep coming
and coming
about you
about how one day
about how it might go if
and whether you'll stay in our house
and whether you'll be on the
and whether you'll have anyone you
and whether you'll leave for parts unknown
and about the road beneath your feet
the food in your mouth
the illness that afflicts you
and about the people
the water

the future
so fast
approaching

// woods

you pick a deer
you grab your knife
it's night so it's time
it's harder and harder to find them
you've heard the stories
about people creeping inside other people
at first just the people they find
the fresh ones
then the people they pick out
the big ones
the ones they can fit a whole family inside
you're alone
not so picky
not so demanding
you're faster
no one on your back
or in your belly
so here you are
still chasing after deer

you're one of the first
they're in our house
they tell you to leave
fifteen minutes
you don't know much
you're not prepared
and it's raining
it's always raining hard

you ask
where can i go?
out the front door
but this is my house
this is my mother's house
they say it doesn't matter
you have to leave
you take your knife
you go
and everything's gone
the dark blue walls
the nicks in the floor
the metal legs of the table
the light through the attic window
the scribbles in your books

you walk the roads
and see other people coming out
with fifteen minutes of stuff
a teddy bear
a suitcase
a scarf
oh shit you think
warm clothes
i have to go back
you turn the corner
you can't go further
border guards
you're dangerous
you want something back
that's not yours anymore
you're nothing now but your own flesh
and a memory of my smile
and it's raining
it is always raining hard
a gust of wind blows you off your feet

the waters are rising
you think about jumping
going wherever the river goes
but then again you know
where that will take you
and you'd rather walk
you look for a hiding place
hear groaning in the distance

you've been walking for months now
you don't know if things will ever
you can only hope
maybe you're not thinking anything
but feeling everything
the seeping cold
the keening wind

// me

thoughts batter their way in
one after another
i see you
later
in a house
in the woods
on a ship
with a child
the world's wetness
is out of balance
half the world is drying up
the other half is drowning
the people on the dry side
are crumbling into sand
the soggy people are fighting

for bits of still-dry land
side by side with the animals
that they try to eat
and use for warmth
sometimes it's ice cold
sometimes burning hot
you don't know when
you don't know why
you have to adapt at the very last minute
again and again
at the very last minute
and hope you're still in time
because if not you'll freeze
or melt
you'll stop existing

you're not a child anymore
not quite
though you've never been anything but young
you used to see
old people around
but the times are too hard for them now
they adapt too late
and go up in smoke
or turn to stone
they won't stand up
refuse to leave
and are demolished with everything else
they know it isn't right
they're used to a better life
they saw this coming
    and never would stand up

// house

there's still television
you're watching it now
always the same
there's sometimes news
but less and less
because none of what they're reporting
is really new
not the heat waves
not the storms
not the flash freezes
you think of the people outside
without television
of their ignorance
you hope they know a few tricks
for protecting themselves
like when swallows fly low
there's a storm coming
and when stags blow steam
it's time to skin one
to stay warm
you just hope
they know
as you sit in someone's chair
watching the news
on someone's television

you wonder how you wound up here
what gave you the right
what gave you this house
whether maybe you should share it
you wonder how to start

the nations tell you to be strong
if you give in there will be chaos

you must take what comes your way
it belongs to you
your eyes must hide any sign of empathy
if they see it
they'll latch onto it
and tug your eyes out of their sockets
and tug you out the front door by your hair
they want it back
what once was theirs
but you have to show them
with your eyes
with the hate in your eyes
that they have no more rights
to that house
it's your house
you paid for it
worked hard for it
it's yours
not theirs
show no pity
send them back
into the woods
if you give in
there will be chaos
power will fall
into their hands
into the hands of the poor
cut them off
as soon as they set one foot inside
one finger
this house will be theirs
don't let them go one step too far
or come too close
more walls
the nations insist
the higher the better

you must not shrink
you are the richest
you are the strongest
if you want to survive
that's how it has to stay

// woods

a mass is bobbing up and down
a heap of clumping filth
you can't see the pieces
that make up the mass
all you see is the horrible whole
and the ducks
and the otters
streaming toward it
and getting stuck
no longer ducks
or otters
but part of the mass
arms try to control it
to scale and climb it
they fall prey to it
get stuck
become mass
you don't want to look
just in case your eyes
get stuck in the horror
so you don't jump
in the water

you walk the roads
you search for the woods
you sigh
a soft sigh
of relief
when you hear the grass under your feet
hear it crunch
and see in the distance the antlers
your first deer fleeing
a stag
you don't stop to think
you rush toward it
with your knife
you're quick
not quick enough
the deer escapes
you climb a tree
and wait for it
when it's just below you
you jump
out of the branches
into the deer

you whisper to the stag
that you miss us
that your father's name was Bunny
that you're grateful
and you sleep
for the first time in nights

// me

is the clock counting up
or counting down

i whisper to your father
he grunts and rolls over

i imagine i'm a tree
blowing gently in the wind

// ship

you made the cut
you're on the crew
you're fertile
receptive
genetically sound
they tested
so you can be sure
there's water
there will be water
they say
clean water
and a protective layer
between the good air
and the deadly gases
you won't feel the sun
or burn your skin there
they told you
all the energy will come
from inexhaustible sources
they gave you a bird

your companion on the flight
your guardian angel
so perhaps if things go wrong
you can borrow its wings
you think about those emotional support animals
you're glad not to have a dog
there are colossal trees there
they tell you
that's where you will live
you can build your home
on one of the branches
try to use the flight
to get to know someone
so you can build a house together
so you hope
that one of the other hundred flighters
can make your dreams come true
and if not
you tell yourself
you'll just have to do the work
to make it work
you tell yourself
that's how you are
that's how you were brought up
you wonder if one hundred's enough
for genetic diversity
for health
in the new place
so we won't all
have to raise
amorphous children
on those giant branches
soon you'll be able to go outdoors
go for walks
with the other flighters

you can look
and know they're looking back at you
wondering if it'll be you
on the branch with them
now all you can see are their faces
on a little screen
right in front of your nose
fifty fertile males
free of genetic defects
twenty-five years old
fifty fertile females
free of genetic defects
twenty-five years old
each holding a different degree
men who fall for men
women who fall for women
women who fall for men
and men who fall for women
and every one of them willing
everyone on board
willing to share cells
willing to accept cells
you know you can't tell a thing
from that photo
on your little screen
that face might be attached to a body
that gives you the shivers
or that head
might contain strange roots
that fill its mouth with absurd pronouncements
or the face you choose
might turn away from you
or curl her lips into a grimace
you know all that
but still
you can just picture it

she's the one you want there with you
on your branch

// child

dew slides from your nose
down to your lips
your daughter licks you awake
and says
i'm thirsty
you open your eyes
it's getting warm
soon enough it will be scorching
the birds are flying low
you stand up
you lift her onto your back
in search of coolness
oxygen
you look around
nothing but charred earth
here and there a blackened tree
you take a step to what you think is north
your daughter asks
are we almost there yet
you still have no idea
where you could go
the question is not
am i happy here
but
can my daughter survive here
that question
non stop
how can she stay alive
you think of past generations

dead generations
as you step
across the dry earth
shriveled lichens
heading north
you think
you think you're heading north

Gravity

AROA MORENO DURÁN

Translated by Kate Whittemore

Aroa Moreno Durán (1981) is the author of *La hija del comunista* (2017), a novel that won her the Ojo Crítico Fiction Prize. She has published the poetry books *Veinte años sin lápices nuevos* (2009) and *Jet lag* (2016). She has also written a biography of Frida Kahlo, *Viva la vida* (2012), and *La valiente alegría* (2011), a life of Federico García Lorca. Her short story "Gravity" (2018), initially published in *Estío*, an anthology of climate fiction, takes place in a future made barely livable by the changing climate.

I can tell by your face that you've seen the dead bird at the edge of the beach, the feathers glued down like a plastic skin. I was witness to how the sea left it there this morning. I don't like birds. When I was a girl, I held a dead sparrow in my hands. Have you ever held a lifeless bird? They don't weigh a thing. I realize now that only life gives a bird any weight at all, that pulse beneath the plumage. You feel the weight of a living bird when they struggle to fly away and you struggle to trap them in your hands. That bird, the one I found in my parents' fireplace, was as light as a dry sponge. That's what I thought it was, a dry sponge in the fireplace, when I stuck my arm in to clean out remnants of wood and ash and pulled it out. I'd like to know how to really explain this to you: I don't like birds because they could die if you tighten your hand around them. Something like vertigo: I don't like heights because I know I could throw myself off, into the void. But I don't tell you any of this, because you're not here to listen to me ramble about birds or what it means to unexpectedly hold a lifeless one in your hand when you are a child. You're dragging your feet, I never should have allowed myself to be touched by a man who drags his feet like that, and you come into the kitchen and open and close the cabinets as if this wasn't your house, what are you looking for, water? I don't know when we stopped speaking to each other. Or why I woke up so early and feel this way. Half my life trying to put a name to this feeling. An anguish. A hollow inside me—next to my heart, or rather, between my ribs—that grows and grows and then vanishes. But you have to stop thinking about it. If you think, it grows. If you stop thinking, it disappears. Unhealthy episodes of an unnamed thing. I felt it many times before all this, but now we're supposedly on alert, evacuated from our routine, watching the fish gasp on the beach before they die and dry out and disintegrate like ash among the seaweed. But the sea always collects its cadavers. The sea is always a little closer. Now everything is high tide, all the time. Like us. Always closer to drowning. But you, the opening and closing of cabinets and the slamming of doors and this house and that's what I'm feeling. You could take out your earbuds, stop listening to the news, look at me and ask me what will happen to us. What will happen to us, in the end. Or, as a minimum, you could pluck up the courage to ask about the water. I can't promise that I'd say anything, but I would probably make some gesture to signal that the water is in the basement. That's what we decided. We'll hide the water, I said. We'll hide the water, you told me. I used to like when you built yourself up with my ideas. Or I thought it was sweet. Not anymore. I turn my gaze back to the window. A dog—thin, alive, shadow of a dog—is scratching at the ground on the beach. I don't want it to find the bird. Do dogs eat birds? I don't know, but I stop watching. I can't bear to see that sort of thing. Maybe it's horrible to tell you this now, but I hate nature when it turns natural. I liked the flowers on our balcony, the fields outside the city, and this sky back then, when it would writhe before a storm, but I am not going to miss seeing two big animals copulate, or insect larvae, soft and secret, or a worm feeding on fruit. You need to know this: why I didn't clean the vegetables, why I didn't dig in the dirt, why I couldn't stand to see a dog's erection in spring. You come back with a glass of water. You're looking out at the beach again. Our narrow beach, now a black strip of death. Your back is beautiful. Remember when we danced at that party, I don't remember whose house, but I do remember when the music started and you, who never dances, pulled me from the couch. And you grabbed me and pressed hard against me and I touched the line that runs down from your neck, dividing your back in two. I can be thinking about this and about all the other stuff at the same time, and even I'm aroused by that night, which wasn't the first night, or the second, but it was at the beginning. I see that line now, furrow of scorched earth. All I have seen for months. You've turned around, suddenly, alarmed. As if you had heard me or as if you had seen the bird stretched between the shimmering fish and the dog sniffing at it and you had wanted to tell someone. But you've seen that it's only me, watching you, and morbidly you turn your eyes back to the window. You swallow the water and leave the glass. I don't know how much longer I can hold on to your back. And it can't be that you're going out there to look at death close up. But you are: you open the door and leave and I don't shut it and a haze enters, unbreathable. You throw a stick for the dog and slowly he moves away after it. You decide to inspect the fallen creature. You lift a wing, get very close to the dead thing. The sun strikes you, too; there, your line has a shadow. You look back toward me. You've sat down next to the bird. The dog returns and you throw the stick again. It's the same thing: I, too, walk in and out and come and go, bringing you that stick. You drive me away and draw me back. Have I become your pet? I approach you and the animals on the beach. We are all together, now. I haven't protected myself from this silence, either, or from this sun. I don't think how my hand has come to rest on your arm. Your arm burns. A gust of wind stirs the bird's feathers and I stop breathing so I won't sense the smell of rot. I couldn't bear it, not now. I only smell you. I breathe you in and you say that the animal is cold. So you've touched it, then. Death is cold, I tell you. And I touch it, too. I want to remember the cold. You lift one of your hands and stroke my head the dog the sand the stick. I know you value the life there under your hand. Your hand could take my breath away. We're burning. Now you know. They have thrown us into the abyss. We have fallen. Nothing has weight.

Under the Seas

DOĞU YÜCEL

Translated by Nicholas Glastonbury

Doğu Yücel is a writer of fiction and screenplays who was born in Istanbul, Turkey, in 1977. He won the Genclik Kitabevi Story Awards in 1997 and the Nostromo Science Fiction Story Awards jury prize in 1999. He is the author of several short story collections, including *Dreams, Nightmares and Future Tales* (2000) and *Sun Thieves* (2014), and novels. His first novel *Ghost Book* (2002) was adapted by the Taylan brothers into a film entitled *Okul* (School). Yücel also wrote the screenplay for *Okul* and the 2006 film *Little Apocalypse*. His other novels include: *Nonexistents* (2011), *Who the Hell Is Mitat Karaman?* (2017), and *God Forbid Mitat Karaman!* (2022). The short story included here comes from the 2019 collection *The Man Who Learned that He Died from Google and Other Weird Stories*.

The sea doesn't belong to tyrants. On its surface they can still exercise their iniquitous claims, battle each other, devour each other, haul every earthly horror. But thirty feet below sea level, their dominion ceases, their influence fades, their power vanishes!

Captain Nemo · Jules Verne's *20,000 Leagues Under the Sea*

I should warn you upfront, you might have a hard time believing what you're about to read. To be honest, even I sometimes don't believe these things happened to me. I just don't trust myself, don't trust those vague images left in my memory.

So then, given how weak even my faith is in the truth of this story, is it fair for me to expect you to believe me? Well, the fact of the matter is that I don't care. Whether you believe me or not is up to you. After all,

I've been tasked with telling this story to you, to humanity, so I'm going to do my best.

In order for you to be able to imagine in earnest what it is that happened to me, we have to go back in time a little bit to get a grasp of the characters and other pieces in the story, and we have to plunge into my history with the sea. What we find submerged there are the '80s, with their unmistakable flamboyance: the years of my childhood.

I first met the sea by way of our black-and-white television. I hadn't yet even dipped my toes in the water, but I felt like I was swimming in the depths of the sea, thanks to the *Man from Atlantis*, which aired every week. When the time finally came for me to meet the real sea in Çeşme, that quaint seaside town in Izmir (it hadn't yet been discovered by high society), I learned to swim in no time, inspired by the fish-man I'd seen on television. You just couldn't get me out of the water. I liked to imagine that if I stayed in the water long enough, webs would open up between my fingers just like the Man from Atlantis, and I'd be able to swim quickly underwater just like him.

My mother always said I was in love with the sea. One by one my friends would get out of the water freezing, their teeth clattering, but I'd still be out there swimming. But one day, my love for the sea, which began with a television show, came to an end with a movie. The movie was called *Teeth of the Sea*. Of course, you must have no idea what movie this is based on the name. Steven Spielberg's *Jaws* was shown in Turkey with the title *Teeth of the Sea*. The movie was forbidden to anyone under the age of eighteen. Still, I found a way to sneak into the theater. Afterwards, I paid a steep price for breaking the rules: Now I was scared of the sea. My love had become a phobia. Whenever I swam out, way out from the shore, I'd hear out of nowhere that terrifying refrain by John Williams, those two simple notes. The teeth of the sea were approaching. Dun dun, dun dun, dun dun . . .

My fear was in vain. The sharks didn't attack Çeşme, but something even more horrible did. Monsters made by men: *beach clubs*. An army of white plastic beach chairs approached the shores with their gaping maws, and the beach umbrellas sprung up one by one all over the bays. It no longer seemed possible for us to enjoy the beach without paying for it or having to hear the horrible music echoing out of those wretched establishments.

We basically had to pay tribute in order to go to beaches belonging to the public. After a while, thanks to those *beach club* blockades, I had a falling out with the sea; I shut myself up at home and, since there was nothing else to do in the summer when the sun was at its peak, I dedicated myself to reading books and watching TV shows.

During this time, the subtitle translators stopped sating my hunger for shows. So I rolled up my sleeves and started working as a translator. You may have seen my work on Divxplanet: psycho_pontiff66, that's me. Over time I distinguished myself with my translations and eventually found myself a professional translator.

It might be hard to believe, but it was thanks to these translations that I met Lara. She was the first (and only) person who took notice of the note I added at the start of films: "Enjoy the show, friends." She really liked my translations and the annotations I added, apparently, and she sent me an email expressing her appreciation. Women are the only ones anymore who hold artistic work in high esteem. There's a term they use these days, sapiosexual, for people who are turned on not by physical appearance but by the mind. An interesting statistic: I've seen many women like that, but not a single man. Even if all the men continue copulating with women whose minds they don't care about, throttling the evolution of the human brain, the mind will continue to make progress thanks to those heroic women.

And Lara, she was one of those heroic women. Her name means "water nymph." Her parents must have been able to see the future because she really was like a water nymph. Aside from her beauty, which seemed right out of the pages of a fantastical comic, her expressions, her smile, and her tone of voice had a dreamlike quality to them.

Since I met Lara that summer, I knew that my only chance at taking our flirtation to the next level and forming a relationship with her would be a vacation featuring the sea, the sun, and the sand. And so, pretending like I had no phobia of the sea, I arranged a vacation in Çeşme with a full itinerary. I put my plan into action by bringing her to the most expensive *beach club* during the day. The price for entry cost as much as three thick books (in those times I always thought of everything in units of books). I couldn't complain. The *beach club* wasn't all that bad, aside from everyone acting like they were at a fashion show for bathing suits. The music was bearable, the sand was clean, and the sea was shining.

With Lara by my side, I had no fear of the sea. The eyes of the Woman from Atlantis made me forget the teeth of *Jaws*.

Lara had enchanted me not just with her beauty but with her mind as well. It was clear she'd surrounded herself with philosophy and literature. How many people read Hannah Arendt on the beach?! And how many people would have looked at the copy of *The Call of Cthulhu* that I brought with me and ask, "Could the myth of Cthulhu represent Lovecraft's loneliness?" Life was truly full of surprises. Who could have imagined that I'd find the woman of my dreams not on Facebook, Instagram, or Snapchat, but on Divxplanet?

It was a very hot day. I hadn't managed to bring our flirtation to the next level on the beach; we were getting on like nothing more than two friends. After baking long enough under the hot sun, we got in the water. We played that childhood game where you talk to each other underwater. I was always really good at it. I understood everything she said. She laughed. "Even underwater it's clear you're a good translator," she said, and gestured with her index finger for me to come to her before diving to the bottom like a periscope. So I dove after her . . .

We shared our first kiss underwater. And our second, and our third. Then I stopped counting.

I don't know if this happens to you, but any time I'm enjoying myself, any time I'm brimming with joy, suddenly out of nowhere unhappiness comes crashing down on me, and I think of all those other people who aren't as lucky as me. There in the middle of the pleasure I'm experiencing, I remember all those people suffering elsewhere, all those people writhing in hopelessness and hunger, all those people who've helplessly bowed down to death while I'm here getting the most out of life, and I'm overcome with a feeling somewhere between sadness and embarrassment.

Lara and I experienced that same shift in emotions at the same time. The excessively upbeat atmosphere surrounding us made both Lara and I uncomfortable. She looked out on the horizon. "While we're here having fun like this, just a few kilometers out on the open waters, they . . ." she said, trailing off. She never said aloud who exactly she meant by "they," but I understood immediately that she was describing the migrants drowning in the Aegean as they attempted to cross from Çeşme to Chios. Lara's ellipsis was pregnant with the Syrians who'd ended up at the bottom of the sea, with their cheap, easy-to-sink boats and their fake life preservers. And somewhere in that ellipsis, I fell in love with Lara.

We got up from our beach chairs and gathered our things to leave this beach of hedonists. Not long had really passed since we'd met but there was a harmony to our movements that could only be described as a form of telepathy.

We carried ourselves to a desolate bay. It was a shallow, narrow bay, reminiscent of a giant swimming pool. We sat between two palm trees and, as the sun set, we opened the bottle of Jägermeister we brought along and began taking shots out of small plastic cups.

Darkness had descended by the time we saw the bottom of the bottle. Our heads were spinning. We lay down and looked up at the stars scattered in the sky. The lanternfish of the cosmic ocean had cast a canopy over this small bay in Çeşme. Among those shining points of light, the moon caught my attention. Though it seemed smaller than usual, it had managed to confidently gather a group of stars around it in the shape of parentheses.

Lara sat up and looked at the sea. A different mayhem of light awaited us there.

"Look! Phosphorescence!" she cried, and pointed at the lights flickering like fireflies in the sea. "The moonlight looks so beautiful scattered on the sea," she added, as if to explain the cause of the phosphorescence.

The ambience was meting out romance in greater and greater amounts. Of course, though, the moment had come for me to spoil the mood by mansplaining it away. "Phosphorescence isn't a natural phenomenon caused by the moon, like most people think. It happens because the kinetic energy of the waves causes tiny, single-celled sea creatures to shine," I said. Bravo, me!

Lara smiled, a weighty expression on her face.

"O wise sir, then would you please prove it to me?"

"But how?"

She stood up and took my hand, pulling me after her. She was dragging me toward the sea!

"Let's see, are there really sea creatures there in all that light?"

I laughed, releasing the full weight of my body to the ground to show that I had no intention of going back in. Think about it, the sea at night. My greatest fear. Nothing for light around us except the stars, the phosphorescent creatures, and the moon. Not even a full moon, either, just a sliver of a crescent.

The sea loomed there in the darkness like an enormous black hole that would swallow anyone who dared set foot in it.

"What happened, are you afraid?" the beautiful girl asked.

What could I say? I didn't want to put an end to a day straight out of a romance film by raising doubts about my manliness. I tossed back the last few sips in the bottom of the Jägermeister bottle and took Lara's hand. Toward the dark water we went.

We waded in up to our knees. I splashed the water with my hand to show how the single-celled sea creatures lit up. With the plankton still shimmering on my palm, I felt like a magician. "You win," said the water nymph, and as she leaned in toward my lips I felt so grateful to those microscopic creatures for not proving me wrong.

Then we went in even deeper, up to our waists. The scene before my eyes was so beautiful that hardly anything remained of my fear: The stars swam in the night sky, the phosphorescence in the sea, and fireflies in Lara's eyes.

With a strength that the alcohol was pumping through my blood, I took Lara into my arms and spun her around as we looked at the stars. Our drunken cries echoed across the bay.

Then I let her go. Looking at me with her shining eyes, Lara ran her hands through my wet hair. She leaned in and solemnly whispered in my ear.

"We should have sex."

I was astonished. "Here?" I replied.

"Why not?"

I panicked, of course, there was no hiding it. What if someone saw, what if a fish bit off my dick, what if I couldn't get it up? We all know what cold water does to the skin! But before I could get a word in edgewise, we'd started kissing. Lara first took off her bikini top, entrusting it to the waves. Then, her bottoms, left to the currents.

I was paralyzed, feeling like I'd seen some extraordinary creature, a mermaid, completely naked. "Looks like I have to do everything," she seemed to be thinking as she smiled at my anxious and motionless state, and she slipped my shorts off me. Then we began having sex in our bed of water.

In the water that night, two land animals were caught among the waves of love, trapped in a riptide of pleasure. The experience was as erotic as it was spiritual, like our minds and our souls had abandoned our bodies. Stars shining in our eyes, alcohol flowing through our blood, bodily fluids mixing together, our moans accompanied by the sounds of the waves, screams of pleasure echoing across the bay, and finally, my sperm set free . . . Like the words of a song, millions of my unborn children merged with the sea.

It almost goes without saying that I'd never had it better. The most enthralling orgasm of my life had assailed my brain. Lara was in the same state. She floated on her back with the grace of a synchronized swimmer. Like her, I relinquished myself to the sea. Our ears were underwater, plunging the world into silence.

The current slowly carried us out into deeper waters. Lying on my back, ferried along by the tiny caresses of the sea, I lost myself watching the stars in the sky. *The Museum of Innocence* is a novel with problematic Turkish, but its catchy, famous opening line came to mind. *It was the happiest moment of my life, though I didn't know it. Had I known, would I have been able to preserve that happiness, would everything have turned out differently?* It was the happiest moment of my life and, unlike Orhan Pamuk, I knew it right there, in that moment itself. Yet even though I knew it, I still wouldn't have been able to preserve that happiness, because a terrifying series of events, events nobody had the power to stop, were awaiting me.

I realized suddenly that I was being pulled down into the water. At first I thought Lara was playing a joke, that classic joke where you pull an unsuspecting victim underwater. But after a few seconds I realized that she was way too good at this game; in fact, no woman or man, even a diver wearing fins, could be this strong, could pull a person with such force down into the water. Something, some power had wrapped itself around my waist and was pulling me under, my body still facing upwards.

Looking toward the surface of the water from the depths into which I was being dragged, I could see the crescent moon, but after some time, it turned into a faint comma in the distance. The water grew darker and darker, and I could no longer see. The moment the pressure began hurting my head, I felt a soft touch wrap around my ears, my mouth, and my nose. It was a stingray, I could tell by its tail. It clung to my face like a suction cup. But it was neither poisoning me nor stinging me; in fact, it was helping me, somehow preventing my head from being crushed under the pressure, even allowing me to breathe underwater.

After being dragged even deeper, I realized that my surroundings were slowly growing brighter. The source of the light was unclear, but it helped me to see that what had wrapped itself around my waist was an octopus. Eventually, the eight-legged creature flipped me over with an agile gesture and I came face to face with the sight of the bottom of the sea.

It was blinding. A riot of light spread out before me. It took a few seconds for my retinas to grow accustomed to the flurry of color, before the web of plants and the phosphorescent sea creatures that were the sources of the light took shape. Fish, seahorses, and seaweeds of every color and type swarmed around me. They emanated light in many different tones: the blues from jellyfish swirling like tiny flying saucers, the greens from strips of seaweed rising like pipes from the seafloor, the reds from clusters of algae. It was like the inside of a snow globe here, an enchanted garden untouched by the current but dancing with bubbles.

The octopus that dragged me here nimbly tied my foot to a length of seaweed before gliding toward the rocks and delicately alighting on an enormous seashell in the center of the rocks. It was a beautiful seashell, reminiscent of those in Renaissance paintings. When the octopus touched the surface, it began slowly to open. Bubbles spurted out from the shell. I imagined some beautiful woman like Venus would emerge from it, but a terrifying creature leapt out. At first I thought it was a shark; it showed off its teeth as it came toward me. Just when it looked like it was going to bite off my head it juked past me, circling me instead. In that instant, I pissed myself. Mercifully, I'm quite good at hiding it when I piss in the sea, and so I kept the sea creatures there from noticing.

I watched the creature that had just pretended to attack me. Settled back in its shell, sitting still, I could make out its shape and appearance. It wasn't a shark, I realized; though its mouth resembled a shark's, its head looked like an octopus's. Its body was thick like a seal's but it narrowed from its stomach onwards, drawing an S shape with its body like a seahorse. The ends of its limbs had shells like crabs' but most of its body was half-transparent. Like a jellyfish, its digestive and circulatory systems were visible. Despite its utterly confusing anatomy, I was surprised that the creature seemed familiar, like a mythological creature. The first thing that came to mind was H. P. Lovecraft's myth of Cthulhu and what that myth describes: the creatures lurking under the seas since time immemorial, waiting to one day take over the lands.

That's when the creature's face suddenly changed. It opened and closed its mouth and whirled its arms around. It seemed like it was making fun of me and laughing. I think it realized I'd pissed myself. But then I heard a voice in my head. At first I struggled to make out the words because the voice was echoing in my skull. Then I figured it out by breaking the words into syllables. But I still couldn't understand it. The strange creature was speaking a language I'd never heard before:

"R'lyeh wgah' naph'nglui."

Interesting. This language reminded me of the language in Lovecraft's Cthulhu stories.

That's when I thought it necessary to translate this language, with an instinct entirely unique to translators, and somehow, I succeeded.

"Oh, that guy again?" the creature said.

How did I understand it? How did it make itself understood to me?

Its response came in short order: "Sound moves more quickly here, underwater, than it does in the air. That's true not just for sound but for thought as well."

And so I had an explanation for how I heard what Lara, and then what this creature, had said underwater: I wasn't reading lips but reading minds. As I dwelled on this revelation, the creature spoke again.

"Lovecraft let us down. You won't, will you?"

I knew I had to reply but the stingray was still on my face and my lips wouldn't budge. Of course! I couldn't speak with my lips anyway. As I looked at the grotesque being before me, I thought hard, releasing that thought to the water such that I could reach its mind.

"No, I won't let you down. Well, I don't know how he let you down, but . . ."

"Lord of the land! Son of Adam!" it interrupted with a loud thought. I was startled by this phrase, which resounded in my skull.

"I'm listening."

"You are here on behalf of the surface of the earth. Are you aware of this?"

"Is that so? Well, then, um . . . yes, lord of the seas . . ."

Rather than being pleased by my flattery, the mongrel being corrected me again: "I am not the lord of the seas, because we have no lords here; we are all lords. Thousands of years ago we entrusted the lands to you who abandoned the seas, and we did so to purge the seas of you. But of course that wasn't sufficient for you."

"I know that our species is greedy; I criticize people for it," I said in my thoughts. With this rather serious reply I imagined that I'd begun to fulfill my duty as envoy to the sea.

"You are here on behalf of the sons of Adam. You may not shift the blame onto others."

"You're right, I apologize."

I saw Lara then; like me, they'd tied her to seaweed, and she also had a stingray on her face. The only difference was that she was unconscious. I was worried about her.

"Fret not, for she is alive. But it's better that she not see this. Because ultimately, she has no culpability. You are the culprit: you, man, son of Adam."

"I understand, of course, but what exactly is our crime, if I may ask?"

"Not knowing what you've done: that's just how you sons of Adam are . . ."

"Well, I mean, if you're talking about the *beach clubs*, yes, their music really doesn't . . ."

The creature extended its arms at me like spears and fixed its eyes on mine. I shuddered.

"No, son of Adam, you're wrong. Listen to me well now. This is my last warning. Never, ever touch the seas again."

"If you mean the disasters at sea and the oil that spills into the water, I'm afraid . . ."

Angered again, the creature shot bubbles at me, interrupting the sentence of my thought:

"What we mean is what you, personally, have done, you chromosomally-lacking homo sapiens."

Okay, but what could I have done? Little old me? I thought to myself, but kept those thoughts from spreading through the water.

That's when I remembered . . .

Oh god, no, they'd realized I pissed myself!

"Lords of the sea, I couldn't hold it in, I was so afraid. That's the human condition. Please forgive me."

The octopus-like thing whirled its arms and spit out bubbles. Sparks flickered through its transparent body. It was enraged.

"You think that's what I mean, you idiot? I'm talking about those damned white seeds of yours!"

White seeds? I hadn't scattered white seeds, in fact I'm no good with plants. As I was readying to send off these thoughts in defense of myself . . . Oh. Of course. I really was an idiot. The mongrel being meant the sperm I'd released into the sea while having sex with Lara.

I blushed, like I'd been caught having sex in someone else's bed.

"Of course you're ashamed," it stated.

"I'm sorry, I hadn't thought of that."

The sea creatures looked quite angry. It seemed we'd broken some divine rule by having sex in the sea. The spokescreature piped up again:

"You sink your ships, spill your oil, mine for precious metals, lay down your waste pipes, dig your tunnels, all in our home, and yet we've said nothing. At the very least, you could refrain from doing what you did!"

Of course, it was right, but wasn't it exaggerating a little bit?

"What harm is a handful of sperm?" I asked.

At this, not just the spokescreature but all of the creatures burst into a frenzy. They snarled angrily, surrounding me with bubbles. It was terrifying.

"Foolish son of Adam. Do you think that's the kind of pollution I mean? What if a dolphin becomes pregnant by your malignant seeds? What do you think would happen if your disgusting temperaments took over the creatures of the sea?"

Was that possible? Or were the sea creatures just being a little uptight?

"But how would I know? I would never have suspected such a thing was possible, hand to god," I replied.

"Oh, son of Adam, lord of the lands, how determined you are to shirk culpability for what you've done."

Okay, that was true. I looked away in shame. My eyes fell on Lara again. She was still unconscious. Realizing I was looking at her, the creature spoke again:

"And, what's more, you made this daughter of Eve complicit in your crime."

That irritated me, though. The creature had been more or less fair in everything it had said up till now, but by exonerating her from this crime it was, quite frankly, being unfair to me. Ultimately, she was the reason we'd committed such a sin tonight, she had taken the first step. I wondered if I should explain this fact to them. Or would it be better to hide it? No, it was best to keep her out of it and to shoulder the responsibility on my own, like a man. But my thoughts slipped out of my mind by accident.

"Well, actually, the idea was Lara's," I found myself saying.

The bubbles stopped. The octopus-like being looked straight into my eyes. I couldn't hear a single thought; it was scaring me with the sheer terror of absolute silence. I cursed myself too, of course. I had taken advantage of Lara's unconsciousness to snitch on her, the woman I loved, to these sea creatures I'd just met! I was the most despicable kind of snitch. These sons of Adam of which I'm a member, we must really be a base, dishonorable, vile race . . .

Then the spokescreature of the seas turned to the other sea creatures.

"And there you have it. He would betray the female he loves; what wouldn't he do to us? Now you understand, don't you, why a handful of seeds is such a cause of concern?"

The many residents of this surreal underwater garden went berserk. Fish flashing their teeth, octopuses spinning their legs like fans, jellyfish pulsing their bells open and closed. Seahorses had lined up like an army ready to attack. The murmur of their thoughts swelled in me. Vengeful thoughts like "You're right!," "We need to get rid of this bastard right away!," "Drag him to the very bottom!," "Let's feed him to the piranhas!" swept through the underwater currents.

It had been decided. The fantasy of it all was over. These undersea beings were going to execute me then and there. Still, I couldn't blame them; even if I wanted to, I didn't object to their decision. Fleeing was no longer an option for me. I was getting what I deserved.

I was in a wonderland who knows how many leagues under the sea, the orgasm and the Jägermeister had left me groggy, I'd had a beautiful night, and in the midst of all that pleasure I should have predicted that I could bring about its exact opposite, horror or even death. I could finally take the place of all the suffering people I fretted over.

"He'll stay with us a little longer," the octopus-like being said to the others, and turned to me.

"Yes, son of Adam, to tell the truth, we were scared at first of your seeds spreading through the sea, but there's no longer any danger. We killed them immediately with the sting of the jellyfish."

The jellyfish had basically killed my unborn children by electroshock. I had no idea what to say.

"We were going to punish you to teach a lesson to all those other people acting out their fantasies in our seas, but we've learned something about you. It seems you're a translator. Is this true?"

"It is."

"Then you will be our translator. Understood?"

They had all fixed their attention on me. It was like I was being sworn into an undersea court.

"Well, of course . . ." I said, not quite knowing what the creature meant.

"Humankind is not to meddle with the seas any longer. I don't mean your waste, though. In the last few days you've sent thousands of people down to the seafloor, most of them drowned. We don't know what on earth you're doing up there, but . . ." and my thoughts accidentally interrupted the creature.

"The migrants . . ."

"We do not want to learn of your devilries. We saw those false life preservers you manufactured using our sponge comrades. No such evil has ever swum through even the darkest underground waters of Jupiter."

"As you know, we are a pitiful race, we haven't yet fully evolved."

"Enough excuses, son of Adam, take this message from us. But don't be egotistical about it! Don't be like that tawdry writer and paint us as hideous monstrosities. Because we don't have any intent of one day taking over the land. We want to forever live and die here in the waters, where life itself was born. But if things continue on this course, we will not hesitate to unleash onto the lands oceanic demons beyond your wildest imaginings."

I repeated the thoughts it sent to my mind over and over in order to keep them in my memory. The creature noticed.

"Well done. Lovecraft made us instruments of his own nightmares. You too, Translator, you must not turn this story from what it is into another story. It is enough to simply be a translator, to transmit our concerns to humankind."

I nodded my head. "As you wish," I added.

That's when I realized the seaweed wrapped around my leg was coming loose all on its own. Lara's was too. We began gliding slowly toward the surface, the stingrays still on our faces.

I heard one last thought as we returned to the surface . . .

"Have a nice swim, Translator."

As I was drawn back to the surface I felt like I was the Man from Atlantis. A childhood dream of mine had come true, you know; like him, I'd breathed underwater, and I'd swum as fast as he had. Plus, apart from the stingray on my face, I hadn't gotten any help from anything or anyone. Lara was there rising to the surface next to me, still unconscious, the Woman from Atlantis . . .

The sun began to appear above, slowly rising in the sky. It was beautiful under the sea, but I'd missed the place where I belonged.

I reached the surface of the water. The stingray fell off my face and glided away, disappearing into the sea. Pure oxygen! I missed it, and took it deep into my lungs. Once I got over the shock, I glanced around me. Lara was floating on her back in the water. The sun was shining on her face. I poked her, and she awoke, straightening up in the water like a synchronized swimmer. "I passed out," she said. "What happened?"

What hadn't happened . . .

"We slept a little while," I said.

"I had the craziest dream," she muttered.

"What was it?" What I really wanted to know was how much she had seen and heard.

She scratched her wet hair. "I don't remember. It was weird, though," she said, and made for the beach, still naked.

She seemed completely unaware of what had happened at the bottom of the sea. "I feel so dazed," she said, losing her balance. I took her arm.

"We went overboard with the Jägermeister, I think," I stated, listing off the many facts from urban legends about Jägermeister, that it contained deer blood and hallucinatory substances. Rather than shouldering what had happened and trying as best I could to explain it all to her, I opted to change the subject to idle chatter. "Got it," she said in reply. "Let's not do that again."

Two land animals who had spent too long in the water finally returned to the land after a night of adventure.

So now you're going to ask me, why should we believe the story you've told? Do you have any evidence? I don't think I'm entirely lacking in evidence. In fact, I have one piece of evidence. It's intangible evidence, but evidence nonetheless. Let me explain.

From that day forward, things with Lara were different from before. And yet, apart from the last-minute interference from the bottom of the sea, the day we'd spent together had been like a fairy tale, and anyway, she didn't even remember what happened underwater. So why did things change so suddenly? I rewound the film of the day to reexamine what we'd done together and found no mistake on my part that would justify these changes to her behavior. Eventually, I came up with some classic son-of-Adam theory about the volatility of women and glossed over the issue altogether. One day, she coughed, even though she wasn't sick. I understood by the sound of her cough what she was about to say. "It's not working... not like before. Something came loose in me. I don't know how to describe it," she demurred. That was the last time we spoke.

Later, I finally understood why her feelings toward me had changed. Though she'd been unconscious at the bottom of the sea, she had certainly heard me tattle on her to the sea creatures. The betrayed woman feels it; even if she can't put what she feels into words, sometimes, she just can't forgive herself if she tries to ignore this truth. Thoughts move more quickly in water than air, that mongrel creature had said. Oddly enough, even though this story is full of so much nonsense it'd be heavy-handed even in an old-fashioned fable, this is my evidence that it really happened.

The undersea creatures gave me no object nor secret to prove what happened to me, they gave me a feeling. A clue to show at the end of the film that the whole thing wasn't a dream, that it had really happened. Lara's inability to forgive me was the spinning top at the end of *Inception*. It was the baseball in *Field of Dreams*. Truth is always more creative, more cunning, than fiction.

How quickly the subject has changed, hasn't it? At the heart of my story I've placed not the message transmitted from the deep seas to the land-dwellers, but the romantic remorse which is the only thing that ought to matter to me in this world. Forgive me, lords of the sea, your messenger has disappointed you yet again. Just like Lovecraft used his experiences with you as the material for his horror literature, so too have I made it a tool of my own romanticism.

But, well, what can you do? Writers and translators who are sons of Adam are like this. Soon as we get hold of our pen, our selfishness comes right out. We are all, as you put it, egotistical.

But there's another reason I changed the subject. I really like telling stories that are hard to believe, that bend and twist the truth. To be honest, I'm really not interested in any stories still connected by their umbilical cords to the truth. The value in listening to and narrating the events of this story stems from their unbelievability. As to which part of the story is hard to believe, that's up for debate. Deep-sea creatures? No, I don't think so. Watch an underwater documentary and you'll see even stranger things. Or is it that they talked to me, that they sent a message to humankind, that seems unreal? I don't think it's that either; every day mother nature sends so many messages, so many warnings; what's unbelievable about that?

That's why, when I think about the day I spent with Lara, the time I spent surrounded by strange sea creatures in some corner of deep-sea paradise pales in comparison. Here's what I believe: that out of everything that happened, what's truly bewildering isn't what I encountered under the sea, but what I've seen and experienced above the sea.

It was a night when stars swam in the sky and phosphorescence swam through the sea. Two land animals got in the water, and they were caught among the waves of love, trapped in a riptide of pleasure. And then, they stretched out in the sea and plunged the world into silence.

Which is when everything went dark, like all those dreams you can't remember when you wake up, like all those memories made meaningless when you break up.

2017

Selections from

Lettrines II

JULIEN GRACQ

Translated by Isabella Huberman

Julien Gracq (Louis Poirier, 1910–2007) was an author of fiction, nonfiction, poetry, and criticism. His short pieces—"lettrines"—reflect a profound appreciation of geography and a remarkable attention to landscape and language. This section includes selections from *Lettrines II*, published in 1974 by José Corti. The selections appear in English for the first time in Isabella Huberman's translation.

I do not like the little plains of Vaucluse, just as I do not like those of Roussillon. The division into parcels, too small, too broken up, is without harmony; nothing of the ample and deep chlorophyllous breath of the Dutch terroir.

It is no longer a countryside—it is not a garden. The idea of *yield*, sordidly present in all of this agricultural factory, is at odds with that of the garden, which breathes only selflessness and time lost with love. Here vegetables, fruit trees, borrow something withered and harsh from the money into which they are converted. The view, in spite of irrigation, remains curiously that of a dry cultivation: nowhere the soft juicy abundance that the word *orchard* or the word *vegetable garden* evoke.

It is a suburb, a vegetable-producing and fruit-bearing *zone*, with all that the word implies of the degraded and leprously functional. Ugly new houses are sown between the cherry and peach trees, upon which they throw a dusty something.

The tree also disgraces, when it is present, this ungrateful and rich country. At times arranged in utilitarian curtains against the mistral, at others clustered in clumps poorly anchored to the ground, the cropped scraps and leftovers of horticultural planks; a singularly inharmonious association is made almost everywhere of sunlight species and hydrophilic species: cypresses, tamarisks, and sycamores on the one hand, willows and poplars on the other.

The *reed fencing*: unfortunate exotic counterfeit, flaccid bamboo, barren cane sugar, whose colorless leaves are foolishly distressed and disheveled by the mistral.

At noon, under the porcelain blue, and the Mexican and violent light of the mistral, there is, for me, in this landscape of the Comtat (all the same very beautiful), under the superficial pleasantness, a touch of the distinctly hostile. What I also felt to the point of anguish in the palace of Avignon and the towers of Aigues-Mortes, in the hollow, indifferent kindness of the native population, and what I call the icy heart of the Midi.

Fountain of Vaucluse: from the depths of the lustrous waters where the locks of hair of green water sprites stir, to the upper lips of the shadowed conch, in two hundred meters all the arpeggios of freshness.

Changes are happening from year to year among the *feathered race* that I observe on my walks in the countryside. This afternoon, it is a vast flock of seagulls that I see grazing along the road in a wheat field of the *Sourderie*: it is said that they progressively change their habitat, and either because of the pollution or the depopulation of the sea, abandon coastal fishing to go further and further inland to graze in the fields. This congregation, all white under the sun, pecking at the green-yellow down of the just-risen wheat, seemed to me curiously exotic: never in the past had one seen a seagull land near the Loire—at most a few swirled above the river upstream of the bridge, always announcing a storm and more infallible than the barometer. At this spectacle, a word came back to me, a word Chateaubriand uses at the beginning of the *Memoirs* and which pleases me: *pelagic countrysides*. And by analogy as well, a passage from *The Opposing Shore* of which the memory amused me: the one about the disaffected sailors of the Admiralty who are rented as shepherds on farms in the steppes. The same lively feeling of decay which then moves through the book was present all throughout my walk, as it is superbly expressed in half the poems in *Amours Jaunes* by

Corbière. Whomever goes from the workings of the sea to those of the soil inevitably derogates: without doubt there is not a people for whom this degradation is not expressed in song or in legend—and the animals themselves are not exempt: to see these magnificent flyers hovering low above the hedges and skipping about so white upon the wet clay, the loss of nobility that man inflicts year after year on the world he defiles appeared obvious: these snowy plumages wading in the mud of the thaw were as sobering to the eye as *sedentarized* nomads.

4

LATIN AMERICA

Introduction

ROBERTO FORNS-BROGGI

Among other possible reasons, beyond the economic benefit or stability that in any case become increasingly more unattainable in developing countries, it seems to me that current practitioners of Latin American speculative fiction find an impulse to write in the fact that it is possible and necessary to resist the seizure, the reduction, and the simplification of the future that the different extremes would like. In that not all of us will continue to deprive ourselves of the right to reclaim for ourselves the possibilities of the imagination and, in particular, those that could be useful for us to ask about our future, our concrete futures.

Alberto Chimal · "On Latin American Speculative Fiction"

The idea that territory is recovered through enjoyment and storytelling seems to me to be of enormous power against all this globalizing madness. The plausible territories of being appropriated by the imagination represent the weakness of the imposing Market.

Lucrecia Martel · "Territorios transitables"

In Latin America, the phrase *buen vivir* describes alternatives to development. It calls for a new ethics that balances quality of life, democratization of the state, and concern with biocentric ideals. Keeping that phrase in mind will allow the pieces in this reader to transmit surprise and emotion. You can learn to pay attention, concentrate, and devote yourselves to those revisited grounds. You can slow down to hear voices that convey new ways to relate to the land, feel the movement of being alive, and enjoy those experiential passages that speak to you. These texts are an invitation to invent new ways of breathing. They allow their readers to carve out spaces of a fuller human flourishing. But it takes years to flourish, and you will not flourish alone. You flourish when you experience surprise and emotion at any life's aura, when you retain deep questions with a quiet body, with a curious mind, and with an open heart. What a precious attempt to strive for a real sustainable way of life! What a humble rehearsal for the harmonizing of human and non-human worlds! I hope this invitation will be an exercise of memory and courage, harnessing imagination in the service of real sustainability.

Crucial to the imagination are rivers, oceans, lakes, or fountains that expose suppressed memories or forgotten histories of landscape and, in so doing, foreground situations of political or environmental conflict, violence, and contamination. For this effect, we can turn to Camila Fadda's liquid poems, works that display a deep true capacity for admiration, enthusiasm, and mourning. Fluidity and liquidity in these poems and this brief collection of fiction and nonfiction texts channel a call for revisions of the history and future of human-nature relations. Like all of the works in this section, they are shaped not only by the apocalyptic imagination but also by admiration and enthusiasm for being alive and connecting like water. They offer glimpses of future ways to occupy and move on the land as well as undercurrents of anxiety and uncertainty about tomorrow.

Abdón Ubidia writes a narrative against the abrupt loss of material and cultural reference points in a global society. His short story about the Neanderthals, published in Quito in 2004, offers an original setting in which the condition of the past is present as a marker of a future without the current dependence on technology. This is not a representation of Ubidia's home country of Ecuador, but a *terra incognita*, an outlandish story. It reveals both our transient condition and, at the same time, our struggles for survival. Ubidia's story is about a scale of otherness, a measure that escapes control or destructive interference. There is a temporal suspension that allows you to see a very different possible world rather than blindly follow the cold-hearted economic system that pretends to own the future.

Edmundo Paz Soldán's science fiction describes the near-future political Latin American reality as an amplified replication of the current situation. In the excerpt from his novel, *There Are Monsters Out There*, published in 2021, you might imagine the future incarnating the present, with the same dreams, anxieties, and nightmares of today. The context belongs to an extractive economy of a fictitious Andean country but eludes concrete references to his home country of Bolivia. It could be Ecuador, Perú, or the north of Chile or Argentina, only with a more moving yet believable future in which people experience what the earth's body would be capable of if human beings changed their relationship with it from exploitation to co-production.

Ulises Gutiérrez Llantoy's characters miss indigenous culture when they live in their own country, and also miss Western culture when they live abroad. "The Journey of the *Muchka*" appears in a collection of short stories that was published in five different editions from 2008 until 2020. The story allows you to deconstruct the supply chain in a way that pays attention to memory and the displaced indigenous cultures that are capable of joining tradition and modernity with creativity and love for the land.

Rodolfo Enrique Fogwill is usually known by his surname alone, Fogwill. His novel *Runa* (2002) describes an urn that contains the remains of voices and things heard long ago, and that may soon cease to be heard. In the selections included here, Fogwill invents a universe of Neolithic voices coming from all the impossibilities, the faults, the denials, the laws that limit, and the differences that deny: these peoples do not count, they do not speak, they do not know, they do not hunt, they can't put together a story, they don't believe, they don't look, and they don't think. Here, we have pieces of an anthropology that does not lead to knowledge. *Runa* is an ingenious criticism of all anthropology and also of all narration.

Gabriela Damián Miravete's work refers to the present moment rather than the possible future and speaks for the current rise of fantastic literature in Mexico. "They Will Dream in the Garden" was published in 2015 and won the 2018 Tiptree Award (since renamed the Otherwise Award). It is not only a potent piece of science fiction but also a very innovative way to change what the reader can imagine about the future: a garden full of memories in Mexico, memories of murdered women that cannot be retrieved completely because there is no imagination to fill in the blanks, unless you dare to do it.

The future becomes palpable when we see the possibility of moving through and appropriating territories: instead of serving depredatory economies, these lands could become public spaces of coproduction, of self-limited consumption; instead of increasing the "gross domestic product," they could become places for the collective experience of "gross inner happiness," or "gross inner mourning." I hope that you enjoy reading these variations on the creative imagination and dare to formulate deep questions to keep in mind: How can the dominant, shallow, exclusively instrumental ontology of land use be transformed to make room for something more sustainable? How to respect and incorporate the enduring and now increasingly relevant wisdom of the indigenous custodians of fragile and biodiverse territories? How to pay attention to what is irreversible and dissipative about our course through time?

We need people who will talk and criticize, who will propose a democratic horizon for our citizens to gaze upon. Those people inhabit these texts that are waiting to be read as the land awaits the sun and the rain. They might incarnate Roberto Bolaño's words in his posthumous novel, *2666*: "They turned the pain of others into memories of one's own. They turned pain, which is natural, enduring, and eternally triumphant, into personal memory, which is human, brief, and eternally elusive" (244).

WORK CITED

Bolaño, Roberto. 2004. *2666*. Barcelona: Anagrama.

Opinions of a Neanderthal

A Narrative Essay

ABDÓN UBIDIA

Translated by Adele Lonas

Abdón Ubidia (b. 1944, Quito, Ecuador) is a novelist, short-story writer, playwright, essayist, researcher, and literary critic. He is considered one of the most important voices of modern Ecuadorian literature. In this piece, a hidden group of Neanderthals try to escape extinction in the near future. These twenty-two vignettes create a very intriguing fiction about the darker aspects of speciesism.

1

Listen, before we are forever lost, to what I'm going to tell you:

The first globalization began 40,000 years ago. There were two species of hominids then: the humans and the Neanderthals. The first were born in Africa and the second in Europe. The first exterminated the second in the first genocide in history. That's what the sages say.

It wasn't like that. They didn't succeed in driving us to extinction. I'm a Neanderthal.

Now that the issue is trendy, many theories try to explain that genocide. Some say that the group instinct of humans moved the balance in their favor. Others say that their build, less robust than that of the Neanderthal, made them more apt to survive the scarcities of the ice age. Since our brain was larger than theirs, they haven't been able to claim having greater intelligence. But a greater imagination, yes.

They rely on an apparent proof: our migrants failed to reach the other side of rivers, lakes, and seas. One scientist maintains, based on that precarious proof, that we were deprived of abstract thought and imagination. Gibberish. The issue isn't about wondering what exists on the other side of a sea. It's crossing it with or without needing to. Regardless of any danger.

I want you to understand that their fundamental mistake consists in believing that their imagination serves them to escape indefinitely from real circumstances, from the limits that all of us living beings have: the time allowed to live, the natural laws that cannot be violated without paying, in the end, great consequences.

I want you to understand that the imagination that denies our most crass realities, serves to "imagine" the impossible. To dream that limits don't exist.

The limit itself. That is the point. Only the hungry beast crosses it. Only the madman doesn't recognize it.

I want to tell you that finding the other side (possibly nonexistent, mistaken, or unknown and it reminds us of Columbus) was the fruit of a brutal and unbridled adventure.

I want to tell you that if the humans pursued and killed us without mercy it was because of the aggressive instinct and barbarity that dominated them. And something else I discovered later.

I want to tell you that if they dominated and plundered the world it was for the same reason. They never understood their limit.

I want to tell you that because of their aggression and insanity, the human species will become extinct.

Thus, we will inherit their world, what they have added to it and have destroyed. Thus, we will also return to live peacefully once again on Earth.

How was it that some of us survived the great massacre?

Because we camouflaged ourselves. The same as certain animals that have developed the perfect camouflage to blend in with their surroundings, we also succeeded in blending in with the humans, assimilating their cultures, their languages, their clothing; living like them and among them.

Certainly, we have a few anatomical differences: our faces are somewhat longer, our bones more robust, our voices less docile. But that isn't much. Sometimes it's possible to find greater physical differences between their own ethnicities, and even between individuals of the same human race.

2

Are we more intelligent than humans? I could say yes. Their average brain weighs 1,350 grams and ours 1,600. But that isn't a valid reason. Because each species has the intelligence that it needs. The brain of a rat is perfect for the rat and that of the elephant for the elephant. Ultimately, there's only one true intelligence: How to survive? And that isn't in individuals but in the species.

My species was able to survive precisely in the midst of our enemies. We couldn't hide from them but, precisely, among them, the bloodthirsty hunters.

Why, then, forty millenniums ago, didn't we defeat them?

For one reason. We weren't (and never will be) prepared to confront the absurd.

Because no one can triumph over a catastrophe, nor can ever be entirely prepared to confront one. What did the dinosaurs know about the meteorite that, 65 million years ago, hit Earth and lifted up a cloud of dust that led to their extinction? What do we know of what is brewing in the dark heart of the universe? What of the cataclysms that the Earth itself is preparing? That belongs to what we don't want to admit nor think about: fate. And with it, our own end. That is the absurd. The eruption of the uncontrollable, of the unexpected, of the untimely. And, unfortunately, that is the law of the world. The human scientists despair. They make calculations. They produce theories. All will be in vain. They themselves estimate that, since life began, 99 percent of the species that inhabited the face of the Earth have disappeared from it. Why would it matter to the universe if another species disappears, even if it's called human?

And I speak from personal experience: that of my species, that of the Neanderthals, that name that humans assigned us.

3

We couldn't predict the aggression or the insanity of the humans. And that was our downfall. Our annihilation.

Who could convince them of a treaty, of an arrangement of coexistence, if when we were already burying our dead (and we had musical instruments), they were still continuing their cannibalistic practices with their own or would leave them to rot from the elements?

Their appearance was similar to ours. That was their camouflage. Face to face with the saber-toothed tiger, we knew how to proceed. But not face to face with those we should have been able to believe were our own kind. At first, we couldn't understand that what was hidden inside a body that was practically the same as ours was the most aggressive and predatory species of all those that have inhabited the Earth. We were, then, decimated without mercy. Neither our corpulence nor skills served us in the least. All understanding takes time, requires moments of calm reflection. When under attack that can be a heavy burden. And it was. Their ferocity won out. Some of ours fled to the glaciers. And, until today, the limited travelers who have seen them haven't wavered in calling them "abominable snowmen" and other similar epithets, without bothering to provide any proof to the contrary. The legend's possibility is clear: that the "yetis" don't exist and are only part of the popular imagination that humans are such enthusiasts of. But, from the depths of my heart, the hope is born that those brothers do exist, that they run free between mountains of ice and secret caves.

4

I'm saying that, in just a few years, they practically erased us from Earth. When we learned to recognize them it was too late. The few of us who survived and didn't flee, we invented a way to assimilate into those distant tribes that hadn't yet discovered our existence. One of ours, dressed like them, alone, and maybe because we had already stopped being so gregarious, approached them in peace and began to busy himself with the hardest and most humble jobs until he was accepted, be it as a slave or as a craftsman because we were always skilled at making utensils and tools. In a way, we did what some wolves did in turning into dogs to survive among humans. Only we did so using other strategies.

When the humans would leave for their hunts and sometimes endless wars, it was easier to slip into a family and partner with a forlorn woman.

Among ourselves, we didn't have the custom of forming permanent groups or families. Groups and families lasted when they were meant to last. However long protecting an offspring required. Furthermore, we were very few, a species in extinction.

We had to turn to other methods. Of one, I am sure. The discreet substitution of Neanderthal babies for human babies, for example.

In contrast to the females of other mammals, human mothers don't recognize their offspring by their individual smell. I am sure that we must have taken advantage of this inadequacy; it is easy to imagine a female Neanderthal laden with her offspring, finding the exact moment to leave her hiding (or take advantage of her servitude) and approach during the night the bedside of a human mother who had also recently given birth, and substitute her child. What would happen to the other offspring? Anything. Maybe she would destroy it. Maybe she would abandon it someplace so someone would adopt it. Remember the old stories of humans. Remember Oedipus, Moses; and also Little Thumb; why not?

That practice must have begun thousands of years ago and been perfected and maintained up to this day. I know it well. I was exchanged in a maternity ward and was raised in a human home. My parents never knew. But I always suspected it because I was never able to understand them. Because I was never able to give them the love that they gave me. In their own way, of course, in own their way. Too much affection and too many rules. Too much fear about my fate. Too many prejudices. Only when X told me the truth, that is to say, that of my secret Neanderthal condition, was I able to understand them. They weren't worried just about my own future. But also about theirs. They feared getting old in desolation, maybe in poverty. I was their guarantee. A life insurance paid in installments. There wasn't any other way to understand the education that they imposed on me. They wanted me to be rich and successful. And I only wanted to be happy. Under a Neanderthal's terms, of course. Something that in humans would look like tranquility. I wanted them to let me live according to my own tastes. Nothing more. I had confrontations with them. They never understood me. A common thing between human parents and their children. I was a resentful adolescent. I believed then that I was human and I came to admire the guys that gathered together in rebellious gangs, even though on many occasions I was the victim of their cruelty. They gave me nicknames and subjected me to humiliating punishments because they couldn't understand my withdrawal and solitude either. Soon, I learned, or rather I imitated, their behaviors. They accepted me when I began to learn the art of cruel nicknames with greater skill than they had. And even more, when I learned to hit them back. Since then, I pretended to share in their stupid wars. Night raids, sieges, stupid adventures, pointless risks, extreme sports. And I was able to adopt, not without a deep repugnance, their coarse habits.

5

Fear guided them like it did my parents. Everything was intimidating. And their easy violence was simply the easy response to their fear. If they're going to attack you, attack. If they're going to destroy you, destroy. If death is after you, go after it.

It took me much more time to discover the deep-rooted cause of that fear.

This is important: they are a threat to themselves. Their own imagination harasses them. They fight, as one of them said, with windmills that they confuse with giants. With frequent ghosts. Also with impossible dreams. Because they never could find the limit between the real and the imagined. That is to say, the limit between the earth they walk on, the river that wets them, the fruit that nourishes them, the weapon by which they die or kill . . . and the fantastic beams that emanate from their troubled heads.

They always confuse reality with the imagination. They imagine reality. They act on their imagination.

That is the mark of their species. Everything has a shadow: a bend, a place, a stranger, for them it is something else: a threat or a place to conquer or dominate.

6

They see what doesn't exist. They invent all the time. That's how they pursue their wars and endeavors. They fear everything and dream of fantasies. Their truth is uncertainty. They fear the present. But much more the future.

X told me this the only time we spoke, when my childhood was just ending.

X is my mother. Or was. I never saw her again. I never knew her human name. I call her this: X.

I remember her well. She appeared in a park. I saw her sitting on a bench, among the old pines. I went to her instinctively, guided by her smell. I had seen her a few times, from a distance, moving away from me. Never before had I allowed myself to get close to her. One of her looks was enough to stop me. It wasn't only her smell. It was her energy, if I can say it like that; something like a special warmth, like a magnetic wave that I could clearly sense.

"I've protected you up until now. I've watched over you from afar. It's no longer necessary. You'll survive among the humans."

We spent the day together.

She spoke quickly. But I understood not only her words, in any case human, made by a human language, but also all she hid between the folds of them: echoes, intonations, innermost cries, a savage murmur, a weaving of vibrant signals; like a radiance that came accompanied with fragrances and something like variations of humidity and temperature that came to me from her body, from her entire trembling being, fully employed to communicate the most information possible in a day, a day that flew as fast as her words.

"I've come to say good-bye," she said. "After today I will no longer be your mother."

"You never were," I should have complained, thinking of the model of human mothers, thinking of the one who, between anguished heartbeats, would be waiting for me at home, wondering why I hadn't appeared yet as always at lunch time, imagining to herself all the dangers that could have caused me to be absent that day at school, because at that hour she would have already spoken with the teachers and would have learned of my absence in class. Tormenting herself in silence, because surely, she wouldn't have said anything to my human father so as not to worry him. That's how they were: my father was tasked with suffering a job he hated and she with working at her daily suffering. Like all humans from that era. Now it's worse, human women dispute with their men over a power that even for them was never just nor good.

Of course, I didn't say anything to X. It wasn't necessary. She knew. Neither did I ask her about her future.

She didn't speak about my father. Like all Neanderthals, he had learned to engender and leave. He had learned the role that he had to fulfill. And nothing more.

7

She told me she was married to a human who feared her. And that he did nothing other than submit to her desires.

"I didn't force that relationship. He, on his own, submitted himself to me. Because the difficulty that humans have separating the spheres of fact and fiction not only results in aggression towards others, but frequently, it turns against them, and they suffer and torment themselves without there being visible cause. Because they carry on their shoulders ghosts that control their lives with imperious standards. My husband drags a burden that no one obligates him to carry: outside of the home he is a master (his employees fear him), but at home he is a slave. That isn't the rule. In general, the opposite occurs. The majority of men want to dominate at work and at home. But I'll tell you one thing: no human behavior should surprise you: there are saints that assassinate and heroes that die of fear."

After a brief silence she continued:

"In these times, after breaking all the limits, crossing all the shores, they are at the point of straining everything and exhausting themselves as a species. They are at the point of abandoning their own scale, the human scale: the one that has allowed them to be on this earth that they have already exhausted."

8

A few decades have passed since that meeting with X. And the humans have already surpassed their own limits. They've heated the Earth with toxic emissions from their industries. They've manipulated their own genetic codes and from there, ultimately, only monsters will come of it. They've turned war into a science, a leading-edge industry and, in the case of the great powers, an engine of their economy. And they've imposed a social system made for inequality, that enriches the richest and impoverishes the poorest, based on that simple determination that whoever has more, earns more. Only hate, envy, robbery, discrimination, and crime can come from that infernal mechanism. And emptiness.

My Neanderthal mother was right. The human scale is already broken. It has broken its own limits.

Then she said nothing more. It wasn't necessary. Everything was clear to me. Since that day I have changed my behavior. I stopped opposing the plans of my parents. I studied what they wanted. I'm speaking of my first career. It never served me in the least. Not even to find a decent job. Afterward I studied other things on my own: psychology, anthropology, history, literature—the sciences called "not exact sciences" that are the only ones that recognize human behavior. I wanted to understand it. It felt so strange to me.

No one should think that Neanderthals form a sect, a fraternity, a parallel and secret society. Nothing like that. No conspiracies nor strange groupings.

We don't need a society. We recognize each other when we're close and that's enough. We obey the law of our species: we wait. Our hour will arrive.

9

My personal experience is enough. I infiltrated them knowing them to be different. I didn't need the surprise of a DNA test. At that time, it wasn't even possible. Only a few scientists were just beginning to learn about it. But I, at twenty-two years old, I already knew I was different. I already knew who I was.

Soon, during a long night of insomnia, I found sense in all the senselessness that surrounded me. I understood that those "loose thoughts" as I always called them then, that came to me from the depths of my heart, were silent, secret, instinctive voices that communicated to me the decisions necessary for my survival.

It's obvious that hundreds of generations of Neanderthals lived and died without knowing what they were throughout their lives. It wasn't necessary for them to know. They knew the fundamental: they were different. And that the only possible way they could survive was by camouflaging themselves as humans, pretending to be humans, blending in with them.

Forgive the paradox. On having to be like them, we learned the enormous distances that separated us. I've already pointed out the fundamental: the human impossibility of separating the real from the imaginary. And I'll always insist on it. I'll explain it.

They only see what they want to see. That's to say, they don't see what they don't want to see (the same individual can be judged a demon by some and an angel by others). Whatever they don't look for doesn't interest them. Even if it exists. Even if their neighbor might be a Neanderthal. And they construct their sciences to find what they want to find. From there they have developed an autophagic thought that feeds on itself forever. They only think what they want to think. And they imagine what they want to and can imagine. Furthermore, the only limits that they set for themselves are also imaginary. There were entire civilizations of Indians that knew of the wheel, for example, but for religious reasons refused to use it. And they even confused their conquerors with gods. That excess of imagination was their end.

The same occurs with their basic necessities: food, sex. They impose prohibitions that don't allow them simple pleasures: hungry Hindus that refuse cow meat, tribes that did the same with pork, Westerners that scorn those who consume insects rich in protein; anorexics that come to hate food against what nature ordains for all living beings. During times of abundance this isn't that important, but during those of scarcity it can mean the difference between life and death.

10

What to say about the self-prohibitions of humans in relation to sex.

The Neanderthals, in contrast, we feel the urge for sex in an imperative way, irrepressible. Suddenly, dressed as humans, "humanized" in appearance despite our heads being somewhat larger, the strength of our bodies and our elongated faces; owners of human jobs, of human families; lost, camouflaged among the human mass that wanders in the streets, plazas, and commercial centers, the Neanderthal male finds the Neanderthal female and she finds him. It's the great hormonal charge that leads them to each other without ever having met. They will go then, urgently, hastily, to the first refuge they find: sometimes a public bathroom, the nook of a garden, the door of an entryway left ajar, a motel, and there they'll copulate with a fury that the humans will never understand. Those meetings are repeated over various days, while heat lasts.

After, the inseminated female loses herself in the world to fulfill her role: ensure that her offspring survives in it.

I learned to be discreet during such encounters. My first marriage was ruined because my human wife found out about one of my inevitable escapades. How to make her understand that I wasn't being unfaithful, that I wasn't going to abandon her, that I didn't "love" anyone else? That I was only fulfilling an imperative desire, a hormonal command? There was no way to convince her. She was prisoner of a blind fury. The same would have happened if I were a run-of-the-mill human. Adultery is among one of the most entrenched human fears. And it's the perfect example of humans' most profound contradictions. Desire and fear are joined in it.

However, they commit it regularly. There's a prosperous gift and motel industry made exclusively for lovers that the mundane, established, routine of human marriage doesn't utilize except at the beginning or in exceptional cases. But both their churches and their laws condemn adultery with extreme severity and there are frequent cases of crimes and suicides committed in its name. From ancient mythology to classic literature, to crime news, they document it well.

11

Thus, one of their oldest institutions, matrimony, is a "should be" that is only fulfilled to guarantee the "imaginary" functioning, I would say, of their societies.

The same happens on a large scale, with their arbitrary and fictitious economies and currencies and the delicate network of what they call their cultures. Meaning: their religions. In other words, their supreme truths, their practices, occupations, and supreme research: science, primarily.

It's almost a rule that in the name of freedom they promote inequality. That in the name of good, they plunder and exterminate entire peoples. That in the name of the poor they enrich themselves without end. That in the name of the weak they become powerful. And that the so-called Truth is the best instrument of the lie. This might sound like propaganda, but it isn't. At night, I rehearse in silence impossible messages—You, human who doubts, maybe you can understand me: look at your opulent palaces and temples and at your miserable slums; look at your history of wars and massacres; look at your own life, judge me well, if you can, if your human head allows you to, and you'll see I am right.

12

Listen to me well, young female, since after these intense days, you'll disappear forever:

I've proved that memory, even in splendid brains, is limited. No one remembers everything. No one knows everything. Thus, the sages have to appeal to other sages who also don't remember everything. Nor know everything. Surrounded by a sea of oblivion, they write books that cite other books. Books that can only hold their memories and their knowledge in writing. In this way, they've created a parallel knowledge, like facing mirrors, in which the books read each other.

And this, which is certain, is only a metaphor since the social knowledge that they've created, that some call History, has not only accumulated in their written words but is engraved in the things that they've made throughout this millennia. Machines, cities, monuments, roads, communication devices, electronic and biological inventions. Thus, all that has been created by human civilization speaks to itself, separating, ultimately, from concrete humans, from individuals, even from their societies and now, from the will, the need to survive, of the human species. That's why I say, I will always say and will repeat that they have already broken the human scale, their own measure of the possibility of their being on Earth.

There is a point that I should clarify. There is a second class of humans. Included in that long history of heroes and assassins—who, in general, are the same—are their sages and martyrs—who almost always are the same—and who, from time to time, brandish what they call "humanism" like a warning call from the mistaken path that their species has taken. They despair. They invent utopias. They try revolutions. They write redundant and useless ethical manifests that always, in every era say the same things, just in another context and with other words: "Don't kill, don't steal," etc. A good number of them take refuge in art or in philosophy. They build, then, a parallel virtual world, an "ideal" representation of the world they've made. But their "real" world is something else. The proof is that many poets, artists, and philosophers have been persecuted to death by their peers.

Or, in contrast, in a worse, more sarcastic version, they've been integrated, coopted, and even celebrated, precisely by those responsible for or representatives of the world denounced by those poets, artists, or philosophers. For the same reason, it isn't strange to find, for example, in the house of a wealthy and powerful man, a painting that shows misery and degradation adorning one of the walls.

This is only understandable because the owner of that painting and the artist who painted it both speak imaginary languages that are incommunicable, that have nothing to do with each other.

13

The prophets, saints, and martyrs—who have said and written so much, used their own sacrifices, their own lives, as ethical and also aesthetic examples for others, always useless of course—belong to that second class of humans.

Because the rest of humanity never understood them. It was immersed in its wars, its conquests, its forbidden businesses, its plundering.

Thus, how were they going to understand that each tenet, each work of art, was a warning or, as I already said or tried to say, a cry, and sometimes of pain.

Young female, though later you'll leave forever, you're with me now and, well, this is important:

I have a suspicion that I might be able to confirm in the near future: I believe that a lot of supposed "humans" were, in reality, Neanderthals. Most of all those who proclaimed human redemption or that believed, until the end, in a humanism that very seldom was understood by their peers. If you want historical names I'll give them to you: maybe Jesus and Mohammed were. They spoke their words to humans who didn't consider them of them but rather sent from the heavens, almost aliens, gods or sons of gods; they saw them as so different. The human mass, which always pays attention to the fanatics, did the rest. In their name, they denied the words of the prophets and transformed, many times, too many times, their message of love into one of hate.

Their message of love? Yes, of love. Because the slogan of love can only be proclaimed from weakness, from the weakness of the persecuted. The strong don't need it because they scorn and subjugate. For me, then, such prophets—in many ways my brothers—were only asking the impossible: mercy.

Remember: "The last ones will be the first ones." It's in the Bible. Remember: "The people will be like scattered moths and not know where to go." It's in the Koran. Remember: "One day the sea will be desert and the desert will be sea." Brazilian lore says it. Such warnings seem to contain secret meanings.

Many supposed "humans" that repeated that sign of love with great success existed or exist mostly among artists. I tell you that I don't have any proof, but to cite one case among a hundred, I believe that Kafka was a Neanderthal. There is a text from him in which a monkey says that it accepted becoming human simply to survive. The message couldn't be clearer.

14

What I'm telling you is only a supposition, and I don't have any way to prove it. But it isn't ridiculous. Because, after so many millennia of secret coexistence, we, the Neanderthals, should have impacted human uses. I'm not speaking of hybridizations, although they have found skeletons of children that had DNA mixed with traces from both species. I'm speaking to you of the Neanderthals that, more out of desperation in facing what they couldn't understand, believing themselves to be human, spoke a word destined to confusion.

And regarding the hybridizations between humans and Neanderthals and given that they've never found hybrid skeletons of adult individuals but only of children, I think that that mix wasn't successful. Nature never wanted it. Like in so many cases of neighboring species: even when they are able to engender offspring, like the mule, let's say, those never could reproduce themselves afterward. Nature imposed its prohibitions, its scales, its inviolable laws—at least until recently when humans began with their genetic experiments. Or maybe, a few centuries ago, when they discovered medicine, whose main purpose is to conquer death, to artificially prolong the life of individuals, beyond the possible, with perverse drugs that every time make them even more dependent on and hostage of those who make the drugs, but also, more vulnerable: in a word, more decrepit. Listen to me well, humans don't want to die. And they're convinced, in their delirious insanity, that they will achieve, step by step, the annulling of the main disposition of Nature: the depletion, the death of individuals so that the species can survive.

15

Humanity never understood the difference between two concepts that, in appearance, only appearance, are the same: man and human. Concepts that I should explain better: "human" is a concrete being, of a concrete species that has a role and a relationship within the group of live beings that inhabits the Earth; and a direct relationship with Earth, with the Nature that it has plundered so much.

"Man," in contrast, is a narrow concept, barely tribal, that leads each tribe no matter how ancient or recent to determine that the members of other tribes are not "men."

They even have a telling saying: "Man is the wolf of man." It summarizes the secret of their misfortune. Any difference: the color of the skin, language, gender, customs, social position, serves some "men" to take advantage of others, to exercise contempt, marginalization, exploitation, or crime. All in the name of the great principles: civilization, ethnicity, creed, and even whimsical slogans like that of "freedom" that each group understands in its own way.

Listen, young female, you who carry in your womb the son I'll never know:

The great burden of humans: their boundless imagination leads them to turn it on themselves. They bewitch themselves, they self-suggest, self-hypnotize, and believe until the end in their own imaginings: their myths, yes; their ideologies, also; but above all, in the "reality" of their imaginations: obsessive, enclosed in their mirrored palaces, convinced of their tenuous reasons—and the so-called "reason" is one of them—they go through the world entrenched in their crazy ideas, prisoners of them, sometimes propagating them however they can; others, suffering them in silence.

16

Since this is just a summary, I'll only tell you about three obsessive ideas of the humans: power, freedom, and passion (mystic or romantic). Take it as you want: they are their three dreams or their three misfortunes.

The first, power, is the imaginary form that humans invent to transcend themselves, to conquer their finitude, to take on more than they can control. Since they know that they must die, they want to "survive" in the memory of others. Since they know they can't truly "own" anything other than their immediate goods, they invent signs, coins, papers, functions, titles, that only "represent" what is beyond their own physical limits. Since they know that they can't dominate others because they are the infinite masses, they recur to systems of domination—it's worth saying inhuman systems—that end up dominating them. The kingdom exists, not the king. The bank exists, not the banker. The dictatorship exists, not the dictator. The government exists, not the governor. Understand me: the powerful are servants of their own power. The proof is that they are willing to die for it.

Their second fantasy: freedom, it's the impossible dream, the extreme word, the eternal fountain of human confusion because anyone can enslave or kill another human in the name of it.

"Defend your freedom," the modern master tells the slave. "I am free," the slave repeats, like an echo.

Listen to me: there is no slave worse than the one who believes himself to be free.

For me, what they call freedom is only the "freedom" of the human imagination: its impossibility of accepting a limit. And like happiness, which can only be understood in misfortune, it's unreachable, undefinable. And it only takes on meaning when it doesn't exist. When you don't have it. Or when it's been crudely lost: the prisoner, the victim of a dictatorship, the one submitted by force, the dominated, the slave himself. When, and this is rare, they understand their real condition, only then do they know what their freedom is. For the rest it's only a slogan that, in general, they use to imprison, submit or—as I tell you so often—to enslave.

In the name of freedom they've annihilated civilizations and entire peoples and it wouldn't be strange if that beautiful word were already its own epitaph.

17

And, finally, I should speak to you of the third human fantasy, passion. If the dream of power and of freedom are their collective insanities, passion is their individual insanity, the means that the individual has to convince himself that he is special, important, unique among his species: the passion of the miser who wants to accumulate everything; the passion of the martyr who believes that his death will redeem all humanity; the passion of the leader who seeks total power; and the worst in terms of suffering and hallucination: the amorous passion of the individual who loves another he believes to be special, important, unique, that is to say, as "individual" as he is. This amorous passion is a way of loving the self through another. For the same reason, lovers invent each other. That's why they even believe in the absurdity that two are one. Bewitched, self-suggested, they are capable of inflicting great suffering. It's one of the human terrors. Death and pain foment it because, as a twentieth-century humanist philosopher, a supposed Sartre, said: "All passion is born to die" and it is that awareness that exalts it and turns it into amorous passion.

Young Neanderthal, girl who still hasn't lived enough, for the same reason, consider that if we learn the human languages, religions, sciences, and customs, we also run the risk of learning love and the other human passions if we don't take precautions. I myself have incurred that risk two or three times throughout my life. And believe me I regret it. It won't happen again.

After these intense days, you'll have to leave because, you and I, we run the risk of imitating the human passion, of learning it, of being influenced by it, of believing that we will be, always, "made for each other," you and I, of the same flesh, undying, unfading, eternal; such is the formidable mutual lie that spouses and lovers invent together. But as time passes, so does the enchantment, the bewitching, and each returns on their own to their unique body, to their individual borders—that is to say, to painfully accept that never, except in the cursed imagination, were they one. They return then to unwalk what they walked, to accept the death of each in the other, the real separation that "separates them," that returns them to their true condition of individuals who only were fulfilling a mandate of their species, that of mating in order to serve their species, the true owner of their disposable bodies.

18

The cursed human imagination. Because of it, each human, each person wants to be more than what they are: to transcend themselves, live beyond death, possess more than what they can hold; to extend their dominion until infinity. All the human empires are the example. Remember Rome and how it fell. Remember Spain, Germany, England, and now the American Empire and how it's falling.

The cursed human imagination. Another proof is current technology. Millions of artifacts made to suppress distances and times. And they only generate anxiety and anguish because you can only suppress distance and time, the idea of them, in the imagination. I'll explain myself: the letter that before took three months to arrive and now, the email that takes three fractions of a second; or the instant international call. Each keeps its correspondents as far away as ever, subject to their respective land and to their different life, to their rain or their sun, to their cold or heat, to their night or day, that is to say to their distance, to their farness. So much that, in truth, their contact is almost illusory, made only of memory, of dream, of precarious phantom companies.

I'll explain myself better: the traveler who today takes a trip in just a few hours, when in the past he took months, isn't saving his time; the only time that matters is the time of his life. What he is doing is simply using those hours to do more things, the majority unnecessary, to come and go more quickly, things that end up burdening him, while "real" time, the hours of his existence, those that have been assigned to him to be on this Earth, continue being the same, so much that he could have employed them the same if he were to have remained still, in the chair of his desk or of a cinema or of the plane that he uses to travel. Just as when some insect prefers to jump instead of going after its food in the usual way, this supposed time saver doesn't mean anything in the real compass of the planet, of the stars, of a universe that continues to be so removed from high-speed travel. Confusing speed with time has been another of the great human errors. Now, humanity runs, each time more quickly, but without knowing where to nor what for.

At this point I should tell you about something apparently contradictory: the limits of his "unlimited" imagination. They exist, though his mind doesn't recognize them. Because humans are only able to imagine that which their mind allows them to. The blind drive to dominate Nature is only achieved with techniques made to the measure of their species: the biggest cranes only increase the force of their arms; the telescopes and microscopes and televisions, of their sight; the radars, sonars, radio receptors, of their hearing; the fastest transportations, of their legs. Based on such evidence, a supposed Borges came to accept that human writing was only an extension of his memory.

I want to tell you that humans use their boundless imagination like a palace of mirrors, only to reproduce themselves. Their tragedy consists in not recognizing that it is "limited" by its own nature. Their crazy dream of wanting to overtake their imagination is too human to be able to see and understand what is beyond the desires of its only species and to predict the costs and sacrifices that they inflict on their planet and, including, on their own lives.

19

Led by that disturbance of their conscience, the imagination, finally they have constructed a machine that wants to imitate, clumsily, of course, their own brain. It is the computer. With it they believe to have enclosed their conscience in a box in which each government, each company, each home, "orders" their lives. Millions of programs—those that sustain the Internet, for example—keep the individual tied to his seat, sure that he has the real world on his screen. Dream keepers, games, and fantasies, distant lands and abbreviated times appear on it. The computerized individual, the "internaut," is the galley slave of today. And he doesn't know it. He lives a prisoner of a delicate "virtual" network that he believes is "real." That's why his chains and shackles are also "virtual." That is to say, imaginary. Never have humans been more subjected and exploited by another human than today. Because the gap between some humans, the rich, and other humans, the poor, has never been greater. Their own measures show it.

The natural human is lost; now you can only speak; as does a supposed Gubern of the electronic man, the *Homo electronicus*, a ghost, like a cloak, superimposed on a body made of flesh and bone and blood and nerves that lives prisoner of its new armor, interconnected to other armors also made of vibrating electrons. This is the true "network," the electronic network. A spiderweb that doesn't connect them, as they believe, but traps them. They can no longer live without this invention that they have constructed just barely two centuries ago. The network that was born from them is their new habitat. Their new nature. Their new ecological system. It means that with only one of the elements of the world, the electrons captured in storage batteries, or channeled, directed, by cables and waves, they believe they have resolved the problem of surviving. And if their creature has already escaped from them? If it already dominates and directs and imposes on their lives? If they've become prisoners of the monster that they wanted to dominate? Listen, girl, two centuries ago, when humans were barely beginning their experiments with electricity, there was a woman, a supposed Mary Shelley, who warned about what was going to happen later in a famous story, *Frankenstein*. I'm not exaggerating. The monster has now escaped and governs the human world. The slave imprisoned by his electronic screen is the example.

20

The *Homo electronicus*. The electronic man. The human who has invented an "ecological" system of electromagnetic waves in order to exist. Cables and wireless connections: millions of devices that function thanks to the incessant flow of electrons and directed waves that feed them. A perfect barrier to isolate him from true Nature. Such is the "ecology" of the *Homo electronicus*. Without it the actual human can no longer survive.

Listen, girl: think for a moment, that one day the electronic flow will cease in all his current devices. Think of the human without his motors, heaters, lighting, refrigerators, radios, radars, telephones, televisions, cars, planes, and the millions and millions of inventions that use electricity to operate. You, a Neanderthal, if you can consider it. An actual human cannot. It's unthinkable. That for him could never happen. Whoever dares say it they'll judge as crazy. However, it will happen. When the great melting begins and their dams and great hydroelectric centers flood and collapse; when, on a planet that is every day hotter, each fuel tank is a threat, a bomb that many desperate people will willingly explode; when they discover their portable batteries to be the poisonous chemicals that they are; when the wars over water and other basic elements, the air included, begin, don't doubt it girl, it will happen. Maybe you or your offspring, or the offspring of your offspring, will see it. Because it will happen. It's already too late for the humans. There's no turning back.

21

Facing the imminence of their apocalypse, the most conscientious try to unite, to create activist groups. But if you look at human history, those will fail, just like all their communities. Because each human group carries the seed of its own destruction. As soon as the objective—almost always a common enemy—disappears, the group turns against itself: the factions appear; the victim and the executioner come out of their lairs; the saint and the warrior too, and always the master and the slave. And the group boils with contradictions on the inside. The warrior will never understand the reasoning of the saint; the saint will never understand that of the warrior. A neighbor tells me stories about the company where he works. Another about his ministry. Another about his sports club. I, in teaching at a school, I see all the rivalries every day between the other teachers, the small hell that reigns there.

Of course, in general, humans try to organize themselves like all the members of the animal kingdom: in colonies (like the bees, termites, and gorillas). But in contrast to others, they always disband each grouping that they construct; they don't set limits on them (and that is my key word), on individual actions or on the collective possibilities, and they destroy, like always, their real scale, their possible group.

Across the world, or globally like they say today, they are fulfilling their nonsense. Now that their planet is running out, they think that they can jump its great shore and colonize other planets: it's easy to predict the monsters that they would engender on them: raised at other gravities, at a different aridity and at extreme temperatures, their bodies will mutate. They will be others: humanoids that will curse their earthly parents, and of course, given that their bodies will be different, their intelligence will be also. The humans will have lost them forever. Their definitive extinction awaits them.

I'm not saying that that future is already arriving. It can take a few centuries. Or, who knows, only a few decades. And then, another history will begin, that of us, the Neanderthals. We will see, then, not only the last humans become extinct (and maybe we will help them to die well), but also what they have constructed: we will let a wild vegetation grow over their cathedrals, skyscrapers, and highways. Like what has already happened with their pyramids. We will let their flying machines rot from the elements, their books disintegrate; only their works of art will endure—like the paintings of Altamira and others, very few others, I assure you—like unique traces of what once existed. And only then will we inhabit a concrete world, with the real times and distances that all the species—except the human species—recognize and respect well.

It is certain that I won't be able to see the extinction of the human species. I am old already and I must die. I won't do anything to impede it. I trust in the natural pharmacopeia, in the natural remedies that each live body keeps inside itself. Because each organism has its own. The proof is that immunological systems exist and antibodies with them. And, furthermore, there's instinct. The little sick animal that eats dirt is looking for the minerals that he lacks. The one that devours grass—alien to its natural diet—knows that it needs certain carbohydrates and proteins to get well. I will do as they do. Just as the other Neanderthals have surely done, to not lose what humans have lost forever, instinct, the instinct of inclusive survival. When my hour comes, when all those aids fail, I will let myself die. I will have fulfilled the bidding of my species. Not forcing the limits of what was assigned to me as a useful life. I won't be a heavy burden for anyone. That, I believe, is already part of our instinct. The messages of adaptation to the changes of the world already are in the child that you carry in your womb. And in all the others that I have engendered along the way.

Facing the sad spectacle of human demise, on my solitary nights I say to him—to a human who will never possibly hear me—in my mind, as always: do something for your species, limit your imagination so it doesn't contradict the real world and transform itself into insanity; limit your wealth to what you can control so it doesn't become abstract and you no longer know nor enjoy what you have, because another suffers the lack of what you have in surplus. Limit your power so you don't become only a servant of it; defend your idea of Good without causing another to see it as another of the multiple forms of Evil; understand the scale in which you move, the human scale, don't break it, don't transgress it, because you will cease being human and will die as a species.

These are, of course, useless cries that only serve me in proving that I am not human and that already it is too late for them, for those who are human.

Because the only way they would have to stay their end, to understand themselves and understand what they call their history, would be that of trying to place themselves outside of their human conscience—not from their "pure reason" but outside of it, looking at it from another place, as though it belonged to one of the other species with which they poorly coexist. In short, putting themselves in the place of a Neanderthal, for example.

That which, in principle, is impossible.

22

Girl, the moment to say good-bye has arrived. Now we have to return to the human homes that house us. Me to my older wife, to the children that she already had when I married her, to the gray job in which I occupy myself, the classes I give where I teach to the little beasts, perfectly ordered at their desks, the future that awaits them. You to your young husband, father already of a child that isn't his.

Your little one will have more luck than I did. One day, seven years after you abandon him in some human home, you will tell him the truth. His true condition. Like my mother did with me and yours would have done with you had you known her. And so, he'll be prepared to face what can already be seen coming: that which, by way of their own genetic searches (DNA, etc.), in little time the humans will achieve: the discovery that we, the Neanderthals, have been coexisting with them. It will be a difficult moment. But it is no longer a moment of great hunts. Soon they will see that we are not any threat to them. Maybe they will accept us as another of their ethnicities. In any case, I am convinced that we will also survive this difficult passage. We will survive. Or better: we will survive them.

One of them wrote a while back that, for humans, life is a dream. Another of ours will repeat it in the future: yes, you dreamed your lives: your imagination was your end.

Selection from

There Are Monsters Out There

EDMUNDO PAZ SOLDÁN

Translated by Adele Lonas

Edmundo Paz Soldán (b. 1967, Cochabamba, Bolivia) is a novelist and literary scholar at Cornell University. This excerpt is from a new novel that focuses on the politicization of a future pandemic. It narrates the confrontation between a president who privileges the economy over health and a ministry with a very regionalist identity that rebels against the decisions of the central power.

I listened to Tomicha's podcast while getting up. My mother had prohibited me from listening to it, saying he was a fairground charlatan, someone who changed doomsday on a whim and still had followers: the world would end in ten months, he said a few years ago. Now he was claiming that the idea was what was most important, not the exactness of the dates.

I agreed with his first two commandments: to preserve the life of animals and plants and insist that Nature has a value beyond its utility. The other two were more complicated: to withdraw from the world and build a shelter. *If you withdraw from the world they'll say you let yourself be defeated. They'll say you're obligated to fight for world peace or the climate or the end of bad times, that to fight is better than renouncing. Ignore them and embrace the old spiritual tradition of withdrawing from the fight. Abandoning everything not in a cynical way, but with an inquisitive mind.*

A friend of my mother's had been in the Tomichá commune. She told us that letting yourself get infected by the bug was part of the ritual, those who survived were seen as beings capable of facing the challenge of a new world in which we weren't central. She was there one month, she lived with that hairless man who had won all the awards in his field but at twenty-nine abandoned the university disappointed in his students because they were incapable of recognizing the change that was coming. He worked as a cook at a nursing home, stopped using banks, and carried wads of money wrapped with rubber bands in his pockets. One day he went to live in the mountains with a tent and a sleeping bag. Soon after he posted on the internet *Ecology for Dark Times*, an eighty-page manifesto that gathered together a thorough work on the destruction of nature with apocalyptic declarations and numerological prophecy. Despite this or maybe because of it a cult was created around him. He mistrusted the state and claimed that only a universal citizenship would save us. When the bug arrived he created a commune of two hundred people in the mountains and called on them to disobey the law that prohibited gatherings of more than ten. We aren't afraid of the bug, he said, we'll learn to live with it: we want the bug, now. The authorities of The Star prohibited people from getting close to the commune under threat of jail, but by the time they reacted it was too late; there was talk of sending in the military and taking them out, but in the end nothing happened.

My mother's friend said that Tomichá had a cruel sense of humor and was brilliant. But she couldn't get over the deaths of so many followers who had gone to the mountains to intentionally seek out the bug, so she abandoned the commune.

Sometimes I walked to the bridge with my ball below my arm and looked at the mountains: the trees seemed to hang over me, and the birds screeched in the treetops as though they were preparing an attack. It still wasn't night and the stars were already appearing. A constant wind circled the guard house then dove deep into the river, smelly and swampy with waste. It was frightening. I heard, or thought I heard, a buzz that shook me and shook the walls and roofs of the houses, and the bells of the churches and the statues of the plazas and towers of the Governor's palace: the bug that weaves its web, I thought, that prepares its net to continue covering the world with its embrace. In the middle of a row of trees a gap opened up, one of the many horse trails crossing the mountains that led to the dispersed indigenous communities in their territory—my mother's grandparents were from there—and to the logging camps.

I camped once in the mountains with my parents; I wondered if one day

I would be capable of going to their deepest reaches. Maybe I was brave or irresponsible or simply curious. In the meantime, I listened to the podcast: *True change only begins with renouncing. Renouncing to prevent the machine from continuing its advance is the right position. Action isn't always more effective than inaction . . .*

Tomichá had followers everywhere. They refused to pay taxes and disobeyed the government; they didn't use face masks or practice social distancing. That's why they often ended up in jail.

When Elsa Acosta rose up, Tomichá refused to support her and there were abuses in the towns. Acosta's people in Nieves urged Tomichá's people to join them. Urbina, the strongman of Tomichá in the town, was wounded and they took him away. He was found dead a few days later. They said that Acosta was really surprised but it was known that that death couldn't have occurred without her permission.

Some got scared because they believed that Tomichá had supernatural powers. Would he send the bug after Acosta? That death had been a mistake.

There were followers of Tomichá who were intimidated and changed to Acosta's side. My mother didn't believe they did it willingly: following Tomichá was a profound commitment.

Santos Ruiz didn't join Acosta. He was from Nieves. My mother's voice would tremble on remembering him: she was friends with his older sisters, she would see him in the patio of their house, barefoot or with his shoes untied, reading or playing alone, inventing mysterious characters for himself to populate his days. In jail, every day they took him a paper and said if he were to sign it that would be enough to get out free and join the revolution. He refused and would utter strange and shocking conjurations. He would say he was a friend of the *suinos* and that they were at that very moment incubating countless different bugs. Humanity's future was full of bugs, one would come every year until they wiped out everything.

They ordered Santos Ruiz to be killed but no one wanted to do it. My uncles tried to intercede and asked for him to be freed. Fifteen days passed. In jail, he read the same novel over and over: *The Three Musketeers.*

One day Santos Ruiz's sister appeared at my aunt and uncle's house. They're going to kill my brother, she said. Her braids were flying in the wind, her black silhouette impressive.

There were three shots at one in the afternoon. My mother was pained when she found out: each death pained her but that of the boy from her town in particular. They told her that Santos Ruiz had shaved two hours before they killed him so his sister wouldn't see him unkempt. Once he was facing the ones who were going to kill him he begged them not to shoot him in the face and explained how they should give him the coup de grace. He said he would have preferred the embrace of the bug to this boring death. He said that true change only began with renouncing. He said that action wasn't always more effective than inaction. My mother grew quiet and couldn't continue. I wondered if she would forgive Acosta.

Metallic and scattered. His resounding shouts, clear, sometimes smooth and vibrant. Tomichá's voice thundered on the podcast. It could be heard from a great distance, his lungs as though of steel. Tomichá was all voice because he never appeared on television, there were almost no existing images of him, only those archived, obtained from the universities where he had studied and worked and from the lost sister who had a grudge against him. I could be convinced of his insanity but there was something in his endeavor that captivated me: *The future presents itself with a strange combination of ongoing collapse, that will continue to fragment nature and culture, and of a new wave of high-tech solutions to control us, biological passports in a failed attempt to prevent the inevitable. Nothing can break this cycle unless there's a thorough reboot of everything like we've seen so many times throughout history. The bug should take us to a lower level of civilizing complexity. The perfect storm is brewing. You're wasting your time if you have a big plan to construct a future world based on science and rational argument. If you try to live in the past, or if you think that the machine can be revamped or domesticated or if you believe that you can get out of the mess with new ideas or technologies, the same. You have to be honest about our infinitesimal place in the great cycle of history and about the things that we can do and the ones we cannot.*

Tomichá issued a statement on his podcast: *we don't understand the bug because we don't understand that it's not being alive and not being dead at the same time challenges us. We live in its world and we must make peace with it to continue. There is no point living on your knees and in fear. The solutions aren't in the government, no leader will liberate us from anything if we don't break the attachments within us. We should adopt a planetary perspective. By only defending the state we don't get anywhere, by only trying to understand the country we don't get anywhere. All the organs and fibers of the earth should be of concern to us, we shouldn't destroy any creature of the universe. There was a time when this forest was full of other animals, but they disappeared. While we are alive we shouldn't let anything or anyone go extinct. Only then will beauty return.*

My vision wasn't global. Neither could I live without fear. Some phrases from Tomichá would come to me, then I would remember what I knew about his commune and the countless deaths from the bug, and I would disregard them.

Ugly rumors arrived of what was happening in Tomichá's commune. The government denied that they had entered the mountains with tractors and bulldozers to help them build a cemetery; they didn't have any idea where the commune was. No one from the community nor any health workers would venture to go there taking the foot paths used by animals that might carry the bug.

One morning I read that a group of scientists from the capital had gone into the mountains to start an investigation on the origin of the bug. The scientists advanced little by little into the mountains. One group would travel five hundred meters, act as a lookout to ensure that the path was clear, and then give the order for the other group to advance. In an interview the head of the expedition said that the most difficult part was advancing with the protective suit on in the extreme heat. His intention wasn't to get to Tomichá, but he did know where the commune was. He had found it on past expeditions.

—There's a legend that they live underground, in caves. I'm taking this opportunity to refute that. They live near the bat caves; I told Tomichá that that could alter the ecosystem and he responded that no one took care of it better than he did.

Vicente drew the scientists as beings arrived from another planet entering the mountains; he interpreted the legends mother told us and said they had fallen to the Earth on facing another collapse of the sky. I told him that was impossible, if the sky were to fall again it would be the end of the world for us. Maybe it is, he said, and started to cry. I want father, he begged in a frightened voice, and I hugged him, pleading with him not to start throwing things or hit his head or have a seizure. How would his little head live through the desolation of these months? I also realized how heavy it was for me but I dealt with it because there was nothing I could do, I had to help my mother with Vincent. I would have time to explode later.

I saw on the internet again the scientists entering the mountains. They sent photos and messages of their route along the narrow paths. They spoke of immense bumblebees and warblers smaller than normal, dwarf trees and giant trees and trees with petrified trunks as they entered further into the mountains. The photos showed twisted trunks, bark overrun by mushrooms and lichens, clusters of trunks and branches that appeared to be used by people to protect themselves under them.

On the second day the communications began to fail. On the third a scientist reported he was wounded:

—We were drinking water from a creek when there was an ambush and shots were fired from within the trees. Two of my partners are dead. They came and searched our pockets and took the equipment. They left me for dead. I don't know where the rest are.

Nothing was heard for days. There was talk of going to look for them but no one had the courage. A week later the head of the expedition informed us in a video of various details:

—We've lost two. The rest of us are safe and we're already returning. We couldn't get to the caves. Tomichá's commune no longer exists. Tomichá no longer exists.

The expedition reappeared along the same path they had taken to go into the mountains. The ambulances took them to the military hospital. There were no more declarations; the government prohibited them from talking. On the internet people were saying that Tomichá was an alien; that in the commune there was a ritual of collective infection that ended badly; that Tomichá was the scientist guilty of freeing the bug as part of a process of population control ordered by the seven families who owned the planet.

A drone filmed a section of a cemetery with graves recently excavated in the depths of the mountains. Tomichá's body was never found. There was no more commune. There was nothing more.

The Journey of the Muchka

ULISES GUTIÉRREZ LLANTOY
Translated by Adele Lonas

Ulises Gutiérrez Llantoy (b. 1969, Colcabamba, Perú) is a sanitary engineer and storyteller. *Muchka*, a Quechua word, refers to an Andean mortar. The many layers of meanings connected to the mortar become tools for understanding a revival of Andean culture under the threat of globalization in Perú.

I called thinking of getting rid of the *muchka*. I was going to accept whatever offer just for them to take it. Depending on its size, its state of conservation, and if it's original, we can pay up to two hundred dollars, he told me, by cellphone, a guy with a French accent I had contacted through a newspaper ad in which he offered to buy them. An ad that was hidden in a corner of the section "Various" of the Sunday edition and that I randomly found and read in the waiting room of the mechanic who was perpetually repairing my car. The word "*muchka*"—written like that, in Quechua—stood out, raised its hand, navigating alone in the middle of a sea of words in Spanish; as soon as I saw it my retina focused on it: "I buy *muchkas*. Will pay good price."

The offer of two hundred dollars surprised me: Not only was I going to get rid of the *muchka* but also they would pay me for it! Excellent!! I answered, without hiding my conformity. I agreed to meet in two days.

What could the Frenchman have meant with that "if it's original or not," I wondered on hanging up. Could there possibly be fake *muchkas*? Could you forge a stone mortar? I laughed to myself and went to look for it in the small space that served sometimes as a laundry room in my reduced apartment. Ignored, beside the trash bin, and covered in dust under the wash sink, the *muchka* lay upside down in a corner. Useless, fallow, abandoned.

There it had remained since the day my grandmother appeared, knocking on my door, dragging it inside a nylon sac as someone would a steel ball. It's a gift for you, son—my grandmother said, you're the one who deserves it the most, and she handed it to me. I tried to refuse it, of course. No grandmother, I can't accept it, I said. It's your *muchka*, only yours. How could I take it from you? I'm offering it to you son, it's for you, she insisted. I tried to make more excuses, but she insisted again and I had to accept it. I ended up promising that I would care for the *muchka* just as my grandmother had cared for it. She was going to live in Australia with her oldest daughter, my mother's sister, who had lived there for years, and in the drawn-out task of saying good-bye to Peru, to family, her things, she had spent her last days in Lima visiting her daughters, grandchildren, cousins, uncles, neighbors, friends, auctioning off her things, divvying up wares, getting rid of her knickknacks. The *muchka* was for me.

It was in the way in the apartment. Whenever I wanted to store anything under the wash sink, there was the *muchka* to prevent it; if I moved it to the cleaning room, to the bathroom, to any hidden corner of the kitchen, to beside the plant stands, it ended up being in the way even more. So I decided to get rid of it. The first time, I took advantage of the deserted mornings: I put it in a sac, covered it with a bag from the supermarket, and abandoned it on the first floor next to the building's trash when I left for work. That night, on returning, I saw that the garbage truck had taken everything else except the sac with the stone; I left it thinking that someone else would take it, hoping that a confused waste recycler could put it to use. I waited for the waste recycler to pass again but nothing; the *muchka* was still there. The porter approached me on the third day, that the neighbors were complaining, they knew the bag was mine and so I had to carry it back up to the apartment. The second time, at the suggestion of my wife I tried to break it into pieces to throw it out piece by piece, but it was the handle of the hammer that broke first and I couldn't find anything else to destroy it with.

I took the *muchka* out of its corner. I had two weeks of vacation from work, my wife was away from Lima due to her work at the bank; I was taking advantage of those days to get repairs done on the car, paperwork, improvements to the apartment I had put off, and so I rescued it from its exile under the wash sink. The dust and lint from its neglect had covered the surface until almost completely hiding its true texture and color. I dusted it, washed and scrubbed it with detergent, and dried it; I left it clean, upside down and right side up, I ensured that even the nooks and crannies were free of dirt, ready for the meeting with the buyer.

The day of the appointment I went by car. I exited Jesus Maria toward San Borja, to the agreed-upon place, and at the pedestrian crossway between Cuba and Arquipa, at the moment when I saw an old lady crossing the avenue at the stoplight, I began to wonder what my grandmother would say if she were to find out about the deal. What would I tell her? What lie would I invent to justify that the *muchka* was no longer with us, that she no longer belonged to us? For the first time, doubt set in about getting rid of the stone, but then I thought about how useless and cumbersome it was in my small apartment and that it was better to give it to whoever could really use it: in a kitchen, in a restaurant. I remembered the offer: two hundred dollars. If one day my grandmother were to return and ask for her *muchka*, I would invent some story; that I had lent it, that I had given it to a friend who enjoyed cooking, that he would return it soon. I was selling it.

I arrived at the place, a restaurant in San Borja. It was still closed and I rang the doorbell as the Frenchman had said. A tall, fat, bald man with abundant eyebrows looked through a window after a few minutes.

"Hi, I'm the one with the *muchka*," I said.

"I'll open the door for you," he responded with a smile.

He stretched out his hand, courteously, as if we already knew each other or were to have already done business before and he asked me to show him the *muchka*. He accompanied me to the car where I had the stone, I took off the nylon bag that covered it, and he picked it up to his shoulders like someone carrying a baby.

"Aha!" he said. "Black, well-carved."

He turned it over, inspected it with curiosity, and then returned it carefully to the floor of the car as if the mortar weren't of stone, but of crystal.

"Nice. How old is it?"

I quickly calculated its age.

"At least fifty years old," I said.

"You can tell."

He patiently felt the edges of the mortar, like a blind man reading braille, and then with the same patience, continued with the inside walls.

"With these stones you can tell the age in the polish of its walls," he said. "They're like wine: the older the harvest, the more ideal taste it will leave on the palate."

His response left me without a response; never before had I heard anything like that about the *muchka*. Not even my grandmother, in her most desperate defenses to leave it with me the morning when she brought it, had she proclaimed such virtues.

"And the *ccollota*?" the Frenchman then asked, interrupting my thoughts.

"Sorry?" I responded, pretending to not understand.

"The *ccollota*," he insisted, with an almost perfect pronunciation in Quechua, and fitting his right fist against his left palm.

He was referring to the stone that always accompanied the *muchka*. An oval rock the size and shape of a turkey egg, a stone sufficiently big and heavy that fulfilled the job of grinding together with the mortar. My grandmother had left me the *ccollota* also, but in being small, it was a while ago that someone had gotten rid of it and we hadn't seen it since. No explanation occurred to me to offer the Frenchman.

"Ah! Of course!" I said. "Excuse me, please, I must have forgotten it at home."

I lied. I thought it was something I could easily get later.

"Okay. You'll bring it later then."

"Yes, of course."

"And so tell me, how did you end up with this *muchka*?" he then asked with interest.

"It belonged to my grandmother," I said.

"Wait," he interrupted. "Come in, please, and let me offer you something to drink while you tell me everything: a thousand stories can fit into fifty years."

I followed him to the kitchen. The cooks and helpers were at work, the kitchens blazing already since these hours of the morning. He prepared an aguaymanto and melon juice in the corner with the blenders, while he told me about the dedication that his business demanded, as well as about the ascent of his restaurant and the gastronomic fusions that he had achieved. Of how he had established himself in Lima after travelling through almost all America: "from Canada to Argentina".

"Now, tell me the story," he said after serving me a second glass.

"See, my grandfather had some land in San Pedro Cachora, in Abancay. To the south," I said, with the intention of locating the town on a mental map of Peru.

"Don't worry," he interrupted, "I know that area and almost all of Peru."

"When he died," I continued, "my grandmother was alone and so my mother and her sisters decided to bring her to Lima. A difficult task because my grandmother had lived almost all her life in that town and she refused to leave her land. When she finally accepted, she sold everything she could, gave away the rest, and was soon ready to live in Lima. But the move led to another problem because the things she wanted to bring with her were countless. She moved over the course of I don't know how many trips. We had to take turns among various of her grandchildren, children, and relatives to accompany her on one journey after another to and from Cachora. Since I was getting ready to go to college and was the oldest of the grandchildren, I accompanied her during the last trip of her move."

I told him the story of that haphazard trip.

We left Cachora early, almost at daybreak, in a rickety truck to Abancay to go from there to Lima. Despite my protests, my grandmother was taking more luggage than necessary; my mother and my aunts had warned me to omit anything beyond her clothing, but the day of the trip I found myself surrounded by sacs with potatoes, corn, and meat for the family; a box with utensils, pots, and mementos that, according to my grandmother were necessary, essential in Lima. Among those essential things was the *muchka*, wrapped up in its own sac, as though it were making the move to Lima on its own. It was toward the end of March, I remember; in the Sierra it had rained a lot and the highways were a dump of water and mud. On the route from Abancay to Chalhuanca, a landslide caught us. The mudflows had devoured various gorges, entire stretches of the highway had disappeared and it was impossible to continue; such that, to get out of there and be able to transfer to the buses camped on the other side of the landslide and continue on to Lima, you had to walk close to a kilometer along various paths also muddy, narrow, and dangerous. The passengers that decided to continue were forced to only take with them the most basic luggage, the most valuable, and to abandon the rest. We had to give away the potatoes, the corn, the meat to a few truck drivers who had been stuck there for days, and we abandoned the utensils and the dishes, the rest of our burden. Everything, except the *muchka*.

"Grandma, it's only a stone!" I told her when she refused to abandon it on the side of the highway.

"No. It isn't a stone, it's a *muchka*," she promptly responded, upset.

She picked it up from the road despite the mud. She insisted that we had to take it with us. I'm not going to carry it Grandmother, I said, and so she took the sac and hauled it over her shoulder. I had no option; I had no choice left but to give in: I lugged the blessed stone for an endless kilometer!

"It was like carrying the platform of The Lord of Miracles," I told the Frenchman.

"I can imagine," he said laughing.

"I'll never forget that trek. My grandmother told the story of the *muchka*, the story of how the stone had come to her."

My grandfather had brought it from Písac. He was a merchant and traveled frequently between Cuzco and Abancay, in the fifties, during the era when traveling to Cachora took various days and was done by caravans of dozens of mules, horses, and various muleteers. My grandfather had studied and lived in Cuzco in his youth and had many friends there; one of them was a famous stonecutter in Písac, with whom he had gone to grade school. When my grandfather asked him for advice about the best anniversary gift for my grandmother, the stonecutter asked him: How's your wife's cooking? Better than my mother's, my grandfather answered. Then we'll give her a special *muchka*, one made by me, the stonecutter told him. He took close to half a year to finish it in his workshop in Písac.

During the trek to transfer, with the stone on my back, my grandmother told me that story. She told me that, among the many things that my grandfather had given to her, the *muchka* had been the one she remembered most.

"She cooked like the gods," I told the Frenchman. "I remember so well her *cuyes chacatados*, her *rocotos*, her *ccapchi*, those dishes with ground herbs that they prepare up in the sierra."

"It's that grinding spices in a *muchka* is the best way to extract their flavor," he said; "and as I was telling you, for that, antiquity is fundamental. You can have a *muchka* made now: they take the stone, they carve it and polish it. But the final shine of the stone, the ideal surface, no file can achieve it other than the years: the friction of stone against stone, *ccollota* against *muchka*."

"Yeah, of course," I said, as though I actually knew that.

"The *ccollota* that you have is just as old?" he asked with interest.

For a minute I thought of telling him the truth, telling him that I didn't have the *ccollota*, but at this point of the interview it seemed stupid to risk my credibility, admitting that I had lied about the stone egg.

"Yes," I responded. "It's the same one that my grandmother always used."

"A *muchka* without a *ccollota* is like a violin without a bow," he joked.

He stood up. He took my empty glass with the intention of offering me another juice, but I begged him for just a little water instead. We toasted the *muchka*.

"I'll come on Friday more or less at this time and we can close the deal," I said, thinking that in the next few days I could find a substitute *ccollota*. One of my aunts had to have an extra one, I thought, I had seen them at their house the many times I visited them.

I returned to my apartment thinking about the offer. I imagined telling the story to my wife on her return, spending the money on something for our apartment, something to spoil her for her two months of pregnancy. I called her by phone, we chatted about how her trip was going and what I was doing, but I didn't tell her anything about the *muchka*, I wanted to surprise her.

That night I called my mother and two of my aunts. I asked them if they happened to have an extra *ccollota*. Oh, son, those things aren't used anymore, my oldest aunt said. Are you crazy? I've had my *ccollota* since I was single, the youngest said. God only knows what your sisters have done with it, my mother said.

I called my sister. She didn't have it either, but she told me that once she had seen them for sale in the artisan stores of Miraflores, on the first block of Petit Thours; the next afternoon, I went there. I asked among the vendors if they had a *ccollota*. I had to explain to them what it was and what a *muchka* was, but no one had any idea what I was talking about. Only one guy with a scraggly beard could tell me anything:

"You aren't going to find those things here. Maybe at the markets of La Marina."

I went there, but I didn't find anything there either. I remembered the comment "a violin without a bow" and thought that once again, I wouldn't be able to get rid of the *muchka*.

The solution was in finding a stone egg, I thought; one that was black like the *muchka*. But how? Where? Could I find and replace it with just any round stone? I remembered Ventura, a friend who had studied with me in high school and who at the annual gatherings of former students of *Melitón Carbajal* would usually talk with passion about his work as a geologist. He wasn't necessarily my closest friend, but he would surely help me.

I got his number thanks to another friend. I called him, I told him the story of the *muchka* and the truncated deal due to the missing *ccollota*, and asked if I could take any stone in the shape of an egg and where could I find it.

"I'd have to see what kind of rock you're talking to me about," he answered. "Not all stones have the same resistance. Not all stones can handle blows, frictions. How are these stones?"

I didn't even know how to describe the *muchka* and the *ccollota*.

"A stone, well, no?" I responded. "A crappy mortar and its round stone, like an egg, that's used to grind spices, those kinds of things."

"I meant the surface of the stones. How are the surfaces?"

"Black stones. Hard. Smooth."

"I'd have to see them. If you want, come to my house tonight. We can have something to drink, talk, and take a look at it."

I went to his house in Los Olivos. It had been years since I had gone to this part of the city and I had no idea of the horrid traffic that awaited me. I went first to the north to arrive on time at the agreed-on hour, crossing through the center of Lima, entering the Caqueta bypass, and after on the Pan-American Highway, cursing the idea of having accepted making the trip. In the middle of the twisted and rushing river of cars, at every complication along the way, regretting going, wanting to forget everything and go back home, the same question kept repeating itself: What the hell am I doing? Why not leave the *muchka* how it was? Or better yet: Why not throw it away once and for all in one of those trash lots along the side of the road?

I arrived at Ventura's house. He received me, intrigued by the stone; he had consulted some history books: the *muchkas* were artifacts that the ancient Peruvians used since time immemorial, pre-Incan; he asked me where I had it.

"It's in the car," I said.

He accompanied me to the car. He took off the nylon sac, observed it from all sides and upside down. He tapped it with his knuckles and turned it like a rudder.

"It's an andesite," he said. "Black andesite."

I didn't understand. For an economist like myself, that sounded like Chinese.

"And that, what does that mean?" I said.

"Igneous rock, intrusive," Ventura said, still analyzing the surface of the *muchka*. "Or rather, those that were formed from pure lava and cooled at great depths in the earth's crust," he added, sensing my confusion. "The greater the depth, the more uniform the color, the harder and more resistant, like this one," he said, hitting the stone again with his knuckles.

He explained that the hardness and resistance of andesite was one of the greatest. Sacsayhuaman, the Cathedral of Cusco and a great part of the walls of the Incan cities were constructed with this type of stone.

"Or rather, you mean that I have to go to Cusco to get a rock like one of these?" I said laughing.

"No, no. You can find it all along the Andes Mountain range, from Venezuela to Patagonia, that's why it's called andesite, because of the Andes Mountain range."

"What I need is a round stone, a stone egg that fits this mortar," I said with the hopes that he would help me to solve my problem, that he would just tell me how to find the *ccollota*.

He explained to me that the ground in Lima was a cemetery of spherical rocks, of "stone eggs," as I called them. For millions of years, the rocks broke off the mountains, the rivers dragged them down from the Andes, they descended rolling and rolling and, as they came into the coastal valleys, they remained strewn along the way, burying themselves in the dirt. That's why the stones were smaller and rounder as they got closer to the sea.

"You want an oval andesite the size of a fist, no?" he asked.

"Exactly," I answered.

"So go to the beaches of Cantolao."

"To Callao? To La Punta?"

"To Cantolao, to the banks of the Rimac River, the Lurin River, the Chillon River, to Costa Verde; in short, to all those pebble cemeteries. There you're going to find, among other rocks, oval andesites of all colors and sizes. Look for one that doesn't have spots, that has a uniform color, black like this one, and done."

The explanation left me calmer. It was an easy task, it was a matter of going to one of those places that he was suggesting and looking for oval stones, "pebbles," as he called them, black and hard, without spots, like the *muchka*, and done. What Liman hadn't seen stones like those before?

Afterwards, he convinced me to have a few beers. We started talking about the same as always, of our days in high school, of the rest of our mutual friends and what had happened to them. But in the end, I listened to more about andesite and the Incan constructions. He gave me advice on how to recognize the stones and even insisted on loaning me a few books on geology.

I glanced at them at home. One explained the classification of rocks, the other explained in detail the physical tests to determine the hardness, the chemical composition of them.

The next morning, I woke up with the memory of a strange dream. I was going on horseback with my grandfather through the ranches of Cachora, he was telling me about the andesite of the snow-capped Salkantay peak, of the canyons of the Apurimac River, of the lost cities of Vilcabamba. I had never dreamt of my grandfather before, whom I had barely seen more than a few times in my life as a child, and I had no further memories of him. But even stranger than that was that he was talking to me about places where I had never been. I attributed the dream to the memories of the conversation with Ventura.

I ate breakfast while reading the newspaper. Someone called my cell phone. It was the Frenchman.

"My friend," he said, "don't forget our appointment tomorrow."

"Don't worry. I'll be there," I said, doubting as to whether to continue with the deal or not because of the *ccollota*.

I agreed to meet him at four, which would allow me to be home before my wife returned from her trip. Afterwards, I began to clean the studio, the library, one of the many pending tasks to do during my vacation. Among my books I found one of those tourist books, one with maps of the highways in Peru. I looked for the one where Písac appeared and I began to follow, on the map, the route that, according to my grandmother and my memories, the *muchka* had taken: Cusco, Abancay, Puquio; Nasca, Ica, Lima: more than five hundred kilometers, including the kilometer that it had traveled on my shoulders. I smiled at the discovery.

I went to the Costa Verde to look for a *ccollota*. I decided to go there because it was closer to home, it was safer than venturing to the mouth of a river. I entered the circuit of beaches going down by Dibos, wondering where to start the search; I slowly drove along the highway observing the sea and cliffs and parked at the edge of Makaha Beach. It looked to me like a good place. Parking was allowed, you could see the pebble beach quite close. It was close to ten in the morning, the day was cloudy and cold, a guy was fishing nearby and a few people were jogging alongside the road.

I went down to the beach. The sea came in and out leaving behind the clean stones, it dragged them out a few centimeters, it returned them to their place. I took a stone and then another to look at them up close, to analyze them how, surely, Ventura would have. I had been there before on that beach, countless times; however, it was the first time that I noticed the variety of colors, textures, and weaves that the rocks had. There were blue-greens, grays, blacks, cherry red; with spots, without spots, with holes, without holes, smooth, rough; each one different from the other in tone, in spots and texture. I looked for an oval one, but I didn't find any; all of them were flat and weren't of any use to me; the friction of stone against stone in the eternal coming and going of the sea had polished their faces until transforming them into circular stones, flat like coins. The stones that separated from the sea, in contrast, maintained their roundness; as I moved farther away from the sea and got closer to the highway, to the cliffs, the stones became oval, spherical.

I went toward the cliffs. I examined one stone after another, but all, on being dusty and dirty, looked the same to me. I tried to search a few more times and abandoned my quest when I felt that I was being observed. Some of the people passing by jogging or in their cars were distracted watching me fishing around among the rocks at the foot of the cliff; a police car slowed down then stopped for a few seconds to watch me, but then continued on its way. I was embarrassed. I felt ridiculous trying to find a black andesite as though I actually knew about these things, as though I really were a geologist; a stone that, furthermore, I never would have the certainty of what it really was and that, surely, the Frenchman would find crude and fake. I started to walk toward the car. I stopped at the edge of the highway waiting for traffic to clear to be able to cross and I looked up at the cliff. The wall of stones, steep, high, vertical, like a rampart. I noticed the cluster of round stones embedded in it; millions of round rocks, oval like eggs; big, medium, small, of all sizes, peeked out of the wall as though waiting for their turn to fall, as though they had spent their life watching the sea. I remembered then the route that the *muchka* had taken, the route that the maternal side of my family had taken, migrating from Cachora to Abancay, from Abancay to Ica, from Ica to Lima. I thought of the things that my mother, my aunts, my grandmother shared about each one of those cities where they had lived, what they meant to them. I felt that I myself, despite having been born in Lima, of only having lived in Lima, in a certain way was one of those stones, one of those pebbles that had arrived stumbling down along the river from Cachora to stay, finally, in Lima—to stay by the sea.

So I returned to the car, filled a gallon jug with sea water and returned to the cliff. I washed the stone eggs that I felt would be of use to me. I selected about fifteen and discarded them as I rubbed them, one against another, to see which of them would remain scratched up—when you scrape two rocks together, the harder one leaves scratches on the softer one, Ventura had told me. I kept four stones, the four finalists of the scratch test and that, in my judgment, qualified as *ccollotas*; those that had remained intact on being thrown against the bigger rocks; more advice from Ventura to test their resistance.

I returned to the car. I chose one of the *ccollotas*, the blackest, smoothest, and most oval, and put it inside the *muchka*. I looked at them together. I knew that they weren't the original "bow and violin," but it was the summary of my family: the original *ccollota* was indefinitely lost, the same as some customs from my branch; but the *muchka* still remained, the true one, the hard one, the unscathed one, the indestructible one, like my memories of Cachora, the memories of my grandmother, the memories of my family. On arriving home, I parked the car in the underground lot, took out the *muchka*, and took it up to the apartment on my shoulders again.

When my wife came home, she asked me what the *muchka* and *ccollota* were doing between the blender and the microwave. I told her the story. You're crazy, she repeatedly told me, laughing. In the middle of the story, I realized that only a few months remained before our first wedding anniversary, that I should offer her a gift. What could encompass her, the son we were expecting, the family that we were forming, more than the *muchka*?

Dedication For the Gutierrez Morales family and their fifth generation

Selections from

Runa

FOGWILL

Translated by Adele Lonas

Rodolfo Enrique Fogwill (1941–2010, Quilmes, Argentina) was a short-story writer, novelist, poet, and businessman. His work was a continuous challenge to established literary traditions. These short texts describe the customs of an almost extinct civilization or perhaps a future culture in which technology does not control daily life.

TO FLOAT

Women don't float. That's why you have to lay them on log rafts to cross the river and creeks going down to the plains. Either a woman's body weighs more or the water of the rivers and creeks doesn't want it because it fears it will be poisoned by the blood it releases.

Children don't float. If they fall in the water, they make swimming movements that they learned watching the adults, but their heads sink them, and they drown. On becoming just old enough to hunt, make a spear, and get a woman, the males can begin to float. At first the water doesn't recognize them, that's why they have to celebrate it, splash it with their legs and explore the bottom of the rivers while holding onto the mane of a diver. Only once the water becomes familiar with them will it allow them to float.

The great blue water of the sand country is different. Not even the best diver should try to submerge himself in it. The great blue water doesn't want the men of the huts and it marks them an area of white foam that they shouldn't cross.

The great water allows those from the sand country to cross over and fish riding in their logs beyond the white foam. But if a man from the huts tries to follow those fishermen, the great blue water will create strong tidal currents that will carry them far away from the sand, and not even the best of the divers will be able to return.

LEARNING AND TEACHING

You can't teach how to make catgut the way the village of huts and fires makes it. It's prohibited to tell the secrets of the preparation and the smoothing of the intestines, of the stretching, the drying, the cutting and twisting of them. But even if someone were to master all the steps of the process and wanted to teach them, it would be difficult to find anyone in another village willing to wait the three full summers needed to complete the work. The peaceful villages don't need catgut for their bows: hemp thread is adequate. And among the warriors, there's never enough patience to learn this type of time-consuming work.

When someone visits the snow country and learns the language, the leaders ask him for the secrets to preparing softening juices. Teaching it isn't prohibited but something happens in the snow country that prevents even the best preparation of fruits, roots, and mushrooms from fermenting. An even soup is obtained, but it never produces bubbles. It's easier to bring the leaders a bowl of juice up from the plains than to waste days waiting for the mix to ferment at high elevation.

And the leaders of the snow village, the same who order killed and mummified those who obtained the juices and drank them in their land, they drink from the bowl in secret and soften like boiled mutton entrails.

In exchange they teach the secrets of mummifying: how to cook the cadavers, how to empty out the viscera and bones through the holes in the neck, how to dry and dye the skin, and where to get the leaves and seeds with which to prepare the juices to wash what remains inside and out.

Those who return come back knowing everything and confident of being able to replicate it in the land of huts and fires. But until now there's been no one who could replicate it here. They did it there and one even brought his own mummy to show he had learned, but it's possible that for the same reason that in the snow country the mushroom, roots, and sweet fruit juice won't bubble, on the plains and in the land of huts and fires you can't finish the task of making a mummy that looks real without it rotting covered with mold and holes made by the worms that enter and leave it and eat everything on their way.

THOSE OF THE PLAINS ARE OURS

No one knows how they survive the winter. There are animals that burrow themselves and sleep and might have taught it to the men of the plains. They are few and they don't sing. The women and the children belong to everyone. They're poor hunters and their spears are twisted branches. They have few cutting stones, and they lose them. Or better said, when one of them dies or disappears, everyone cries and jumps for days and no one worries about recovering the cutting stone, the spear, or anything else that he might have had that would still be of use even though the owner has died.

They keep everything buried in the ground and they forget where they buried it. That's because they don't have huts, tents, or caves for everyone. They don't want to learn: they watch the hunters and warriors of the huts and fires and they laugh and shout, but they don't copy them.

They see one of ours following the tracks of a ram on the plains, and they in turn follow him and celebrate when he kills his prey and carries it, with the sticky blood running down over his shoulders. But they don't know how to follow a track. That's to say, they don't want to believe there was a track. It seems they live convinced that the track is made by the hunter as he advances in circles crouching down every now and then to smell the grass or turn roots over.

No one adopts children from the plains men and there is no swapping of children or women with them. They don't come to the huts and fires because they haven't learned to scale the cliff. Those of the plains aren't named in songs brought from elsewhere, nor in celebratory, marching, or war songs. That's why it's as though they don't exist. No warrior would ever kill anyone from the plains, nor taste any of their meat.

COUPLING WITH ANIMALS

There are villages that couple with animals. It's not that the men live with the animals as though they were their women. That happens in all the villages. They couple with them by lying on top or by sitting on an animal and making their feet walk for them or by jumping wells and ditches so big that not even they, running, could jump. Before, near the sand country there was one of those villages that would come down from the red mountain at the beginning of every summer. They no longer come now. Maybe the animals took them to another place forever. Since they were never seen again, it's impossible to know. And when you don't know, anything could have happened. You believe me? Here, no one was able to couple with an animal in that way. The hunter Oiás made his wife raise a bear cub along with their children. And the bear cub ate the food they ate, slept in their huts next to them and their children. She was gentle and obedient and even learned, in summer, to shit and pee behind the reeds, like the children. But in winter she would go into a burrow and wouldn't go down to the plain where they carried her a few times tied up, asleep. Later, when the snow was melting, she began walking and obeying again. Bears grow slower than people and this bear grew big much later than Oiás' oldest daughter. The bear would eat all their food and sometimes escape and bring them pieces of a dead deer, or wasp hives that she took down from the tallest trees. Bears grow slower than people but eat more than a whole handful of people. They should have eaten her beforehand. When she stopped growing, Oiás and his son, who is now also a hunter, started to sit on her, but they never were able to get her to take them where they wanted to go. No one knows the language of bears and one summer when there were many males pursuing the females and the fish along the cliffs of the creek, the bear went with them, following a bear in heat as if she were a male, and she never appeared again. They had even given her a name, a female name, not a bear's name. Now they think also that it would have been better to have eaten her when she was fat and tender.

Those who had come down from the red mountain to the sand country coupled with animals weren't riding bears nor deer but big animals, with a big mouth, that instead of having feet like bears' feet, they had paws as though from clay, similar to the hooves of goats but big and round. They spoke to them in their own language and the animals obeyed, opening their enormous mouths and taking them wherever they wanted to go.

WHERE THEY COME FROM

It's known. The old women don't. The sages do, the leaders do, they know it. The women and even some children know where they come from. The warriors don't care. You all come from the birds of brilliant stone, from the air. Those birds that move through the sky and on passing, a thunder is heard that echoes in the mountains: birds of brilliant stone with long wings near the head and short ones at the tail. Wings that almost don't move but shine and inside carry feet on which they stand when they touch ground, running more than the deer and the tigers along the ground, making thunder, a noise that frightens all the birds; of a size that frightens all the birds, all the animals and the men.

They don't come from the plains, nor from the mountains beyond the snow country, nor from the sand country or the great blue water. The old women say that beyond the great blue water there is another sand country and after, mountains and beyond that, other plains, other sand and another big blue water that you have to cross to find other countries with plains and villages. But if it's from there that they bring those enormous birds of brilliant stone it must be a country with mountain-sized trees, with branches as high as the mountains. Not even the warriors want to know that country. They frighten with their thunder and the enormous things out of brilliant stone that they make there. That's why they don't eat you all nor even kill you: because inside you come full of fear.

EXCHANGES

Let them believe what they believe. What someone believes can't be known. It's always more important what a man wants than what he can or wants to believe. And it's even more important what he does. Look at what they do. What's that one doing? You see him: he always walks by whenever we're talking. Now he's going to crouch down at the entrance to the hut where the two old women live who no longer have husbands. He's going to try to make you believe that he's telling them about something that happened or that's about to happen, or a secret of the *buúlg* or of the warriors and he does it so you'll believe that he knows, and you'll start to ask him and will also give him things. He must want your brilliant cutting stones, the green transparent stones that are put over the eyes to look at the sun, or those sticks that you use to paint words, those that can paint on your note boxes and on stone but that can't paint in the air, in the water nor in the dirt. They are things that everyone wants, hoping to be near you when you die to keep some of those things. Kill him, no, because the leaders already ordered that no one kill him and that they teach him to speak. The elder *Aúmm* said that it is written in the sky that when you learn to speak you'll make the bird of brilliant stone come again laden with more things to exchange and with gifts for everyone. For everyone, no: for the leaders. The gifts are for the leaders. It always has to be that way. They decide afterward what they should share.

SPEAKING OF THINGS

The same happens when you speak about the colors. It seems that you all have more colors than things. Here we have the blue of the sky that is the blue of the great blue water, the green of the plains after rain, the color of blood that is the same color as the earth, the color of white things, and no other colors are needed for anything, and even less for speaking. If there are different things and they are the same color, they are recognized by their shape, by their smell, by the purpose for which someone wants them or by the name of their owner. The name of the owner is always more important than the color when people speak of the things they want. And of the things that no one wants, if they aren't harmful, it's not worthwhile to speak of them.

SENSOR

. . . you don't look at others in the eyes nor are you able to tell what he who talks with his eyes, hands and nose tells . . .

BATTLES IN THE SKY

The leaders see the sky because they always walk in the night to talk among themselves without being seen nor heard. That's why they know more than the men. But the old women who don't sleep know more than they do. You're going to stay and when winter comes, you'll see if they tell the truth. They said that along the stars' longest path an extinguished sun passed that laid two seeds that will make it rain two times before winter. Hopefully that's true. Those who don't sleep watch over the sky and if there is a battle between stars, they run to wake up the warriors to warn them. Then the warriors watch over. It's been a while since there were any battles in the sky. When there are battles in the sky a star might escape, and after it follow stars that sometimes lose their way, slip from the sky and fall. That's where the birds of brilliant stone come from that land on the plain. The warriors always wait for them to fall and they go out to find them in the mountains or plains. The brilliant stones are the best at cutting because they cut the meat of trees and the meat of animals, but they can also cut other stones and are useful to make spears, arrows, and the points of fighting sticks. You have a lot of brilliant stone because you bring it down from the sky with your birds of brilliant stone. If you name them "metal" as you do, it's impossible to know what they are. "Brilliant stones" means that they are made with parts of the light from the sky and that they are hard and last forever, like the stars that battle and battle and never die. With the way you all speak it's impossible to understand what's true. Saying like we do here, brilliant stone, we know what it is and where it came from.

YOU CAN'T HAVE EVERYTHING

You all deceive by putting your names on things and using names that aren't the true names of things. Those of the plain, who forget everything and almost never speak, always lie. Those of the snow country lie to deceive, and so that no warrior or traveler will know where they hide their grains and the deer mummies and the *patapeludas*—the Bigfoot—that they keep in the snow to eat in the winter. Those who travel to trade lie to get more and, sometimes, to eat a part of what they should take to the village of huts and fires. But everyone knows and says the true names of things and when they lie they don't forget what the true name is. You all lie without knowing the truth. That's why the women laugh when you come down to ask them something, and they say anything in response. And that's why those of your country come and ask as if they wanted to know what they don't need to know. But they don't want to know. They want to have everything in their voice boxes and paint the noise of the words on their note boxes. And they can never have everything. And if they had everything, they still would have nothing.

They Will Dream in the Garden

GABRIELA DAMIÁN MIRAVETE

Translated by Adrian Demopulos

Gabriela Damián Miravete (b. 1979, Mexico City) is a writer, editor, and scriptwriter. She also works as a culture journalist, writing about literature and film for publications including *Letras Libres*, *Lee+*, *Cine Premiere*, and *Confabulario*. Her book of children's stories, *La tradición de Judas* (The tradition of Judas), illustrated by Cecilia Varela, was awarded the Premio de Cuento en la Feria del Libro Infantil y Juvenil de la Ciudad de México. In 2010, she won a Jóvenes Creadores grant for narrative and wrote the short-story collection *Pequeños naipes de ópalo* (Little opal playing cards). In 2012, she was a finalist for the World Fantasy Award for her story "Future Nereid," which was featured in the anthology *Three Messages and a Warning*. Her essays and stories have been translated into English and Portuguese. This story proposes a not-so-distant future, focusing on a garden of holograms programmed with the data from thousands of murdered women. Artificial intelligence allows those women whose lives were taken to create a dialogue with visitors and raise their awareness of femicide.

Long and short-term goals:
—Get into swimming
—Work hard to pay school enrollment fees
—Scrape up money for El Cervantino
—Build the closet
—Paint the house in September
—Buy the dining room chairs
—Buy some shoes
—Read Plato
—Talk to and be friendly with people

Handwritten note by Erika Nohemí Carrillo
(in a photograph by Mayra Martell)

The orange trees will be heavy with fruits, and their flowers will fill the humid air of the western garden. A silky fog will cool the ends of the grass, of the herb grown from that meadow. The sun will always come out behind the almond tree and the branches of the oldest tree, a stocky *ahuehuete*, will extend first toward its rays, lengthening like a girl who wants to stretch. Around nine the garden will become populated with silhouettes. Some will greet each other. Others will be frightened by the falling of an orange, and they will run away laughing toward the shadow of other leaves. Some more will look toward the sea that, beneath the slope that elevates the western garden over the beach, will roar and will extend enough to climb up to the grayish blue of the sky.

The assistants will check that everything is in good condition to receive the visitors, because in the mid-morning many groups of first-graders will arrive accompanied by their Teachers, some of them still apprentices. They will come out of the vehicles between tiny shouts of excitement and stumbles. The apprentice Teacher will warn them "No running!" with a girl in his arms who had fallen asleep during the trip, her mouth half-open and cheeks colored.

The Caretaker of the garden, a smiling old woman with a steady gait despite using a walking stick, will give the assistants the rigorous recommendation: support the apprentice Teachers at all times, accompany the children in their emotions, have the snacks ready at 2:00, every hour distribute water to slurp. Later she will quicken her step and stand at the front of a long line of children who will sing thunderously and off-key in a joyful procession on the pebbled path before arriving at the western garden. Some children will lose the rhythm, one girl will get distracted by a lizard hidden beneath a rock, and the apprentice Teacher will have to guide them again to the path, mark their steps, their palms. The small steps will be heard in unison over the gravel. The children's laughter will float in the air, mixed with the scent of honey and the salty aftertaste of the breeze. The temperature will be very pleasant, a comforting warmth.

Before the tall brass bars that shelter the garden, the party will stop. A pair of Teachers will continue entertaining the children, the rest will turn to listen to the warnings of one of the garden assistants.

"As you all already know, the idea is to let the children interact with them and intervene only when necessary. Do not be afraid of the reactions of the children or try to limit them, they are part of the educative process. We will be close by and aware of what they need at all times."

The brass doors will open slowly with the magnetic key that The Caretaker carries like a necklace. The infantile ruckus will disperse through the western garden until the children notice the presence of *them*.

The silhouettes will shine with pearly glimmers that will enchant the visitors. They will be made, as in all the old tricks, of lights and mirrors, a complex mechanism that will remain hidden to the visitors. In the open air they will possess a subtle transparency which perhaps will permit a view of the landscape through them, but even taking a closer look will make one appreciate their defined features, they will seem solid, *alive*. Beneath a tree will be the ones who study; moving from one side to the other the ones who play; sat on the grass the ones who speak to others. Upon moving too fast they will emit a tenuous gleam which will leave in their steps a brief luminous wake.

The Caretaker will walk toward the apprentice Teacher, who will continue juggling the sleeping girl in his arms and the boy who hangs on his leg like an anxious dog.

"Do you need help? You could share a bit of that love," she says to him as she opens her arms as if to receive the girl.

"Thank you. Maybe one of the assistants could help me check if I have something on my right leg. Oh, it feels so heavy! What could it be? I think I've been climbed by a Tommy!"

The boy in question will be so entertained by the joke that he will cling even more to the game. But finally one of the assistants will take him with her. The Caretaker and the apprentice Teacher will observe them getting lost between the rest of the people and the silhouettes.

"You're very kind. I'd like to take this opportunity to tell you that it is a true honor to meet you, ma'am. Your work in . . ."

The Caretaker of the garden will smack her lips and with a gesture ask that he not continue, because she will find the recognitions uncomfortable for reasons more than mere modesty. But as she won't want the guy to feel scorned, she will take him by the arm so that they can walk together.

Marisela, better known as The Caretaker, was born in September of 1985 in Veracruz. She was the last of three children. Her favorite memory of that time was to hang out the laundry in the sun with her mother: the smell of soap, the sound of the fabric as it extends, like the wings of a bird, and also the games of her mother, who disguised herself as a ghost hiding under the bedsheets to scare her. This way they forgot the daily routine, which was heavy. Every day Marisela and her mother served the food and ironed her brother's shirts, which they wore to the movies when they had time, on special occasions. One night, in her relatives' house, one of her mother's brothers entered the room in which she slept. She didn't know exactly what it was the man did standing there next to her in the darkness, because she was too small to understand it. She got the impression that her uncle was squeezing what he had between his legs like a wet rag. She was scared but she never told anybody. And she felt guilty of keeping a secret. When she was fifteen she and her mother moved alone to Mexico City. Marisela had to get a job to support them, first in a shoe store. Her boss soon wanted *something else* from her, he said it spitting into her ear, between the stacks of merchandise in the stockroom, smelling of new leather. She refused. In the truck ride home she was so worried about what would become of them that she didn't realize until much later that the man had put his hand between her legs. Thanks to her uncle (the one who had done *that* in her room), she started working at a Big Telecommunications Company. At first it was simple to answer telephones and push buttons, but then technological advances complicated everything. They said goodbye to many girls who didn't know how to use the new machines (among them, to a friend of hers who was also from Veracruz, Paquita). She decided she would take all the available courses. At night she studied the functions of cables and computers, of mirrors and laser lights. She wanted to learn the function of what the company called "the image of the future," holograms. She got the highest grades in her classes. She got promoted. Married. She had kids. Her husband was "a good man" (being a good man meant he washed his own underwear and cared for her and her daughters if they were sick and made dinner once in a while and almost never reproached her for spending too much time outside of the house).

The Caretaker and the apprentice Teacher will observe a typical scene: the boy will run, will play at touching the silhouette and immediately take away his hand.

"Hey, don't do that, Thomas! You don't even know her yet. Greet her, tell her your name first." The tone of the assistant will not be one of reproach and she will be able to ignore the pouts of the boy produced by the electric current.

The apprentice Teacher will want to approach Thomas, but The Caretaker will hold him back.

"Surely this touching thing wasn't around in your time. The first thing the kids tend to do is go through them with their hands, but upon crossing the meadow, the system emits a current. The stings aren't very pleasant, but they're tolerable. They always think twice before putting their little hands in again. The instruction at all times is that they treat them just like people of flesh and bone."

"Okay." The apprentice Teacher will then furrow his brow, considering a new problem. "But what if they want to touch them?"

The Caretaker will offer him a melancholy smile.

"They can't. It's part of the lesson."

It will be a little hard for the apprentice Teacher to understand why. But finally he will admit to its logic: the dead will never be able to receive our caresses again. Not even them, even though they're "back."

One morning Marisela arrived to work and was met with the news that Paquita had been murdered in Mexico State. Her body was found recently thrown to the sidewalk, like people do when they run over an animal. They had done horrible, horrible things to her.

Paquita had gripped in her fist the keys to her house, the place to which she hoped to return. She had used them to defend herself. What if she were heading down the wrong path, they said, what was she doing alone at that hour? But what if she were on her way to work! said the Teacher, and if she were walking on the "wrong path" (*and it would be your fault, because you fired her*, although she didn't say that) what, she deserved it? The rest shrugged their shoulders. They quickly continued minding their own business. But she still could not stop seeing the absence of Paquita, nor the corpses of one and another and another woman. There were too many. And all of them, in the eyes of decent people, seemed to be at fault for what had happened to them. They didn't even recover their names in the footnotes of the newspapers: "Drug Addict Murders His Mother," "Ex-Girlfriend Slain out of Spite," "Woman Who Reported Rape Killed for Being a Gossip."

The key will be in combining the dynamics of play and conversation to maintain the children's attention. The Teachers will seem affectionate to communicate security. And although they will keep their distance, they must be within reach at all moments.

"Hello, what's your name?"

"Thomas, but everyone calls me Tommy. What do people call you?"

"My name is Ruby Marisol, and everyone calls me Ruby. What pretty eyes you have, Thomas."

"My mom packed cookies in my lunch, want one?"

"I would, but I can't eat."

"Why not?"

"Because I don't have a body like you." She joins her hands in front of herself with her palms facing upward and then slides one through the other, passing through them. "See? But we can still talk."

The boy will be perplexed. He will try to do the same, and then will want to touch Ruby's silhouette, but he'll remember that the sensation is not pleasant.

The apprentice Teacher will seem to become uncomfortable with the situation. The Caretaker will try to alleviate the tension.

"Do you remember the first time you came here?"

"Yes. I never forgot. I was ten. But bringing them at this age seems dangerous to me. They don't yet have all of the cognitive tools to understand the significance of this place, we haven't told them the meaning of death, just of the death of all of them."

The Caretaker will listen attentively. Meanwhile she will observe the numerous tiny white butterflies that will fly around the silhouettes, the children, the flowers. They will look beautiful, but she will not stop asking herself if they won't be, perhaps, a plague.

One day they found the body of Dulce, who to be able to pay for her computation classes on the weekends worked Monday through Friday cleaning offices, among them, Marisela's. Dulce's friends (most of them were barely just girls; they weren't even fifteen) started to meet every Tuesday to remember her and to practice punches, kicks, slaps, whatever kind of defense would protect them. The first days they finished the sessions with red faces, disheveled and sweaty, crying together from pure fear or pure courage. After a couple months they laughed a bit more, punched harder and finished the training by eating something sweet to recover. They searched for a name. They liked The Gossips, because that was a word that people used to judge them, to tell them to conform, that they'd better be still and shut up. One evening Marisela came to the door and asked to join the group. Those girls taught her to kick well with her stockings and uniform and everything, to throw her elbows, to be brave and to cry in good company.

"Why don't you have a body?"

"Because it was taken from me. I'm dead."

Upon detecting the boy's silence, the silhouette of Ruby will emit more concrete answers.

"That means that I can't eat, or play, or kiss my mom."

The boy will look around, as if searching for some key. He will look toward the sea and then he'll study the appearance of his interlocutor.

"Are you a ghost?"

"No. I'm a memory. Like a photograph."

"Like a video of before?"

"Yes, exactly that. Thomas, do you have grandparents?"

The boy will ignore the question.

"Why were you killed?"

"I don't know. Why do you think it happened?"

Thomas will think of the answer squeezing his lips together, furrowing his eyebrows.

"Because you did something bad. Maybe you made someone really, really mad."

The silhouette of Ruby will consider those options.

"It wasn't my fault. It was they who did something very bad."

"They hurt you?"

"Yes."

"And your mom made it better?"

"When you're killed, it can't be made better."

The Gossips made a pact: they would take care of each other. Girlfriend- or daughter-beaters, abusive bosses? They'd find out if they could take all of them at once. When one of them asked for help, the rest would show up en masse to make it clear to their aggressors that they would not leave her alone. They grew until they formed an army made of women of all ages who went where their presence was missing. They started to appear in the news, to be considered, to give advice.

The years passed, and the friends of Dulce, those prep-school girls, turned into mature women who made people listen, who demanded justice. People learned to look at them with respect, and that respect was slowly extended to the rest of the women like the humidity of the waves of the ocean reaching the hot, distant sand.

Marisela got older too. She kept working at the Big Telecommunications Company, in her laboratory of mirrors and laser lights. She saw her daughters grow up, she saw her mother die, always accompanied by her friends. A longing emerged in her. She had a plan.

The apprentice Teacher will also notice the white butterflies, the unpredictable dancing of their flight, the aroma of flowers and salt that will float in the western garden. The Caretaker and he will enjoy all of that during an activity in which the assistants will have the children sing a very old song, one that will talk of planting a seed, and leaving it to grow in peace, and knowing to wait to see what it turns into.

"You're probably right," The Caretaker says to him in response to his worry about the age of the children. "And the people who decided to start bringing them at earlier ages were also probably right. Learning that there are different paths of life, that there are alternatives to violence, takes time. Better to start immediately, I guess." The Caretaker shrugs her shoulders.

"You don't sound so sure . . ."

"I am. It's just that, in the beginning, the objective of this place was different."

Marisela's plan consisted of obtaining resources to construct the holographic memorial that she designed along with The Gossips and other organizations who carried a reliable record of the victims. Every one of the murdered women, with her body and her name, would be replicated in a three-dimensional hologram using testimonies and materials provided by their relatives, friends and, above all, the information recovered from their personal email accounts and social media: photographs, videos, letters, conversations . . . everything would be used to recreate in the most precise way their voices, their movements, their reactions; to, in some way, *bring them back to life*. If they got enough money they could use the more advanced technology that allowed them to set up the system in the open air, in nature. Maybe in a garden by the sea. It would have to be a beautiful place, the closest thing to a paradise that they could give to them and their families to remember them alive and happy.

The apprentice Teacher will imagine the placid memorial that this garden once was. He will appreciate the idyllic scenery with its trees and its beach, the peaceful wandering of the silhouettes.

"The place is just as pretty as I remembered. There are more trees, sure, the ones we planted have grown. Everything is very well conserved."

"It's true," responds The Caretaker proudly. "Although I don't know what's more astonishing: that its beauty is being conserved or that it's being conserved even though it's *in Mexico*."

The apprentice Teacher will laugh more because of the ease with which she says these things than because of the joke itself: he will not consider it implausible that Mexico could keep anything in good condition. Between her generation and that of the apprentice Teacher there will be an abyss.

"It must be surprising to you how the country has changed. You've seen it all."

"Well, I'm ninety-four years old. If I hadn't seen it all, I'd ask for a refund on my admission ticket."

"I imagine that that era must have been terrible."

"Yes, it was."

There was a time when nobody called them *silhouettes*. Their families came to visit them and they felt almost happy. The Caretaker saw The Gossips' wish fulfilled when the mothers and fathers, and the brothers and sisters, and their friends, saw them inside the garden, *alive*, smiling. They felt the joy that justice had not been able to give them. As is natural, many families disappeared with the passing of the years, pulled by the river of life, by their chores, their loved ones. But some did not return because the garden did not compensate for them in any way. "It's not them," they said.

The problem is that Marisela had been naive: it wasn't possible to make up for everything. For some they barely had a name, a blurry photograph. Of others there were only bones. From those who had left an ample testimony of their path through the world there were almost perfect, precise holographic replicas, but even then: a life is a unique weave, a thread within a great tapestry, and if it breaks, the thread that replaces it will not by the same. It isn't possible to patch up their flesh, blood, breath, learning, desire. Their future.

When few families were left, the State decided that the memorial should serve an additional function to earn the right to permanence. It would serve as an educational space against violence. The younger population would come, mandatorily, to learn the history of the murdered women of Mexico with the purpose of it never happening again. The Caretaker would understand the intention of this change, and what's more: as part of The Gossips, she would believe it necessary. But she detested feeling like they were being used. She refused to reprogram them, to convert them into textbook chapters. She cried and fought to keep them intact.

In the end she had to do it so their memory wouldn't disappear. From that point on the silhouettes would have to repeat to the children, time and time again, that they were dead.

"The country came out on top because of people like you, people who never tired of demanding justice."

The Caretaker will make another incredulous gesture.

"There's no merit in that. It was the only thing we had left. So much horror left us with no purpose, no meaning. Conserving the memory was the only way out."

"At least the deaths of all those women were good for something."

Clinging to her cane, The Caretaker will turn brusquely to respond.

"*Good for something?* For what? To teach us that we're a horror? We already knew that. It's one thing to voluntarily give your life for a cause and it's another to be killed for it. Which would you like more? That your life had been good 'for something' or to have lived? Bite an apple, smell the rain on the dirt, know the sea. I don't know. As I get older I think that transcendence is overrated. It's a comfort of fools, a comfort for the living, but not for the dead. If they could really speak (*them*, not the silhouettes), what would they say to us? 'Listen, it's nice that my death was good for something, but I didn't want to die.' This," she said, extending her arms and the cane, as if trying to encompass the whole garden, "is not enough. How can I fix the damage? Can you imagine that at one time they piled them up in a tower of anonymous bodies? Can you believe that they were blamed for their own deaths? Nobody can imagine the pain they experienced in their final moments, and you all, the young, don't know the horror of knowing that those who did it weren't monsters, it wasn't Jack the Ripper: they were their classmates, their boyfriends, their relatives, the friendly taxi driver that you chatted with yesterday, the police officer on the corner. It was the world, an environment that made us beauty queens while they kicked us in the ribs, and called us crazy if we complained. It was that horrible."

The apprentice Teacher will listen to the reprimand without looking at her face. He will look at the children, who will keep digging holes in the dirt, singing the old sowing song.

"I'm sorry, it's true. Of course they didn't die in vain." The Caretaker gave a long sigh before continuing. "The anger it caused us to lose them was the start of it all. We rose up, repeated their names in the streets, we got to change the path. They were the wind that propelled the sail of this boat, of our future. I just wish that we had learned before the lesson, that all of them could have kept living. That they could have had, at least, the possibility of doing what they dreamed of."

The apprentice Teacher will look in her eyes and agree respectfully. He will note that many silhouettes listen to the children who are singing and even applaud them; others continue about their business mechanically, somewhat estranged from the present tense, trapped in the programming of the tasks that they themselves decided on a long time in the past, when they were alive and confessed, in many spaces of online life, what they liked, to what they were dedicated, or what they wanted for the future. He will rummage in his memory:

"You know what I want to do? Study to be an engineer." Mariana Elizabeth had said that to him when he was a ten-year-old boy (he never forgot her name).

"I don't really know what that is."

"Someone who builds things, like bridges or machines."

"If you study, my mom says that when you grow up you can do whatever you want."

"I'm not going to grow up because I'm dead. But how I would like to . . ."

The seed song will finish. He will ask the children to gather up everything and say goodbye. They will react in different ways. Some will start to cry, some will say goodbye with an indifferent gesture. A pair of girls will want the silhouettes to keep their drawings.

The apprentice Teacher will have to approach Thomas because he will sense his confusion: he will be there, looking at the nothingness. Before he takes a step, the boy will wrap his arms around the silhouette, and feeling nothing, he will hug himself inside Ruby's luminous silhouette.

"I want to hug you because it's really mean that they killed you. I want to hug you because they hurt you and left you all alone."

Tommy will feel the electrical currents through his whole body and will resist them until the apprentice Teacher takes his hand, separates him from Ruby.

At six in the evening the sun will begin to hide itself in the western garden. The visitors will have to go just as the darkness arrives, which will make the silhouettes even more beautiful. Their luminous colors will stand out, refined and clear, before the nocturnal sky. They and the children will wave goodbye, and for The Caretaker everything will have the appearance of a movie from way back when, where everything was happy and the people on the dock waved goodbye to the boat setting sail, and there was music and streamers.

The assistants will make sure that everything is clean and in order before leaving. Marisela, who will insist until the end of her days that she be the one who leaves last every day (they call her The Caretaker for a reason), will wander around the garden as is her custom, making a sound with her cane on the stone paths, recharging every so often by a tree.

With the magnetic key that she carries on her chest she will lock the brass doors that separate the control room from the garden. The silhouettes will sleep by the sea, lying on their sides, mouths half-open, hands under their chins or over their laps, a nice illusion that occurred to her when she updated some of the systems, an image that day by day allows her to stop the motors without feeling that she unplugs them, that she erases them, that the world will once again be without them. Just like that, it will be like she turned off the lights so they could sleep after telling them a story. Oh, if only life would allow her to finish the program that will make them dream!

But Marisela, just like The Gossips, is very old, and there is still so much to detail. Others will have to finish it and take the risk of putting it into action. During the day they will be heroines, silhouettes, memories, they will say that they are dead, but the nights will be theirs. They will construct what was taken from them. In the garden they will dream of their future.

Marisela will watch them sleep. And then she will press the button. The silhouettes will shrink until they become miniscule points of light mixed up with the stars that hang over the sea. After a bit everything will be dark without them.

"Rest, my girls," The Caretaker will murmur. "Rest."

Selections from

Moving the Water

CAMILA FADDA GACITÚA

Translated by Roberto Forns-Broggi

Camila Fadda Gacitúa (b. 1969, Santiago, Chile) writes poems that focus on nature, courses (riverbeds), woman, and water. Her verses create waves that go deep and then expand on the surface. She introduces being-river as a possible future.

WOMB

Nor light nor shadow nor noise
not a thing moving.
Quietness and silence and water
without above without beneath
without vertigo nor gravity.
Nothing that could stay raised
nothing that could be torn down.
Nor cold nor warmth nor hunger nor thirst.
Just
liquid and beat.

GRAVITY

Tossing the word hard
to sink her into the softness
it's a serious act that affects
expansive and silently
all the loving territory
encompassing from very much here
how far a heart is lost
over there on the other shore.

Imagine yourself on your shore
imagine the word as stone
imagine the softness as water
and gravity as gravity.

It can't fall without affecting
not without moving the water from my shore.

5

NORTH AMERICA

Introduction

KURT CAVENDER

For most of the past two centuries, North American literature's environmental imagination generally has circulated within and between the entangled, mutually constitutive modes of elegiac pastoralism and apocalyptic fatalism. This dynamic is our literary inheritance from Thoreau and Melville and their contemporaries, or rather from their solutions to the aesthetic task that confronted them: that of bringing modern concepts of beauty, genius, purposiveness, and the sublime to bear upon the old problem of humanity's relation to the non-human world. Humans are locked in unresolvable antagonism with our environment, this tradition seems to conclude; we mourn the permanent loss of something ineffable when nature's creative powers submit too readily to modern scientific discipline, and we alternately shudder and rage when they do not.

Since the birth of the modern environmentalist movement in the early 1960s, North American literature has increasingly turned its ecological attention from the challenges of colonizing, pacifying, and modernizing an unruly continent to the disastrous environmental consequences of this process: the intersecting and compounding catastrophes of industrial contamination, commercial despoliation, anthropogenic climate change, and broad-based ecosystemic collapse. Climate scientists and environmental sociologists often speak of our present situation in terms of a set of ecological rifts—climate change predominant among them but also ocean acidification, stratospheric ozone depletion, loss of biodiversity, and others—disrupting the metabolic relation between human social activity and the non-human world to the point where the depletion and degradation of this world become irreversible and modern society becomes unsustainable. Recent North American literature has increasingly sought to bear witness to these rifts, whether that takes the form of Thoreau's pastoralism echoing through contemporary nature writing from Joan Didion and Wendell

Berry to Jedediah Purdy or reflections of Melville's dark vision in fictions of ecological despair by Margaret Atwood and Cormac McCarthy.

But the texts included in this section attest to another kind of ecological rift, not in the social metabolism between modern society and a broader *oikeios* that sustains it but in the cultural metabolism between the broad multiplicity of ways North American peoples figure their place in the non-human world and a mainstream literary culture that privileges a much narrower set of ecological representations. Bound up as it is with the history of colonization and capitalist modernization, the North American literary mainstream routinely fails to read those communities whose ecological imaginations have been systematically plundered and erased by these very processes. This section seeks to begin to set this omission right—not by offering an exhaustive catalog of neglected or plundered North American literatures but by gesturing toward their multiplicity.

Indeed, abject urban subjects appear regularly in this section in various guises: the Laguna Pueblo villagers begging water from a local priest in order to mourn their dead properly in Leslie Marmon Silko's "The Man to Send Rain Clouds," the north-bound barefoot traveler in Jamaica Kincaid's "What I Have Been Doing Lately," the laid-off night watchman devolving into an ape in David Clerson's "The Ape Within." The term *abject-subject* has been developed by the *Endnotes* collective as a way of pushing back against the expectation that surplus populations are invested by their structural superfluity with any sort of particular revolutionary potential. In contrast to visions of something like a revolutionary *lumpenproletariat*, abjection is meant to highlight how postindustrial economic precarity paired with increased police oppression means various fragments of the population are "cast off, marked as contingent or lowly, without actually being exteriorized," in the words of *Endnotes*. Forcibly corralled into the reservation and the ghetto, the redlined neighborhood and the urban food desert and the migrant detention camp, the abject-subject is the human remainder of capital's self-valorization, internal to the system but having no place within it. And, as the succession of ecological horrors from Hurricane Katrina to Flint, Michigan, to the annual West Coast firescapes demonstrates, the abject-subject is frequently made to cover capital's ecological bill as well.

Under these conditions, the familiar elegy-apocalypse dynamic that has characterized so much North American environmental literature all too easily resolves into a kind of imaginative closure, a paralyzing sense of either nostalgia or futility that paradoxically reinforces the very social-ecological trajectory it dreads. But as the following pieces demonstrate, the ecological experiences of indigenous peoples, migrants, racial or ethnic minorities, and the otherwise socially abject can offer a variety of alternatives to the political dead-end of dystopianism. We encounter one such alternative in Robin Wall Kimmerer's "In the Footsteps of Nanabozho," where indigeneity and myth represent a kind of radical antidote to the environmental destructiveness of the Western colonizing ethic. Kimberly Blaeser's "Growing Things" offers another alternative when an encounter between Western and tribal horticultural practices serves as an occasion for reflecting on potential intersections between science and indigenous environmental knowledge. Traditional agricultural practices, indigenous science and mythic conceptions of the natural world, and salvage and scavenging culture all constitute ways of knowing and relating to the non-human world that are to some extent incommensurable with the valorization of value that impoverishes our imaginations as it orders modern life. Of course, this is why such forms of human and non-human coexistence are always targeted for suppression by colonizing and modernizing forces, clearing the way for value's not-so-long march toward ecological crisis. It is also why it matters that we learn to read certain literary forms and modes—for instance, myth, oral tradition, the dreamwork, the eyewitness account, the personal reflective essay—as potential repositories for a kind of collective ecological imagination that has no place (except as self-parody) in a modern North American culture that has yet to reckon with its colonialist foundation.

Each of the pieces gathered in this section might be taken as one starting point for such a reckoning and, through it, a more robust way of conceiving our relationship to the non-human world. Centering the experiences of the abject-subject, each takes up in some way the question of how our modern ecological regime appears, not to its beneficiaries but to those for whom it has had little use in recent history. Read alongside one another, they give rise to a host of interrelated concerns: for negotiations over the sacred and our relation to it; for what it means to inhabit or belong to a place; conversely, for what it means to traverse a landscape as a migrant or colonizer; for different ways of knowing about the natural world, as well as for their (in)commensurability and instrumentalization; for what social forms care (for the human and the non-human alike) might assume if divorced from the valorizing imperative. Most importantly, they raise these concerns as productive lines of inquiry with no fixed endpoint, unlocking a manifold of hidden pasts, opening onto a manifold of possible futures.

This, then, is the crucial contribution of these pieces to our ecological imagination: that they disrupt the temporal framing of environmental catastrophe implicit in the old elegy-apocalypse dynamic. The ecological crises that will shape our future are not to be located with some atmospheric carbon tipping-point in ten years, they suggest, nor even with the industrial revolution and the emergence of the carbon economy, but with the four-centuries-long colonization of the globe by a set of social relations whose comportment toward the world entail only abstract domination and extraction. We are living inside the catastrophe; everything we know and anticipate and fear and miss—even the supposedly natural ways of being in the world whose loss we mourn—has been contemporaneous within the catastrophe. This is what it means to be modern, and we don't need an apocalypse to tell us this.

WORKS CITED

"An Identical-Abject Subject?" 2015. *Endnotes*, 4 (October): 298.

Clark, Brett, John Bellamy Foster, and Richard York. 2010. *The Ecological Rift: Capitalism's War on the Earth*. New York: Monthly Review Press.

In the Footsteps of Nanabozho

Becoming Indigenous to Place

ROBIN WALL KIMMERER

Robin Wall Kimmerer is a writer, botanist, and professor of environmental biology at the SUNY College of Environmental Science and Forestry. A member of the Citizen Potawatomi Nation, she has authored two acclaimed books, the first of which was awarded a John Burroughs Medal for outstanding nature writing, as well as numerous essays. "In the Footsteps of Nanabozho: Becoming Indigenous to Place" first appeared in her 2013 book *Braiding Sweetgrass: Indigenous Wisdom, Scientific Knowledge, and the Teachings of Plants*. In this piece, Kimmerer uses the indigenous myth of Nanabozho to propose an alternative way of conceiving humanity's place in the various ecologies we inhabit. European settler society is presented as transient in its relation to the earth, and as a culture that could learn from Maple Nation how to adopt a more permanent ecological presence.

Fog shrouds the land. There is just this rock in the half-darkness and the surf, rising and falling with a thunderous roar, reminding me how tenuous my perch is on this tiny island. I almost feel her feet on these cold, wet rocks instead of my own; Skywoman on a speck of land, alone in a cold dark sea, before she made our home. When she fell from Skyworld, Turtle Island was her Plymouth Rock, her Ellis Island. The Mother of the People was first an immigrant.

I'm new here too, on this shore at the western edge of the continent, new to how land appears and disappears in this place with the tides and with the fog. No one knows my name here, and I don't know theirs. Without this exchange of the barest recognition, I feel like I could disappear in the fog along with everything else.

It is said that the Creator gathered together the four sacred elements and breathed life into them to give form to Original Man before setting him upon Turtle Island. The last of all beings to be created, First Man was given the name Nanabozho. The Creator called out the name to the four directions so that the others would know who was coming. Nanabozho, part man, part *manido*—a powerful spirit being—is the personification of life forces, the Anishinaabe culture hero, and our great teacher of how to be human. In Nanabozho's form as Original Man and in our own, we humans are the newest arrivals on earth, the youngsters, just learning to find our way.

I can imagine how it might have been for him in the beginning, before anyone knew him and he did not know them. I too was a stranger at first in this dark dripping forest perched at the edge of the sea, but I sought out an elder, my Sitka Spruce grandmother with a lap wide enough for many grandchildren. I introduced myself, told her my name and why I had come. I offered her tobacco from my pouch and asked if I might visit in her community for a time. She asked me to sit down, and there was a place right between her roots. Her canopy towers above the forest and her swaying foliage is constantly murmuring to her neighbors. I know she'll eventually pass the word and my name on the wind.

Nanabozho did not know his parentage or his origins—only that he was set down into a fully peopled world of plants and animals, winds, and water. He was an immigrant too. Before he arrived, the world was all here, in balance and harmony, each one fulfilling their purpose in the Creation. He understood, as some did not, that this was not the "New World," but one that was ancient before he came.

The ground where I sit with Sitka Grandmother is deep with needles, soft with centuries of humus; the trees are so old that my lifetime compared to theirs is just a birdsong long. I suspect that Nanabozho walked like I do, in awe, looking up into the trees so often I stumble.

The Creator gave Nanabozho some tasks in his role as Original Man, his Original Instructions. Anishinaabe elder Eddie Benton-Banai beautifully retells the story of Nanabozho's first work: to walk through the world that Skywoman had danced into life. His instructions were to walk in such a way "that each step is a greeting to Mother Earth," but he wasn't quite sure yet what that meant. Fortunately, although his were the First Man's prints upon the earth, there were many paths to follow, made by all those whose home this already was.

The time when the Original Instructions were given we might call "a long time ago." For in the popular way of thinking, history draws a time "line," as if time marched in lockstep in only one direction. Some people say that time is a river into which we can step but once, as it flows in a straight path to the sea. But Nanabozho's people know time as a circle. Time is not a river running inexorably to the sea, but the sea itself—its tides that appear and disappear, the fog that rises to become rain in a different river. All things that were will come again. In the way of linear time, you might hear Nanabozho's stories as mythic lore of history, a recounting of the long-ago past and how things came to be. But in circular time, these stories are both history and prophecy, stories for a time yet to come. If time is a turning circle, there is a place where history and prophecy converge—the footprints of First Man lie on the path behind us and on the path ahead. With all the power and all the failings of a human being, Nanabozho did his best with the Original Instructions and tried to become native to his new home. His legacy is that we are still trying. But the instructions have gotten tattered along the way and many have been forgotten.

After all these generations since Columbus, some of the wisest of Native elders still puzzle over the people who came to our shores. They look at the toll on the land and say, "The problem with these new people is that they don't have both feet on the shore. One is still on the boat. They don't seem to know whether they're staying or not." This same observation is heard from some contemporary scholars who see in the social pathologies and relentlessly materialist culture the fruit of homelessness, a rootless past. America has been called the home of second chances. For the sake of the peoples and the land, the urgent work of the Second Man may be to set aside the ways of the colonist and become indigenous to place. But can Americans, as a nation of immigrants, learn to live here as if we were staying? With both feet on the shore?

What happens when we truly become native to a place, when we finally make a home? Where are the stories that lead the way? If time does in fact eddy back on itself, maybe the journey of the First Man will provide footsteps to guide the journey of the Second.

Nanabozho's journey first took him toward the rising sun, to the place where the day begins. As he walked, he worried how he would eat, especially as he was already hungry. How would he find his way? He considered the

Original Instructions and understood that all the knowledge he needed in order to live was present in the land. His role was not to control or change the world as a human, but to learn from the world how to be human.

Wabunong—the East—is the direction of knowledge. We send gratitude to the East for the chance to learn every day, to start anew. In the East, Nanabozho received the lesson that Mother Earth is our wisest teacher. He came to know *sema*, the sacred tobacco, and how to use it to carry his thoughts to the Creator.

As he continued exploring the land, Nanabozho was given a new responsibility: to learn the names of all the beings. He watched them carefully to see how they lived and spoke with them to learn what gifts they carried in order to discern their true names. Right away he began to feel more at home and was not lonely anymore when he could call the others by name and they called out to him when he passed, "*Bozho!*"—still our greeting to one another today.

Today, far from my neighbors in Maple Nation, I see some species I recognize and many I do not, so I walk as Original Man may have done, seeing them for the first time. I try to turn off my science mind and name them with a Nanabozho mind. I've noticed that once some folks attach a scientific label to a being, they stop exploring who it is. But with newly created names I keep looking even closer, to see if I've gotten it right. And so today it is not *Picea sitchensis* but *strong arms covered in moss. Branch like a wing* instead of *Thuja plicata*.

Most people don't know the names of these relatives; in fact, they hardly even see them. Names are the way we humans build relationship, not only with each other but with the living world. I'm trying to imagine what it would be like going through life not knowing the names of the plants and animals around you. Given who I am and what I do, I can't know what that's like, but I think it would be a little scary and disorienting—like being lost in a foreign city where you can't read the street signs. Philosophers call this state of isolation and disconnection "species loneliness"—a deep, unnamed sadness stemming from estrangement from the rest of Creation, from the loss of relationship. As our human dominance of the world has grown, we have become more isolated, more lonely when we can no longer call out to our neighbors. It's no wonder that naming was the first job the Creator gave Nanabozho.

He walked the land, handing out names to all he met, an Anishinaabe Linnaeus. I like to think of the two of them walking together. Linnaeus the Swedish botanist and zoologist, in his loden jacket and woolen trousers, with felt hat cocked back on his forehead and a vasculum under his arm, and Nanabozho naked but for his breechcloth and a single feather, with a buckskin bag under his arm. They stroll along discussing the names for things. They're both so enthusiastic, pointing out the beautiful leaf shapes, the incomparable flowers. Linnaeus explains his *Systema Naturae*, a scheme designed to show the ways in which all things are related. Nanabozho nods enthusiastically, "Yes, that is also our way: we say, 'We are all related.'" He explains that there was a time when all beings spoke the same language and could understand one another, so all of Creation knew each other's names. Linnaeus looks wistful about that. "I ended up having to translate everything into Latin," he says of binomial nomenclature. "We lost any other common language long ago." Linnaeus lends Nanabozho his magnifying glass so he can see the tiny floral parts. Nanabozho gives Linnaeus a song so he can see their spirits. And neither of them are lonely.

After his eastern sojourn, Nanabozho's footsteps took him next to the South, *zhawanong*, the land of birth and growth. From the South comes the green that covers the world in spring, carried on the warm winds. There, cedar, *kizhig*, the sacred plant of the South, shared her teachings with him. Her branches are medicine that purify and protect life within her embrace. He carried *kizhig* with him to remind him that to be indigenous is to protect life on earth.

Following the Original Instructions, Benton-Banai recounts that Nanabozho also had the task to learn how to live from his elder brothers and sisters. When he needed food, he noticed what the animals were eating and copied them. Heron taught him to gather wild rice. One night by the creek, he saw a little ring-tailed animal carefully washing his food with delicate hands. He thought, "Ahh, I am supposed to put only clean food in my body."

Nanabozho was counseled by many plants too, who shared gifts, and learned to treat them always with the greatest respect. After all, plants were here first on the earth and have had a long time to figure things out. Together, all the beings, both plants and animals, taught him what he needed to know. The Creator had told him it would be this way.

His elder brothers and sisters also inspired Nanabozho to make new things in order to survive. Beaver showed him how to make an axe; Whale gave him the shape for his canoe. He'd been instructed that if he could combine the lessons from nature with the strength of his own good mind, he could discover new things that would be useful for the people to come. In his mind, Grandmother Spider's web became a fish net. He followed the winter lessons of squirrels to create maple sugar. The lessons Nanabozho learned are the mythic roots of Native science, medicine, architecture, agriculture, and ecological knowledge.

But true to the circle of time, science and technology are starting to catch up with Native science by adopting the Nanabozho approach—looking to nature for models of design, by the architects of biomimicry. By honoring the knowledge in the land, and caring for its keepers, we start to become indigenous to place.

To each of the four directions Nanabozho wandered on long, strong legs. Singing loudly as he went, he didn't hear the bird's chirps of caution and was duly surprised when Grizzly challenged him. After that, when he came near the territories of others, he did not just blunder in as if the whole world belonged to him. He learned to sit quietly at the edge of the woods and wait to be invited. Then, Benton-Banai recounts, Nanabozho would rise and speak these words to the citizens of that place: "I wish not to mar the beauty of the earth or to disturb my brother's purpose. I ask that I be allowed to pass."

He saw flowers blooming through the snow, Ravens who spoke to Wolves, and insects who lit the prairie nights. His gratitude for their abilities grew and he came to understand that to carry a gift is also to carry a responsibility. The Creator gave Wood Thrush the gift of a beautiful song, with the duty to sing the forest good-night. Late at night he was grateful that the stars were sparkling to guide his way. Breathing underwater, flying to the ends of the earth and back, digging earthen dens, making medicines. Every being with a gift, every being with a responsibility. He considered his own empty hands. He had to rely on the world to take care of him.

From my high bluff on the coast I look east and the hills before me are a ragged range of clear-cut forests. To the south I see an estuary dammed and diked so that salmon may no longer pass. On the western horizon, a bottom-dragging trawler scrapes up the ocean floor. And far away to the north, the earth is torn open for oil.

Had the new people learned what Original Man was taught at a council of animals—never damage Creation, and never interfere with the sacred purpose of another being—the eagle would look down on a different world. The salmon would be crowding up the rivers, and passenger pigeons would darken the sky. Wolves, cranes, *Nehalem*, cougars, *Lenape*, old-growth forests would still be here, each fulfilling their sacred purpose. I would be speaking Potawatomi. We would see what Nanabozho saw. It does not bear too much imagining, for in that direction lies heartbreak.

Against the backdrop of that history, an invitation to settler society to become indigenous to place feels like a free ticket to a housebreaking party. It could be read as an open invitation to take what little is left. Can settlers be trusted to follow Nanabozho, to walk so that "each step is a greeting to Mother Earth"? Grief and fear still sit in the shadows, behind the glimmer of hope. Together they try to hold my heart closed.

But I need to remember that the grief is the settlers' as well. They too will never walk in a tallgrass prairie where sunflowers dance with goldfinches. Their children have also lost the chance to sing at the Maple Dance. They can't drink the water either.

In his journey to the North, Nanabozho found the medicine teachers. They gave him *Wiingaashk* to teach him the ways of compassion, kindness, and healing, even for those who have made bad mistakes, for who has not? To become indigenous is to grow the circle of healing to include all of Creation. Sweetgrass, in a long braid, offers protection to a traveler, and Nanabozho put some in his bag. A path scented with sweetgrass leads to a landscape of forgiveness and healing for all who need it. She doesn't give her gift only to some.

When Nanabozho came to the West, he found many things that frightened him. The earth shook beneath his feet. He saw great fires consume the land. Sage, *mshkodewashk*, the sacred plant of the west, was there to help him, to wash away fear. Benton-Banai reminds us that Firekeeper himself came to Nanabozho. "This is the same fire that warms your lodge," he said. "All powers have two sides, the power to create and the power to destroy. We must recognize them both, but invest our gifts on the side of creation."

Nanabozho learned that in the duality of all things, he had a twin brother who was as committed to making imbalance as Nanabozho was dedicated to balance. That twin had learned the interplay of creation and destruction and rocked it like a boat on a choppy sea to keep people out of balance. He found that the arrogance of power could be used to unleash unlimited growth—an unrestrained, cancerous sort of creation that would lead to destruction. Nanabozho vowed to walk with humility in order to try to balance his twin's arrogance. That too is the task of those who would walk in his footsteps.

I go to sit with my Sitka Spruce grandmother to think. I am not from here, just a stranger who comes with gratitude and respect and questions of how it is we come to belong to a place. And yet she makes me welcome, just as we are told the big trees of the west kindly looked after Nanabozho.

Even as I sit in her still shadow, my thoughts are all tangled. Like my elders before me, I want to envision a way that an immigrant society could become indigenous to place, but I'm stumbling on the words. Immigrants cannot by definition be indigenous. *Indigenous* is a birthright word. No amount of time or caring changes history or substitutes for soul-deep fusion with the land. Following Nanabozho's footsteps doesn't guarantee transformation of Second Man to First. But if people do not feel "indigenous," can they nevertheless enter into the deep reciprocity that renews the world? Is this something that can be learned? Where are the teachers? I'm remembering the words of elder Henry Lickers. "You know, they came here thinking they'd get rich by working on the land. So they dug their mines and cut down the trees. But the land is the one with the power—while they were working on the land, the land was working on them. Teaching them."

I sit a long time and eventually the sound of the wind in Grandmother Sitka's branches washes words away and I lose myself in just listening—to the crisp voice of laurels, the chatter of alders, the whispers of lichens. I have to be reminded—just like Nanabozho—that the plants are our oldest teachers.

I get up from my needle-soft nook between Grandmother's roots and walk back to the trail, where I am stopped in my tracks. Bedazzled by my new neighbors—giant firs, sword fern, and salal—I had passed by an old friend without recognition. I'm embarrassed to not have greeted him before. From the east coast to the edge of the west, he had walked here. Our people have a name for this round-leafed plant: White Man's Footstep.

Just a low circle of leaves, pressed close to the ground with no stem to speak of, it arrived with the first settlers and followed them everywhere they went. It trotted along paths through the woods, along wagon roads and railroads, like a faithful dog so as to be near them. Linnaeus called it *Plantago major*, the common plantain. Its Latin epithet *Plantago* refers to the sole of a foot.

At first the Native people were distrustful of a plant that came with so much trouble trailing behind. But Nanabozho's people knew that all things have a purpose and that we must not interfere with its fulfillment. When it became clear that White Man's Footstep would be staying on Turtle Island, they began to learn about its gifts. In spring it makes a good pot of greens, before summer heat turns the leaves tough. The people became glad for its constant presence when they learned that the leaves, when they are rolled or chewed to a poultice, make a fine first aid for cuts, burns, and especially insect bites. Every part of the plant is useful. Those tiny seeds are good medicine for digestion. The leaves can halt bleeding right away and heal wounds without infection.

This wise and generous plant, faithfully following the people, became an honored member of the plant community. It's a foreigner, an immigrant, but after five hundred years of living as a good neighbor, people forget that kind of thing.

Our immigrant plant teachers offer a lot of different models for how *not* to make themselves welcome on a new continent. Garlic mustard poisons the soil so that native species will die. Tamarisk uses up all the water. Foreign invaders like loosestrife, kudzu, and cheatgrass have the colonizing habit of taking over others' homes and growing without regard to limits. But Plantain is not like that. Its strategy was to be useful, to fit into small places, to coexist with others around the dooryard, to heal wounds. Plantain is so prevalent, so well integrated, that we think of it as native. It has earned the name bestowed by botanists for plants that have become our own. Plantain is not indigenous but "naturalized." This is the same term we use for the foreign-born when they become citizens in our country. They pledge to uphold the laws of the state. They might well uphold Nanabozho's Original Instructions, too.

Maybe the task assigned to Second Man is to unlearn the model of kudzu and follow the teachings of White Man's Footstep, to strive to become naturalized to place, to throw off the mind-set of the immigrant. Being naturalized to place means to live as if this is the land that feeds you, as if these are the streams from which you drink, that build your body and fill your spirit. To become naturalized is to know that your ancestors lie in this ground. Here you will give your gifts and meet your responsibilities. To become naturalized is to live as if your children's future matters, to take care of the land as if our lives and the lives of all our relatives depend on it. Because they do.

As time circles around on itself again, maybe White Man's Footstep *is* following in Nanabozho's. Perhaps Plantain will line the homeward path. We could follow. White Man's Footstep, generous and healing, grows with its leaves so close to the ground that each step is a greeting to Mother Earth.

Growing Things

KIMBERLY M. BLAESER

Kimberly Blaeser is a professor of English at University of Wisconsin-Milwaukee and an MFA faculty member at Institute of American Indian Arts in Santa Fe. She is also an Anishinaabe activist and environmentalist and an enrolled member of the White Earth Nation. Her short story "Growing Things" first appeared in *Reckonings: Contemporary Short Fiction by Native American Women* in 2008. In addition to numerous other works of fiction, Blaeser has published five poetry collections, and is a past Wisconsin Poet Laureate and founding director of In-Na-Po, Indigenous Nations Poets. In "Growing Things," an indigenous woman calls an arborist to care for some trees on her rural property, and likens him in her mind to the tribal tree doctor she remembers from her youth. During a second visit, they discuss the relationship between science and indigenous environmental knowledge.

"You have to go deep to do any good," Spanish heard him say. He went on gesturing and explaining to her about fertilization. She found it hard to meet his eyes, so she turned small rocks over with her toes, half alert for a fossil. Every so often she would look up at the old oak—seventy-five to a hundred years old he had told her.

Now he was writing things down: formulas, brand names, equipment she would need. She wanted to laugh every time she looked at him. It's the way she felt ever since he came down the drive in that sporty Mazda. Like his shirt, it was some kind of blue she couldn't name—one of the designer colors invented in some laboratory, custom made for yuppies. For this yuppie tree doctor.

She stood squinting trying to superimpose some distinctive character over his smooth, round, dimpled cheeks. She tied a bandanna pirate-style over his head. No, that didn't work. She rolled it into a headband, but that looked silly on his close-cropped hair, made his little bald spot more prominent. Well, maybe a hat . . . an Aussie hat . . . or a scar across his cheekbone . . .

"Well, that should do it. Got it? I'd bring the mulch out to here if you don't mind the looks of it. Miss?"

"Hmmm? Oh, I think so. Mulch, fertilizer injections, pruning . . ."

"In the dead of winter."

"Right. But you say you can't promise it will do any good."

"Know in three to five years—if you're still here. I'll leave you my card if you think of something you forgot to ask."

And then he was bending over his notebook again. Suddenly she wanted to touch the little hollow on his chin, fill it with her finger. Feel the smooth curve of it. A tree doctor after all. Some ancient blood, some spirit must have left its mark, somewhere palpable. Her hand moved to caress the cold smooth dip of the brown spirit stone in her pocket.

He himself had hardly touched anything. The bark for no more than a few seconds. A branch pulled down for a hasty look at the leaves.

"*Boozhoo*, my friend Oak," her grandpa would say as he grasped a bare low branch in a handshake. "This here is my little Spanish." He would lift her giggling to the handshake, to the solemn introductions he used to make. "Good day, Mrs. Birch. What fine dress you wear."

"Grandpa, her dress is torn," she would whisper, knowing he must pretend to correct her manners.

Because of her grandpa, the world of Spanish's childhood was furry, prickly, sticky with life. A place of rocks, cold and wet, their colors made vibrant by the waves breaking over them, rocks to be turned and admired in the hand, to be felt and heard with the hands. The world she knew was a place of sharp thorns, coarse or sleek animal fur, slippery bodies of fish. It was mossy forest floors upon which they lay, bodies cushioned, remembering a nest of crisp fall leaves, imagining the soft bed of clouds.

To know the world by touch is to know it by heart. That, thought Spanish, was the single lesson her grandpa taught. Did he realize the many troubles she would encounter because she learned it so well?

Touch was of the devil—the lesson the nuns taught. Keep your hands folded on your desk in the classroom, in your lap when you sit, in front of you when you walk. Wear white gloves to church like nice young ladies do. Keep your hands clean. Don't play in the mud, don't put your fingers in the food, don't play with your hair, and don't touch boys—ever.

And yet, Spanish remembered how all the miracles in the Bible stories came about because of touch. Jesus touched the blind man's eyes, the dead, the lame, the sick. He blessed the loaves and the fishes. He broke the bread with his hands. The Bible knew the power of touch.

Was this power what the nuns feared? The reason Spanish spent so many afternoons writing one declaration or another five hundred times, saying in words what she wouldn't say with her heart, that she wouldn't hold hands behind the silo, wouldn't swing on birches, wouldn't touch the Host with her fingers. Wouldn't trail her fingers along the tree doctor's palm during their parting handshake until he looked up startled and laughed uneasily.

"Well, goodbye then. Call me if you want . . . another checkup. If you have questions. If you . . ." He closed the car door on his own half-expectant mumbling. Spanish held up her left hand in farewell, her right hand again fingering the stone in her pocket. She stood squinting into the sun, watching the yuppie tree doctor drive off and wondering what she had expected.

Spanish had prepared for his arrival as if he were deserving of ritual honor, as if she had summoned him with a gift of tobacco—like a sucking doctor called to heal the sick. She had not completely settled in, so her preparation required she search the still-packed boxes for the odd group of items she thought appropriate. On the built-in side table she placed special teas and a tumbler of whiskey. She filled a kettle for the stove, set out a turtle-shaped bowl, matches and cedar. She dressed carefully, slipping a heavy silver bracelet onto her wrist, wearing the dream catcher earrings given her by cousin Julia, and pulling her hair back in a beaded barrette with a thunderbird pattern she had designed herself. Dragon, her mixed-blood spaniel, she closed in the loft. "Sometimes them doctors need it real quiet." Her grandma's voice, consoling Spanish when she must tie her old reservation dogs away from the house before a medicine man was due to come.

Old habits. She laughed as now she sat on the steps, her fingers buried deep in the hair around Dragon's neck, her caresses a peace offering for his recent banishment. The tree doctor—*Shelby Mathews, Arborist,* his card said—had not come into Spanish's new log home, had not tasted tea or whiskey, had not made any offering, told any story, done any healing.

Spanish told herself she was being unfair. She knew where she was coming when she moved here. The lake country of southern Wisconsin: rural, but still Middle America. Maybe her romps in the surrounding woods had tricked her, brought back memories, built her expectations. But Shelby Mathews was an arborist, not really a tree doctor as she had thought of him, certainly not a *jiisakiiwinini* or conjurer.

"Still he has potential, eh, Dragon?" Spanish said, thinking of his hard-muscled legs and the quiet feel of his spirit. But then she laughed when she recalled his notebook and yuppie earnestness. "Should have asked him in for tea anyway. Maybe I could teach him what I know about the healing touch. Well let's get about this mulch thing. Wanna ride in the wheelbarrow, Dragon?"

In the weeks that followed, Spanish would gaze intently at the oak, trying to see signs that her care was working. She felt what she knew was an inordinate amount of guilt for its threatened health. Even though she had fenced an eight-foot-wide circle off limits for the heavy equipment during building, the oak's root system must have suffered.

Proximity, such a tricky business. Seven cousins layered together in the back of that old rusty pickup, their three moms crowded into the cab. Kids bouncing along singing to hear their voices jar and crack with the bumps. Going to town, going fishing, going visiting, just going along. Spanish thought about the close kin system of her childhood. Three generations sharing beds, clothes, chores, food, and fun, living together in tight quarters. What made it work? Living in Texas with cowboy Dale, the whole ranch hadn't been big enough for the two of them. She had fumbled through several relationships—the watercolor artist in Colorado, the school teacher in Illinois—always one or the other party began to feel threatened by the closeness. Claustrophobia. Not the classic panic in small spaces, but some fear of personal closeness. A need for freedom, for personal space—my space.

Last time, with Jim Snow, Spanish was the one who ran. She ran here. Built a cabin. Did freelance editing on her PC. Fished. Roamed the countryside. Looking for that space. Constantly reminded of the problems of proximity by this damn oak tree.

The arborist came back in late January—the dead of winter. Spanish had called him about the pruning. Small preparations this time and Dragon at her side, where she kept her nervous hands busy in his winter coat.

"How you liking it out here?" he asked while setting up. "Pretty quiet in the winter, isn't it?"

"I keep myself busy. I like quiet." Dumb answer, Spanish, dumb. She watched him find the rhythm of his pruning routine. Lotsa science in this guy, she thought, but some music too, maybe a little bit of magic he doesn't acknowledge yet.

It hurt her to watch the cutting, so she turned away, performing small duties about the grounds as she listened to his movements. Pruning wasn't in her blood. Not like it must be in the blood of the bonsai masters, and maybe in the blood of Shelby Mathews. She remembered the hollow feeling that came the first time she saw a woodchipper at work. Branches gobbled up by the shrieking machine, spit out as bits and sawdust. That was true modern magic, she supposed, but not for her. But this, this pruning for health was a different kind of cutting, maybe an art. *Shelby Mathews, Tree Doctor, Artist.* Spanish smiled as she conjured the business card in her mind.

He was done. It didn't look like art, not yet anyway. Poor stump branches, she thought. Together Spanish and Shelby carried the fallen pieces to her woodpile.

"Come in for coffee or hot chocolate while I write you a check?" she offered.

"Sure, thanks."

He was fingering her chess set when she returned with the serving tray. He had removed his gloves and held an onyx knight in his hand, following its lines. "Pretty set."

"Thanks. You play?"

"A little, sometimes."

"Want to?"

"What? Oh, play? Now?"

"Or . . . sometime."

They both laughed then at the awkwardness.

"I'm sorry," Spanish began. "Out here, conversation, well, isn't my strong suit these days."

"No, I'm sure it's me. Pruning puts me in a bit of a trance, I guess."

A trance. It was a perfect answer. An arborist yes, but a tree doctor maybe a little, too.

They didn't play chess. Just talked a little about the area, his business, her house, and about Dragon when he demanded attention. Shelby didn't stay long, but he admired a lot of things in her house: the wood finishes, fish decoys, black ash baskets, books. Maybe one of them would bring him back, she thought when he left. Maybe she would.

Maybe if she knew about love medicines. Sympathetic magic was what the anthropologists called it when dolls were tied together to conjure a bond. Did those dolls break their leather ties when one of the lovers fled in search of personal space? What kind of love was it that created such a largeness in a relationship that no one became afraid? What kind of love had eluded her? Would this tree doctor who knew about root systems know about that magic?

As a child she had watched her old cat Mrs. Tom give birth and lick each newborn kitten dry. "Why does she do that, Grandpa? Doesn't she get tired?"

"She's waking up their blood, Spanish, the way you wake yours up each morning when you stretch. She's gettin' that blood to move around in their bodies . . . bringing them life."

Science would later tell her that the mother cat was stimulating her offsprings' circulation, but Spanish would always think about it as waking up their kitten blood. And when later she would lie with a lover whose hands gently petted and caressed her, who ran kisses down her neck and arms, she knew he was waking up her kitten blood, too, and filling the life vessels of her body. What stopped that magic?

The tree doctor came back a week later, pulled into the yard in a brown four-wheel-drive Bronco. "Mazda's kind of impractical in this weather," he told her when she asked.

"I had a job down the road a ways, saw you in the yard . . ."

"I'm glad you came. I was just studying this tree."

"You won't know for awhile, I thought I explained."

"You did, but I can't help searching for a sign." Spanish traced the bark pattern lightly with her fingers. "I try to encourage it, it's too grand to be destroyed by humans crowding in."

"I saw the tobacco."

"Huh?"

"The first day I came. You had some kind of ceremony."

"Made an offering. Appeasement, I guess."

"I wondered. And me? Hedging your bets?"

Spanish glanced up at his face and his raised eyebrows. But before she could respond, he laughed.

"It's okay. I'm as used to skepticism as well as you are, I guess. After you've explained to forty people about some invisible fungus invading through the root system or tried to counter the story of some TV fertilizer wizard, you just accept it: some people are going to think you inhaled too much nitrogen or something."

She could have told him then, but he didn't seem in any hurry. If anyone did, he knew about waiting. Three years healing for the tree if she helped it along. "Oh, I believe in science," she could have said, "just not by itself."

Someday she might show him the tamarack stands, the jackpines, the maple sugar grounds of her childhood. He might burn with fury when he saw the scars of clear-cutting in her homeland. Or they might sit together watching the waves of heat, wiping their foreheads with a folded red bandanna, and singing for rain to feed the rows and rows of saplings set before them. "Feel these furrows, Child. They are the same on the great oak, on the marked land, and now on the forehead of your *mishoomis*."

"Grandpa, are you turning to bark?" They laughed then. As Spanish did now with this smooth-faced tree doctor. She could almost see him turning to bark, too. And waited.

What I Have Been Doing Lately

JAMAICA KINCAID

Jamaica Kincaid is an Antiguan-American writer and Professor of African American Studies in Residence at Harvard University. Author of five novels and numerous short stories and essays, Kincaid has been the recipient of numerous awards, including a Guggenheim Fellowship for Creative Arts in Fiction. "What I Have Been Doing Lately" first appeared in the winter 1981 issue of *Paris Review*. Its unnamed narrator describes a surreal sequence in which she is awakened by a doorbell, leaves her house, and passes through a surreal landscape. Eventually, she encounters a figure on the horizon, and describes the sequence again to this figure.

What I have been doing lately: I was lying in bed and the doorbell rang. I ran downstairs. Quick. I opened the door. There was no one there. I stepped outside. Wither it was drizzling or there was a lot of dust in the air and the dust was damp. I stuck out my tongue and the drizzle or the damp dust tasted like government school ink. I looked north. I looked south. I decided to start walking north. While walking north, I noticed that I was barefoot. While walking north, I looked up and saw the planet Venus. I said "It must be almost morning." I saw a monkey in the tree. The tree had no leaves. I said, "Ah, a monkey. Just look at that. A monkey." I walked for I don't know how long before I came to a big body of water. I wanted to get across it but I couldn't swim. I wanted to get across it but it would take me years to build a boat. I wanted to get across it but it would take me I didn't know how long to build a bridge. Years passed and then one day, feeling like it, I got into my boat and rowed across. When I got to the other side, it was noon and my shadow was small and fell beneath me. I set out on a path that stretched out straight ahead. I passed a house, and a dog was sitting on the verandah but it looked the other way when it saw me coming. I passed a boy tossing a ball in the air but the boy looked the other way when he saw me coming. I walked and I walked but I couldn't tell if I walked a long time because my feet didn't feel as if they would drop off. I turned around to see what I had left behind me but nothing was familiar. Instead of the straight path, I saw hills. Instead of the boy with his ball, I saw tall flowing trees. I looked up and the sky was without clouds and seemed near, as if it were the ceiling in my house and, if I stood on a chair, I could touch it with the tips of my fingers. I turned around and looked ahead of me again. A deep hole had opened up before me. I looked in. The hole was deep and dark and I couldn't see the bottom. I thought, What's down there?, so on purpose I fell in.

I fell and I fell, over and over, as if I were an old suitcase. On the sides of the deep hole I could see things written, but perhaps it was in a foreign language because I couldn't read them. Still I fell, for I don't know how long. As I fell I began to see that I didn't like the way falling made me feel. Falling made me feel sick and I missed all the people I had loved. I said, I don't want to fall anymore, and I reversed myself. I was standing again on the edge of the deep hole. I looked at the deep hole and I said, You can close up now, and it did. I walked some more without knowing distance. I only knew that I passed through days and nights, I only knew that I passed through rain and shine, light and darkness. I was never thirsty and I felt no pain. Looking at the horizon, I made a joke for myself: I said, "The earth has thin lips," and I laughed.

Looking at the horizon again, I saw a lone figure coming toward me, but I wasn't frightened because I was sure it was my mother. As I got closer to the figure, I could see that it wasn't my mother, but still I wasn't frightened because I could see that it was a woman.

When this woman got closer to me, she looked at me hard and then she threw up her hands. She must have seen me somewhere before because she said, "It's you. Just look at that. It's you. And just what have you been doing lately?"

I could have said, "I have been praying not to grow any taller." I could have said, "I have been listening carefully to my mother's words, so as to make a good imitation of a dutiful daughter."

I could have said, "A pack of dogs, tired from chasing each other all over town, slept in the moonlight."

Instead, I said, "What I have been doing lately: I was lying in bed on my back, my hands drawn up, my fingers interlaced lightly at the nape of my neck. Someone rang the doorbell. I went downstairs and opened the door but there was no one there. I stepped outside. Wither it was drizzling or there was a lot of dust in the air and the dust was damp. I stuck out my tongue and the drizzle or the damp dust tasted like government school ink. I looked north and I looked south. I started walking north. While walking north, I wanted to move fast, so I removed the shoes from my feet. While walking north, I looked up and saw the planet Venus and I said, "If the sun went out, it would be eight minutes before I would know it." I saw a monkey sitting in a tree that had no leaves and I said, "A monkey. Just look at that. A monkey." I picked up a stone and I threw it at the monkey. The monkey, seeing the stone, quickly moved out of its way. Three times I threw a stone at the monkey and three times it moved away. The fourth time I threw the stone, the monkey caught it and threw it back at me. The stone struck me on my forehead over my right eye, making a deep gash. The gash healed immediately but now the skin on my forehead felt false to me. I walked for I don't know how long before I came to a big body of water. I wanted to get across, so when the boat came I paid my fare. When I got to the other side, I saw a lot of people sitting on the beach and they were having a picnic. They were the most beautiful people I had ever seen. Everything about them was black and shiny. Their skin was black and shiny. Their shoes were black and shiny. Their hair was black and shiny. The clothes they wore were black and shiny. I could hear them laughing and chatting and I said, I would like to be with these people, so I started to walk toward them, but when I got up close to them I saw that they weren't at a picnic and they weren't beautiful and they weren't chatting and laughing. All around me was black mud and the people all looked as if they had been made up out of the black mud. I looked up and saw that the sky seemed far away and nothing I could stand on would make me able to touch it with my fingertips. I thought, If only I could get out of this, so I started to walk. I must have walked for a long time because my feet hurt and felt as if they would drop off. I thought, If only just around the bend I would see my house and inside my house I would find my bed, freshly made at that, and in the kitchen I would find my mother or anyone else that I loved making me a custard. I thought, If only it was a Sunday and

I was sitting in a church and I had just heard someone sing a psalm. I felt very sad so I sat down. I felt so sad that I rested my head on my own knees and smoothed my own head. I felt so sad I couldn't imagine feeling any other way again. I said, I don't like this. I don't want to do this anymore. And I went back to lying in bed just before the doorbell rang.

The Man to Send Rain Clouds

LESLIE MARMON SILKO

Leslie Marmon Silko is a Lagunita Pueblo author of numerous novels, short stories, poems, and essays. A pioneer of contemporary indigenous American literature, Silko is the recipient of many literary awards, including an inaugural MacArthur Fellowship. "The Man to Send Rain Clouds" first appeared in *New Mexico Quarterly* in 1968. In the story, Teofilo is found dead under a cottonwood tree, and given a traditional Pueblo funeral ceremony (in which the dead are understood to help their living community by sending rain clouds). The local Catholic priest is asked to play part of the ceremony by sprinkling water on the body, initially refuses, then reconsiders without quite understanding why he has been invited.

I

They found him under a big cottonwood tree. His Levi jacket and pants were faded light-blue so that he had been easy to find. The big cottonwood tree stood apart from a small grove of winterbare cottonwoods which grew in the wide, sandy arroyo. He had been dead for a day or more, and the sheep had wandered and scattered up and down the arroyo. Leon and his brother-in-law, Ken, gathered the sheep and left them in the pen at the sheep camp before they returned to the cottonwood tree. Leon waited under the tree while Ken drove the truck through the deep sand to the edge of the arroyo. He squinted up at the sun and unzipped his jacket—it sure was hot for this time of year. But high and northwest the blue mountains were still deep in snow. Ken came sliding down the low, crumbling bank about fifty yards down, and he was bringing the red blanket.

Before they wrapped the old man, Leon took a piece of string out of his pocket and tied a small gray feather in the old man's long white hair. Ken gave him the paint. Across the brown wrinkled forehead he drew a streak of white and along the high cheekbones he drew a strip of blue paint. He paused and watched Ken throw pinches of corn meal and pollen into the wind that fluttered the small gray feather. Then Leon painted with yellow under the old man's broad nose, and finally, when he had painted green across the chin, he smiled.

"Send us rain clouds, Grandfather." They laid the bundle in the back of the pickup and covered it with a heavy tarp before they started back to the pueblo.

They turned off the highway onto the sandy pueblo road. Not long after they passed the store and post office they saw Father Paul's car coming toward them. When he recognized their faces he slowed his car and waved for them to stop. The young priest rolled down the car window.

"Did you find old Teofilo?" he asked loudly.

Leon stopped the truck. "Good morning, Father. We were just out to the sheep camp. Everything is O.K. now."

"Thank God for that. Teofilo is a very old man. You really shouldn't allow him to stay at the sheep camp alone."

"No, he won't do that any more now."

"Well, I'm glad you understand. I hope I'll be seeing you at Mass this week—we missed you last Sunday. See if you can get old Teofilo to come with you." The priest smiled and waved at them as they drove away.

II

Louise and Teresa were waiting. The table was set for lunch, and the coffee was boiling on the black iron stove. Leon looked at Louise and then at Teresa.

"We found him under a cottonwood tree in the big arroyo near sheep camp. I guess he sat down to rest in the shade and never got up again." Leon walked toward the old man's bed. The red plaid shawl had been shaken and spread carefully over the bed, and a new brown flannel shirt and pair of stiff new Levis were arranged neatly beside the pillow. Louise held the screen door open while Leon and Ken carried in the red blanket. He looked small and shriveled, and after they dressed him in the new shirt and pants he seemed more shrunken.

It was noontime now because the church bells rang the Angelus. They ate the beans with hot bread, and nobody said anything until after Teresa poured the coffee.

Ken stood up and put on his jacket. "I'll see about the gravediggers. Only the top layer of soil is frozen. I think it can be ready before dark."

Leon nodded his head and finished his coffee. After Ken had been gone for a while, the neighbors and clanspeople came quietly to embrace Teofilo's family and to leave food on the table because the gravediggers would come to eat when they were finished.

III

The sky in the west was full of pale-yellow light. Louise stood outside with her hands in the pockets of Leon's green army jacket that was too big for her. The funeral was over, and the old men had taken their candles and medicine bags and were gone. She waited until the body was laid into the pickup before she said anything to Leon. She touched his arm, and he noticed that her hands were still dusty from the corn meal that she had sprinkled around the old man. When she spoke, Leon could not hear her.

"What did you say? I didn't hear you."

"I said that I had been thinking about something."

"About what?"

"About the priest sprinkling holy water for Grandpa. So he won't be thirsty."

Leon stared at the new moccasins that Teofilo had made for the ceremonial dances in the summer. They were nearly hidden by the red blanket. It was getting colder, and the wind pushed gray dust down the narrow pueblo road. The sun was approaching the long mesa where it disappeared during the winter. Louise stood there shivering and watching his face. Then he zipped up his jacket and opened the truck door. "I'll see if he's there."

IV

Ken stopped the pickup at the church, and Leon got out; and then Ken drove down the hill to the graveyard where people were waiting. Leon knocked at the old carved door with its symbols of the Lamb. While he waited he looked up at the twin bells from the king of Spain with the last sunlight pouring around them in their tower.

The priest opened the door and smiled when he saw who it was. "Come in! What brings you here this evening?"

The priest walked toward the kitchen, and Leon stood with his cap in his hand, playing with the earflaps and examining the living room—the brown sofa, the green armchair, and the brass lamp that hung down from the ceiling by links of chain. The priest dragged a chair out of the kitchen and offered it to Leon.

"No thank you, Father. I only came to ask you if you would bring your holy water to the graveyard."

The priest turned away from Leon and looked out the window at the patio full of shadows and the dining-room windows of the nuns' cloister across the patio. The curtains were heavy, and the light from within faintly penetrated; it was impossible to see the nuns inside eating supper. "Why didn't you tell me he was dead? I could have brought the Last Rites anyway."

Leon smiled. "It wasn't necessary, Father."

The priest stared down at his scuffed brown loafers and the worn hem of his cassock. "For a Christian burial it was necessary."

His voice was distant, and Leon thought that his blue eyes looked tired. "It's O.K. Father, we just want him to have plenty of water."

The priest sank down into the green chair and picked up a glossy missionary magazine. He turned the colored pages full of lepers and pagans without looking at them.

"You know I can't do that, Leon. There should have been the Last Rites and a funeral mass at the very least."

Leon put on his green cap and pulled the flaps down over his ears. "It's getting late, Father. I've got to go."

When Leon opened the door Father Paul stood up and said, "Wait." He left the room and came back wearing a long brown overcoat. He followed Leon out the door and across the dim churchyard to the adobe steps in front of the church. They both stooped to fit through the low adobe entrance. And when they started down the hill to the graveyard only half of the sun was visible above the mesa.

The priest approached the grave slowly, wondering how they had managed to dig into the frozen ground; and then he remembered that this was New Mexico, and saw the pile of cold loose sand beside the hole. The people stood close to each other with little clouds of steam puffing from their faces. The priest looked at them and saw a pile of jackets, gloves, and scarves in the yellow, dry tumbleweeds that grew in the graveyard. He looked at the red blanket, not sure that Teofilo was so small, wondering if it wasn't some perverse Indian trick—something they did in March to ensure a good harvest—wondering if maybe old Teofilo was actually at sheep camp corraling the sheep for the night. But there he was, facing into a cold dry wind and squinting at the last sunlight, ready to bury a red wool blanket while the faces of his parishioners were in shadow with the last warmth of the sun on their backs.

His fingers were stiff, and it took him a long time to twist the lid off the holy water. Drops of water fell on the red blanket and soaked into dark icy spots. He sprinkled the grave and the water disappeared almost before it touched the dim, cold sand; it reminded him of something—he tried to remember what it was, because he thought if he could remember he might understand this. He sprinkled more water; he shook the container until it was empty, and the water fell through the light from sundown like August rain that fell while the sun was still shining, almost evaporating before it touched the wilted squash flowers.

The wind pulled at the priest's brown Franciscan robe and swirled away the corn meal and pollen that had been sprinkled on the blanket. They lowered the bundle into the ground, and they didn't bother to untie the stiff pieces of new rope that were tied around the ends of the blanket. The sun was gone, and over on the highway the eastbound lane was full of headlights. The priest walked away slowly. Leon watched him climb the hill, and when he had disappeared within the tall, thick walls, Leon turned to look up at the high blue mountains in the deep snow that reflected a faint red light from the west. He felt good because it was finished, and he was happy about the sprinkling of the holy water; now the old man could send them big thunderclouds for sure.

The Ape Within

DAVID CLERSON

Translated by Katia Grubisic

David Clerson is a Quebecois author of two novels and one collection of short fiction. His debut novel, *Frères*, won the Grand Prix littéraire Archambault in 2014, while his third book, *Dormir sans tête* was a finalist for the Grand Prix du livre de Montréal in 2019 and was published in Katia Grubisic's English translation under the title *To See Out the Night*. The first short story from this collection, "Le singe intérieur," appears here as "The Ape Within." Examining the relationship between humans and other animals, the story describes how Louis loses his job as a parking garage attendant after permitting a homeless man to take shelter in the garage. After watching a television program about apes, he begins to feel an ape growing within himself, and gradually assumes its behaviors as he struggles to adapt to life as an unhoused person.

On January 6, 2016, Louis, a night watchman, lost his job in a downtown parking lot after he let in a homeless man. The man was hunched over, and a messy beard covered half his face. He smelled revolting. Louis felt sorry for him, and didn't say anything when the man walked by his booth, watching as he shuffled into the depths of the parking garage. Three floors down he fell asleep over a heating grate. When he woke up he shat, leaning against a Mercedes and smearing the car with his excrement.

Louis didn't really try very hard to find other work. He had a little money saved up, and his employment insurance benefits were good enough. At first he hung out with a few former colleagues with whom he used to go for a beer, but he stopped answering their emails, and they stopped asking him along. Although it was cold, he spent his days walking across the city, through Jarry Park, along the train tracks, and up to the top of the mountain, sometimes staying until nightfall.

At night, on Chambord Street not far from the Metropolitan expressway, he ate pasta, sitting alone at his kitchen table, his computer open in front of him. He usually watched nature documentaries, on bears or hyenas, lampreys, other animals. Maybe it was a way of revisiting his childhood, the fascination he'd had for exotic beasts, or trying to relive his university years. He had briefly taken biology because he thought he wanted to be a zoologist, though he gave up in the end. As his schoolwork became less important and he became used to the routine and atmosphere of the underground parking garage, he let the night-watchman gig take over.

One evening in April, four months after he was fired, he was watching a documentary on endangered species of Southeast Asia when an orangutan appeared on the screen, a hulking male squatting heavily on a branch. The camera panned along the ape's body: the wide facial disc, its texture like leather, and the tiny eyes shoved deep into the skin, as if they were about to disappear. Louis met the animal's stare, those eyes in which he saw nothing, a blankness that frightened him. Although other images blinked across the screen, Louis felt that his gaze remained plunged into the orangutan's, that the dark eyes were a parasite inside him, as if the primate's pupils had lodged themselves in his.

Louis's body was racked with shivers. His chest grew tight, his fingers shook. He suddenly hated the reek of his breath, which smelled like an animal's. That night he had trouble falling asleep, and woke shortly before dawn convinced that the orangutan now lived within him.

In the days that followed, Louis felt his limbs growing languorous. They no longer seemed to move the same way; his gestures seemed at once more fluid and much slower. His habits changed. He almost never went out, only to get groceries on Jarry, and he started spending less time online. One Saturday at the beginning of May he dropped his fork on the floor and found himself eating with his hands. The next day he injured his shoulder after trying to hang from his shower-curtain rod, which ripped out of the wall from his weight. A few days after that, he woke up wet, which hadn't happened since childhood. He decided that the incontinence wasn't him; it was the ape within that had needed to urinate. His sheets and his mattress were wet too, and the next night he decided to sleep on the floor in a nest of blankets.

The other anthropoid showed itself gradually. It wasn't so much the sometimes out-of-control behavior that worried Louis, but the feeling of a presence that was growing inside him, and taking up all the space. His limbs hurt. Sometimes he woke up in the night thinking his skin was tearing. Every day he ran his hands over his body, squeezing his arms and legs as if to make sure they belonged to him. Louis could feel the ape stretching within him, the ape's joints moving, the ape's head thinking inside his own. Its proportions were almost human; the ape filled his entire body. Sometimes it seemed like the orangutan would kill him, that it was feeding on him from the inside. At other times Louis had the impression that what was growing under his skin was the emptiness left by an animal dying. He saw again the dark face, the eyes. He was lost in the orangutan's small bright eyes, and he imagined being inhabited by a dying animal.

Several times Louis shoved his fingers down his throat, as if he could vomit out the ape, but he only spat up a trickle of saliva. He wondered what effect abortion pills would have, or whether he should try some kind of antiparasitic instead. He also thought of his father's gun—his father, who'd been a hunter—and he visualized pushing the gun all the way into his mouth to kill the ape. But that would accomplish nothing; to dislodge it he first had to get to know the foreign presence.

The summer was unbearably hot. Louis's apartment was an oven, and he sat in the sweltering heat reading about primates. He learned that orangutans were solitary and territorial, that they ate fruit, shoots, eggs, insects, and invertebrates, and that they were constantly on the move, building a new nest of branches every night. The cries of the males were powerful, and could carry over a kilometer or more. Louis could almost hear them in the distance. The fangs of an ape in one photograph terrified him. He saw others, victims of hunters or held in poacher cages. What struck him most was a piece he read on animal trafficking. The exotic-animals trade was strictly regulated, and in some countries offenders were punished with jail time, but across the world, the market brought in millions. Hidden in the trunks of cars, in the holds of ships, or in the back of delivery trucks, all kinds of creatures were being smuggled across borders—reptiles, rainbow-feathered birds, felines, amphibians, monkeys. Orangutan babies were especially sought after as pets. Separated from their mothers, most died during the journey. Some were rescued by border guards but they were too young and couldn't be released back into the wild.

Although Louis had never left the country, he knew the Canada–U.S. border's reputation: American customs officials were tough. A former colleague of Louis's, Rawi, who was Lebanese, had been turned away when he tried to go on vacation in Maine. Louis figured that venomous spiders or reptiles could get across pretty easily, and maybe smaller primates, like lemurs or marmosets, but a big ape would be difficult to sneak over the border. He had to get to the United States as soon as possible.

That evening he found a rental agency online, with an office less than a kilometer from his place, and he reserved a car. He found his passport in a drawer under a pile of socks, without a single stamp. He didn't sleep that night, spending most of it in front of his computer. He read about exotic-animal trafficking laws, and felt better. The next day Louis drove to the States.

Sweat poured down his forehead. He gripped the steering wheel, but his limbs felt like they were being stretched from the inside out, and his fingers were too tight. Three times he stopped to pee, afraid that the ape would force him to urinate. The border crossing seemed to take forever. When the customs officers asked him why he was going, he said something vague about the beaches of Maine and New Hampshire, the Bronx Zoo, a zoo in Queens. He was surprised that they let him through, even as the ape stirred within him. He could feel his heart beating in his head. His skin was slick with sweat. But as soon as he set foot on American soil, a weight lifted from his shoulders. He laughed unexpectedly, suddenly convinced that the orangutan had been intercepted at the border.

Louis pulled over on the side of the road. He took a deep breath, folded and unfolded his hands and rubbed them over his face. He stuck out his tongue in his rearview mirror. He was free. He couldn't remember ever feeling so light.

He slept in a motel near the interstate. He drank beer in front of the TV and ate a hamburger and fries coated with ketchup and mayonnaise. Louis rarely drank. Although he had sometimes had one too many with guys from work, his drunkenness had always been circumstantial. That evening, however, he downed one beer after another. When he finished the cans he'd bought, he went to the motel bar and came back with a bottle of cheap whiskey. He was drinking, he was drunk; he was drunk and he was laughing, he was surprised by his own laughter. He lay back on the bed and flipped through American reality shows, the secret life of Britney Spears, a story about a refugee boat sinking in the Mediterranean.

When he woke up, the screen was still flashing. It took a long time to find the remote control to click the TV off. Louis's head was on fire, and he wanted to throw up. He had dark circles under his eyes. His face was pale, his limbs leaden, his mouth pasty. Everything about him disgusted him. He wanted to go back to sleep, but couldn't. It occurred to him that the orangutan's disappearance hadn't freed him. Now he was suffering from the animal's absence, he'd been abandoned.

At eleven o'clock a hotel clerk knocked on his door: time to check out. He decided to pay for another night, and asked for some ibuprofen. After taking a couple of pills, he was able to sleep. When he opened his eyes, it was night again.

In a dream he'd climbed mangroves and meranti trees, screaming under the branches and ripping into the flesh of exotic fruits. His arms were agile. On the mossy ground of a swampy forest, he had copulated with a female. He was awake now, and went into the bathroom to splash water on his face. In the mirror he stared at his black eyes, and he thought he recognized the eyes of the ape. He stretched out his hands and opened his mouth wide. When he raised his arms over his head, he was surprised to find them so long, and he laughed again. He knew that the orangutan was still living in him, clinging to his body. The animal had been able to get across after all. In hindsight, Louis was perplexed that he'd wanted the orangutan to leave at all. He'd felt so deserted when he thought the ape had left. He wanted to learn to live with the other.

The rest of the story is a rebirth. Back home, Louis bought ferns, alocasias, and hibiscus to decorate his apartment. His diet changed, and he ate nuts and fruit rather than the omelets, rice, or pasta that had once been his staples. He felt stronger, more alert, more confident. Sometimes, usually shortly after waking up, it seemed to him that the orangutan was overflowing, pouring out over his body, that it engulfed him. He thought he was carrying out a mission, as if he'd found in the ape an answer to his life.

One evening in August, he was listening to an expert online who explained that orangutans would be extinct within ten years from poaching and habitat loss. There is no hope, the biologist said, but for Louis the words were a revelation: the species would survive in him.

His apartment looked like a jungle. He patted dirt everywhere, and plants started growing along the walls. Sometimes he defecated on the floor. He never washed or changed his clothes anymore, and his beard and hair were long and dirty. His appearance and his smell were repulsive. When he went out, people avoided him. He liked the disgust and the fear he elicited. To those around him, it looked like Louis was losing it.

At night he dreamed of Borneo, but by day he never thought of returning to the forest, where the last wild primates would perish. He rejoiced: exile was a refuge for the ape, and it gave meaning to his legs, arms, belly, and head.

The rest might seem obvious. Louis was evicted from his apartment, Louis ended up on the street, eating out of the garbage, Louis was cloaked in his filth. He sometimes thought he was dressed as a monkey. Louis caught scabies and Lyme disease, Louis lived out a few summers and winters before he was found dead in the middle of the detritus. What's less predictable is that before he died, he prowled across a strange, unnameable Earth. He lived among humans like a beast. His feet were prehensile and his arms even longer than orangutans' arms, his blackened skin became leathery, his head grew wider. As his understanding of reality changed, he thought he could glimpse the delirious landscapes of worlds to come, where he roamed, half-man, half-ape, beneath the sultry sun that set the earth and the sky ablaze.

I'd worked with him for a long time, and I saw him now and again during the last years of his life. He wandered downtown, and he often walked by the entrance to the underground parking lot where I still worked. I always said hello. Most of the time he avoided me, but sometimes he would whisper what was going through his head, bits and pieces of his life.

I saw him one last time shortly before his death. I was walking down an alley between Stanley and Peel on my way home from work as the sun came up when I saw something moving through the garbage. At first I stepped back. But I recognized him, and I went over. I can hardly repeat what he said to me, his words were so garbled, but my eyes met his. I saw a deep darkness, an emptiness into which I started to sink. I believe his eyes were acknowledging the imminence of death. Just as I was about to leave, to leave him to the squalor, I was afraid his eyes had inseminated me, just as the ape's eyes had inseminated him. He would die within me as he died amid the trash, and his death would settle inside of me.

Acknowledgments

Investments in the present are necessary to build bridges to the future. For this project, funds were generously provided by the Dean of Arts and Sciences at Brandeis University, the Brandeis Latin American, Caribbean and Latinx Program, the Brandeis Department of English, the Social Sciences and Humanities Research Council of Canada, the Department of English at Yale University, and the Department of English and Comparative Literature at Columbia University.

For essential administrative help, tidal waves of gratitude go out to Lisa Pannella, Barbara Strauss, Mangok Bol, Brian Schutter, Anik Chartrand, and Anthony Lipscomb. Sue Ramin had the initial idea for this project and kept the faith for longer than anyone has a right to expect. Ashley Burns, Peter Fong, Hannah Krasikov, and Anthony Lipscomb all made this project immeasurably better. Jorge Marcone, Imre Szeman, Sabine von Mering, and Jennifer Wenzel provided guidance and input at just the right moments. The anthology would never have come together without the energy of the editorial team; Kurt Cavender, Roberto Forns-Broggi, Cajetan Iheka, Pablo Mukherjee, Irina Sadovina, and Shaobo Xie deserve deep appreciation. For deepening the vision of environmental literature that shapes this reader, not enough can be said about the merits of Chris Barrett, Glyn Davis, Jonathan Flatley, Laura Harris, and Kylee Weiss. Finally, for the energy, passion, and ever-growing worldliness with which they demand a contemporary reboot of green action, the students of Generation Z deserve a shout-out—in particular, my beloved Alaska.

For permission to reprint or excerpt works included in this volume we recognize the following:

Africa World Press, Inc: Selections from Ogaga Ifowodo, *The Oil Lamp* (2005). Published by permission of the publisher, Africa World Press, Inc.

Anna Carlier: *Hertenleer* by Anna Carlier. Copyright © 2020 Anna Carlier. Translation of a selection published as "from *HIDE*" in *Asymptote*, October 2021. Translation copyright © 2021 David McKay.

Aroa Moreno Durán: "La gravedad" by Aroa Moreno Durán, 2018. Copyright © Aroa Moreno Durán. Published in *Estío. Once relatos de ficción climática* (Episkaia 2018), pp. 27–32. Translation copyright © Kate Whittemore. Translation published as "Gravity" in *Los Angeles Review*.

David Clerson: "The Ape Within" from *To See Out the Night*. Published by QC Fiction, an imprint of Baraka Books.

Doğu Yücel: *Denizler Altinda* by Doğu Yücel. Copyright © 2018 Doğu Yücel. Published in *Öldüğünü Google'dan Öğrenen Adam ve Diğer Tuhaf Hikâyeler* (Can Yayinlari). Translation copyright © 2022 Nicholas Glastonbury.

Editions Corti: *Lettrines II* by Julien Gracq. Copyright © Editions Corti, 1974. Translation copyright © 2022 Isabella Huberman.

Evgenia Nekrasova: *Музей московского мусора* by Evgenia Nekrasova. Original text copyright © 2019 Evgenia Nekrasova. Translation copyright © 2022 Jane Costlow and José Vergara.

Henrietta Rose-Innes: For her story, "Poison. Copyright © 2007 Henrietta Rose-Innes.

Jamaica Kincaid: "What I Have Been Doing Lately" from *At the Bottom of the River* by Jamaica Kincaid. Copyright © 1983 by Jamaica Kincaid. Reprinted by permission of Farrar, Straus and Giroux. All Rights Reserved.

Kimberly M. Blaeser: "Growing Things" by Kimberly M. Blaeser. First published in *Blue Dawn, Red Earth: New Native American Storytellers*. New York: Anchor Books, 1996.

La Escala Humana: Autorizamos la traducción y publicación de los fragmentos 1, 3, 5, 12, 13, 16, 17, 21 y 22 del cuento "Opiniones de un neandertal, un ensayo relatado," de Abdón Ubidia, publicado por Editorial El Conejo. Abdón Ubidia, "Opiniones de un neandertal, un ensayo relatado," en *La Escala Humana*. Quito: Editorial El Conejo, 2018.

Maarja Pärtna: Selections from *Vivaarium*. Copyright © 2019 Maarja Pärtna. Translation published as *Vivarium* by The Emma Press. Translation copyright © 2020 Jayde Will. And "talv" by Maarja Pärtna. Copyright © 2021 Maarja Pärtna. Published in *Looming*, May 2021. Translated by the author.

Mahasweta Devi: Used with permission of Taylor & Francis Group LLC – Books, from *Imaginary Maps: Three Stories*, Mahasweta Devi (1994). Permission conveyed through Copyright Clearance Center, Inc.

Milkweed Editions: Robin Wall Kimmerer, "In the Footsteps of Nanabozho: Becoming Indigenous to Place" from *Braiding Sweetgrass: Indigenous Wisdom, Scientific Knowledge and the Teachings of Plants*. Copyright © 2013, 2015 by Robin Wall Kimmerer.

Tlotlo Tsamaase: For her story "Eclipse Our Sins." First published in the December 2019 issue of *Clarkesworld Magazine*.

White Pine Press: *Juolgevuođđu* by Niillas Holmberg. Copyright © 2018 Niillas Holmberg. Translation published as *Underfoot* by White Pine Press. Translation copyright © 2022 Jennifer Kwon Dobbs and Johanna Domokos.

Wylie Agency: Excerpt from "Alla afuera hay monstruos" by Edmundo Paz Soldán. Copyright © Edmundo Paz Soldán. Used by permission of The Wylie Agency LLC.

Wylie Agency: "The Man to Send Rain Clouds" by Leslie Marmon Silko. Copyright © 1981, 2012 Leslie Marmon Silko. Used by permission of The Wylie Agency LLC.

Contributors

KURT CAVENDER is an independent scholar and writer living in Sharon, Massachusetts. He holds a PhD in modern and contemporary American literature from Brandeis University, and his work has appeared in *College Literature*, *Post45*, and *Arizona Quarterly*, as well as the edited collections *Reading Modernism with Machines* (Palgrave Macmillan, 2016) and *Literature and Event* (Routledge, 2022).

Straddling between Canada and China, LEILEI CHEN 莫译 (her pen name in Mandarin) lives her life learning the philosophy of the in-between space and its potential contribution to social progress. She translates Margaret Laurence's short stories, Steven Grosby's *Nationalism: A Very Short Introduction*, and contemporary Canadian poetry and essays. She is the English translator of modern and contemporary women writers such as Ling Shuhua (凌叔华) and Zhang Li (张莉) as well as MA Hui's (马辉) *I Have Forsaken Heaven and Earth, but Never Forsaken You*. She publishes poetry, short memoir writings, and *Re-orienting China: Travel Writing and Cross-cultural Understanding*. She teaches at the University of Alberta.

JANE COSTLOW has written and edited books and essays on Russian literature and culture, including histories of water and the forest, Russian women's writing, and classic writers including Ivan Turgenev and Vladimir Korolenko. She won the American Association of Teachers of Slavic and East European Languages prize for best translation in 1999 for her translation of Lydia Zinovieva-Annibal's *The Tragic Menagerie* (Northwestern University Press). She recently retired from teaching Russian literature and environmental humanities at Bates College in Lewiston, Maine.

ADRIAN DEMOPULOS was born in Dallas, Texas. She graduated from the University of Oklahoma with BAs in Spanish and communication. Her translations have appeared in *Latin American Literature Today* and in the anthology *A Larger Reality: Speculative Fiction from the Bicultural Margins* by The Mexicanx Initiative.

JENNIFER KWON DOBBS is the author of *Interrogation Room* (White Pine Press, 2018); *Paper Pavilion* (White Pine, 2007), winner of the White Pine Press Poetry Prize; and the chapbooks *Notes from a Missing Person* (Essay Press, 2015) and *Necro Citizens* (German/English edition, hochroth Verlag, 2019). *Interrogation Room* received mention in *The New York Times*, was praised by *World Literature Today* for "a vigorous restlessness," and won the Association of Asian American Studies Award in Creative Writing: Poetry. She also co-translates Sami poetry with poet-scholar Johanna Domokos, and their translation of Niillas Holmberg's *Juolgevuođđu* is published as *Underfoot* (2022) by White Pine Press. Currently, she is professor of English and race and ethnic studies at St. Olaf College and poetry editor at *AGNI*.

JOHANNA DOMOKOS is a comparative literary scholar of indigenous cultures and minority literatures with expertise in Scandinavian and Central European areas. She wrote her PhD on the translatability and multicultural dynamism of Sámi literature (1999, University of Szeged). She is currently affiliated with Károli University in Budapest and coordinates Gruppe Bie Translation and Book Production Laboratory at Bielefeld University. She is author of four monographs related to Sámi literature, and has edited more than twenty books. She translates from and into English, Hungarian, German, and Sámi languages.

ROBERTO FORNS-BROGGI has been a writer and professor at Denver Metropolitan State University since 1998. He teaches several advanced classes in Spanish, including Latin American cinema. His works of ecological perspective applied to literature, cinema, and new media aim to investigate alternative epistemologies and their influence on reading and writing practices. He has published *Knots Like Stars: ABC of the Ecological Imagination in Our Americas* (2012). An enlarged and corrected version came out in English in 2016. His work is nourished by curiosity, the crossing of disciplines, and the weaving of knots between ancient and contemporary cultures. He is currently preparing a workbook on environmental writing and film in Latin America and a series of experimental eco-shorts.

NICHOLAS GLASTONBURY is a cultural anthropologist of sound, media, empire, the Middle East, and the former Soviet Union. He is currently a postdoctoral associate at the Center for Cultural Analysis at Rutgers University. He holds a PhD in anthropology and a graduate certificate in women's and gender studies from the Graduate Center of the City University of New York. He is a translator of Turkish and Kurdish literature and the chair of the advisory board for the PEN/Heim Translation Fund. His translation of Sema Kaygusuz's novel *Every Fire You Tend* (2019) was the recipient of the 2020 TA First Translation Prize from the Society of Authors. He is also an editor of the e-zine *Jadaliyya*.

KATIA GRUBISIC is a writer, editor, and translator. Her work has appeared in Canadian and international publications. She has been a finalist for the Governor General's Literary Award for translation and the A. M. Klein Prize for Poetry, and her collection of poems *What If Red Ran Out* won the Gerald Lampert award for best first book.

ISABELLA HUBERMAN is an assistant professor of French studies at the University of British Columbia. She has published numerous articles on Indigenous literatures of Quebec. Her current research examines narrative and visual art by Indigenous creators from communities in Canada living with the consequences of hydroelectric development. She is the author of *Histoires souveraines: poétiques du personnel dans les littératures autochtones au Québec* (Presses de l'Université de Montréal 2023).

CAJETAN IHEKA is professor of English at Yale University, specializing in African literature, ecocriticism, ecomedia, and postcolonial literature. He is the author of *Naturalizing Africa: Ecological Violence, Agency, and Postcolonial Resistance in African Literature* (Cambridge University Press, 2018), winner of the 2019 Ecocriticism Book Award of the Association for the Study of Literature and Environment, and the 2020 First Book Prize of the African Literature Association. His latest single-authored book is *African Ecomedia: Network Forms, Planetary Politics* (Duke University Press, 2021). The monograph, which positions Africa at the center of discourses on media ecologies, materiality, and infrastructure, received several awards. It won the 2022 Ecocriticism Book Award of the Association for the

Study of Literature and Environment, and the Ronnie Heyman Prize for Outstanding Scholarly Publication in the Humanities. *African Ecomedia* was also awarded honorable mention for the Association for the Study of the Arts of the Present (ASAP) Book Prize, and was a finalist for the Media Ecology Association Book Awards. Professor Iheka is editor of the MLA volume *Teaching Postcolonial Environmental Literature and Media* (2022). He also coedited *African Migration Narratives: Politics, Race, and Space* (University of Rochester Press, 2018), and *Environmental Transformations*, a special issue of *African Literature Today*.

CAREN IRR is Kevy and Hortense Kaiserman Professor of Humanities at Brandeis University. She is the author of several monographs on political fiction and the editor of four collections of essays on contemporary literature and culture—most recently *Life in Plastic: Artistic Responses to Petromodernity* (University of Minnesota, 2021).

ADELE LONAS was born in Burney, California and has lived in Virginia, Maryland, New York City, and Mexico. For the last nine years, she has lived in Colorado, where she completed a joint master's degree in teaching English as a second language and Spanish language and literature. She currently works as an early childhood family specialist with families from Mexico and Central and Latin America. She does translation work for the same early childhood program—of everything from event flyers to grant narratives and parent handbooks—and for a local immigration lawyer. She has completed various literary translations and is currently working on a group translation project along with the editor of a compilation of Elena Garro's (Mexico, b. 1916) poetry. In her free time, she paints and explores Colorado's countless mountains.

DAVID MCKAY translates novels, plays, short stories, a wide range of nonfiction, and poetry from Dutch and Frisian into English. He received the Vondel Prize in 2017 for *War and Turpentine* by Stefan Hertmans, which was also nominated for the International Booker Prize and shortlisted for the Best Translated Book Award. His co-translation with Ina Rilke of *Max Havelaar* by Multatuli was shortlisted for the Oxford-Weidenfeld Prize 2020, and in 2021 he received an ICM Global South Translation Fellowship from Cornell University for Anton de Kom's classic anti-colonial manifesto *We Slaves of Suriname*, published by Polity Press in January 2022. Other publications planned for 2022 include *Bold Ventures* by Charlotte van den Broeck and *The Ascent* by Stefan Hertmans. His translation of *The Wetsuitman*, a four-act play by Freek Mariën published online in *The Mercurian*, was staged in 2022 by Foreign Affairs in London and The Cherry Arts in Ithaca, New York. His website is www.openbooktranslation.com.

UPAMANYU PABLO MUKHERJEE is professor of Anglophone world-literature at Oxford University. He researches across four interrelated fields—colonial and postcolonial literatures, environmental humanities, world-literary studies, and Victorian studies. He is the author of five monographs—*Crime Fiction and Empire* (2003); *Postcolonial Environments: Nature, Culture and the Contemporary Indian Novel in English* (2010); *Natural Disasters and Victorian Imperial Culture* (2013); *Combined and Uneven Development: Towards a New Theory of World-Literature* (with the Warwick Research Collective, 2015); and *Final Frontiers: Science Fiction and Techno-Science in Non-Aligned India* (2020, winner of the Science Fiction Research Association's 2021 Book Award). He has also edited three essay collections and anthologies, and written a wide range of articles in leading academic journals. He co-edits Palgrave Macmillan's book series *New Comparisons in World Literature*. He is currently developing a project on anti-colonial world literatures, and working with colleagues at the New School of the Anthropocene in London to develop the role of arts and humanities in popular understanding of climate change. He was elected Fellow of the British Academy in 2022.

IRINA SADOVINA is a researcher and translator. She has a PhD in comparative literature from the University of Toronto and a PhD in folklore from the University of Tartu. She teaches at the University of Sheffield.

GAYATRI CHAKRAVORTY SPIVAK is University Professor at the Department of English and Comparative Literature at Columbia University and a founding member of Columbia's Institute for Comparative Literature and Society. A proponent of a "practical deconstructivist–feminist-Marxist position," Spivak gained international recognition with her translation and extended introduction of Jacques Derrida's *De la grammatologie* (1976). She has helped shape several academic fields such as postcolonial studies, and her publications include the seminal essay "Can the Subaltern Speak?" (1988), *Outside in the Teaching Machine* (1993), *Critique of Postcolonial Reason: Towards a History of the Vanishing Present* (1999), *Death of a Discipline* (2003), *Other Asias* (2008), *An Aesthetic Education in the Age of Globalization* (2012), *Readings* (2014), and *Du Bois and the General Strike* (forthcoming). She received a Lifetime Scholarly Achievement from the Modern Language Association of America (2018), the Kyoto Prize in Arts and Philosophy, and the *Padma Bhushan* (2013). The translator of several works from Mahasweta Devi, Ramprasad Sen, and Aimé Césaire, she received a translation award by Sahitya Akadami, the Indian National Academy of Letters (1997).

JOSÉ VERGARA is assistant professor of Russian at Bryn Mawr College. He specializes in prose of the long twentieth century with an emphasis on experimental works. His first book, *All Future Plunges to the Past: James Joyce in Russian Literature*, examines Russian writers' reception of Joyce's fiction. He has published on authors including Vladimir Nabokov, Mikhail Shishkin, and Sasha Sokolov, among others, and his writing and interviews can also be found in the *Los Angeles Review of Books*, *Asymptote*, *Words Without Borders*, and *Music & Literature*.

KATE WHITTEMORE is a translator from the Spanish. Her translations include *The Communist's Daughter* by Aroa Moreno Durán, *Four by Four* and *Bad Handwriting* by Sara Mesa, *World's Best Mother* by Nuria Labari, *Last Words on Earth* by Javier Serena, *Mother's Don't* by Katixa Agirre, and *Wolfskin* by Lara Moreno. She lives in Valencia, Spain.

JAYDE WILL is a writer and translator. Recent translations include Alberts Bels's novel *Insomnia* (Parthian Books, 2020), and Arvis Viguls's poetry collection *They* (Valley Press, 2020). His poetry, short stories, and writing about Baltic literatures can be found in *Words Without Borders*, *In Other Words*, *Five Books*, punctummagazine.lv, satori.lv, and *Panel Magazine*.

SHAOBO XIE is professor of English at the University of Calgary. He teaches literary theory, postcolonial literature and theory, and translation studies. His articles have appeared in journals such as *Boundary 2*, *New Literary History*, *Cultural Critique*, *Telos*, *Neohelicon*, *Semiotica*, *Canadian Review of Comparative Literature*, *Science & Society*, *Asia Pacific Translation and Intercultural Studies*, *Theoretical Studies in Literature and Art*, and *International Social Science Journal*. Among his recent publications are "Translation and Globalization," "Green Religion as a Way of Life: Thoreau and his Ecocentric Aesthetics of Existence," "Chinese Beginnings of Cosmopolitanism: A Genealogical Critique of *Tianxia Guan*," and "*Tao*, *Parrhēsia* and the Chinese Intellectual."